W9-APH-177

"Friends don't want to kiss the living daylights out of one another,"

Alex said, quiet enough for only her ears.

Halona's heart raced at his words, and the closeness of their bodies, and because this was Alex. He was the first guy who ever caught her attention and the only one who'd sparked any interest inside of her since her late ex-husband died.

"Who's ready to light this tree?" Claire called over the crowd. Then she started a countdown on the mic. "Five...four..."

"I probably shouldn't have said that," Alex said.

"Three..."

"I want to kiss you too," Halona admitted, swallowing and instinctively wetting her lips. "But we probably shouldn't."

"Two..."

"It's probably a really bad idea," he agreed, his gaze dropping to her mouth and staying there. Then their lips collided, almost accidentally except it didn't feel like an accident at all. It felt amazing. Right. Like magic.

"One!" Claire shouted into the crowd. "Let there be light!"

Everyone oohed and aahed as they watched the town square tree with great excitement. Everyone except Alex and Halona, who were making a light show of their own.

PRAISE FOR ANNIE RAINS AND HER SWEETWATER SPRINGS SERIES

Springtime at Hope Cottage

"This delicious rom-com has plenty of heart and is ideal comfort reading."

—*Publishers Weekly*

"Annie Rains puts her heart in every word!"
—Brenda Novak, *New York Times* bestselling author

"Such a sweet romance!"

—TheGenreMinx.com

"A touching tale brimming with romance, drama, and feels!...I really enjoyed what I found between the pages of this newest offering from Ms. Rains, her words warmed my heart and her characters had me smiling and swooning throughout! Highly recommend!"

—RedsRomanceReviews.blogspot.com

"A wonderfully written romance that will make you wish you could visit this town."

—RomancingtheReaders.blogspot.com

"Annie Rains is a gifted storyteller, and I can't wait for my next visit to Sweetwater Springs!"
—RaeAnne Thayne, *New York Times* bestselling author

Christmas on Mistletoe Lane

"Top Pick! Five stars! Romance author Annie Rains was blessed with an empathetic voice that shines through each character she writes. *Christmas on Mistletoe Lane* is the latest example of that gift."

—NightOwlReviews.com

"The premise is entertaining, engaging and endearing; the characters are dynamic and lively...the romance is tender and dramatic...A wonderful holiday read, *Christmas on Mistletoe Lane* is a great start to the holiday season."

—TheReadingCafe.com

"This first installment of Rains's Sweetwater Springs series is cozy and most enjoyable. A strong cast of supporting characters as well as expert characterizations and strong plotting will have readers looking forward to future installments."

—*Publishers Weekly*

"Settle in with a mug of hot chocolate and prepare to find holiday joy in a story you won't forget."

—RaeAnne Thayne, *New York Times* bestselling author

"Don't miss this sparkling debut full of heart and emotion!"

—Lori Wilde, *New York Times* bestselling author

"How does Annie Rains do it? This is a lovely book, perfect for warming your heart on a long winter night."

—Grace Burrowes, *New York Times* bestselling author

SNOWFALL ON CEDAR TRAIL

ALSO BY ANNIE RAINS

SNOWFALL ON CEDAR TRAIL

ANNIE RAINS

FOREVER

NEW YORK BOSTON

This book is a work of fiction. Names, characters, places, and incidents are the product of the author's imagination or are used fictitiously. Any resemblance to actual events, locales, or persons, living or dead, is coincidental.

Copyright © 2019 by Annie Rains
Excerpt from *Two Peas & Their Pod Cookbook* copyright © 2019 by Maria Lichty

Cover design and illustration by Elizabeth Turner Stokes
Cover copyright © 2019 by Hachette Book Group, Inc.

Bonus novel *Then There Was You* copyright © 2018 by Miranda Liasson

Hachette Book Group supports the right to free expression and the value of copyright. The purpose of copyright is to encourage writers and artists to produce the creative works that enrich our culture.

The scanning, uploading, and distribution of this book without permission is a theft of the author's intellectual property. If you would like permission to use material from the book (other than for review purposes), please contact permissions@hbgusa.com. Thank you for your support of the author's rights.

Forever
Hachette Book Group
1290 Avenue of the Americas, New York, NY 10104
read-forever.com
twitter.com/readforeverpub

First Edition: September 2019

Forever is an imprint of Grand Central Publishing. The Forever name and logo are trademarks of Hachette Book Group, Inc.

The publisher is not responsible for websites (or their content) that are not owned by the publisher.

The Hachette Speakers Bureau provides a wide range of authors for speaking events. To find out more, go to www.hachettespeakersbureau.com or call (866) 376-6591.

ISBN: 978-1-5387-1402-7 (mass market), 978-1-5387-1400-3 (ebook)

Printed in the United States of America
OPM
10 9 8 7 6 5 4 3 2 1

ATTENTION CORPORATIONS AND ORGANIZATIONS:
Most Hachette Book Group books are available at quantity discounts with bulk purchase for educational, business, or sales promotional use. For information, please call or write:

Special Markets Department, Hachette Book Group
1290 Avenue of the Americas, New York, NY 10104
Telephone: 1-800-222-6747 Fax: 1-800-477-5925

*For my readers. May the season
of hope surround you and stay
with you throughout the year.*

Acknowledgments

Thank you to my family for supporting me in every way. I love you and I couldn't do any of this without you. Thank you especially to my husband, Sonny, for being the man behind every hero I write. I couldn't live out this dream without you by my side, offering limitless advice and support.

I would also like to thank my amazing and talented editor, Alex Logan, at Grand Central / Forever for making my work shine. Thank you to Estelle Hallick for your PR expertise, Monisha Lakhotia for your social media genius, Elizabeth Turner Stokes for your beautiful work on this cover, and everyone else on the Grand Central / Forever team for all your hard work!

Thank you to my tireless literary agent, Sarah Younger. I'm so fortunate to have you in my corner! I'm so thankful to have my critique partner and friend, Rachel Lacey, by my side on this writing journey as well!

Thank you so much to the wonderful Maria Lichty for

allowing me to reference the *Two Peas & Their Pod* blog and cookbook. It's a huge honor to have your Triple-Chip Chocolate Cookie recipe included in this book for my readers to make and enjoy for themselves!

Last but not least, thank you to my readers, who are the reason I get to tell my stories and put them out in the world. Your support is the best gift you could give me, and it means more to me than you know.

CHAPTER ONE

*S*omething crashed in the kitchen.

Halona Locklear cracked open an eye as she listened and debated whether the sound warranted getting out of bed. Before she could decide, her alarm clock started to shriek from across the room. She'd put it there so that she couldn't press Snooze and make herself late for the morning drop-off at her son's school.

She groaned and burrowed deeper into her covers. She'd gotten up with Theo and his nightmares four times in the night, and she was exhausted. *Just one more hour.* Another crash in the kitchen launched her out of bed. She slid her feet into a pair of slippers and hurried down the hall.

"Theo?" she called. "What are you doing?"

She squinted in the harsh overhead lights, seeing her son sitting on the kitchen counter. There was a carton of milk at his side and a box of Cheerios. Without a word, he grabbed a bowl and hopped down. There was another dish on the floor, the culprit of the crash she'd heard in her bedroom. Thankfully, it was plastic.

"To the table," she ordered, grabbing the milk and cereal and following behind him. She couldn't be mad. At seven, he was finally at the age where he was doing more stuff for himself, even if it meant chipped plates and a few spills here and there.

Halona poured them both a glass of orange juice and then sat down alongside her son and drank as she talked to Theo. He smiled up at her intermittently while he ate. He didn't speak. The only time she heard his voice anymore was during his nightmares, which were the source of his dark eyes underscored with blue half-moons. She imagined hers looked the same right now.

"Hurry up," she prodded after a few minutes, standing up from the table. "I've got to get you to school."

Theo lifted his gaze and started shoveling the cereal into his mouth faster than he could chew and swallow. Milk dribbled down his chin, and he quickly wiped it away with the sleeve of his pajama shirt.

Halona laughed despite her bone-deep fatigue. Then she retreated to her bedroom and dressed herself before helping Theo pick out something to wear.

On the way out the front door, she grabbed the lunch she'd packed for him last night, his backpack, and her purse. Then they loaded in her car and headed down the road.

"Have a good day," she said cheerfully as she pulled up at Sweetwater Elementary ten minutes later.

She saw the corners of his mouth lift just a touch in the rearview mirror.

"I love you," she added as her breath suspended in

her chest, waiting and hoping this time that he'd return the words.

Instead, a teacher working with the car pool line opened the passenger-side door for him to exit.

"Good morning, Theo," the teacher said, helping him step down onto the school's curb.

Theo's greeting came in the way of another smile as he pulled the straps of his backpack over his shoulders. Then he glanced back at Halona and waved before heading off.

"Bye, sweetie!" She watched him until the car behind her beeped its horn. Halona cast an irritated glance at the driver behind her and then drove to the Little Shop of Flowers on Main Street. There was usually an uptick in business in the winter months heading into the holidays. People were more generous this time of year. They looked for ways to say *I love you*, and what said it better than flowers?

She unlocked her door and stepped inside.

She knew better. Nothing replaced those three little words, not even roses. What she wouldn't give to hear Theo whisper them again. His doctor had diagnosed him with selective mutism last year, and she'd been working with every professional in the area who might be able to help. So far, nothing had made a huge difference, but she wasn't one to give up easily, especially where her son was concerned.

Her nerves calmed a touch as she inhaled the sweet floral aroma of her shop. Then she walked to the back room. The smell of roasted beans would also perk her up. She poured water and grounds into her coffee maker and flipped it on. After a moment, the machine started funneling its dark brew into the pot.

The coffee next door at the Sweetwater Café was far better, but that would require running into half the people in town, including Chief of Police Alex Baker, who appeared to have a small addiction to Emma St. James's brew. Or maybe for the café owner herself. Not that Halona was jealous. The last thing she needed was romance intertwining with her heavy load of responsibilities.

When the coffee was done, she poured a cup. No sooner had she taken her first sip than the bell above the door rang with an incoming customer. Halona put her mug down and dutifully put on a smile as she approached the front counter from the back room. Her breath stumbled along with her feet when she locked eyes with the man who'd just walked in. So much for avoiding Chief Baker by settling for mediocre coffee.

"Hey," he said, his deep voice a product of his six-foot-plus body and broad quarterback-size shoulders.

"Hey," she echoed back, feeling a bit foolish because a thousand butterflies, usually dormant, suddenly fluttered around inside her chest. She'd always had a thing for her brother's best friend but he'd only ever looked at her as a little kid when they were growing up. And just like her brother, Alex was overprotective. Perhaps to a fault.

Resentment over what happened two years ago festered up, which she suppressed along with those annoying butterflies. "To what do I owe your visit? Business or personal?" she asked.

"A little of both, I guess. I need an arrangement for a fellow officer's wife. Mary Beth Edwards."

"Oh. She just had surgery, right? That's nice of you to think of her," Halona said.

"It'll be from the whole department."

"Well, I'm sure she'll appreciate the sentiment. I'll

get that arrangement for you right away." Halona stepped toward her cooler of fresh flowers to get started, feeling the coolness of the air contrasting with the burning of her skin.

"I thought I'd grab a coffee from next door while I wait," he said behind her. "Would you like some?"

She turned to face him. "No, thanks. I've got a machine in the back."

"Not the same," he coaxed. "Let me grab you a coffee. How do you take it?"

He stared at her from the other side of the counter, his blue eyes shining brightly beneath his rust-colored hair.

Overprotective and hard to resist. "Medium-dark roast with three raw sugars and a splash of cream," she finally conceded.

"You got it. I'll be right back."

She watched him walk out of her store and exhaled softly. She wanted to be mad at him but she knew he was only doing his job when he'd arrested her late ex-husband. Overprotective, hard to resist, and unbending when it came to the law—that was Chief Alex Baker.

* * *

Alex's blood felt electric, and it had nothing to do with the smell of fresh coffee and the promise of its jolt of caffeine. When was he ever going to stop reacting to Halona this way? He'd known her when she'd been a tomboy irritating him, her brother Tuck, and the last of the three musketeers, Mitch Hargrove.

She wasn't boyish in any way these days though—that was for sure.

"Hey, Chief Baker," Emma St. James said as he reached

her counter. She always smiled a little wider when he was around. Why couldn't he have a thing for someone uncomplicated like Emma? The only thing the beautiful café owner stirred for him, however, was his coffee. Halona, on the other hand, whipped up a variety of unsettling emotions: attraction, need…confusion. He didn't understand her choices. All he knew was that *he'd* made the right one. He would never regret arresting Ted for hurting her.

"Your usual?" Emma asked.

He gave a nod. "And a medium-dark roast with a splash of cream and three raw sugars."

Emma lifted a thin brow. "That's the way Halona takes her coffee."

He shoved his hands in his jeans pockets. "Do you know how everyone in town takes their drinks?"

She turned to start pouring. "It's my job to know, Chief Baker," she called over her shoulder. A moment later, she exchanged two coffees for his debit card. She swiped it and handed it back. "Tell Hal I said hello."

Alex didn't respond. Instead, he said a polite goodbye and started toward the door just as Mayor Brian Everson was pushing through in his wheelchair. Alex held the door as a courtesy, not that Brian needed help. Brian had more strength and endurance than most men with two able legs.

"Thanks, Chief," Brian said as he looked up. "You've been dodging my calls. I figured I'd run into you sooner or later."

"I'm actually in a hurry this morning," Alex lied. He liked Brian but he knew what the Sweetwater Springs mayor wanted to discuss. Apparently, Alex had gotten the reputation of being hard-nosed with some town members. He didn't bend the law for anyone, including eighty-year-olds who spiked the punch at public gatherings. Janice Murphy hadn't learned her lesson with all of Alex's many warnings over the years so he'd taken her to jail a couple of months back. It was just a scare tactic, of course. He hadn't actually charged Janice with anything, and afterward, he'd taken her to Dawanda's Fudge Shop. Was that the behavior of a hardened cop?

Brian angled his wheelchair to pin Alex with an assessing stare. "Call me. Better yet, stop by my office. This is your friend talking, not the mayor. You're good for this town, and we need to make sure everyone knows it."

Alex shifted the carrying tray of coffee in his hands. "I'll be in touch." Right after he figured out who was vandalizing the town and solved the cold case that had been in his desk drawer haunting him since he was nineteen years old. Every December, as the anniversary of his father's death loomed, he reassessed the facts and interviewed old witnesses. Yet the case wasn't any closer to being solved.

One day.

Alex stepped out of the coffee shop and walked back into the Little Shop of Flowers. Halona looked up with those honey-colored eyes of hers that seemed unnaturally bright against her inky black hair and tanned skin. She had high, defined cheekbones characteristic of her Cherokee heritage and petal-pink lips that none of the flowers in her shop could ever match.

His lungs constricted, making it hard to breathe for a second. She had this effect on him. Every. Single. Time. And he reckoned she always would.

Never going to happen.

"Here you go," he said, clearing his throat as he

approached the counter and setting the cup of coffee in front of her.

"Thank you." Her gaze flitted up to meet his. Then she pointed to a small table set up next to the flower cooler. "Your arrangement is over there. No charge. Please send Mary Beth my best wishes."

"You don't have to do that," he said.

"I want to. For her." There was a sharp note in her tone that he didn't miss. She reached for the coffee that he'd placed before her. "Thank you for this. Emma's brew is so much better than the stuff I have."

"I like to tell people I go so often because I'm secretly investigating her. Her coffee is too addictive to be legal."

Halona's face contorted with a small laugh that punched him as forcefully as a gunshot into his bulletproof vest.

"Well, I better get back to work. There's a graffiti incident to investigate."

Halona's brows lifted. "Sounds urgent."

Alex smiled at her teasing tone. "To Mrs. Roberts it is."

Halona's lips parted. "At the seamstress shop? That's right next door to A Taste of Heaven Catering."

"Don't worry. Brenna's business survived the incident unscathed. Hopefully, I'll catch the perp before their can of spray paint strikes again." He turned and headed toward the arrangement that she'd prepared. If he didn't leave now, he was at risk of doing something foolish like asking her out. Her answer would be no, of course. While she seemed to have forgiven him for arresting Ted, that didn't mean she wanted to date him. In fact, Halona didn't seem to want to date anyone.

"Good luck!" she called after him, her words muted by the sound of a cell phone ringing. "Hello," he heard her say at his back. Her sharp intake of breath made him turn to face her. "Yes. Is he okay?...I'll be there as soon as I can."

"Everything all right?" Alex asked once she'd disconnected the call.

"No. Theo threw up at school. I need to close up shop and go get him." She hesitated. "I have a customer coming in anytime to pick up an arrangement I promised her." She nibbled her lower lip and then pulled her phone back out of her pocket. "Maybe Mom can come watch the store," she said to herself.

"Not necessary. I'll watch it for you," Alex heard himself say.

Halona looked up with surprise in her eyes. He was a little shocked at the offer too. He didn't have time to take on extra work. Yet, here he was, offering to do exactly that for Halona.

"That's not necessary. I don't need your help," she said, that sharp tone returning, even if her smile was firmly in place.

"No, you don't. But you could get to Theo's school a lot faster if you let me do this for you."

Halona's shoulders rounded. "Are you sure?"

"Positive. Go get Theo. I'll try not to burn the place down while you're away."

Halona smiled, and it actually reached her eyes this time. That felt like a small accomplishment. "Thank you."

"Of course." He watched her grab her keys and hurry out. Then he looked around the store, completely perplexed at how the town's chief of police had suddenly gotten himself into running a flower shop.

* * *

It wasn't even an hour ago that Halona had dropped Theo off. Now here she was again, picking him up. He'd been having stomach pain a lot lately. His therapist believed it was anxiety induced, just like his refusal to talk. In his short life, Theo had been through a lot. At the parent-teacher conference last month, his teacher reported that Theo didn't have any friends. She'd described him as a good student who kept to himself.

Kids were supposed to have friends though. They were supposed to act up and get into trouble. Halona certainly had. She'd prefer to get called to the principal's office because Theo was misbehaving than because his emotions were eating away at him little by little.

Halona opened the door to Sweetwater Elementary and stepped inside, hearing the cacophony of school-related sounds: the buzzing of overhead lights, the sound of children's voices and laughter, the intercom calling for a custodian.

Veering into the front office to her right, Halona straightened her shoulders and put on a smile. Masking her feelings was something she'd come to do well. She wasn't sure if that was an attribute or a character flaw.

"Good morning, Ms. Locklear-Byrd," the front office secretary said.

Halona decided not to correct the secretary for the tenth time. In a small town, everyone knew your name and, apparently, couldn't remember if you had decided to change it. After her divorce, she'd dropped Ted's last name. She'd wanted a clean break from her past, not realizing until later that one never truly broke free. "I got a call about Theo?"

"Yes, he's in the nurse's office." The secretary pointed to a room down the hall but Halona knew her way.

"Thank you." She took quick steps until she was standing in the doorway.

Theo looked up while holding his little hands over his belly, his face scrunched up tightly.

"Hey, buddy. How are you doing?" She walked over and kneeled in front of him.

"He doesn't seem to feel well," Nurse Johnston said. "No fever though."

Halona could've guessed that much. He had been fine when he was eating Cheerios at breakfast earlier this morning.

"He threw up?" Halona asked.

Nurse Johnston nodded. "Just a little bit. Could've been something he ate or maybe a little bit of nerves." She winked. "I hope he feels well enough to return to class tomorrow."

Halona stood, keeping her gaze on Theo. "Yeah, me too. Want to come work at the flower shop with me today, bud?"

Theo's face relaxed, and a smile touched the corners of his mouth. Nerves it was. Halona almost would've preferred he had a virus. At least then she would know what to do for him.

Grabbing his hand, she stopped back in the office to sign Theo out. Then she walked him back to her car, buckled him in, and cranked the engine. "School is important, you know. You can't keep coming home just because you're not happy." She looked at him in the rear-view mirror. The only sign that he'd even heard her was the stubborn lift of his chin.

With a sigh, she pulled out of the parking spot and drove back to the Little Shop of Flowers. Despite her worry, a little flutter of anticipation batted around in her belly at the knowledge that Alex was inside waiting for her. She ignored it, parked, and helped Theo out of the car. As soon as he darted into the store, he froze at the sight of Alex behind the counter.

"Hey, buddy," Alex said.

After a moment's hesitation, Theo took off running toward him, making Halona's heart squeeze. Theo was shy with most people, even before his selective mutism diagnosis, but he'd never been that way with Alex. There was something between them that Halona didn't quite understand. The same was true between *her* and Alex.

"Give me five, little man," Alex said after the hug.

Theo gave the hit everything he had.

"Down low." As Theo tried to hit him again, Alex yanked his hand away. "*Ohhh*, you're too slow."

Theo giggled happily.

"As you can tell, he's sick," Halona told Alex, approaching the two of them.

"Oh, yeah." Alex's face turned solemn. "Guess you better stay in bed all day and eat nothing but chicken soup. That's what my mom used to say."

No longer smiling, Theo's eyes widened.

Halona redirected her attention to Alex. "Thanks for watching the store. Did anyone come by?"

Alex shook his head. "I had it easy. Just me and the flowers. They're good listeners, you know."

Halona gave him a curious look. "You talked to my flowers?"

"Of course. Told them all my secrets. They promised not to tell." He winked at Theo, whose cheeks puffed back up into a wide grin. "Well, I'll see you later." Alex grabbed his flower arrangement for Mary Beth Edwards and headed out the door.

Watching him, Halona reminded herself to breathe. The flowers knew his secrets, and Alex knew hers. Well, one of them, at least. She'd made a promise never to tell anyone the rest of the story, and she intended to keep it.

CHAPTER TWO

I don't want to know," Alex said as he walked into the Sweetwater Springs police station and past the front desk secretary, Tammy Duncan.

"Five," she told him anyway.

He stopped and gave her a look that would frighten some. Tammy didn't even bat one of her long, black eyelashes. She was a tall and slender African American woman who kept her hair cropped short and her nails long and painted. Alex had gone to high school with Tammy. They hadn't had much in common back then. He'd been into sports, and Tammy had been a thespian. Since she'd come to work at the station a few years back though, they'd developed a sort of sibling relationship. "I said I didn't want to know."

"It's my job to tell you how many missed calls you have. Five," she said again, and if he wasn't mistaken, she seemed to be enjoying herself. "Mayor Everson is one of them. I'd recommend you return that call first."

Alex shook his head. He'd already run into Brian earlier. He didn't consider that an urgent call to return.

Tammy flashed a bright smile in his direction. "Sharlene Anderson also called."

He felt his shoulders tense now. "What'd she say?"

"She said she wanted to talk to you—that's all. You know she won't talk to anyone else."

And unfortunately, she wouldn't even talk to Alex. Not yet.

"She sounded upset though," Tammy continued.

"She called from her home number?" he asked, turning from the direction of his office and heading toward the back exit.

"I think so...Hey, where are you going? Don't you want to know about your other three callers?"

"They can wait," Alex called back. Sharlene might not be able to.

He climbed into his police SUV and drove five miles per hour above the speed limit. This wasn't an emergency, but he'd been watching Sharlene for the last year. She'd almost talked to him a number of times, especially right after she'd gone to the hospital with a sprained wrist. She'd been so close to telling him the truth that night. The truth was not that she'd tripped over their new puppy on the way out the back door. Not even close.

Tony Anderson wouldn't like having a police vehicle pull up in his driveway. He'd suspect that his wife had called, which might make things at home worse for Sharlene.

Alex lifted his foot off the gas pedal. He wanted to help Sharlene, but he couldn't without her testimony or any evidence of wrongdoing.

Instead of turning down Pine Cone Lane as planned, Alex continued driving. Tomorrow he'd stop at the post office where Sharlene worked. It was on the same strip as the Sweetwater Café—and the Little Shop of Flowers. He could get a cup of joe and stop in to check with Halona on Theo's sickness.

After circling back, Alex walked into the police station twenty minutes after he'd left. "How many?" he asked as he came toward the front desk.

Tammy's gaze slid toward him. "Thought you didn't want to know."

"I changed my mind."

She shook her head. "You said not to tell you earlier so I'll just wait until—"

Alex growled, and Tammy started laughing.

"You're up to seven now, Chief. The list is on your desk along with a roast beef sandwich. I made the roast last night. It has my secret ingredient, too, that keeps people asking for more."

He pointed a finger at her. "*This* is why I let you stay despite your troublemaking ways."

He was only teasing, of course. Tammy was the best secretary he'd ever had. She was organized and professional.

He closed his office door, sat down at his desk, and unwrapped the sandwich she'd left for him along with an ice-cold Coke. Not only was Tammy good at her job, she was also a talented chef, who graciously shared her delicious creations with everyone she knew.

After taking the last bite, he threw away his trash and reached for the list of missed calls. Halona's name caught his eye. Without hesitating, he picked up the phone and dialed.

"Hello?" Her voice hit a note inside him that resonated through his entire body.

"You called?" he asked, clearing his throat.

"Yes. I hope I didn't disturb you."

"You didn't. Is everything okay?"

"Everything's fine. I just wanted to thank you for earlier. For watching the flower shop."

"Don't tell anyone, okay?" He heard the drop of his voice, unintentionally flirtatious and completely out of his control.

"Oops. I already spoke to Serena Gibbs at the news station. Your lapse of the tough-guy act will be on the evening news at five."

Alex laughed. It felt good, like all the pent-up tension he tended to carry around just rolled right off his shoulders. "You don't have to thank me. I didn't mind."

"Well, if I can ever return the favor, let me know."

He had a few ideas that he kept to himself. "How's Theo?"

"He's going to school tomorrow, and if he wants to be able to read his books this weekend, he'll stay all day."

"When I was in school, the threat was *making* me read books, not taking them away," Alex said.

"Well, Theo is not your normal child."

Alex already knew this about young Theo. Tuck had informed Alex of the boy's emotional issues. It only made sense. Theo had been through a lot in his young life. "I'm happy to help any time you need it," he said. "No thanks necessary."

"Well, I'll, um, see you around." There was a hesitation in her voice that had him wondering if she had more to say. There was always more to say between them though. Things unspoken, at least on his part. "Have a good rest of your day."

"You too." He hung up the phone and then looked up when someone knocked on his open door.

"Was that my sister you were on the phone with?" Tuck asked.

Alex cleared his throat and straightened in his office chair. "What tipped you off?"

Tuck chuckled. "Your body language. The only time you ever look vulnerable, like someone stands a chance at taking you down, is when she's around."

This wasn't the first time Tuck had called Alex out on having a thing for his sister. Alex had always denied it, of course. It wasn't something he could act on. Back in school, he'd held back because of his friendship with Tuck. A guy didn't go after his best friend's little sister. It was an unspoken rule, and Alex had never been a rule breaker. Then Halona had married Ted, and they'd had a child.

Even though she was no longer married, she still had a lot on her shoulders. She wasn't available for dating. That didn't stop Alex from checking in on her every now and then though. Or from the occasional fantasy that he couldn't seem to help entertaining.

"You'd think I threatened you to stay away or something," Tuck continued, oblivious to Alex's sidetracked thoughts. "I'm completely okay with you dating Halona if you need my permission."

Alex frowned, wishing Tuck had closed the door to his office before ribbing him. Tammy had uncanny hearing, and she teased Alex harder than anyone else in his life. "I don't want to date your sister," Alex lied. If things were different, he'd ask her out, and he didn't think he'd lose interest in her after one or two dates. "Did you come here to spy on me or was there something else?"

Tuck nodded. "You haven't been to the Tipsy Tavern with us in a while. You've been putting me off when I call. So, since my ten o'clock patient canceled their physical therapy appointment this morning, I thought I'd come down here to hassle you in person."

"I have a lot on my plate," Alex said with a shake of his head.

Tuck lowered his voice and leaned over Alex's desk. "I know it's a hard time of year for you, man. You don't have to deal with things on your own though. You have friends you can lean on."

Tuck was talking about Alex's father, and he was right. The month of December seemed to suck Alex in every year. While everyone else celebrated and seemed consumed by joy, Alex was swept away by the past.

He sighed heavily, not wanting to discuss this right now. It was too early in the day. "I'm fine. Just let me know the next time you go out, and I'll meet you."

"Great." Tuck straightened. "Maybe Mitch can pull himself away from Kaitlyn long enough to hang out with us too. Might be nice for her and Josie to get together for one of their movie marathons at the inn while we knock back some beers." Josie was Tuck's fiancée. After losing his wife to cancer, Tuck deserved some happiness in his love life. Mitch too. Alex was glad for both of them. Maybe he was also a bit jealous, but none of the women in town caught his interest. None but one.

"Sounds good."

Tuck pointed a finger. "I'll call you about it. No backing out."

"I won't." Alex waved as Tuck left his office. A minute later, he listened to Tammy say goodbye to Tuck on the way out of the building.

Alex leaned back in his chair and expelled a heavy breath. Maybe going out with the guys one night soon would be good, especially as the anniversary of his father's death approached. It'd been eleven years, and no new evidence or witnesses had come forward. The case probably wouldn't be solved this Christmas either, but it was the season of hope, even if Alex's was dwindling more each December.

* * *

Theo was finally asleep, but who knew how long that would last?

Halona sat at the kitchen table with a cup of herbal tea. She had a book in front of her that she'd ordered from the local bookstore. *Unspeakable: How to Help Your Child with Selective Mutism.* It wasn't the first book that she'd read on her son's diagnosis, and it probably wouldn't be the last. She'd also scoured the internet and had Theo in counseling. But was it enough?

She sipped her tea and opened the book to the page she'd bookmarked earlier and started reading where she'd left off. She already knew the facts. Selective mutism wasn't an inability to speak. It was considered an anxiety disorder. Theo had always been timid, but his speech development had been normal until his father's death. After Ted's skiing accident, Theo had slowly stopped talking to acquaintances, his peers, and then his own family. Now he didn't even speak to her. His therapist, Dr. Charwood, called it progressive mutism. It didn't mean he would never talk, but there was no guarantee that he would either.

He will, Halona told herself. She wouldn't rest until

she'd helped her son get back to normal, whatever that was.

The words blurred as she stared at the page, and her focus scattered along with her thoughts. At first, she'd assumed Theo's withdrawal was a phase. Part of the grief process. Then she'd gotten worried after weeks of not hearing his voice. She'd even threatened to punish him before taking him to counseling and realizing what was going on. Now she just felt helpless. She wanted to do something, anything, to make him better.

Halona closed the book and then reached for her laptop instead, opening a browser and looking for something, anything, to rest her mind before bed. After checking her email, she went to one of her favorite blog sites called *Two Peas & Their Pod*. She loved all the fun recommendations for shopping and family outings but especially the recipes. The blog even had a new cookbook that Halona had been drooling over.

Halona clicked on the link and hesitated only a moment before ordering. It wasn't exactly impulse shopping, considering that she'd been wanting the cookbook for a while. Maybe she and Theo could find a new cookie recipe to make together during the holidays.

She continued to peruse the site, stopping short when she heard Theo's cry down the hall. She jumped up from the table and hurried to his bedroom. He'd only made it an hour before his first nightmare. That didn't bode well for the night ahead.

Stroking his black hair off his forehead, she watched his shadowed face contort and flinch in the darkness. She waited for him to speak. Sometimes he did when he was dreaming. His voice was sweet and small, just like she remembered. She hung on every word, even though he was troubled by whatever thoughts or memories were circulating in his mind.

"Daddy," he finally cried quietly. "No, Daddy."

Was he dreaming about Ted's death? Or about things he'd seen before?

No. She'd made sure that Theo never witnessed any of Ted's violence. Theo wouldn't have understood. Neither had Alex, but only because Ted had made Halona promise not to tell anyone that he was sick. Ted was a proud man who'd risen above poor circumstances to become a local football star. His NFL career had only lasted a couple of years before his last head injury. He was a success story in town, and people admired him. Ted didn't want that to be shadowed by his diagnosis or spiraling behaviors. He loved being a hero and never wanted to be seen as weak.

Halona tried not to blame him for that. She'd admired so much more about her late ex than his athletic ability though. He was a great dad and husband, and he'd fought against the medical challenges he faced just as fiercely as he had fought on the football field. This was the one field where he couldn't win, however.

"Daddy, don't go!" Theo whimpered in his sleep.

Halona swallowed painfully. "It's okay, Theo," she whispered even though he was still asleep and she wasn't sure he could hear her. "Shh, shh. Everything is all right."

Eventually, Theo's breathing pattern evened out, and his body relaxed into the mattress. Once he'd returned to a peaceful sleep, she got up and walked down the hall to her own bed. She hoped sleep would find her fast. She needed as much rest as she could get before Theo woke again.

* * *

"Oh, this sketch is just gorgeous!" Carrie Summers said the next day, standing with her sister Maggie in the Little Shop of Flowers. Halona had spent the last couple of days creating a blueprint of sorts for the bride-to-be's upcoming wedding bouquet.

"Are you sure?" Halona asked.

"Absolutely. This is perfect!"

A thread of pride weaved through Halona. She loved pleasing her customers and rarely ever got a complaint. When she did, it was usually from her clients who couldn't be pleased even if Halona cut her flowers fresh from the royal gardens in England. "Wonderful. I'll prepare the bouquet and other arrangements on Friday morning to ensure freshness. Then I'll set up the church that evening before your rehearsal."

"What do you need me to do?" Carrie asked.

Halona shrugged. "The only thing a bride has to do on her wedding day is arrive on time and say *I do*."

Carrie tsked. "I *wish* that were true. I'm juggling a ton of appointments this week to make sure everything goes off without a hitch. I'm also hosting relatives as they arrive. My parents are divorced and argue nonstop when they're together. Keeping things civil between them is going to be a challenge. I keep telling Jacob we should've just eloped."

Halona had done that with Ted. They hadn't wanted to waste time in planning an event, because Ted had been so busy with football obligations. Even so, their wedding day had been full of hope and promises—all broken toward the end of their marriage.

"When you're eighty years old and looking back on

your life," Carrie's sister, Maggie, said, "you'll be happy to have pictures of the wedding."

Pictures. All this fuss for the sake of an album. Of course, in Halona's heart, she knew it was more than just that. She loved weddings. She really did. A large part of her business revolved around supporting the happy union of two people in love. A big, beautiful wedding day didn't equal a perfect life though. Falling in love was the easy part. Things got hard after the *I do*.

Halona watched as Carrie looked down at the sketch once more. Her client hadn't specified which type of flowers she'd wanted, only that the colors be reflective of the upcoming holidays. Her bridesmaids were wearing deep crimson gowns. Halona had designed the bouquet to match, using blush and ivory roses with dark berries interspersed. In her sketch, she'd been careful to place the berries deep inside the arrangement to make sure they didn't rub on Carrie's dress on Saturday. The arrangement would be tied with a lovely ivory ribbon.

"It's just beautiful," Carrie said with a bright bride-to-be smile.

"I'm glad you're happy."

"Everything looks perfect. I'll see you soon."

Halona nodded. "Yes, you will."

"Now we're off to Taste of Heaven to make sure Brenna is all set with the catering for the reception."

Brenna McConnell owned A Taste of Heaven Catering, which was located at the opposite end of the downtown strip of stores from the Little Shop of Flowers. She and Halona grew up together but had only become close friends as adults. Halona enjoyed her company when she stopped in the shop, and they texted back and forth on an almost daily basis.

"Brenna is one of the most organized people I know. I'm sure she has everything set for your special day."

Carrie shrugged her shoulders to her ears and clasped her hands at her chest. "I'm just so excited."

"As you should be." Halona waved goodbye as the women exited her store and then her vision snagged on a familiar face walking outside. Alex stopped midstride and glanced inside her window, pinning his gaze on her. After a moment, he lifted his hand and waved.

Halona returned the gesture and mentally chanted, *Keep walking, keep walking, keep walking.* True to his nature not to be told what to do, however, Alex walked right into her store.

"Good morning," he said as the bell chimed overhead.

"Hi." She fiddled nervously with some ribbon on her counter. "How are you?"

He glanced around her shop, seemingly interested in the flowers on display. "Good. Just on my way to get a coffee and then go to the post office."

Her gaze fell to his empty hands. "But you don't have a package."

"Yeah. I need to find one. It's a ploy to check on Sharlene." His gaze sharpened when he looked at her.

She didn't have to ask why he needed to check on Sharlene and didn't like knowing that he automatically put her in the same "victim" category. Halona wasn't a victim and never had been.

"Got anything that needs to be shipped?" Alex asked. "I'll take it for you."

"I do, actually." She shook her head. "I already owe you for watching the store yesterday though."

"Letting me send off your package would be doing *me* a favor. We'd call it even."

Yeah, right. She wasn't sure which direction the scale was tipping these days, but she was positive that this gesture wouldn't make them even. "Just give me a second." She walked to the back room to retrieve the package she'd prepared for a childhood best friend. Then she walked into the front room and laid the package on the counter. "Ground shipping is fine. Let me get some cash from my purse."

Alex held out a hand. "You're doing me a favor here, remember? I'll pay." He took the box and looked at the address. "How is Marlena these days?"

"Good." Halona and Marlena had many a sleepover while Tuck, Mitch, and Alex had done the same at her parents' house. Halona hadn't realized it at the time but her parents were saints for entertaining simultaneous sleepovers so often. "She's planning to come down for Kaitlyn and Mitch's wedding after Christmas. I can't wait to see her," Halona told him. "It's been a long time."

Alex nodded. "I'd love to say hello. Let me know when she arrives."

"As if anyone enters your town without you knowing it," Halona said.

Alex gave a half shrug. "That used to be true until Josie's article about Sweetwater Springs increased the tourism here last year."

"And sales for me," Halona pointed out. "Which is good because Theo's wish list gets longer every Christmas."

Alex hugged the package to his side. "I'm hitting the café first. Do you want a coffee?"

Halona held up a hand. "I've reached my caffeine limit for today. If I have too much, my hands get shaky with the shears."

"That doesn't sound good." He chuckled and took a few steps toward the exit.

She couldn't wait for him to leave almost as much as she hated to see him go. Were these unexpected visits from Alex a ploy to check on her just like he was checking on Sharlene? If so, she didn't need a protector. What she needed was a way to get through to her son, and while Alex could offer her coffee and free package delivery, Halona seriously doubted he could give her that.

* * *

The post office was at the end of the string of stores downtown. The coffee in Alex's hand served two purposes: It woke him up and it made it appear less like he was here for the sole reason of checking on Sharlene and more like a casual coincidence.

He juggled the package and the coffee to open the door to the post office and headed toward the front counter.

Buck Miller grinned wide. "Hey, Chief Baker."

Alex returned the smile, all the while looking for evidence of Sharlene. "Good morning. Just you working the counter today?"

Buck's smile slid away. The older man was sharp minded. He likely knew exactly why Alex was here. "I'm afraid Sharlene is out sick today."

"I see," Alex said, his worry kicking up a notch.

"Not sure if she'll be back tomorrow or not." Buck took the package that Alex had set on the counter, weighed it, and printed out a label that he placed on the front.

Alex pulled out his wallet and paid the shipping cost.

"Is that all?" Buck asked.

Alex took a sip from his coffee. "For now. I might have more to send off tomorrow."

Buck nodded, seeming to understand. "I'll look forward to seeing you, Chief."

Alex left the post office and got into his SUV. He sat behind the wheel for a long moment with his cup of coffee, contemplating what to do.

Tony Anderson worked at the local mill. Sharlene would likely be home alone. It wasn't exactly the chief of police's job to check on the sick, but neither was a long list of other things that Alex found himself doing during the day.

He cranked his vehicle and drove to Pine Cone Lane. The Andersons lived in the last house on the cul-de-sac. As Alex rounded the bend and saw their house, his gut twisted. Tony's white pickup truck was parked out front, but thankfully there was no one outside to see Alex.

Alex's jaw clenched as he slowed. If he turned around and left, he might be leaving Sharlene in a dangerous situation. If he stopped, he might be putting her in more danger.

Following his instincts, he pulled in behind Tony's truck and headed toward the front door. He listened before knocking, hearing no sign of distress inside. After he rapped his knuckles on the door, a dog started barking excitedly.

It sounded ferocious, but Alex knew that the puppy, which appeared to be a cross between a German shepherd and a border collie, was harmless.

Tony barked louder than the dog inside. "Shut up!"

Anger knotted in Alex's chest. Most of the citizens in Sweetwater Springs were good, honest, respectable people. Tony Anderson, however, was an unhappy, mean-spirited, nasty guy. And Alex was pretty sure he used more than his words to lash out at those who lived under his roof.

The door opened, and Tony looked at Alex. Tony was tall and thin. He had a thick five o'clock shadow covering his face, and his breath smelled of whiskey even at the safe four feet of distance between them.

"What do you want?" Tony asked with a sneer.

Alex gave a curt nod. "Good morning to you too." The puppy that had barked excitedly a minute before peeked at him from behind Tony's legs, its head held low in the shadows. "I heard Sharlene was sick. I came to check on her."

Tony folded his arms at his chest. "She's my wife. I'll take care of her."

"I wanted to make sure she was okay," Alex said pointedly.

"She is." Tony puffed out his chest beneath his folded arms. "And unless you have a warrant, you aren't coming inside my house."

Alex gritted his teeth. "Why would I have a warrant to visit a sick townsperson?"

Tony shrugged a nonchalant shoulder. "The thing about being sick is if you get too close, you might find yourself sick too."

Alex shifted restlessly on his feet. His fists reflexively balled, and he dropped his keys accidentally. When he did, the puppy came forward to sniff the item. It put its nose to Alex's keys and then whined softly as Tony grabbed its collar and yanked it back.

"Get out of here, mutt!"

Alex bent to pick up his keys, keeping his gaze trained on Tony the whole time. "He was just seeing if my keys were bacon flavored. He looks a little hungry," he said as he straightened.

"None of your business if my dog is hungry or not. Or if my wife is sick."

Alex shoved his keys into his pocket to free up his hands just in case he needed to protect himself. "Sharlene's a friend. I check on friends who are sick."

"You aren't fooling anyone, Chief. And you aren't coming inside so I suggest you get in your vehicle and get out of my driveway."

The dog inched forward and poked its head out from the side of Tony's leg once more. This time, Tony knocked it back with the heel of his shoe.

"Easy there," Alex warned.

"It was an accident. The dog ran into my foot." Tony cocked his head to one side. Then he stepped off the threshold and onto the porch to stand just inches from Alex. "I'd hate for you to have an accident, too, and maybe trip down those steps."

Alex shook his head. "Threatening a police officer can get you thrown in jail, Tony." And if Alex's gut was correct, that's exactly where Tony belonged.

"Threatening *me*, Chief? If you lock me up, you better lock up my uncle too. You know how he feels about family."

Alex knew the senior Anderson well, although Steve didn't live in the Sweetwater Springs jurisdiction these days.

The puppy limped back onto the porch. Before Tony could act, Alex pushed a hand to his chest. "You're not hurting that dog again."

Tony's face was just a couple of inches from his. "Get your hands off me."

"Matter of fact, animal cruelty is against the law. I'm going to need to take you down to the station for questioning."

"You serious?" Tony scoffed. "I barely touched it. Am I under arrest?"

"Not yet." Alex was sure any good lawyer could probably have Tony released from police custody within hours, but he'd worry about that later. The adorable puppy couldn't protect itself, and detaining Tony would give Alex time to have a chat with Sharlene—*if* she was willing to talk this time.

CHAPTER THREE

$\mathcal{T}$heo had been in the therapist's office for the last hour. Halona usually brought him once a week while her mom closed up shop. Now that Theo felt comfortable with Dr. Natalie Charwood, Halona sat in the waiting room while Theo went in alone.

This was technically free time for her. She usually brought a book, even though she rarely ever read it. She couldn't concentrate long enough to get through one page. Instead, she watched the clock, checked her phone, watched the clock some more, and mentally begged for something to click inside that room to bring her boy back.

In some ways, he was the same old Theo. He still smiled and laughed. He still loved to snuggle up with her and watch movies during the weekends with a huge bowl of popcorn. It was mostly the nightmares and the no-talking thing that worried her.

Halona's phone beeped on her lap. She lifted it, thankful for any distraction, and giggled at a text from

Brenna—a GIF of a woman fanning herself. You should be here with the LDO. It's EXTREMELY HOT!

Brenna was, of course, speaking of the Ladies' Day Out group that she was involved with. The group of women picked an activity and went out a couple of times a month. Halona's mom was also in the group and had been bugging Halona to get involved for a while. Now Brenna also pleaded the case. Sometimes people didn't understand the single-parent life. It wasn't as easy as just leaving Theo with a random babysitter, especially when he wouldn't talk.

Halona stared at her phone, confusion making her eyes squint as she tried to remember what her mom had told her the LDO would be doing this afternoon.

Aren't you eating hot fudge sundaes at Dawanda's Fudge Shop? Halona asked.

We are. And guess who just walked in?

Who? Halona texted back.

Chief Frisky.

Halona was still squinting, this time because she had no idea who Brenna was talking about. Who is that?

You haven't heard the story? Brenna texted back. How is that possible?...I've failed you as a friend. Let's have coffee at the Sweetwater Café in the morning before we open our shops...I need to see your face for this!

Halona laughed out loud in the empty waiting room, the sound filling up the silence. Sounds good! But at least tell me who Chief Frisky is.

Alex Baker, of course. Who else? See you tomorrow!

Halona should've been tipped off by the word *chief*.
It was the adjective *frisky* that threw her. Alex, frisky?
She texted back a quick goodbye and then found herself
needing a distraction from the mention of Alex. Some
part of her wished she was with the LDO right now,
seeing him. And she didn't want to wait to hear the story
behind his nickname either. That definitely had sparked
her interest.

She glanced around the room, and her eye caught on
a pile of pamphlets nearby. She reached for one, reading the announcement of a new community program on
the front.

Mentor Match.

Sweetwater Springs was always coming up with new
events and programs to help the community. This one
was geared toward kids in need of a role model. It offered
once-a-week, one-on-one attention by an adult who'd had
a background check and was good with kids.

Theo might benefit from something like this, she
thought.

The door to the office area opened, and Halona looked
up. "Hey, buddy," she said as Theo came walking toward
her. "Did you have fun?"

He gave an enthusiastic nod, his dark hair falling onto
his forehead.

"Great." She stood and pointed to the chair that she'd
just been sitting in. "You can sit here and read while I
chat with Dr. Charwood for a moment, okay?"

He gave another happy nod.

Once he was settled, Halona stepped out of earshot
and lowered her voice. "Anything?"

Dr. Charwood smiled warmly. "It was a good session. He drew and we played LEGOs. I know it doesn't feel like anything is happening, but Theo is working through things at his own pace. Having another adult that isn't family is sometimes helpful."

"I agree." Halona held up the pamphlet. "What do you think about me signing Theo up for this new Mentor Match program?"

Dr. Charwood glanced down at the material in Halona's hand. "I wasn't sure you'd be interested in that. Honestly, I think it could go either way, depending on who Theo gets matched with. I could put in a call to Jessica Everson, who's running the program, and see if she has any spots left for mentees."

Halona nodded, feeling a spark of hope ignite inside her chest. She'd thought she'd exhausted every resource, but here was a new one. "That would be wonderful."

Dr. Charwood retreated into her office and brought out some paperwork. "While we wait to hear back from Jessica, here is some paperwork to complete for the program."

"Thank you." Halona hugged it to her chest. After saying goodbye, she and Theo walked through the parking lot, got in the car, and drove toward their home on Cedar Trail. "Good session?" she asked, glancing in the rearview mirror.

Theo answered with a smile. He was a happy boy on the outside, and no matter what, Halona would make sure he was the same on the inside too.

* * *

Alex tugged on the collar of his shirt as he headed out of Dawanda's Fudge Shop with his bag of goodies. He hadn't missed that the women inside were staring and whispering about him. He looked down at his shirt to see if there was a stain of some sort. Then he checked his pants to see if there was an embarrassing rip that would warrant their undivided attention. As far as he could see, there was nothing.

He stopped at the bench outside and untied the leash of the little dog he'd confiscated from Tony and Sharlene Anderson's house earlier today. After swinging by the animal shelter and seeing the full cages and lonesome stares between the bars, he hadn't had the heart to leave the puppy there. So, somehow, Alex had found himself temporarily fostering the little guy until the court decided if it would be returned to Tony.

Not happening.

Alex opened the brown paper bag of fudge and pulled out a piece, popping it into his mouth. The small dog looked up with large, wishful eyes. "Sorry, pal. Chocolate is bad for dogs," he said as he and the pup walked down Main Street. "Besides, you shouldn't be hungry after that huge bowl of food I gave you earlier." Alex had never seen a puppy scarf down a bowl of kibbles so quickly. That made him wonder how long the little guy had gone without. "You need a name," he told the pup as they walked. "Whatever Tony was calling you probably wasn't ideal...Comet? What about Pete?"

The dog seemed to roll his eyes as it looked up at him. Then, as if finding something better to attend to, he ran slightly ahead of Alex.

Alex looked up, seeing Theo first. Halona was a couple of steps behind and...the puppy was right. She was definitely worth attending to.

"You got a puppy?" she asked as Theo dropped to

his knees on the pavement and loved on the currently unnamed dog.

"Not exactly. I took this little guy from a bad situation this morning. I'm taking care of him until the court rules on where he goes next."

"Poor little guy," Halona said as a gentle breeze blew dark pieces of her hair around her face.

It took all his willpower not to take his finger and swipe those strands off her cheeks. That wasn't the way he and Halona acted with each other though, not in real life at least. How they behaved together in his mind, however, was a different story. He looked down at the puppy. "I've never had a dog before, but I'm pretty sure I can do a better job than Tony."

Alex looked up to meet Halona's widened eyes. "I wasn't supposed to tell you who the owner was."

She smiled. "I won't tell. Besides, I'd already figured it out. I saw Sharlene walking a puppy who looked a lot like this one the other day."

He nodded, feeling a touch of guilt. It wasn't just Tony's pet he'd taken. It was Sharlene Anderson's too. "Have you by chance seen Sharlene today?"

Halona thought for a second. "No, I don't think so. Why?"

"She wasn't at work, and when I stopped by her house this afternoon, no one answered the door." That was after Alex had taken Tony to the station for another officer to question while he returned to their home on Pine Cone Lane. Either Sharlene was home and pretending she wasn't or she'd left town. Maybe she'd finally decided to leave Tony.

"I hope she's okay," Halona said quietly.

"Me too." But Alex's gut was usually pretty accurate

about people in trouble, and Sharlene fell into that category. Halona didn't these days. She had a lot on her shoulders, that was easy enough to see, but she seemed to be doing well. Still, Alex felt the need to keep coming around and checking on her.

"All right, Theo." Halona tapped Theo's shoulder. "We need to get home and make dinner, and Chief Baker needs to go home and make room for his new puppy."

"It's just temporary," Alex clarified.

Halona grinned as she finally lifted a hand and secured her hair behind her ear the way he'd been itching to do for the last several minutes. "You might realize you like having a dog, Chief Baker. You never know."

Alex seriously doubted it. He liked being able to go home after a long day at the office and relax without needing to cater to another's needs. At least that was the story he told himself. The truth was he wouldn't mind catering to the right pet or person's needs.

His gaze snagged on Halona, and he shook the start of a risky thought away. His head told him she wasn't the right person, but there was a disconnect between his head and his racing heart. Something about Halona Locklear had always short-circuited that connection.

"See you later," she called, taking Theo's hand. Theo waved enthusiastically. The kid had always seemed to like him but Alex thought maybe he'd gained a few points by having a puppy in tow. Perhaps that would also work for some of the folks in town whose bad side he'd gotten on lately by upholding the law no matter the perpetrator.

"Have a good dinner," Alex called as he watched them leave. Then he forced himself to keep walking in the opposite direction and not glance back at Halona, even though he *really* wanted to.

* * *

Halona dragged herself into the kitchen—because skipping dinner was only an option for singles, not doting mothers. With the busy week she'd had so far, however, she hadn't had time to go grocery shopping. The shelves and drawers of her fridge were practically bare. Hard as she tried, she wasn't winning the Mom-of-the-Year award anytime soon.

The doorbell rang, pulling her from her small pity party. Maybe her thoughts were on speed dial, and it was the pizza delivery guy that she hadn't yet called. She walked through the front of the house and opened the door.

"My arms are too full to hug you," Lula said in lieu of hello. She was instead carrying a large pot of something that smelled delicious.

Better than pizza. "What do you have?" Halona asked, opening the door wider so that her mom could step inside.

"Oh, you know, I was cooking and made too much. I thought you and Theo might be hungry."

Halona closed the door behind her and followed her to the kitchen. "You sure you weren't worried that I was starving my son?"

Theo looked up from the kitchen table where he was drawing. Seeing his grandma, he jumped up and darted toward her. Once upon a time he would've ran while shouting, *Elisi, Elisi!* That was the Cherokee word for grandmother, something Lula had taught him as soon as he'd started talking.

"Hold on," Halona told him. "Let Elisi Lula put whatever she has in her hands down first. I'm guessing that's our dinner."

Lula placed it on the kitchen counter and then turned

and opened her arms to Theo. Theo adored his elisi Lula, and she thought he hung the moon every night. They had quite the bond, these two. Theo needed more than a doting grandmother and a tired mom though. Maybe the Mentor Match would fill that need for him.

"Mom, this looks amazing," she said as she lifted the lid to the pot of sweet corn succotash. "There's enough here for a small tribe."

Lula was a community educator, and she loved to teach the people in Sweetwater Springs about her Cherokee heritage. The dances, songs, language, folk stories, and especially the food. "Your dad is on his own tonight. I told him I'm eating with you two. If that's okay."

Tom Locklear wasn't Cherokee and, as such, didn't usually share Lula's passion for food and communing. They couldn't have been more opposite, but it didn't matter. Love was what bound them, and Halona had never questioned her parents' happiness.

Halona shook her head as she looked from her mom to the pot of food.

"No?" Lula asked.

Halona laughed softly. "Yes, of course. Having you over for dinner would be wonderful. I'm just shaking my head at the week I've had," she said as she took the pot to the stove and turned the burner on. "Theo, go get your notebook," she called over her shoulder. "I'm sure Elisi Lula would love to see your artwork." She waited until he was out of earshot before saying anything more.

Halona turned to face her mother. "This dinner is so appreciated. Some weeks I feel like I'm all by myself and barely scraping by. But this week, I've gotten help in unexpected ways."

"Oh?" Lula took a seat at the barstool. "Like what?"

"Well, Theo left school sick yesterday. And, um, *someone* stayed and watched the store for me while I picked him up." Heat tore through Halona's body, and she regretted even bringing the topic up because her mom was as caring as she was nosy.

"It's not like you to let just anyone run your store. Who was it?" Lula asked. She was the only person that Halona ever trusted to run the shop.

Halona returned her focus to the pot full of beans, scallions, peppers, and corn. "Alex Baker," she said, keeping her voice neutral.

"Oh?" Her mom's tone lifted with a hopeful note. It was no secret that Lula loved Tuck's best friends, Mitch and Alex. Between the two of them, Mitch got her brother in trouble and Alex was the one who got them both back in line, winning the greater favor in Lula's eyes.

"It was no big deal," Halona continued. "It's just unexpected help."

"That's quite a favor for a busy police chief," Lula said. "What was he even doing in your shop?"

Halona glanced over her shoulder. "Oh, well, he came by to order an arrangement for the wife of one of his officers."

"That was awfully nice of him," Lula said with a knowing look in her eye. Whatever she thought she knew was wrong though. Or mostly wrong.

"Yes, it was." Halona faced her mom. "When I got back to the shop with Theo, he just ran right up to Alex and gave him a huge hug."

"Maybe Theo is missing a male influence in his life. It would be natural for a boy to think about his father, especially this close to Christmas."

Halona nodded. "He's been calling out for his daddy during his nightmares lately."

Lula leaned forward and propped her elbows on the counter. "When I was growing up on the reservation, we used to do a seven-day cleanse after someone died."

"Mom, it's been two years since Ted's accident, and *I* didn't grow up on the reservation."

"I know." Lula held up a hand. "You and Tuck don't keep to most of the tribal traditions, and I'm not suggesting that you do a cleanse. It was part of our tribe's grief process though. We allowed ourselves to mourn before moving on. I'm certainly not telling you how to mother, but I don't think Theo has had that chance."

"He has therapy sessions every week," Halona pointed out.

"And yet he's still holding everything in along with his words."

Halona stirred the contents of the pot as she considered what her mom was saying. "Maybe so. But I've exhausted everything I can think of. I don't even know what to do anymore."

"This is just a suggestion but you could talk about Ted. The person, not the football star that everyone else in town remembers."

Ted was so much more complicated than the sports hero everyone admired. Halona didn't talk about him much, because along with the good memories came the bad.

Lula cleared her throat, gaining Halona's attention. "Maybe Theo needs to see his mom moving on as well."

"Mom..."

"Maybe not today, but you can't stay single forever. Tuck found love again after Renee."

Halona's brother had a different story though. His

wife had died of cancer, and he didn't have a child to raise. Ted had divorced Halona before his death. He'd said that she and Theo were better off without him. She hated to admit that sometimes she thought maybe he was right. Ted was having a harder time controlling his angry outbursts, and the medication that the doctors prescribed wasn't helping.

Theo padded back into the kitchen with his notebook and climbed up on the stool beside his grandma. He slid the notebook in front of her.

"Want me to take a look?" Lula asked, thankfully dropping the subject of Halona's dating life. Theo nodded at his elisi Lula.

Halona continued to absently stir their dinner as it heated on the stove, the aroma of spices wafting under her nose and making her stomach twist with hunger. Had she eaten lunch today? She'd made sure that Theo had, but she thought maybe she'd forgotten herself.

"Oh, I like that one." Lula pointed at a drawing that Halona couldn't quite make out across the distance. "And that one." Lula continued to flip the pages, oohing and aahing. Dr. Charwood had come up with this idea. Theo used his notebook to draw pictures and write what he wanted to communicate.

Lula stopped on the page where Theo had drawn a picture of Alex with the puppy he was temporarily fostering and glanced up at Halona with that knowing look in her eyes again.

What in the world did she think she knew?

"It seems everyone in the Locklear family enjoys Chief Baker's company," Lula said.

* * *

Alex climbed into his vehicle and drove to his home. He lived on a large lot surrounded by mature trees that provided shade during the summer months. During the winter months, such as now, they seemed to wrap him and his house into their cozy crook and insulate them from the cold. The puppy darted up the front porch steps, tail wagging and already acting like this was his new home.

Don't get attached, pal.

Alex opened the door, and the pup ran inside. No one had offered to take the puppy home, but one of the officers at the station had given Alex a Ziploc bag of dog food. Alex walked into the kitchen and grabbed a mixing bowl to pour the contents of the baggie into. Then he set up a water bowl. When he was done catering to his temporary houseguest, he turned to the refrigerator and briefly considered opening it up. The fudge had hit the spot though. When he was younger, his mom would've had words about him counting his treat from Dawanda's Fudge Shop as dinner, but he was a grown man and his mom lived in Florida now. He needed to call her, but he was too drained to do so tonight. Too drained to stand behind the stove or grill either.

Instead, he grabbed the case file he'd brought home with him and headed onto the back porch to allow the puppy time to run around the yard and get acquainted with the squirrels who were still stowing away acorns for the winter. The squirrels taunted the pup in the same way that this file taunted him.

He sat at the table on his deck and leaned back in his chair, propping one foot over the opposite knee. Then he opened the file. He knew it inside and out, had every word memorized. And still, some days, he thought maybe, just maybe, he'd happen upon a clue, see it in a different way, and the entire mystery of his father's death would finally be solved.

Alex had just graduated from the police academy and couldn't wait to work under his dad's command, but he'd never gotten that opportunity. The following weekend, his father was run down in the street. The vehicle, a truck, had accelerated prior to impact. His father was knocked a hundred feet from his police cruiser, which was pulled to the side of the road. He'd just stopped someone to inform them of a broken taillight. That car had already driven off, leaving no witnesses to whatever happened. He'd been found lying inches deep in the new fallen snow just a few days before Christmas.

It wasn't an accident. It was intentional. How could Alex be a good cop, the chief of police, if he couldn't even solve his own father's murder?

A few feet away, the puppy barked ferociously at a silvery-gray rabbit that sprinted across the lawn and disappeared into the woods. He didn't chase after it, just guarded what he regarded as his turf.

Alex returned his attention to the file. He'd already interviewed the driver, Granger Fields, whom his father had pulled over for the broken taillight just minutes before his death. His father had informed him of the light and let him go on his merry way. Granger hadn't seen anything. Even so, Alex would pay him another visit sometime in the next week. Granger and his father owned Merry Mountain Farms. He wasn't a suspect, wasn't even a witness, but he was the last person to see Alex's father before the hit and run.

Alex continued thumbing through the contents of the file, stopping on the picture of his dad's shoe in the snow where it had landed after impact. This particular piece of evidence had always bothered him. Only one shoe had been found on the scene. The other was missing, and there'd been footprints leading to and away from his dad's body. Whoever hit his dad had stopped to check on him. Then, for a reason Alex couldn't explain, the perp had taken one of his father's shoes. Why?

The prints in the snow had been useless. Other prints had trampled over them as passersby came to help his father. Then the paramedics had rushed him to the hospital.

Alex had already interviewed those passersby and the paramedics, more than once. He sighed, his breath coming out in a white puff. He could interview the emergency crew again, but they'd tell him the same thing. His father had been unconscious the whole time he was in the ambulance; he hadn't said a word. The detectives working the case had found no evidence on his dad's clothing either. Every lead was a dead end.

The last document in the file was something Alex had only added last year. It was a list of all the cases his father had been working at his time of death. Maybe whoever hit him had a vendetta. He'd checked out everyone on the list, but only one name stood out.

Steve Anderson.

Steve was Tony Anderson's uncle. Alex had interviewed him last year, and his gut told him there was more than Steve was saying. For the most part, Steve was quiet these days. Alex couldn't get a search warrant without probable cause, and Steve had an alibi for the evening that Alex's dad was hit. He'd also been none too happy about Alex coming around and questioning him.

Too bad. Alex would be paying Steve another visit this year. He'd also check that alibi once more, looking for discrepancies. And maybe, just maybe, he'd find a reason to get a search warrant to tear apart Steve Anderson's home.

An incoming text got Alex's attention. It was from Brian Everson. The good mayor apparently wasn't going to give up.

I'll be in my office most of the morning tomorrow. Come by first thing.

When Alex had seen Brian at the café, the request to talk had sounded more like an invitation. This sounded like a direct order, and coming from someone who was technically Alex's boss, he couldn't ignore it.

Alex frowned. Being summoned to the mayor's office sat about as well with him as Steve Anderson's flimsy alibi.

CHAPTER FOUR

$\mathcal{T}$he next morning, Halona stepped inside the Sweet-water Café and breathed in the heavy aroma of freshly brewed coffee. She spotted Brenna already seated at a table in the corner, nursing her own beverage. In fairness, Halona was running about ten minutes late. She'd had to drop Theo off at school and then run home to fetch the lunch box that he'd forgotten.

Halona stepped up to the counter and smiled at the café owner.

"Good morning, Halona," Emma said with her usually bright smile. "What can I get for you?"

Halona furrowed her brow. "You mean you don't know? This is a first."

Emma laughed. "Let's just say I haven't had *my* coffee yet this morning. Sniffing it in the air doesn't count."

Halona placed her order and watched Emma buzz around. Caffeine or not, she still had more than her fair share of energy.

"I hired Kyle Martin to start helping me over the weekends," Emma told her as she worked.

"Aw, that's great." Kyle had gotten into trouble with the law last winter. He'd been robbing downtown stores to pay for his mom's cancer treatment. Last Halona had heard, his mother, Cassie, was doing better.

"I might need to hire more help during the week too," Emma continued, sliding Halona's cup of coffee and muffin in front of her.

Halona handed Emma her debit card. "It does get busy in here."

"Busy is good," Emma said, swiping the card and handing it back. "But now that the morning has lulled, it's time for me to make my own cup of java."

Halona took her breakfast. "Enjoy!"

"That's my line," Emma called as Halona turned and headed toward the table.

"Sorry I'm late." Halona took the seat across from Brenna. It faced Main Street, and Halona was able to see community members as they passed by.

"You're right on time," Brenna said. "I was early. Couldn't sleep."

Halona sighed softly. "I could but my little boy wouldn't let me."

"So we'll both be having refills before going to work this morning."

"How was Ladies' Day Out yesterday?" Halona asked.

Brenna unwrapped her breakfast bagel. "A lot of fun. Lula is a hoot, by the way."

Halona picked a piece off her muffin and popped it into her mouth. "That's one word for my mom...No, she's great. Truly. I couldn't make it some days without her."

When Halona looked up, she saw sympathy in Brenna's

eyes. Brenna knew most of Halona's struggles with being divorced and a single mom. She didn't know the details of Ted's illness or their marriage though. No one did. Some things you kept private, even from one of your best friends.

"You really should come out with us next time," Brenna said. "It's only once or twice a month, and it's so good to be with these ladies. I literally feel like I did a huge ab workout last night because I laughed so hard."

Halona smiled. "I'll think about it."

"I know it's hard with Theo, but I'm sure you could find someone you trust to watch him. I've heard Maisey Landover's teenaged little sister babysits for others. I see Maisey all the time. I can get her number for you," Brenna offered.

"I already have it. Maybe I'll check with Maisey," Halona said, before taking another bite of her muffin. She already knew she wouldn't check though. Maisey had been a couple of years younger than Brenna and her in school, but she'd been a hellion back then, and rumor had it that her little sister was following in Maisey's footsteps.

Brenna leaned back in her chair, her dark hair falling over the back rungs. "I'm not going to quit bugging you, you know. Joining the LDO is one of the best things I've done for myself."

Halona had to admit she was curious and envious of all the fun that the ladies seemed to have together. She needed more fun in her life. "I'll try to come along soon. So...tell me about Chief Frisky."

Brenna choked on her bite of bagel for a brief second. "Oh, that's right," she said after she'd swallowed. "You don't know."

"And that's the reason you suggested meeting here for breakfast," Halona reminded her.

"No, that was the excuse. I really just wanted to chat before going to work. Some days it's just me cooking at the oven all day."

"And some days it's just me talking to the flowers," Halona said, reminding herself of what Alex had said when he'd tended her shop for an hour.

Brenna lifted one dark eyebrow. "Talking to flowers? You might be crazier than I am."

They both burst into laughter.

"Okay, here's the Chief Frisky story, as promised. Do you know Greta Merchant? Pushing eighty and walks with a cane even though she's more physically fit than most twentysomethings."

Halona nodded.

"Well, she has a huge crush on Chief Baker. But who doesn't, right?"

Halona averted her gaze. She didn't even want to admit her attraction to Alex to herself, much less Brenna.

"So a couple of months ago, Greta decided to go shoplifting."

"What? Sweet little Greta?"

"Don't worry—Sophie was in on it. Alex had happened to come into the boutique looking for a gift for his grandmother's birthday, and Greta and Sophie exchanged some conspiratorial whispers. Sophie knew Greta was going to be stuffing costume jewelry in her pockets. Then Sophie called Greta out on it loud enough for Alex to overhear."

Halona covered her mouth with one hand. "That's so wrong."

"But also hilarious. Being the dutiful chief of police

Alex is, he headed over and spoke to Greta. He asked her to empty her pockets but she refused. She demanded that he frisk her instead. From the way Greta tells the story, it was the most action she's had in decades."

Halona laughed so hard that she had to press a hand to her side. "Did he arrest her?" she asked when she could breathe again.

"Nah. Sophie told him she wasn't pressing charges."

Halona and Brenna chatted a little more and then both women got refills on their coffees before heading in separate directions to open their stores.

Halona felt lighter as she entered the Little Shop of Flowers, still giggling to herself at the image of Greta Merchant getting frisked by Alex. That image turned to thoughts of him frisking Halona as well.

No, no, no. Not going there.

She turned on the OPEN sign and headed to the coolers to check on her flowers. She removed the select few that would only stay fresh another day or two and put them into an arrangement that she'd offer some lucky customer for free later this morning.

Her phone rang as she worked, and she hoped it wasn't Theo's school. If she continued to have to leave her shop to go deal with him, she really would need to think about hiring part-time help.

She glanced at her caller ID, not recognizing the number. "Hello?"

"Hi, Halona. This is Jessica Everson. I'm calling about the Mentor Match application that you filled out for Theo."

Halona squeezed her cell phone a little tighter. "Yes. I wasn't sure if the program was full or if you could squeeze him in." She crossed her fingers beside her, hoping she wasn't too late in enrolling Theo.

"We can definitely squeeze him in. I'm matching up mentors and mentees right now and wanted to know a little bit about the kind of person Theo gets along best with."

"Oh." Halona sat on a stool and looked out on her shop full of vibrant colored flowers as she considered the question. "Well, he loves to be outside, but he's not great with large crowds. He loves to read, loves animals, and watching Christmas movies is a big hit with him this time of year."

"Of course it is. Do you think a male mentor would be best or a female? Not that I can make any promises in that department."

Halona hesitated. Theo did well with females but he had enough women in his life. The only guy he had was his uncle Tuck, who came around as often as he could, but between work, his fiancée, and his teenaged daughter, it wasn't as often as Theo needed. "I think a male influence would be really good for him."

* * *

Alex stepped up to Mayor Everson's office door mid-morning and knocked three times.

"Come in," Brian called from inside.

Alex and Brian were friends well before either held prominent positions in town. Once upon a time, Brian was on the path to the Olympics. Fate had twisted and turned along with a winding mountain road, however, and left him in a wheelchair.

"It's about time you came to see me." Brian grinned

from behind his large cherry-stained desk. The wheel-chair hadn't slowed him down one bit. Not only was he the mayor of Sweetwater Springs but he and his wife, Jessica, also headed the Special Olympics in town for children with special needs. "Have a seat."

Alex dutifully sat down in the chair across from Brian. He'd left the puppy he was caring for at the station with Tammy. He'd tried to get her to foster the puppy since she seemed to like him so much but she'd shot that idea down immediately, claiming she didn't have the time or patience at home.

Alex could relate to that but he was really getting attached to the little guy. He'd already stopped at the local pet store to get him a bed and chew toys.

"You know what I want to talk to you about," Brian said. "I'm worried because of the year you've had."

Alex nodded. Over the past twelve months, the local media had caught him in less than favoring circumstances. "Janice has been spiking the punch at community events for years. It was time to make her understand that she couldn't do that anymore."

"I agree," Brian said, folding his hands together.

"Then why are you lecturing me about it?"

"I wouldn't be if it were just one isolated incident that raised some eyebrows but there was also what happened at Sophie's Boutique earlier this year."

Alex massaged his forehead with one hand. "Greta and Sophie set me up. Not my fault." And now the women in town had nicknamed him Chief Frisky. How much respect could a chief with that kind of title possibly get?

"Tony Anderson is also upset with you right now. Before you know it, he'll be spreading some nasty rumors about you."

Alex folded his arms across his chest. "Seriously? No one listens to him."

"Some do." Brian leaned forward. "Not me, of course. I know his character, and I know yours. You're one of the best guys I know. I just want to make sure that's how everyone else sees you. You need an image reset," Brian said.

"You want me to stand on the corner dressed like Santa and ring a bell?" Alex asked.

"Not exactly what I had in mind."

Alex raised a brow. "So you have something in mind already? What is it?"

Brian reached for a file on his desk. "Jessica is putting together a new program that I think is going to be amazing for this community. Working with the Special Olympics, we see a lot of kids who struggle with more than just their physical disabilities. Some come from broken homes. The idea is that these kids need someone to look up to, to take them under their wing a couple of times a week and give them a new view on the world."

Alex sat back in his chair. "This is a great idea but I'm not a babysitter, Brian. I deal with criminals, not kids."

Brian chuckled. "Maybe in your mind's eye, you do. But the crime rate in Sweetwater Springs is at an all-time low, another reason you need to stay in your position. This would be after your duty hours. You would be assigned as a mentor for one child and take them out regularly. Spend some quality time with them. That's it."

"How will this help my image?"

"We need to promote the program. We'll use you and a few other prominent citizens to do it. As a result, you'll be associated as a mentor for a child in need and not a police chief who harasses little old ladies. Win-win."

"I don't harass anyone," Alex bit out.

"Christmas is fast approaching. I can't think of a better time to give these kids the TLC they need."

Alex's argument stuck in his throat. Maybe he didn't care if some town members thought he was a hardened police chief but he did care about the kids in his community. "It sounds like a worthwhile program."

Brian smiled. "I think so. We already have a list of kids who need a mentor. Their parents have signed the permission slips for the program, and we're ready to roll it out. Jess has also come up with a list of suggested mentor activities. All we need is a few good men and women to say yes. You'd be setting the first example."

First, he'd taken a dog under his wing, and now he was going to be mentoring a kid? How had this happened?

He really wanted to say no. Some part of him couldn't though. If there was a kid who'd benefit from a few hours of his time, then he couldn't refuse. "Fine."

Brian chuckled. "I knew you'd come around."

"When do I get started?"

Brian tapped the file again. "After you do the training."

"Training?"

"It's mandatory for the program. To provide the mentors with guidelines and rules. We're giving the first one tonight. After that, you receive a certificate, and we give you a kid to mentor."

Alex wondered at the tightness in his chest, suddenly making it hard to take in a full breath. Nerves or fear? He wasn't sure. But how hard could mentoring one kid be?

* * *

Halona glanced in the rearview mirror as she drove along the curving roads. Theo was in the back seat with a new book in his lap. He'd likely read all afternoon while she prepared the chapel for Carrie and Jacob's wedding rehearsal later this evening. "If you finish that tonight, we'll stop at the library tomorrow," she told him.

He met her gaze in the mirror and smiled back. She took that as a yes. The library was his favorite place, and the town's librarian, Lacy Shaw, was one of his favorite people. They were both shy by nature and also avid readers. Two of a kind.

She smiled at the beauty of the drive as she disappeared back into her own thoughts. The weather tomorrow promised to be gorgeous. Chilly, yes—it was the North Carolina mountains after all—but not so much that the bride and groom would have icicles collecting on them if they stood outside for too long.

After a couple more bends and curves, Halona turned onto Chapel Road and pulled into the church parking lot. She was usually the first to arrive at events like this, setting the stage for everything that followed. Sometimes she enlisted the help of her mom or even her sister-in-law-to-be, Josie. Carrie and Jacob's wedding was a small one though. Halona could do it on her own while Theo read quietly. She'd be finished long before the rehearsal in a couple of hours. Hopefully by that time, she and Theo would be snuggled on the couch and watching a movie. *That* was her idea of a good Friday night.

She backed her car up to the front steps of the church so she could easily unload the arrangements that she'd finished up last night before closing the shop. Then she opened Theo's door. "Ready?"

He nodded and unbuckled. A moment later, he wandered out of sight with his book. They had rules established for situations like this. He had to stay inside the building. No going outside without her permission for any reason.

Halona put her earbuds in and turned on some light music on her phone. Then she set about carrying the boxes of flowers into the sanctuary. This was the easy part of her job. No matter where she put them, it brightened and transformed the room.

She sang as she worked, the advantage of being the first to arrive. On Sunday mornings in this very church, she sang traditional hymns. On weekday nights, however, she sang alternative tunes that would probably make Pastor Phillips cringe.

Theo had earbuds of his own so there was no risk of him hearing her. He tended to prefer classical music. Sometimes she wondered where he'd come from, because his preferences were so different from her own. And he certainly hadn't gotten his love of reading or Beethoven from Ted, whose primary passions had been football and family.

A puppy dashed past Halona as she knelt next to the podium with red dahlias in hand.

Halona screeched at the unexpectedness of the animal and then lost her balance and tumbled to the floor. She caught herself on her elbow to avoid crushing the delicate flowers. Once she'd regained her composure, she faced the dog that wiggled and wagged in front of her.

"Where did you come from?" she asked. Had she left the front door open? It must have wandered through. She recognized it from yesterday, and her heart skipped before she saw its temporary owner coming toward her.

Was it just her or was she running into Alex Baker on a daily basis these days? Coincidence or something more?

"Sorry. We're working on obedience," he said.

Halona looked between the pup and his temporary master. "How's the dog-watching going?"

"Good. He has a name now."

"Oh?"

Alex gave a curt nod. He was wearing a jacket this afternoon that hugged his arms and chest. Why did he have to be so attractive? It wasn't just his looks; it was the way he carried himself, his smile, and that voice that seemed to rumble on the air. "I've realized that puppies like to chew," he said.

Halona felt herself grin, knowing exactly where this was leading.

"My favorite pair of tennis shoes were a great teether for this little guy."

"Oh no." Halona stood to face Alex while still holding the dahlias in her hand. "I'm sorry."

He shrugged. "I can always get another pair. I have invested heavily in real dog chew toys though." He looked down affectionately at the pup and then bent to collect it in his arms. Halona melted a little bit at the sight of a big, strong police chief holding an energetic ball of fur that desperately wanted to lap its tongue over his cheek.

Alex kept the dog pinned firmly against his chest, holding him a few inches from his face. "He's also a big hit at the police station so we've made him an honorary officer." Alex glanced down, and this time the pup leaped in his arms, its tongue making contact with Alex's cheek, evoking a deep, sexy laugh from him.

Heart, be still.

"So I'm calling him Officer Chew." Alex put the puppy back down and then looked up at Halona.

She hoped she didn't have drool coming from the

corner of her mouth like Officer Chew did. "That's a great name. Do you know if you have to give him back?"

"The vet has already done X-rays and a wellness check. It looks like the little guy has already suffered a couple of broken bones in his short life. We have a strong case."

Halona frowned. "And Sharlene? Did you ever find her?"

"Apparently, she has a sister in Wild Blossom Bluffs. At least that's what she claimed when I spoke to her on the phone. She'll be back in town this weekend."

"You think she was lying?" Halona asked.

"I think she was protecting Tony. But for the life of me, I can't figure out why."

Halona felt the need to look away. She hated knowing that Alex thought the same about her. It hadn't been that way with her ex at all.

"Madonna, huh?" he finally said, changing the subject to something that made her squirm just as much.

Her cheeks burned hot as she met his gaze again. "Hmm?"

"I heard you singing when I walked in."

"Oh." She swiped her hair out of her eyes and shrugged, her fingers curling around the stems of the dahlias. Officer Chew propped his paws on her leg, whining softly for her attention, but she was completely focused on the man in front of her. "It helps me work, for some reason."

"You don't have it playing in your store," he noted.

Alex Baker was never one to miss a detail. Except he'd missed so many in her marriage to Ted. Everyone had. That was more of a credit to her ability to keep personal things private than to his powers of observation.

"Not that you can hear." She winked. "When the earbuds are in, it's a safe bet that Madonna's playing."

"The things I never knew about Halona Locklear." Alex patted his thigh. "Come here, Officer Chew. Leave the pretty woman alone."

She swallowed hard at the compliment.

"I just saw your vehicle here and guessed that you were preparing for Carrie and Jacob's wedding tomorrow. I'm on my way home to drop Chew off and then go to a training."

"Always on the job," she commented, "keeping the citizens of Sweetwater Springs safe."

She thought she saw something dark pass over his expression, there and gone. Tomorrow was the start of December. It was the warmest month to some despite the dropping temperatures outside. It was the coldest to others whose memories hung over the festivities like dark shadows.

"Say hello to Theo for me," he said, taking a few retreating steps.

"He drew you in his journal yesterday," Halona told him before thinking.

Alex seemed to freeze. "How do you know it was me?"

Halona shrugged. "Let's see. Tall, yellow hair, and a big badge on the shirt."

"I don't have yellow hair."

She grinned. "Crayola doesn't make strawberry-blond-colored pencils. He drew a dog next to you as well that looked just like this one." Without thinking, Halona stepped forward to pat the pup's head, the movement bringing her close enough to catch the scent of Alex's aftershave. Mint leaves and pine sap, nature at its finest.

"This little dog is going to make me very popular with the kids," he said.

And with the ladies.

Alex held her gaze a second too long, and she wondered if he could hear her blaring thoughts. She hoped not. His eyes were more than a simple blue, she realized, unable to break contact. They had depths of color like the ocean, bending in the light and offering shades that ranged from gray to an almost turquoise.

Officer Chew barked.

"Right. Right." Alex looked down at him. "The pretty woman needs to work, and I have training. You can return to your Madonna music. I won't tell Pastor Phillips." One side of his mouth turned up in a soft smile before he turned and exited the room.

Pastor Phillips also shouldn't be informed about the tingly sensations zipping from her toes to her chest as she watched him walk away or about the lustful thoughts popping up in her mind like dandelions in an open pasture.

CHAPTER FIVE

Alex still couldn't quite believe he'd agreed to mentoring a kid. There was a handful of adults in the room for the mandatory training tonight. All of them would be great role models for a child.

Bo Matthews was an architect in town. His brother Cade, a landscape designer, was seated beside him. Kaitlyn Russo, the owner of the Sweetwater Bed and Breakfast, was standing at the table of complimentary coffee and cookies chatting with Paris Montgomery, a local graphic designer.

Granger Fields walked in and sat a few chairs down from Alex.

Alex waved and headed over to say hello. "Should've known I'd see you here."

Granger smiled widely. "Alex, gotta say I'm surprised to see you. You're a busy guy."

Alex nodded. "And it's the busiest time of year too."

Granger's smile faltered a little. "I've been expecting

you to stop by the Christmas tree farm. I'll save you a trip though, Chief. Your dad told me about my broken taillight; I thanked him and continued driving to my girlfriend's house at the time." He shrugged and offered a half smile. "That's all I got. I'm sorry."

Alex nodded. "I know. There's not much to go on though, so I gotta ask. Maybe on your way you passed a truck on the side of the road. Maybe someone was waiting for you to leave so they could go after my dad."

Granger shook his head. "I was young. My attention was one hundred percent on seeing my girlfriend, who broke up with me that Christmas."

"Smart girl," Alex teased, attempting to lift the mood of the conversation. "Thanks anyway."

"Sure. Feel free to question me every December. I don't mind. I just wish I had more information to offer you."

Alex nodded. "Thanks."

"Also feel free to come get a tree at the farm. We've got a large lot of evergreens."

Alex hadn't been one to put up a tree or celebrate since he was an adult. His mom had always done the decorating when he was growing up, but after his dad's death, even she had lost her holiday spirit. She didn't even come to Sweetwater Springs for Christmas anymore. "Maybe so," Alex said, not committing.

"Great," Granger said. "See you at Merry Mountain."

Alex said goodbye and headed back to his seat. A minute later, he felt someone beat a hand on his back.

"Hey, bud." Tuck sat down in the chair beside him.

"You got roped into this too, huh?" Alex asked.

"Actually, I volunteered," Tuck said.

"I would think that you have your hands full with Maddie."

Tuck laughed. "And you'd be right about that. But it's just a couple of hours a week. And I want to give back. I wasn't there for Maddie growing up. I'm thankful that other people were. I want to be that person for someone else. I think it'll make me feel better about the time I missed with my daughter."

"Makes sense."

"And you?" Tuck asked.

"Mayor Everson thinks it'll be good for my image. Soften it up a little bit."

"Thought this was for the kids," Tuck said, arching one dark brow.

"Well, he thinks I'll be good for that too. I don't know why. I don't know the first thing about kids. Going into the schools to talk to them is the most nervous I ever get."

Tuck folded his arms over his chest and leaned back in the chair. "I don't know. I hear my nephew loves you."

"Theo is great," Alex said.

Tuck nodded. "I think he's going to follow in his father's footsteps and be a football legend." He poked an elbow into Alex's side. "If you can tear him away from his books, that child has quite the arm."

Alex's jaw tightened at the mention of Ted. Everyone in town was fooled by Ted's charm. Not Alex. Ted had a hidden side to him. Alex had taken him to jail once, but Ted's fancy lawyer had gotten him out and made sure the whole thing was hush-hush. Before Ted had walked free, Alex informed him that if he ever harmed Halona again, there would be consequences. Ted was such a good actor that he'd almost fooled Alex that night when he'd claimed he loved his family and would never willingly hurt them.

What did that even mean? Nobody held Ted at gunpoint and made him hit Halona.

Regardless if Ted's act was sincere, he had died in a skiing accident later that same year. He'd always been athletic and a little bit of an adrenaline junkie but he'd never acted recklessly before that night. Ted had been skiing on one of the highest slopes during severe weather, almost as if he had a death wish.

Breaking Alex's train of thought, Jessica Everson walked to the front of the room and waved an arm to gain everyone's attention. "Looks like we're still missing a couple of people. We'll wait a few more minutes before getting started. Please help yourself to refreshments," she said.

Tuck hopped up. "Want anything?" he asked Alex, who didn't budge.

Yeah, Alex wanted out of here. He had work to do. And Officer Chew was probably missing him at home. "No, thanks."

Two more people entered the room. Dr. Andrea Lauren was a pediatrician in town. Luke Marini was new in town and worked in fire and rescue. Alex had only exchanged greetings with Luke to this point but he seemed like a nice enough guy.

Five minutes later, Jessica went back to the front of the room.

"Thank you all so much for coming tonight. I'm very excited about this special project. I think it'll benefit you all as much as the kids. At least I'm hoping that's true."

The meeting lasted an hour and a half. They reviewed what to do, what not to do, and a few solutions for situations that might occur—like the child demanding to go home or asking you to buy them something. The answer to that was to always check with the parents if you would like to buy something. The parents kept complete control over all issues, and they were to be kept in the loop about anything important that went on during the outing.

"Lastly," Jessica said, "parents are not to come along on your Mentor Match outings. The mentees need time away. That's the point. I know it's busy over the holidays, but this is the time that kids need someone the most. I chose you all because you're dependable, good, and caring people. I know all of the children will be so lucky to have you on their side."

Alex left the meeting with a pamphlet to review at his leisure. On Monday morning, Jessica would be calling with the name of the child assigned to him.

"Hey, Al?" Tuck ran up beside Alex as he was leaving. "Trying to slip off without saying goodbye?"

"Sorry." Alex turned to his friend. "I was just lost in thought."

"I don't know about you but I'm excited about this Mentor Match thing," Tuck said.

Alex laughed. "Heaven help the kid that gets you."

"And the one that gets you," Tuck teased. "It's Friday night. Let's go to the Tipsy Tavern for that drink you agreed to the other day. I'll buy."

"Can't. I have a puppy at home."

Tuck frowned. "Officer Chew has only been alone for a couple of hours. And, knowing where he came from, he probably doesn't mind it. Come on."

Alex hedged for just a moment. "A drink actually sounds good right about now."

"That's right," Tuck said. "Nothing wrong with a little liquid courage before we embark on this new mentoring endeavor."

Fifteen minutes later, Alex felt relaxed with a beer in one hand and good conversation from Tuck and Mitch, who'd also agreed to join them.

"I feel a little offended that I didn't get asked to help start this Mentor Match program," Mitch said. "I'm good with kids. Why did Kaitlyn get asked instead of me?"

Tuck and Alex shared a look.

"You're great with kids but I think your grumpy disposition might scare them," Tuck said. He measured an inch between his thumb and index fingers. "Just a little bit."

Alex shook his head. "Kaitlyn has changed that for the better. And you'd be a great mentor. You're one of my best officers at the station."

Mitch tipped the neck of his bottle at Alex. "Thank you."

"I'll tell Jessica to set you up with a kid next time," Alex said.

Mitch's jaw slackened. "I wanted to complain but I don't actually want to be a mentor."

Tuck chuckled. "That's probably why she didn't ask you, buddy. Plus you have two jobs. You're a police officer, and you help Kaitlyn host the bed and breakfast."

"That's all Kaitlyn and my mom," Mitch told them. "Well, except for the yard work and the heavy lifting. And whenever something is broken and needs fixing." He nodded. "Yeah, I'm pretty busy."

"Not too busy to hang out tonight though." Tuck lifted his drink to his mouth. "We should do this more often," he said before taking a drink.

"Josie and Maddie might have something to say about that," Alex argued.

"So how is Grandma Baker these days?" Mitch asked then.

Alex peeled the label on his bottle. "She's part of the Ladies' Day Out group, which is really good for her."

"The more women that are added, the more out of control they get," Tuck said.

Mitch agreed. "They didn't even whisper the other day when I walked past them. I won't tell you some of the inappropriate things I overheard."

Both Alex and Tuck howled with laughter.

"Kaitlyn really enjoys being part of the group." Mitch narrowed his eyes at Tuck. "She wasn't checking you out when you saw them, was she?"

Tuck grinned. "Relax. She only has eyes for you, buddy."

And since before he could remember, Alex only had eyes for one woman, who wasn't part of the women's group.

* * *

Halona walked into the Sweetwater Café on Monday morning and looked around. Brenna waved from the same table where they'd sat the other day.

After getting her usual, which Emma remembered this time, Halona headed over. "Fancy meeting you here."

"Sit," Brenna said, gesturing to the chair across from her. "I was hoping you'd show up."

Halona took a seat and smiled back at her friend. "I wondered if I'd run into you as well."

"Match made in heaven."

"Speaking of matches, I'm supposed to find out who Theo's Mentor Match is at some point today," Halona said.

"I trust Jessica. She'll set Theo up with the perfect person for him," Brenna offered. "Any business-related events over the weekend?"

"Just Carrie and Jacob's wedding and a funeral on Sunday." Halona lifted her coffee to her lips and took a taste. "I got orders all last week for flowers to be delivered to the funeral home. Family and friends catered it," she added so that Brenna wouldn't worry about competitors.

Brenna nodded. "I catered a baby shower. They invited me to stay for the party and eat Snickers poop out of diapers."

Halona felt her face twist uncomfortably. "Did you?"

"Oh yeah; I love Snickers bars." Brenna giggled. "And babies." She sighed dreamily. "What girl doesn't?"

"I'm not sure I could eat a candy bar smashed up and labeled as poop though," Halona pointed out. "And this is not an appetizing breakfast conversation."

Brenna laughed. "No, it isn't. I do have something else to discuss with you though. Lights on Silver Lake is this weekend. Are you staying open for it?"

Lights on Silver Lake was the opening event for the Christmas season in Sweetwater Springs. The Christmas tree in the town square was lit for the first time, and all the downtown stores stayed open for extended shopping hours. Halona usually sold quite a lot of poinsettias that weekend.

"Of course. You?"

Brenna shrugged a shoulder. "I didn't last year but I thought I would this time. Maybe put out a spread of holiday-themed hors d'oeuvres. Maybe people will keep me in mind for catering their Christmas parties."

"Great idea. It's a lot of fun." Halona still hadn't

figured out who would take care of Theo that night though. Lula was active with the event. Last year, Tuck had taken Theo. He might be busy this year with his Mentor Match though.

"Well, I have to get to work. I have a potential bride and groom coming in today. I'll send them your way for their floral needs," Brenna promised.

"Thanks. I have to get to work too. Hopefully I'll see you again this week?"

"Hope so," Brenna said with a wave.

Halona grabbed her coffee, called a goodbye to Emma behind the counter, and walked out onto the sidewalk to head to her store.

It was a beautiful morning. The air was cool on her face, a little breeze lifting her hair and tickling her neck. She fumbled for her keys to the store and pushed the right one inside the lock. It sprung open, and Halona stepped inside where it felt and smelled just as fresh as the outdoors.

No sooner had she opened the door than her phone started buzzing inside her purse. Halona pulled it out and sighed when she saw the school's number on her caller ID.

"Hello?"

"Ms. Locklear? This is Chris Nelson, the school's principal."

Halona had come to expect a call from the school's nurse but not the principal. "Is everything all right?"

"Don't worry. Theo is fine but he is in trouble."

Halona's knees weakened a little bit. "What did he do?"

"I usually make the students tell their parents them-selves," Principal Nelson said.

"Oh, no, Theo doesn't—"

"I know Theo isn't much of a talker these days but he can write it down. I'll fill in the gaps if needed. It makes a bigger impact on the students if they have to look you in the eye and see your reaction. We'll be waiting here at the school office for you."

Halona sucked in a deep breath. The air didn't smell so sweet anymore. "I'll be there as soon as I can."

She disconnected the call and stood rooted in her store for a moment. She couldn't shut down her store every time there was a crisis at the school. Something needed to give.

With a heavy sigh, she locked the store back up and headed to her car in the parking lot. Ten minutes later, she parked and walked into the main entrance of Sweetwater Elementary.

"Good morning, Ms. Locklear," the school secretary said with a cheery smile. Halona was surprised that she got her name right this time. "Principal Nelson said to send you right back when you got here." The secretary pointed down a long hallway. "Last door on the left."

Halona turned in that direction. She'd only gotten sent to the principal's office once, and that was during her high school year. She'd been caught smoking in the bathroom. It was her best friend Marlena's idea and Halona's first and last puff. It just so happened that puff was witnessed by the school's librarian at the time.

It was mortifying when Halona's mom came to the school that day. No matter how hard Halona had tried to explain that she was just *trying* the cigarette, it didn't matter. She'd broken a school rule and her mother's trust. Halona had been grounded for two weeks.

Marlena didn't get caught, of course. She'd offered to go to the principal and explain that it was all her fault but Halona had refused. No need for them both to get in trouble.

Halona stopped in front of Principal Nelson's office door and took in a deep breath. Should she present herself as angry with Theo? Should she be compassionate and offer him a hug when she walked in? He was likely terrified in there. Maybe she should be neutral and listen before reacting.

She knocked softly on the door.

"Come in!" a man's voice called.

Halona opened the door and saw Theo seated across from the principal's desk in an oversize chair that made him look smaller. His gaze flicked to meet hers and then back to his fidgeting hands on his lap. Halona looked to Principal Nelson.

"Please, have a seat," he said, gesturing to the chair beside Theo.

Halona did as he asked, reminding herself to breathe. Just because Theo had been sent to the principal's office didn't mean she was a bad mom or that Theo would end up in jail one day.

"Theo," Principal Nelson said as he slid a pad of paper and a pen to the opposite side of the desk, "why don't you tell your mom what happened this morning. In your own words."

Theo just looked at the paper and pen for a long moment.

"Theo, sweetheart, tell me," Halona prompted.

Theo shook his head, still keeping his eyes downcast.

"Whatever happened, I'm sure you didn't mean it. I just need to know."

Theo's little body trembled as he sat in the chair. Finally, he grabbed the pad of paper and the pen and placed it in his lap. Then he started to write.

I punched Willy in the nose.

Halona gasped at the words. "What? Why would you do that?" she asked.

Theo didn't look at her but he started writing again.

He said I didn't talk because I was stupid. His mom told him Daddy died because he was stupid too.

A knot of emotion formed in Halona's chest. It wasn't just one emotion; it was a blend of too many to process at once.

"Did this Willy kid get in trouble too?" she asked, looking up at Principal Nelson.

Principal Nelson frowned. "No, ma'am. I think a bloody nose was a big enough punishment for him."

"And how are you planning to discipline Theo?" she asked.

Principal Nelson looked at Theo. "I think coming to my office today was also a big enough punishment. If it happens again though, the consequences will be much more severe."

"It won't happen again. Right, Theo?"

Theo shook his head and looked between them.

"Willy shouldn't have said those words but fighting is never the answer," Halona said.

Theo looked at her with wide eyes. What was he thinking? Where had he learned that hitting was okay?

That question sent her mind in a direction that she didn't want to go in.

"Thank you, Principal Nelson. I'm very sorry," Halona said, shame washing over her along with guilt and frustration.

"Don't worry, Ms. Locklear. You'd be surprised how many of Sweetwater's parents end up in my office." Principal Nelson leaned in toward Theo. "Can you keep a secret?"

Theo nodded, dark eyes rounding.

"When I was your age, I landed myself in that very seat for the exact same reason."

Theo's mouth dropped open. Halona's did too as she exhaled softly, relief pouring over her. A little worry still niggled at the back of her mind though. Theo had never acted aggressively before. Had he witnessed some of his father's violence before his death? She'd tried to shield Theo as much as possible back then. Ted had broken some things and punched a wall before he'd laid hands on her. He'd only hit her once, and Theo had been asleep at the time. He hadn't seen anything except the aftermath of Ted's outbursts, which she'd explained away.

Theo had always accepted the explanation. Everyone had—except Alex.

* * *

Coming to the hospital always reminded Alex of the day his dad had been left for dead in the snow. Alex had no idea he'd be helping his mom plan a funeral when he'd come inside the building that day.

His dad was invincible. The strongest man Alex had ever known. Alex had been told over the phone before heading to the hospital that the situation wasn't good but it never occurred to him that it was as bad as it was.

Within an hour, his father had passed away from his injuries.

Mary Beth Edwards was only here for hip surgery. She'd had a few minor complications and was staying longer than expected, but surely, she'd walk back out the same way she came—except maybe with a walker and a prescription for a good physical therapist. There wasn't a better one in town than Tuck Locklear, in Alex's opinion.

Alex stepped into the elevator and pushed the third-floor button, still entertaining memories of his father's last day here. His dad had been unconscious when Alex had walked into his room. He'd briefly opened his eyes when Alex had grabbed his hand.

"There's my favorite officer," he'd croaked in a whisper.

Alex was so fresh from graduating from the police academy that he hadn't even started at the department yet. "Hey, Dad. How are you?"

"Proud as any father could be."

"I mean physically," Alex had said with a humorless laugh. "You were involved in a hit and run. Do you remember anything?"

"Already working the case, huh? Whoever hit me doesn't stand a chance."

Alex took a seat by his dad. His mom was out of town but on her way. "We'll catch whoever hit you—don't worry about that."

"I remember a truck," his father said.

"What color?"

His father closed his eyes, his lips pulling in a frown as he seemed to search for the answers in his mind. "I don't know."

"Someone got out. Did you see them?"

"I...don't remember anything after being hit."

His dad looked pale and pretty beat-up but he was talking. The whole situation had been deceiving. Alex didn't think for a moment that his father would die. If he had known, he would've told his dad how much he loved him. Told him that he was the best dad a kid could ask for. Told him that he was the reason he'd gone into law enforcement in the first place. He looked up to his father and wanted to be just like him.

Alex blew out a breath as he got off the elevator and walked to Mary Beth Edwards's hospital room. He knocked once and waited to hear her voice answer on the other side before peeking his head in.

"I don't have flowers this time," he told her in lieu of hello.

"As you can see, I have plenty of flowers," Mary Beth said on a chuckle.

"I see that. It looks like Halona has been busy."

"I should say so." Mary Beth gestured at her collection of roses, wildflowers, and daisies. "Oh, she makes the loveliest arrangements. She's also a lovely woman."

Even in her sickbed, the older woman was trying to be a matchmaker just like every other female in this town. If they weren't checking out the single men for themselves, they were checking them out for others.

Alex pulled up the chair beside Mary Beth's bed and sat down.

"It's so good of you to come visit me here, Chief Baker. You didn't have to. I know you have more important things to be doing."

"My officers' families are what keep them going. That makes your recovery a police matter," Alex told her. "I take care of my officers' families the same way I take care of them. If there's anything I can do for you, Mary Beth, you name it."

She smiled warmly. "I told my bunco club that you were the sweetest. Some of them didn't agree with me but it's the truth."

Alex shifted uncomfortably. The women Mary Beth were talking about were probably the same ones who'd put in a few complaints to Mayor Everson.

"And when I see them again, I'm going to make sure to tell them that you came to visit me in the hospital twice, and once with flowers. You are a great police chief. Every bit as good as your dad was."

Alex looked at his hands in his lap. "I don't know about that." In fact, he was sure that wasn't the truth. His father had never had a case that he couldn't solve, and ironically, the only case Alex had yet to crack was his father's hit and run.

A nurse walked in, and Alex took that as his cue to leave. "Call me if you need anything, Mary Beth. Takeout, more flowers—you name it," he reiterated.

Mary Beth nodded. "I will, Chief Baker. Thank you."

He left the room and passed the nurse's cubicle, which was in the process of being decorated for Christmas. A woman dressed in scrubs was hanging garland with big red velvet bows meant to cheer up the sick who were stuck here this time of year. Holiday decorations hadn't made him feel any better when he'd come after his dad's accident though.

Needing to get out of here, he hurried toward the elevator, took it down to the ground floor, and exited the building. Then he got into his vehicle and headed to Jessica Everson's office to get the Mentor Match file that she'd prepared for him. On Friday night, she'd told all the mentors to stop by today and get the information. It would give the child's name, address, and a little bit of their personal information. Since most of these kids had a troubled background, Jessica wanted to make sure that the mentors were fully aware of any underlying emotional or behavioral issues.

What am I getting myself into?

A few minutes later, he parked and walked into the nonprofit building where Jessica ran a few of her charitable causes.

"Chief Baker!" she exclaimed. "I'm so excited that you agreed to do this. I know you'll love the experience just as much as the child we've chosen for you."

Alex nodded. "I appreciate you and Mayor Everson thinking of me for this opportunity. I'll do my best to be a good role model."

Jessica smiled. "I'm sure you'll do wonderful. What child wouldn't want to have a police chief as their buddy?"

Alex shrugged. "Your husband seems to think that some people in town have gotten a muddy image of me over the past year." And Mary Beth had just confirmed that statement when he'd visited her. "Maybe my mentee's parent will have issues with me."

"Stop worrying. I know your mentee's parent, and she won't disapprove."

Alex lifted a brow. "Who is it?"

Jessica reached for a large manila envelope on her desk and slid it over. She opened her mouth to speak and then Alex's walkie-talkie went off, signaling an emergency.

"I'm sorry. I have to go." He picked up the envelope.

"Duty calls," Jessica said. "I understand. Take today

and tomorrow to look over the information inside the envelope. Then, when you're ready, you can call the child's family and schedule your first Mentor Match outing."

"Sounds good. Thank you," Alex said as he waved and hurried back outside into the cold. He needed to handle this call first. After that, he planned on paying the main suspect of his father's murder a visit.

CHAPTER SIX

*S*teve Anderson lived on the town border of Sweetwater Springs. Technically, jurisdiction went to Malachi James, the sheriff for Wild Blossom Bluffs, but Malachi had given Alex the green light on talking to Steve last year.

Alex pulled into the driveway of Steve's brick ranch home and parked. He doubted Steve would appreciate the unexpected visit but Alex was getting used to not being high on some individuals' list of favorite people. A dog barked in the distance, heightening Alex's awareness. He'd been in sticky situations with canines on home visits before.

He climbed the steps to the front door and rang the doorbell.

Steve opened the door and nodded, not looking surprised at all to see Alex standing there. "I thought I'd be seeing you again this year. You're still not welcome here, Chief."

Alex didn't budge. "Hey, Steve. How are you?"

"Cut to the chase. You and I both know you're not here for a friendly visit."

Alex smiled, despite the urge to do otherwise. "Mind if I come in?"

"I do, as a matter of fact. You have a warrant?"

"Do I need one?" Alex asked. He'd tried and failed to get a warrant last year. He had no damning evidence against this man. No reason for a court to agree to letting Alex go through Steve's belongings.

"Like I told you last year, you ain't coming in here and nosing round my stuff. So it's best you mosey back over to your vehicle there and get off my property."

At least Steve was refraining from using curse words this time. "You told me last year that you don't have anything to hide. So why not invite me in?"

"Because I don't like you." Steve folded his arms over his chest. "And that's all the reason you need. I'll tell you once more, for the record," Steve said, tensing the muscles along his jaw. "I didn't kill your father but I didn't cry at the news of his death either."

Alex's smile dropped now, and he ground his teeth. The Anderson men weren't on his list of favorite people either.

"Do you have any idea who would want my father dead?"

Steve shrugged, his shoulders reaching his overgrown hair. "A man like your dad probably had a lot of people who weren't happy with him. Anyone he ever arrested. His bedside manner wasn't exactly the best. Kind of like yours."

Alex nodded. "I'll never take offense to being compared with my father."

"Keep on the way you are, and there might be more

comparisons to be made," Steve said, his dull eyes lighting up with his sick humor.

Alex nodded and descended back down the creaky steps. It was best he left before he said something he shouldn't. "Have a good day, Steve."

"See you next year, Chief," Steve called before slamming the door.

* * *

Halona looked over her shoulder at Theo, who was sitting at the kitchen table.

"Keep working," she prodded. She wasn't sure what the most fitting punishment was for a little boy who'd punched another child in the nose today. Even if the kid had deserved it.

A little smile quirked at the corners of her mouth. She believed in natural consequences, and if you called a little boy and his deceased father stupid, then it only made sense that you got a bloody nose.

Not that she condoned violence. Theo needed to be responsible for his actions. So tonight, he was sitting at the kitchen table and writing an apology letter to Willy while she cooked dinner at the stove. After that, he would write an apology letter to his teacher for breaking the rules of the classroom and then to Principal Nelson. That was his punishment.

Halona returned her attention to the potato soup that she was cooking. It was one of Lula's favorite Cherokee dishes. She'd passed it on along with a few dozen other recipes, including her Three Sisters Stew, to keep their heritage alive. Whenever someone in town got sick, Lula was there with a big pot of the stew. Whenever someone lost a family member, Lula brought them a meal. Whenever a young couple got married, it wasn't long before Lula showed up with something delicious tasting in tow. Following in her mom's footsteps, Halona did the same with her flowers.

Theo put his pencil down loudly on the table, a cue that he was finished.

Halona wiped her hands on her apron and walked over to inspect his work. "Good enough," she said. Then she grabbed another piece of paper and handed him the pencil again. "Now write a letter to your classroom teacher. Then it'll be time for dinner."

Theo nodded dutifully and started writing. He was such a good boy. He always did as he was told and rarely asked for anything. Once upon a time, Halona and Ted had wanted a large family with four or five children. Halona had changed her mind about that, however. First off, Ted was no longer in the picture. Secondly, Halona already had the most amazing little boy in the entire world. She didn't need more children to make her heart feel any fuller. She had everything she needed right here in this kitchen.

After dinner, Theo took his bath and then got ready for bed. Halona read a chapter from the Harry Potter series that they had started right after Thanksgiving and then turned off his nightstand light.

"Good night, sweetheart," she said as she made her way to the door. "Sweet dreams."

As she walked down the hall, she sent up a little prayer that Theo would actually have a good night and sweet dreams. For his sake and hers.

* * *

Summer Rivera stood across the counter from Halona the next day. "I'm doing the finishing touches on this year's events," she said, "and, as you know, this weekend is Lights on Silver Lake."

Halona nodded. "Yes, I'm ready for it."

"I'm sure you are. That night is good for business owners like you." Summer's smile stretched impossibly wide. "It won't be long after that and we'll be doing the annual Hope for the Holidays event to give back and support people other than ourselves."

Halona nodded, feeling somehow like she was being lectured.

"We're choosing between two community members in need right now, and I know this year's event will make a huge difference in their holiday." She pulled out a notepad and pen. "So how many plants can you donate for the cause this year?"

"Oh, um, probably the same number as last year," Halona said.

Summer looked up from her writing with a disapproving face. "I don't mean to be pushy but we usually like for our donators to increase their donations every year. It's for a good cause, and it benefits the giver as much as the receiver," she said, her voice climbing the octave scale with each word.

Halona held her tongue for a moment. No, she wasn't needy by any means but she was a single parent and a small-business owner. The amount she gave last year had been a stretch for her. "The same as last year will work for me again this year," Halona repeated, keeping her smile secured in place.

"I see." Summer's expression turned crestfallen. "Well, we're thankful for everything that's given, of course. No matter how big or *small*."

Was it just Halona or was Summer calling her donation small?

She sucked in another deep breath as she listened
to Summer drone on about Kaitlyn Russo making her
grandma Mable's famous gingerbread cheesecakes for the
benefit. Brenna was offering catering services to not one
but two recipients this year. Bo Matthews was offering a
free architectural consultation, and Paris Montgomery was
offering his graphic design services. The list went on.

"You'll be there, I hope," Summer finally said.

"I'll try. If I can find someone to care for Theo."

"Oh, bring him with you. He's no trouble," Summer
insisted. "Even though I hear he landed himself in Principal Nelson's hot seat."

How would Summer even know that? The gossip chain
in Sweetwater Springs never ceased to amaze Halona,
even though she'd been born and raised here.

"Well, I need to get started on arrangements for this
weekend's upcoming ceremony," Halona said, prompting
an end to the visit.

"Oh, for the Landemyers? I'm so excited for this
wedding that I can hardly stand it. Aren't you?"

"Mm-hmm," Halona said, disappointed that the conversation didn't seem to be wrapping up. Instead, she'd
unintentionally segued into a new topic. *Save me!*

As soon as she'd had the thought, the bell above the
entry door jingled, announcing a new customer.

Halona could kiss whoever was coming to her rescue.
Then her thoughts stuttered to a halt. As luck would
have it, her rescuer was none other than Alex Baker. She
should've known he'd be the one to hear her silent SOS.
He was *always* the one.

* * *

"Good morning," Alex said as he stepped inside the Little Shop of Flowers. He immediately regretted doing so when he saw Summer Rivera. She was nice enough but she could be a little pushy, especially this time of the year.

"Oh, Chief Baker," Summer exclaimed, turning to him. "I've been meaning to talk to you. I was just asking Halona about the Hope for the Holidays event and what she was willing to donate this year." Summer glanced over her shoulder at Halona and then returned her gaze to him. "We encourage you to offer as much as you can. It's for a good cause, you know."

"I know." He shared a glance with Halona as well. There was more to what they'd been discussing than Summer had divulged.

"And what will you be offering this year?" Summer asked.

Alex scratched the side of his face where new hair was growing despite having shaved this morning. He considered telling her he'd offer up a puppy. Depending on the court's decision, Officer Chew would need a forever home. Alex wanted to make sure Officer Chew went to responsible and loving owners though, especially after all that the little dog had been through.

"Some of the ladies suggested that you might want to offer self-defense lessons. Several of them said they would bid a lot of money to get private lessons with you." Summer winked.

Yeah, that sounded like a way to land himself another nickname among the ladies and possibly another reason to ruffle feathers among his critics. "The truth is I'm very busy this season."

Summer looked disappointed. Then her face lit up. "I know," she said, lifting her index finger. "How about you make a batch of homemade cookies? The people in town will go crazy to know that their own chief of police put on an apron and baked a batch of special Christmas cookies. Oh, and we can even take pictures of you in the apron to help make the donations go even higher. It won't take very long. You can even use ready-made dough, although homemade is always best."

Alex was just about to protest when Halona spoke up.

"I think that's a fantastic idea," she said, sliding her gaze to meet his. There was a playful twinkle in her brown eyes that told him she knew he was very uncomfortable with the request, and she was loving every second of it.

He shook his head. "I'm afraid I don't have an apron. Sorry to disappoint."

"Don't worry," Halona said. "I have lots of aprons. And I think I know just the one for you."

"I really don't—" Alex began to argue.

Summer cut him off. "Great!" She clapped her hands together in front of her with excitement. "Oh, this is going to be the best Hope for the Holidays event ever! I'm so excited." With that, she waved and walked out, leaving Alex alone with Halona in the flower shop.

"Thanks for throwing me under the bus," he said.

"It's for a good cause."

He nodded and shoved his hands into his jeans pockets. "I guess so. I'm not really much for baking cookies though."

"Do you know how to turn on an oven?" she asked.

"Yeah."

"Then you'll do fine. And I just ordered a new

cookbook. I'm sure there are some great cookie recipes in there to choose from."

Alex lifted a brow.

"I'm eager to try the Triple-Chip Chocolate Cookie recipe, and it would be perfect for the auction."

"That does sound good."

"Well, if you want, you can come over and Theo and I will help, seeing that I kind of volunteered you."

He narrowed his eyes. "Kind of?"

She laughed. Then she looked at him for a long moment, as if waiting for him to say something more. "What brought you to my shop? Was there something you needed? Flowers?" she asked.

Alex shook his head. "No, I was just passing by and thought I'd stop in. I felt like you needed me, to tell the truth."

Halona laughed quietly. "Well, Summer was grilling me pretty good about not upping my donation this year."

"She's a bulldog, that one. Guess that's good for the charity. It seems to keep growing every year. Mary Beth might not be able to help her this year either."

"How is she?" Halona asked.

"She's doing well, but I highly doubt she'll be participating in the event."

"I guess I can just be thankful that Summer didn't try to recruit me for help, then." Halona laughed. "I really do have an apron you can borrow. Christmas trees or reindeer? Which do you prefer?"

Alex grimaced. "Got anything more masculine? Maybe with mountains, bears, or a pack of wolves?"

"Now what fun would that be?" she asked. "I think Summer would agree that people would pay more money to see you in an apron with Rudolph on it. For charity."

"I guess the chief of police doesn't need to act like a scrooge. Just let me know when you're ready, and I'll come do my part." Even though he didn't have time for baking cookies. Or for fostering puppies and entertaining young mentees, for that matter. There were cases on his desk that required his attention. "I guess I better get back to work."

"Thanks for saving me," Halona called.

"Anytime." With a wave, he walked outside and got back into his SUV. Since he was on Main Street, he completed a few errands before heading back to the station.

"You just missed Summer Rivera," Tammy said as he walked inside.

"I saw her at the flower shop already."

Tammy pointedly looked down at his hands and back up at him. "Obviously the flowers weren't for me. Who were they for?"

"I didn't buy any," he admitted.

Tammy simply nodded. "I guessed as much."

Alex didn't take the bait. "What are you donating to the Hope for the Holidays charity?" he asked instead.

"My home cooking, of course."

Alex nodded. "I might be bidding on that."

She laughed. "Don't be greedy, Chief. You get my home cooking for free all the time."

"Can't get enough," he called, heading down the hall toward his office.

* * *

Later that evening, when Alex finally got home, he grabbed his Mentor Match file and took it inside.

Officer Chew barreled toward the back door. The pup had spent all day at the police station, splitting his time between Alex and Tammy. Now he turned circles and barked, begging to go in the backyard, which appeared to be his favorite place here.

"Let me grab a Coke first, will you?" Alex said, heading toward the fridge. He grabbed a cold can from the bottom drawer and popped the top. Then he took the large manila envelope, flipped on the outside light, and opened the back door. He sat at the patio table and finally turned his attention to his Mentor Match. After leaving Jessica's office to go on a call yesterday, the day had only gotten busier. Then he'd accidentally left the envelope at his office. Today had been just as busy and he still hadn't gotten to peek inside to see who his young mentee would be.

The anticipation rose suddenly inside him as he unsealed the envelope. He wondered if he knew the kid already. He knew nearly everyone in town. He pulled out the papers inside, focusing on the picture of the little boy first. Confusion sparked inside him, and for a moment, he thought maybe Jessica had handed him the wrong envelope.

His mentee was Theo.

* * *

Halona had been expecting a call from Theo's Mentor Match since yesterday. Tonight, her phone hadn't buzzed since she'd left the flower shop. She picked it up to make sure it wasn't dead. It wasn't but she'd missed a text from Brenna that made her smile.

My neighbor has no idea that walking to the mailbox at the same time every day is no coincidence.

Halona lay sideways across the recliner with her legs dangling over the arm and texted back.

Maybe you should ask him out.

Nooo. He's the look-but-don't-sample kind, **Brenna said.**

Comparing men to food, huh? You work too much.

You're one to talk, **Brenna texted back along with a winking-face emoji.**

Halona glanced over at Theo on the couch. His eyes were drooping as he tried to stay awake for the rest of *The Nightmare Before Christmas* movie. Her phone buzzed in her hand again.

If he's so cute, why is he single? Must be something wrong with him.

You're single, and you're terrific, **Halona pointed out.** Have you found out his name yet?

Yes. Only because his mail landed in my box the other day. His name is Luke Marini.

Well, maybe Luke needs a friend. **Halona sent a smiling emoji with her text.**

Maybe so.

You're the best friend I know, **Halona texted, meaning it.** See you for coffee tomorrow?

Sure.

Halona placed her phone back in her lap and let her own droopy eyes close. No sooner had she relaxed into a presleep state than the phone startled her back awake. She glanced down at her caller ID, squinting at Alex's name. Maybe she was still sleeping, because it didn't make sense for him to be calling her right now. Unless something had happened.

She bolted out of the chair and hurried to the kitchen before answering, not wanting to disturb Theo, whose eyes were now fully closed.

"Hello?"

"Hey, Halona," Alex said, "am I calling too late?"

"No. Is everything okay?"

"Yeah. Sorry if I scared you. I guess I have that effect on people."

"It's okay," she said, exhaling softly. "If everything is fine, then what's going on?"

"I wanted to talk to you about the Mentor Match program that the Eversons have started."

Halona leaned against the kitchen counter. "Yeah. I've actually got Theo enrolled."

There was a long pause on Alex's side of the conversation.

"Is something wrong with the program?" she asked, pulling in a breath and holding it again. Had she made a mistake in signing Theo up?

"No. I've actually been roped into participating in it myself."

"Oh? That's wonderful. You'd be great with a kid shadowing you. Theo adores you."

There was another long pause. Then Alex cleared his

throat on the line. "I'm, uh...I'm Theo's Mentor Match," he finally said.

Halona gripped the cell phone in her hand more tightly. "You?"

"Yeah. Unless you want someone else," he clarified.

"No. Why would I want someone else?" she asked, posing the question to herself as well. "Like I said, Theo looks up to you." Alex was actually the perfect mentor for her son. The only reason she wouldn't want Alex to be Theo's mentor was because it would mean seeing him more often and feeling her heart skip foolishly around in her chest the way it always did when he was around. He would be hanging out with Theo though, not her. "You're a busy man. Are you sure you have time to do this?"

"I'll make time...and I'm looking forward to it."

There was a hesitation in his voice. She knew he liked her son but didn't think he had any real experience taking care of a child. "Maybe I could swing by and take Theo out this Friday night?"

Halona stared at the refrigerator across the room. No matter his experience or what had happened between them in the past, she trusted Alex. "That sounds perfect. I'll be working late that night preparing arrangements for another wedding anyway," she told him.

"It's a date, then."

There went that foolish heart of hers. It was a date with her son, and that was for the best. The last thing she needed was a date with Alex for herself.

So why was she suddenly jealous of her son?

CHAPTER SEVEN

*H*alona glanced at herself in the long mirror in her bedroom. She was being silly. Alex was coming to her home to pick Theo up, and then they'd leave. Alex probably wouldn't even give her a second glance.

Except she'd always noticed the way his gaze lingered on her too long. Or was that just her imagination?

"Why am I wearing a dress?" she muttered to herself. Even though her outfit was casual, she was working tonight, and she never worked in a dress.

Theo entered the room and sat on the edge of her bed to watch her.

"Are you excited?" she asked, as she pulled open her dresser and grabbed jeans and a cotton shirt to put on instead.

She saw him nod enthusiastically from the corner of her eye. How she wished she could ask him what he was most looking forward to. Was it the fact that he got to spend time with Alex, or that they were going out to do something fun, whereas otherwise he would've been stuck at the community center while she decorated for tomorrow's wedding?

Halona slipped into her bathroom to change. As she walked out, the doorbell rang. Her heart flew up into her throat. She took a few deep breaths as she walked to the front door and opened it. Before she could utter a hello, Theo barreled into Alex's waist and gave him a big hug.

Alex's eyes widened, and he laughed softly. "Hey, pal. Ready for an adventure?"

Theo looked up, his head bouncing with a *yes*. Then he removed his arms from around Alex's waist and bent to pet Officer Chew's head.

"I see you still have the puppy," Halona pointed out.

"For now. The court just ruled in the department's favor. Tony didn't even attend the hearing." Alex looked from her to Theo. "I hope you don't mind Chew crashing our outing tonight."

Theo shook his head and then giggled as the dog licked the side of his face.

"I think it's probably the opposite," Halona said on a laugh. "He's added a dog to his ever-growing Christmas list. I hate to break it to him but it probably won't happen this year."

Theo's lower lip turned down as he looked up at her.

"You sure about that?" Alex asked her quietly once Theo was distracted by Officer Chew again. "I know where you can find one."

Halona narrowed her eyes. "Not this year."

"Too bad. And what's on *your* Christmas list?" he asked her.

The question and its flirtatious tone sent a buzz of

awareness zipping through her. "I don't really make Christmas lists anymore," she said, securing a strand of her hair behind her ear.

"Why not?"

She shrugged. "My only wish is that Theo has a great holiday."

Alex nodded. "*You* deserve to have a great holiday as well, Halona."

She looked away, surprised at the emotion rolling through her. Her life revolved around her son. She knew she needed to take care of herself, too, but it was hard sometimes. "I'll have my cell phone on me the whole night. Just call if you need anything. Where are you two going?"

Alex rubbed his hands together. "Ice-skating. I wish you could come with us . . . for Theo's comfort, of course."

Halona felt her cheeks flush for a reason she couldn't explain. "It's not advised in the Mentor Match code of conduct. I'm supposed to give you two space, and besides, I have a job to do." Her gaze flicked from Alex to Theo. "Do as Chief Baker says, okay?"

"Alex," Alex said, correcting her. "The Mentor Match code of conduct also says to drop the usual titles and go by first names. Tonight I'm just Alex." He jutted out his hand for Theo to shake. Then he lifted his hand and offered it to Halona.

She stared at it for a moment before realizing she had no choice but to take it. She took in the feel of his skin slipping against hers and felt light-headed.

"Just Alex," he said, his voice dropping low as he gave her hand a gentle squeeze before letting go.

He'd never been just Alex to her though. There'd always been something more to him that she didn't dare explore for reasons that seemed to shift and change like the colors in a kaleidoscope. More and more, she was starting to have a harder time remembering what those reasons were.

* * *

What had Alex been thinking? He'd thought ice-skating would be a fun adventure but Theo couldn't communicate with him using his notepad while on the ice. The whole point of being a mentor was to get to know each other. The only clue Alex had that Theo was even enjoying himself was the wide, gap-toothed smile on his face. It was enough to warm Alex even on this freezing-cold night.

"This is fun, isn't it, buddy?" Alex called to Theo, who was making large strides while struggling to keep up. Halona must have taken him a lot in his short life, because he was a really good skater. Or maybe it was Ted that had taken Theo once upon a time.

Different emotions tugged inside Alex's chest. He was sorry that Theo had lost his father. He knew how that felt and wouldn't wish it on anyone, especially not a seven-year-old boy. But he wasn't sorry that Ted was no longer in the picture to push Halona around anymore. How long had the abuse been going on? Why hadn't she come to him?

From his peripheral vision, Alex saw Theo plop down. Alex spun in his direction and scraped the brakes of his skates along the ice, assessing quickly to see that Theo wasn't hurt. "You okay?" he asked as he reached out a hand.

Theo nodded but his smile had slighted.

Alex didn't want to return Theo home injured or with

a frown. He helped Theo to his feet. "Hey, I'm tired anyway. Want to go check on Officer Chew and grab a cup of hot chocolate?"

Theo grinned in response.

They skated toward the outer guardrail where Alex had leashed Chew to a bench. It was standard procedure around Sweetwater Springs. You could trust your bikes and your dogs to still be wherever you left them. Cars too, probably, but Alex didn't recommend it.

Woof!

"Yeah, yeah. I'm sorry, pal. No dogs on the ice. No hot chocolate for you either." He winked at Theo. "But maybe Dawanda will have some sort of dog treat that's suitable."

They headed on foot to Dawanda's Fudge Shop and went inside. It was busy tonight, which was good because the store owner had been trying to sit Alex down and give him one of her cappuccino readings for years. Alex didn't need to know his future. If looking down into a cup of frothy milk would reveal the past and maybe tell him who'd run down his father, however, then sure, he was more than willing to have a go.

"Two of my favorite people!" Dawanda exclaimed as Alex led Theo through the front door and up to the counter. "Where's Halona tonight?"

"She's working. Theo and I just went ice-skating," Alex told her, "and we're a bit cold. We were wondering if you had any hot chocolate to help us out?"

"Well, that's a silly question." Dawanda looked from him to Theo. "Of course I do. I might even have a piece of fudge for you both as well."

Alex chuckled at Theo as he bounced in place. "Sounds wonderful."

She prepared and handed them their drinks and a little baggie of fudge. Cups and bag in hand, Alex turned to survey the seating area. He picked a table along the wall where he thought they wouldn't be disturbed. As the chief of police, he couldn't seem to go anywhere without running into someone who wanted to talk to him. Sometimes they had a complaint, and other times they just wanted to tell him a funny story. He loved the interaction but he remembered how it felt to be a child when this was happening to his own father. Alex would just want a little alone time with his dad to talk about building forts or maybe a kid who was giving him trouble in class. But they'd never finish the conversation, because someone else always intruded. Alex didn't want that to happen to Theo tonight.

Once Theo had a thick chocolate mustache in place, he pulled his notebook and pencil in front of him and started writing.

Alex craned his neck to read the writing upside down.

I know what my mom wants for Christmas.

Alex lifted his eyes to meet the boy's. "You do? What's that?"

Theo began to write again.

Snow.

"Hmm. I didn't know that about your mom." A white Christmas wasn't exactly Alex's favorite. It meant more fender benders and more people calling the police station because they were snowed inside their homes. A thick layer of the white stuff could be full of headaches but he had to admit that snow made the holidays more beautiful. It reminded him of simpler times before he'd taken an oath to serve and protect. Before his father had died. "Well, maybe Santa will deliver that for her this year," he said.

Theo picked up his pencil once again. *I know that Santa isn't real.*

"What makes you say that?"

Theo rolled his eyes. Maybe the kid didn't use words but those dark eyes of his spoke volumes.

I'm not a baby. I just don't talk.

Alex scratched the side of his face and then reached for the last half of his fudge square. He took a bite and chewed. Then he gestured for Theo to hand him the pencil. Theo placed it in his palm, and Alex took the notebook. He wrote, *Why don't you talk?*

Next, it was Theo's turn to write. *I can't.*

Alex visually assessed the boy's features. He knew that Theo physically *could* talk if he wanted to. Alex had done a few Google searches on selective mutism, which usually stemmed from anxiety. The boy didn't appear upset by the line of questioning so Alex continued, writing instead of speaking. *My mom used to say I talked too much.*

Theo giggled. *My mom used to say that too.*

But then sometimes I would get really sad, Alex wrote. *I sort of shut down. I didn't want to talk to anyone.* Alex looked up at Theo. "Does that sound familiar?" he asked out loud this time.

Theo hesitated and then nodded slowly.

"It's okay, buddy. Happens to the best of us. But tonight is about having fun. What should we do next?"

Theo grabbed the notebook and started writing. *The community center.*

That was where Halona was working tonight. "I guess if we give your mom a little help, she can finish early. We can't deliver snow to her tonight but we can bring her hot chocolate and fudge. Do you think she'd like that?" Alex asked.

Theo nodded emphatically, no words needed.

* * *

In just a couple of hours, Halona had placed most of the arrangements she'd prepared around the large, open room in the community center, transforming it from plain to an explosion of bright reds and deep greens for the Christmas holiday.

"Wow!" a deep voice said behind her.

Halona whirled to find Alex and Theo at the door. "Is everything okay?" She looked at her watch. They'd been together for only two hours. She wasn't expecting them back until nine, and she was supposed to meet them at her place not here.

Alex held up a hand. "Everything's fine. We've skated and satisfied our sweet tooth at Dawanda's Fudge Shop." He lifted a cup-holder tray and a small white bag. "And we came bearing treats for your sweet tooth as well."

Halona stepped closer. "You didn't have to do that."

"It's hot chocolate," Alex told her.

"Oh, that sounds heavenly right now." She took the cup he handed her, enjoying the heat against her palm. Then she turned her attention to Theo, relieved to find him in one piece and smiling. "Did you have a good time?"

Theo nodded.

She tapped the notebook tucked under his arm. "You'll have to tell me how many times Chief Baker—"

"Alex," Alex corrected.

Her gaze flitted up to meet his. "How many times *Alex* fell on the ice."

"I'll have you know I didn't fall at all," he told her.

"Impressive. How about you, Theo?" She glanced down at her son standing alongside Officer Chew.

Theo held up one finger.

"Once? That's not too bad. I probably would've hit the ice half a dozen times if I were there. You would've had to keep circling back to help me up."

"I wouldn't have minded," Alex said, snagging her gaze and making her heart do a full somersault.

The chemistry was what made being in the same room with him so uncomfortable. Maybe if they finally kissed, it'd be out of their systems. But like this, it was like an ever-building pressure that threatened to explode one of these days, and that day was coming sooner rather than later.

"We thought we'd help you finish up," Alex said. "But it looks like you're already done."

"Almost. I need to place some flowers on the three light fixtures on the walls."

Alex looked around the room. "I can do that while you eat your fudge."

"Fudge too?" She opened the bag and peered inside. "Be careful. I'll expect something every time you and Theo go out."

"I can manage that," he said with a wink.

Halona blew out a pent-up breath as he headed to the ladder, and then she realized that Theo was watching her. He was too young to understand physical attraction and chemistry, wasn't he? "Wanna bite?" she asked, holding her piece of fudge out to him. He shook his head. "You must've had quite a big piece at Dawanda's to turn down even another bite. Dawanda is known to spoil you."

Halona popped another piece of her fudge into her mouth. She'd gotten used to Theo's silence but it sometimes felt like she was talking to herself. She returned to watching Alex as he hung the flowers on the fixtures. It really couldn't be done wrong; no one scrutinized every arrangement. It was the bride who got all the attention.

Fifteen minutes later, he folded the ladder and walked back over. "Done."

"Looks great. Thank you for the help and the treats. This is dinner," she admitted.

He lifted a brow. "I won't tell Lula."

"Please don't. She'd be so disappointed in me," Halona said on a laugh. They both knew the Locklear matriarch's views on family and food. Never miss a meal or a chance to spend it with the one you love.

"Well, I guess I'll wrap up here and take you home, little man," Halona finally said. "I bet you're tired."

Theo shook his head even as a yawn tumbled off his lips.

Alex patted his back. "Don't worry. We'll hang out again soon. What about tomorrow night?"

Halona looked up. "You're only obligated once a week according to the handbook."

"It's not an obligation. I'm not working the event tomorrow for the first time in years, and I'm guessing you are."

Halona nodded. "Theo will probably spend most of the night in the back room with a book."

"When there's fake snow and hot chocolate to be had?"

Alex shook his head. "Why don't you let me take Theo off your hands?"

"Yeah!" Theo said, jumping up.

Halona's heart flew into her throat. He'd spoken! One word, but that was enough. She blinked past the sting in her eyes, keeping her emotions at bay. Then she looked up at Alex. "I guess I can't argue with that. Thank you."

$\mathcal{C}$HAPTER EIGHT

$\mathcal{J}$ust because it was Saturday didn't mean Alex had the day off. Being chief of police was a job that demanded he be working at all times. His brain apparently hadn't gotten that memo though. He'd tried to give his attention to the tasks piled up on his desk for the last hour, and instead he'd continually had to refocus his wandering mind away from Halona.

Alex's phone rang. He reached for it, thankful for the distraction.

"Get to work," Tammy said from her desk down the hall. She didn't usually work weekends but the part-time helper had called out for the month to go visit family outside of the state. Lucky for Alex, Tammy didn't mind the overtime. She was as reliable as she was feisty.

"What makes you think I'm not working?"

"Because if you were, you would've called back the list of people I put on your desk. Instead, they're calling a second time and asking why you haven't called."

Busted.

"Yes, Chief," Alex joked. "Anything else I can do for you?"

"I'll let you know." With that, Tammy hung up.

Alex chuckled to himself. Then he reached for the list that she was referring to and started calling each person back, one by one.

By lunchtime, he was tired of sitting and needed to get out. He also needed to send a package at the post office before closing. Not that the package was urgent but he wanted to lay eyes on Sharlene Anderson. Tony hadn't caused any trouble lately. Honestly, Alex was surprised at the lack of response for taking his dog.

Picking up the package with one hand and Officer Chew's leash in the other, Alex headed past Tammy at the front entry. "I'm going downtown. Need anything?"

"Only if you're buying," she said, lifting one eyebrow.

"Depends on what you're asking for."

"A sandwich from the café? I forgot my home-cooked lunch at home. There was something for you in there too." She winked.

Alex shifted the package underneath his arm as Officer Chew tugged the leash in his opposite hand. "I'm sorry to be missing out on that."

"Yes, you are. I'd like a bag of baked chips too, please," she added.

"I didn't say yes yet," he pointed out.

"But you will."

"Remind me who's the boss around here again?" he called over his shoulder as he and Officer Chew left the building. He didn't wait for her answer, because he suspected he knew what it would be.

It was a beautiful day out. The air was chilly, reminding

him that Christmas was just around the corner. Another reminder was the red bows tied to all the light posts. After driving to the downtown area and parking, Alex noted that the storefront windows displayed holiday decorations as well. Halona had poinsettias in the window. Emma advertised that her gingerbread mocha was back for the season. Sophie's Boutique boasted a sale on ugly Christmas sweaters.

Bah humbug.

The anniversary of his father's death and the holiday ticked down simultaneously, and it was hard for him to get into the Christmas spirit. He wasn't exactly a grinch. It was just his heart that never seemed to celebrate.

Just before reaching the post office, he looped Officer Chew's leash onto one of the sidewalk benches. No need to rub in the fact that Sharlene no longer had her pet thanks to her mean-tempered husband.

Sharlene looked up with hollow eyes as he entered the post office.

"Good afternoon," Alex said, pretending not to notice that she looked less than thrilled to see him. "How are you, Sharlene?"

"Good, Chief Baker. Do you have a package to send off?" she asked, averting her gaze and exuding nothing but professionalism.

He nodded and plopped the shoebox-size box on the counter. Truthfully, he could've driven it to Grandma Baker's house. She only lived a few miles away but then he'd have no excuse to be here.

Sharlene took the package and looked at the address. Her gaze briefly flitted up to narrow in on him. She didn't say anything though. Instead, she weighed the package and printed a label. "Anything else?"

"Not today." He inserted his debit card into the card reader and glanced up, scanning Sharlene for visible signs of abuse. He didn't see any marks or bruises. "You called me last week. I tried to stop by but Tony answered the door."

Sharlene kept her eyes trained on the task. "I heard. I'm sorry to worry you, Chief Baker. It was nothing."

"Must have been something. Tony was pretty mad when I got there."

Sharlene looked up. "He got over it. I should tell you, though, he isn't happy that you took our dog."

"Well, I wasn't too happy with the way he was treating the little guy," Alex said.

Sharlene squirmed in the spot where she stood. "He has a temper."

Alex shoved his card back into his wallet and then slid it into his back pocket. "He needs to learn to control it."

She averted her gaze.

"Don't hesitate to call me again if you need to, Sharlene. I can handle Tony."

She nodded, her hands shaking a little as she took the package and placed it behind her. "Thank you, Chief Baker. I'll get this out for delivery today," she said, meeting his eyes once more. She lifted her chin subtly. "If that's all…"

Alex didn't want to leave. He wanted to stay and convince her to let him help. Some might consider that bullying but all that mattered was Sharlene's well-being.

Another customer walked in and headed toward the counter.

He didn't have a choice but to end the conversation. "You know how to reach me," he said. As he walked out of the post office, he felt heavier than when he'd walked in, even though his hands were now empty.

* * *

That evening, the sounds and smells of Christmastime were thick in the air as Alex strolled alongside Theo and Officer Chew.

He'd offered Halona a quick greeting before taking Theo. She'd already been busy with customers, and they hadn't had time for anything other than niceties. Certainly no time to make flirty conversation the way they had lately.

"Chief!" Mitch walked up Main Street toward them, dressed in his police uniform tonight.

"Hey, Mitch. How's it going?" Alex asked.

"Calm so far. I've got my eye on Janice Murphy though. I'm sure she's learned her lesson but I'm still guarding the eggnog just in case she gets the notion to add anything."

Alex chuckled. "I wouldn't put it past her. She's sneaky."

Mitch looked down at Theo. "Is Chief Baker treating you okay?"

Theo nodded and reached for Alex's hand.

The gesture clawed into Alex's heart, making it hard for him to speak for a moment.

Mitch grinned when he looked back up. "I'm patrolling tonight. *Your* job is to relax and show my buddy Theo here a good time." Mitch pointed at him and offered a stern look. "That's an order."

Alex shook his head. "Tammy is rubbing off on you. Before you know it, I'll get no respect at the station."

"Not true. We have the utmost respect for you, boss."

Alex grinned. "Let me know if there's any trouble. I have my cell phone on."

"Will do."

Theo didn't let go of Alex's hand as they continued walking. Alex noticed a few stares from onlookers. No doubt people would find a reason to talk about this and make it into a bigger deal than it was. So he had a puppy and was caring for a child. So, for the first time in years, he wasn't working the Lights on Silver Lake event. It didn't mean that there was anything going on that needed to be talked about.

Theo tugged Alex's hand to get his attention and then pointed at the carolers that stood near the huge Christmas tree in the town square. It had paper angels hanging off its branches with a local child's list of needs and wants. Alex usually pulled one off and bought the items on the list plus some.

Heading over, Alex reached for a pale blue paper angel and put it in his pocket. Then he looked down at Theo. "Want to pull one off for your mom?"

Theo reached up and picked out a pink paper angel. He slid it into his coat pocket and then looked back up at Alex.

"The tree won't be lit up for another hour. Let's nab a bench and listen to the carolers."

Theo smiled up at him, once again making it hard for Alex to speak for a moment. Then hand in hand, they found a park bench to settle onto. It was a nice change of pace for Alex, and for a moment, all his cares floated away into the night.

* * *

There had been at least three customers in Halona's shop at all times since the event started at six p.m. Now, at quarter to eight, she was nearly sold out of poinsettias, tired from dealing with excited customers, and needed to use the bathroom.

The bell above her door jingled with another incoming customer.

"Welcome to the Little Shop of Flowers," Halona said with all the holiday cheer she could muster. It didn't feel like Christmas just yet. The decorations had just started going up this past week, and she'd barely started shopping for Theo.

"It's just me," Lula called as she headed over.

"Mom!"

Lula opened her arms and enveloped Halona in a big embrace. As a teen, Halona had been embarrassed by her mom's frequent PDA. Now she didn't mind it. She needed the hug tonight too. She was glad for the sales but also ready for closing time at nine o'clock.

"What are you doing here?" Halona asked.

"I just finished telling the Christmas story in our native language. The kids loved it even if they didn't understand what I was saying. There were pictures and candy too, of course. Now I'm here to relieve you so that you can take Theo to look at the displays."

"Oh. Actually, he's with Alex tonight."

"Oh?" Lula lifted one eyebrow.

Halona looked away from her mom's scrutinizing gaze. "I guess I haven't told you yet. Alex is Theo's new Mentor Match."

"Really?" Lula looked delighted by this fact. Halona was a little surprised her mom hadn't already heard through the Sweetwater Springs grapevine. "Well, isn't that wonderful? Why don't you go join them? I can run this store of yours—you know that."

Halona looked around at the steady influx of customers. "It's really busy tonight."

"Even better. It'll make the time fly by as fast as this year has." Lula walked behind the counter and set her things down as if the decision were already made.

Halona suddenly felt re-energized. "Okay. Thank you. We're running low on poinsettias but I'm taking orders."

Lula waved a hand. "I've got it. Go have fun. You deserve it."

Without letting herself debate the choice a second longer, Halona went to the bathroom and then put on her winter coat. She headed outside with the lights, music, and various smells of yummy things. Most notably were those of nutmeg and cinnamon. Her stomach rumbled its protest as she walked past tables full of treats along Main Street.

The best part of Lights on Silver Lake was about to happen. The lighting of the town tree was in five minutes. Alex and Theo would be there, and she didn't want to miss her son's face when he saw the big display.

Hurrying, she weaved between young couples and families as excitement grew in her chest. The feeling was because of the tree lighting and had absolutely nothing to do with the anticipation of seeing Alex. That was the lie she was telling herself, at least.

When she reached the town square, she saw a group of bikers gathered around. She spotted Paris Montgomery among them. Paris was a graphic designer and motorcycle hobbyist who'd come to town last year for this very event and never left. That's exactly what happened to Tuck's fiancée, Josie Kellum, too. Halona guessed there were plenty of other similar stories. There was a lot to love about Sweetwater Springs.

Her gaze stopped searching when it landed on Alex and Theo sitting on a park bench. "Hey, you two!" she called as she approached.

Theo's eyes lit up when he saw her. One might've thought *she* was the main event. Alex's eyes seemed bright too or was she imagining that?

"My mom took over the store so I thought I'd come hang out with you. Looks like I'm just in time."

Alex scooted over, making room on the bench beside him. The bench was big enough for three, but barely.

"I don't bite," he added, his voice dropping.

She sat down, her thigh knocking against his. Her body hummed with awareness.

"An added bonus is that we can keep each other warm," he said, not in a flirtatious way. He was just being friendly. Wasn't he?

Claire Donovan got on the mic in front of the tree. Claire was a local event planner that handled all of the community's big events. "Everyone having a good time?" she asked.

The crowd whooped and hollered.

Claire laughed into the mic. "Great! Did you all pull an angel off the tree?"

Judging by the crowd's response, everyone did.

"Oh, I need to do that," Halona said, leaning into Alex so he could hear her.

"Theo got you one. I hope that's okay."

"Sure. That's good." She leaned forward to glance at her son whose attention was on Claire and the town tree. "Has he been okay for you?" she asked quietly.

"Of course. Officer Chew was a little skittish with all the commotion. Dawanda said she'd keep him for me until we're done."

Halona rubbed her hands over her thighs in an attempt to warm them. "That's nice of her."

"It is. She gave us a cup of hot cocoa too." Alex's gaze stuck on hers, even though Claire was still talking. She was saying something about this being the twentieth annual Lights on Silver Lake. And how many children the event has helped over the years...Christmas was almost here...last-minute shoppers get busy.

Halona didn't care about any of that with her thigh rubbing against Alex's and his mouth so close to hers that she could practically taste the hot chocolate on his lips. "You got a little...smudge there." She pointed at the corner of his mouth where a five o'clock shadow was filling in.

"I would've gotten you a cup had I known you'd be joining us. I can still go get one if you like."

"No. You'll miss the lights," Halona said.

"It'd be worth it to see you smile."

At his words, she felt her cheeks lift.

"There it is," he said quietly, and maybe he was being more than nice. Maybe he really was flirting.

She swallowed past the growing lump in her throat. She'd seen him nearly every day lately. Was that coincidence? Intentional? Did she like the attention? Did she want it to stop?

No, she didn't want it to stop. "Alex...what are we doing?"

"Talking isn't a crime, Ms. Locklear."

"But it feels like more than talking," she said as a shiver ran over her. It had always felt like more than talking between them.

Alex's blue eyes narrowed. "I don't want to do anything you're not ready for. As far as I'm concerned, we're just friends." He looked away and blew out a breath as Claire continued to talk at the front of the crowd. Then he turned to look at her again. "That felt like a lie, and I'm a sucker for the truth. Let me try again."

Halona's chest lifted on a heavy intake of breath.

"Your brother and I are friends."

"And us?" she asked.

"Friends don't want to kiss the living daylights out of one another," he said, quiet enough for only her ears.

Halona's heart raced at his words, and the closeness of their bodies, and because this was Alex. He was the first guy who ever caught her attention, and the only one who'd sparked any interest inside of her since her late ex-husband died.

"Who's ready to light this tree?" Claire called over the crowd. Then she started a countdown on the mic. "Five…"

"I probably shouldn't have said that," he said. "I blame it on whatever Dawanda puts in her cocoa."

"I feel the same way," Halona told him, her face just a couple of inches from his.

"Four…" Claire shouted.

Alex leaned in a little closer. "About which part? Me kissing you or the fact that I probably shouldn't have said that?"

"Three…"

"I want to kiss you too," Halona admitted, swallowing and instinctively wetting her lips.

"Two…"

"But we probably shouldn't." Halona was finding it hard to breathe.

The corners of his mouth twitched. "It's probably a really bad idea."

"Horrible," Halona practically hummed, hovering a few centimeters from his face.

"The worst," he agreed, his gaze dropping to her mouth and staying there. Then their lips collided, almost accidentally except it didn't feel like an accident at all. It felt amazing. Right. Like magic.

"One!" Claire shouted into the crowd. "Let there be light!"

Everyone oohed and aahed as they watched the town square tree with great excitement. Everyone except Alex and Halona, who were making a light show of their own.

CHAPTER NINE

$\mathcal{A}$lex scooped up a handful of fake snow and formed it into a ball. He looked around for Theo, ready to toss it at his young mentee, when something cold and wet splat on his back. Alex whirled to Theo's childish giggles. "You got me!" Alex said. "My turn!"

The little boy took off running, laughing hysterically all the way. The sound warmed Alex's heart even though he was pretty sure the rest of him was frozen solid right now.

They'd been having a snowball fight while Halona sat and watched from the bench with Officer Chew at her feet. Before coming here, they'd retrieved Chew from Dawanda's Fudge Shop but he wasn't allowed to play in the fake snow set up for the Lights on Silver Lake event. Soon enough the puppy would get to experience the real stuff though.

Another snowball hit Alex's shoulder. He had a lot of adrenaline to work off right now, thanks to that kiss with Halona at the tree lighting ceremony. He and Halona hadn't gotten a chance to talk about it yet but she could've immediately requested to go home after the lighting. Instead, she'd opted to stay and enjoy the festivities a little more with him. He took that as a good sign.

Alex raised his snowball at Theo, whose eyes lit up. Then he smiled and pointed at Halona. Theo nodded excitedly. He scooped up some snow of his own, formed a small ball, and followed Alex toward the bench.

Halona was looking at something on her phone.

"Let's make sure to avoid hitting her face," Alex whispered. "And her phone. Let's just aim for her legs."

Theo nodded, and they crept forward until they were only a few feet away. Theo giggled once more, alerting Halona to their presence. Officer Chew stood at attention and gave a soft *woof*.

"Now!" Alex said. Then he and the boy both pulled back an arm and aimed at Halona's legs.

She shrieked before submitting to a laugh. "I'm going to get you two!" she called, putting her phone inside her purse.

The three of them scooped more snowballs and pummeled each other for another five minutes before Alex raised his arms. "I surrender."

Theo took that opportunity to drive another snowball into Alex's chest.

"Hey. I was surrendering," Alex said with a large smile.

Halona nodded. "Alex is right. We better head home. It's way past your bedtime, Theo."

Theo's expression reminded Alex of the one that Officer Chew had made when they'd left him tied to the bench while they played. Theo's smile easily returned though as they walked through the crowd and back to

Halona's car in the parking lot. Theo gave Officer Chew a huge hug and then turned and did the same to Alex before climbing into the back seat.

Halona didn't immediately move to get into the driver's seat. "Thanks again for taking him tonight," she said. "I know he had a wonderful time."

"I had fun too." His gaze slid to Theo, who was watching them closely.

"I guess the Christmas season has officially started. This is always where I start to feel overwhelmed by the list of things I need to do." She leaned against the car door as she stood in front of him. "Shopping, cooking, wrapping presents, getting a tree of our own."

"I can help you with the tree part," Alex said. "How about tomorrow?" Maybe he was talking out of turn but they'd just kissed and she didn't look regretful. If he had to say good night to her right now, he wanted to secure another way to see her the next day.

Halona hugged her arms around her body. "Okay."

Alex turned his ear toward her to make sure he'd heard correctly. "Okay?"

She nodded with a small shrug. "I'll take you up on that offer. Tuck helped us get a tree last year, but if you're willing..."

"Great. Will tomorrow night work?" he asked. "I'm driving Grandma Baker to church in the morning. She can't see well enough to stay on the road these days. Then I'm going back to her house to tick off the to-do list she has waiting for me."

"You're a regular hero." She looked up at him through thick, black eyelashes.

"That's not heroic."

"I bet Grandma Baker would disagree." She smiled,

her eyelids drooping lazily, and he got the undeniable green light that she wanted him to kiss her again. But that had to be a mixed signal because Theo was watching.

Her neck was exposed, long and narrow as she tipped her face up, eyes searching his. It would be so easy to curl one hand behind her head and touch his mouth to hers. So natural. So right.

Woof!

Halona laughed as she broke eye contact. "I think Officer Chew might be cold."

"You have a fur coat, buddy," Alex said. "But he's right. It's freezing, and you need to get Theo to bed."

"Tomorrow then?" Halona asked.

Alex searched her face one more time, looking for any hint that she might be uncomfortable with their plans. They'd always had a push-pull relationship that kept each other at arm's length but something had changed tonight. "I'll pick you up in the truck. That way you can get the biggest tree on the Merry Mountain Farms lot if you want."

"Theo will be thrilled about that." Halona lowered into the driver's seat.

Alex secured a hand on her open door and dipped inside to look at Theo in the back seat. "Night, Theo." He straightened back up. "Night, Halona."

Tension buzzed in the space between them.

"Night."

He closed her car door and then headed to his SUV completely baffled. Just like the town square tree had been plugged in and had gone from ordinary to something wondrous, a switch seemed to have flipped on inside Halona. She wasn't resisting him anymore, at least not tonight.

* * *

Halona had done a good job remaining calm on the outside but inside she was freaking out. She'd kissed Alex! The only thing she could do afterward was smile and act like it was no big deal. Thank goodness that Theo hadn't seen her and Alex kissing. Hopefully, no one else in town had either.

"You doing okay, sweetie?" she asked, flicking her gaze to Theo in the rearview mirror.

He nodded as she returned her vision to the road. Cedar Trail was only about ten minutes from downtown. She navigated the mountain roads as her mind refused to let go of that kiss. Finally, she turned on their road and drove all the way to the end. Theo was nearly asleep by the time she opened his door and tugged him out.

"You can go straight to bed," she said, helping him along.

Once they were inside, they removed their coats, gloves, and shoes, and Halona helped Theo change into a pair of pajamas and tucked him into bed. Then she made her way back to the kitchen where she sat at the table with a glass of water.

After all this time, she and Alex had kissed. When she'd seen him and Theo together, looking so natural and happy, her attraction had skyrocketed off the charts. She'd been telling herself that Theo needed her full attention but he adored his new mentor, always had. Dating Alex might not be the devastating thing she'd assumed it would be, she thought before a rush of competing objections swam into her mind.

Once she'd drained her glass, Halona tiptoed down the hall and climbed into her own bed. She had a feeling that it wouldn't be Theo that kept her from getting a full eight hours tonight. Instead, she'd be batting around thoughts and memories of Alex and that kiss that she couldn't bring herself to regret.

* * *

The next morning, Halona stirred with the sun beating down on her closed eyelids. She eased into wakefulness, holding onto a wonderful dream she'd been having until her eyes popped open. She didn't have dreams anymore. She didn't stay asleep long enough. And she didn't get the luxury of waking with the sun anymore either.

"Theo!" She shot up out of bed and jammed her feet into a pair of slippers. Then she hurried across the hall to the room adjacent to hers and peeked inside. There was still a visible lump under the covers. She held her breath as she watched, willing the lump to move so she could be sure that he was still breathing. When he did, she exhaled and turned to press her back against the hallway wall.

He'd slept through the night. For the first time in months, he'd actually slept a full eight hours. She wanted to shout it from the rooftops. She'd be able to tell Dr. Charwood next week, of course, but she wanted to tell her good news now.

Halona hurried into the kitchen and set the coffee maker brewing, and then pulled up her mom's contact information on her phone. No answer. She tried to call Tuck. Surely he'd appreciate the news about his nephew. His phone went straight to voicemail.

Halona nibbled on her lower lip. Alex came to mind next. He was Theo's Mentor Match after all. He knew how much she'd been struggling with Theo's sleep. He'd get it. Not giving herself another second to debate the decision, she pressed Call and waited as her heart skipped around.

"Halona? Is everything all right?" he asked.

"Um, yeah. I just couldn't wait to tell you what happened."

"Sounds like good news," he said. His voice was still gravelly, and she wondered if she'd woken him. Surely, he'd already been up and probably out for a jog by now. She'd seen him on the road before when she'd had to set out early to decorate a venue. He ran as the sun was rising, always with sunglasses and a ball cap. The memory made her suddenly want to kiss him again. Her unruly attraction was out of its cage and seemingly couldn't, wouldn't, be contained.

"It is. Theo slept through the night. He's actually still sleeping."

"Whoa. That is good news," Alex agreed.

Halona felt herself grinning from ear to ear. "I don't know if it's because we wore him out completely during the Lights on Silver Lake, or if it was all you. I mean, he spoke his first word in forever after being with you. He said 'yeah.'"

"I seriously doubt it was all me," Alex said.

Halona wondered though. Alex seemed to have the ability to make her do things she normally wouldn't too. "Anyway, I just needed to tell someone."

"I'm glad you told me," he said.

A silence fell on the line between them.

"Am I still seeing you tonight?" he asked. "To get the tree? Or has something come up?"

There was a teasing tone in that last question. She hadn't had time to come up with a valid excuse to cancel on him yet, and she didn't want to. On the contrary, she couldn't wait to see him again.

"Nope. We'll be ready and waiting when you get here," she said.

"Good. Glad to hear it. I also plan to pick out a tree for Grandma Baker while we're there."

"You're taking her to church this morning and getting her a tree later. Who says Chief Alex Baker doesn't have a soft, mushy"—*very kissable*—"side?"

He chuckled into the receiver, the sound tickling her senses. "Only when it comes to my favorite women."

This was definitely flirting, and for some reason, she didn't mind so much anymore. Being with him didn't appear to confuse or upset Theo. In fact, it had the opposite effect. And being near him made her feel giddy and happy and alive.

"Thanks for the good news. See you tonight."

They said their goodbyes and Halona disconnected the call. Then she exhaled the breath that had ballooned inside her chest and carried her cup of coffee to the table to savor it all by herself—something else that hadn't happened in a very long time.

* * *

Alex started to worry after he'd knocked several times and his grandma still hadn't come to the door. He tried the doorknob, and the door opened easily. He stepped inside and looked around. "Grandma? It's Alex. You okay?"

He heard rustling from the living room and headed in that direction, finding her lying on the couch.

"I'm sorry. Is it time already?" she asked groggily. "I must have fallen back to sleep after breakfast."

Alex took a few more steps inside. "You doing all right?"

"Oh, fine." She sat up and smoothed her hair on her head. "Well, maybe not the best, but that's okay." She looked at him. "It's a hard month, as you know. Sometimes it gets the best of me."

Alex sat in the recliner across from her. He didn't have to ask. She was referring to his dad. "Yeah, I know."

Grandma Baker shook her head. "I'm really sorry. I don't think I'm up to going to church today."

"You don't have to apologize to me, Grandma."

"I know. And I try not to have a pity party. I had a wonderful son, and he had an amazing life. He did great things while he was here." She smiled softly. "I just miss him—that's all."

"Yeah," Alex said. He knew that too. "What do you need me to do for you? Want me to make you some tea? Something to eat? Want me to leave you alone so you can sleep some more?"

She laughed, which he considered progress. "I'm feeling better already just by having you here. But that doesn't mean I need you to stay either. I have company coming over this afternoon."

"You do?" Alex asked.

"Yes. Gina Hargrove and her sister Nettie are paying me a visit. I'm so excited I can hardly stand it. I wish I'd started putting out my holiday decorations though. Gina runs that beautiful bed and breakfast with Kaitlyn. I'm sure that place is already decked out by now, and I don't even have a tree yet."

"Well, I'm going to help you with that. I'm going to Merry Mountain Farms this afternoon, and I plan to get you a tree while I'm there."

"Oh, you are such a sweet boy," she said. In her eyes, he guessed he'd always be a boy. "Always so doting. Janice Murphy is wrong about you."

Alex felt a frown weigh on the corners of his mouth. "She's just mad because I've been catching her before she's able to spike the public beverages these days. It's a crime."

Grandma Baker raised a gentle brow. "I'm not criticizing. I think you're doing a fine job but she's not the only one who thinks you need to relax."

Alex sat down on the couch across from her. "You can't be relaxed with the law, Grandma. If you're lenient, crime will grow."

"I know. I just worry about you."

"Well, you shouldn't."

"That's like asking the sun not to rise or set. Or for a grandmother not to completely adore her grandson. It's impossible. But you're a grown man, and you're good at what you do. Just like your father."

"I'm trying."

"You're succeeding. Let me balance out what I said about Janice Murphy. She was wrong about you but Alice Hamilton was right."

Alex wasn't sure he wanted to ask. "What did Ms. Hamilton say?"

"That there's never been a better chief of police in Sweetwater Springs, and that the town is safer than it's ever been with you in charge."

Alex looked at his feet as he swallowed a huge lump in his throat. He'd never feel like that was true until he found his dad's killer.

"Now go. I'm going to shower and get my home ready for my visitors this afternoon. You have a good time at the farm. I like a little tree," she told him. "It's easier to reach the top when I'm hanging my ornaments."

"I can hang the ornaments for you," he said.

"I'm not so old where I can't decorate my own tree. As long as you get a little one."

Alex walked over to her and bent to kiss her cheek. "I'll drop it by tomorrow sometime. You can do the decorating."

"Thank you."

Alex closed the front door behind him as he left and headed to his vehicle. Since he didn't want to walk in late for church and Grandma Baker didn't need him to take her, he went home. Maybe he'd take Officer Chew for a long walk and clear his head.

Grandma Baker wasn't the only one weighed down by memories. His were competing, though, between the ones of his dad and those of that kiss with Halona. After all these years, he was ready to investigate this thing between them. Going too fast would only push her away though. Best to take things slow and follow her lead.

CHAPTER TEN

*H*alona sucked in a deep breath of mountain air as she stepped out of Alex's truck. It was thick with the scent of evergreens. She opened the cab door for Theo and then they walked around to where Alex was waiting for them. This evening, he was dressed casually in jeans and a polo top beneath a brown leather jacket.

She had Off-Duty Alex tonight. Off-Duty Alex was the one she'd found herself lip-locked with. On-Duty Alex was the one who'd taken Ted to jail and threatened to take her to the hospital. That would've placed Theo in protective custody. There would have been questioning. It would've been traumatic for a little boy.

Theo reached for her hand as if sensing the emotion behind her stream of thoughts. Somehow, despite her best efforts, he'd been traumatized anyway. It was in no way Alex's fault; she knew that. He couldn't have known the truth behind the situation.

"There are a million trees out here to choose from,

buddy," Alex told Theo as they walked. "We don't want the biggest or the smallest. In my experience, we want the tree that's right smack-dab in the middle."

Theo seemed to hang on Alex's every word. And why wouldn't he? Alex Baker was a stand-up guy. There weren't any hidden dark sides to him. What you saw was what you got, and Halona had always liked what she'd seen in Alex.

"I love live Christmas trees," she said as they strolled through the lot, letting Theo scrutinize each one. "They make the holidays feel that much more special. We need a good holiday this year." She glanced over. "Last year was tough, with it being the first for Theo without Ted," she said, surprising herself. Her personal life wasn't something she usually talked about.

"I can only imagine. I thought about you a lot last year. Hoped you were doing okay."

"We got through it. Mom always says people come through the fire stronger." Halona swallowed. "Anyway, I want to make this year as special as I can. A live tree is a good start. You should see Theo's list," she added, desperate to swing the subject toward something more neutral because her eyes were suddenly stinging against the cold. Showing outward emotion was also something she didn't normally do. Alex had an effect on her that most didn't. "Theo's list is numbered in order of importance. The number reaches almost to one hundred."

"Whoa," Alex said on a laugh.

"He doesn't expect it all, thank goodness, but he has a lot of wants. And not all of them are material."

"What do you mean?" Alex asked.

Theo was a few steps ahead, touching the evergreen branches and inspecting them thoroughly.

"Well, for instance, he wants a brother." Halona's cheeks flushed immediately upon saying it. That would involve her finding and sleeping with a man, and the only man she'd come close to having those kinds of feelings for was Alex. "He wants to go camping. He wants a fish and a dog. He wants to see a shooting star. And, um..." Halona paused.

"What?" Alex prodded.

She swallowed past the growing emotion once again. "He wants to go skiing." She shrugged. "I'm not sure why." Except that wasn't true. She suspected it had to do with Ted's death. Halona looked over at Alex. "I should probably take him. I just...I don't ski. Theo does. Ted took him every year."

"I haven't been in a while but I hear it's like riding a bike," Alex said.

"Oh, no. I wasn't asking you to take him." Halona released a soft laugh.

"I know but I'm offering. As his Mentor Match. I'll take you too and teach you so you can continue taking him every year. I'm not sure when we can make it happen though. It's a busy time of year right now. Maybe January."

Halona nodded. "You've already been so generous with your time. I'm not sure how I'll ever repay you."

She felt inclined to take a step toward him but they were in public and drawing closer might make her want to kiss him again. So instead she stepped back, right into a man with a video camera. "I'm so sorry," Halona said, stepping toward Alex once more.

"What's going on?" Alex asked.

"Just doing a news story on finding the perfect tree, Chief Baker," the cameraman said. Serena Gibbs was with him. Serena was a local newscaster. She was beautiful and always perfectly polished no matter whether you ran into her at a convenience store at ten p.m. on a Sunday night.

"We would love to add you to the piece," Serena said. "The town will eat up the fact that their very own chief of police is shopping for a tree too."

Alex shook his head. "My personal life isn't news."

Serena kept her beautiful smile despite Alex's frown. "It will be to those who think you live and breathe your job."

"That's all people need to know," he countered.

Halona reached for his hand before he could continue protesting. "It'll be nice to show the public a different side to you, don't you think? It will make you more approachable, which is a good thing."

Alex looked down at her hand on his for a moment, his serious expression softening as he relented. He looked back at Serena. "Just a brief clip."

"Perfect." Serena held her microphone up to Alex and gave a nod at the cameraman. "So, Chief Baker, tell us: What do you look for in a Christmas tree?" she asked.

Alex shrugged. His expression was so serious that Halona wanted to laugh. "I guess I'd like for it to be standing upright."

Serena took his sarcasm without skipping a beat. "Well, as long as you have a tree stand, you should be fine."

"Honestly, I don't put up a Christmas tree at my place," he said.

Serena's mouth popped open.

So much for softening Alex's image.

"Then what are you doing at Merry Mountain Farms?" the newscaster asked.

"He's helping me," Halona said quickly, bumping her shoulder against his as she continued to hold his hand. She hadn't intended to draw attention to herself in this segment, but Alex needed rescuing.

He looked over at her, meeting her eyes. For a moment, Halona had a hard time looking away. She swallowed and turned back to the news crew. "My son and I don't have our tree yet so Alex— Chief Baker offered to assist us."

"Well, that's very kind of our local police chief," Serena said, smiling again. She returned her attention to Alex. "I hear you're also involved in the Eversons' new Mentor Match program, Chief Baker. Is that true?"

Alex nodded, still looking adorably uncomfortable. When he was on the news discussing a crime, he had no difficulty. But when the spotlight shone on him, he looked nervous. Halona gave his hand a soft squeeze of support. "It is. It's a great cause," he said.

"Well, we are a town that loves a good cause," Serena agreed. "Good luck picking out that tree, Chief. Maybe you'll fall in love with one to bring home with you as well."

Halona looked up at Alex. The perfect tree might not be the only thing she fell for tonight.

"Sorry about that," Alex said as Serena and her cameraman finished with them and continued down the rows of evergreens.

"No, it's okay. I think it's great, actually. The town is used to seeing you on the news when something bad happens. It's nice to see you during the good things too.

It'll show them the human side of Alex Baker. The big heart behind that shiny badge of yours."

"I've lived in Sweetwater Springs my entire life. This town knows who I am."

Halona lifted a shoulder. "People can be forgetful. You have to refresh their memories sometimes."

"You're good with public relations," he noted.

Halona looked at him. "I have to be. As the only florist in town, I've worked with quite a few bridezillas. No matter how they feel when they enter my shop, I make sure they're always happy when they leave."

"I should put you on staff at the police station. To make me look good."

Halona grinned. "I think the news segment will do that for you. A police chief helping a friend find the perfect tree for her little boy's Christmas is sure to win you points." Her heart jumped in her throat as soon as the sentence tumbled out of her mouth, and her gaze darted ahead looking for her son. "Where is he?"

"Theo?" Alex called.

"Theo!" Halona echoed. "Theo, where are you?"

"I'm sure he's just moved on ahead of us." Alex started walking faster, calling her son's name every few seconds. Finally, he stopped a few trees past her.

Halona ran forward, suspecting that Theo was there.

"Theo! How many times have I told you not to wander off?" Halona snapped.

Theo looked between them, confusion woven into his expression.

"We got sidetracked. That's my fault," Alex said, attempting to diffuse the tension. "Theo has a one-track mind tonight. It's all about finding the perfect tree. Isn't that right, buddy?"

Theo nodded.

Halona exhaled softly. "It doesn't matter. You still have to stay with us, Theo," she said. "You worried me."

Theo's previously cheerful expression was now crest-fallen. And that made her feel awful. Tonight was for him. It was supposed to be fun.

"Is this the tree?" Alex asked.

Theo looked up at him and nodded quietly.

"It's a fine tree. A really good choice," Alex said.

The light in Theo's eyes returned as Alex continued to praise his choice. Halona watched, feeling a weight lift off her shoulders. Alex had taken that weight. Usually, she would've had to tend to Theo's fragile emotions and help him work his way back to a smile. This time, Alex took the lead. He was good with Theo. Good with her.

Timber! One kiss and all her resolve was gone. She was falling hard for this hardened lawman. She'd seen a different side of him though.

Alex looked at her with a large grin as he wrapped an arm around Theo's shoulders. "I'd say the search is over. It's the perfect one," he declared.

And she agreed. Except instead of looking at the tree, she was looking at Alex.

* * *

Alex got back behind the wheel and looked at his passengers. "Okay. We got our trees so I guess I'll take you home."

"What about Grandma Baker's tree?" Halona asked.

"Oh, I'll drop that off tomorrow sometime." Alex started his vehicle and navigated down the dark mountain back roads toward Cedar Trail.

"I'm sure she'll appreciate that. It would be hard for her to get one on her own."

"That's true but I doubt she'd agree. She may be pushing eighty years old but she's just as strong and independent as ever."

Halona laughed.

"I think the only reason she wants me to take her to church every Sunday is to make sure I go."

"Sneaky."

Alex glanced over. "I didn't make it this morning. Grandma, uh, slept in."

"Theo did too. I didn't have the heart to wake him."

Alex pulled onto Cedar Trail and slowed at the end of the dead-end street. As Halona helped Theo out, Alex walked around to the tailgate and got the tree.

"I'll open the door for you. I already cleared away a space for the tree this afternoon and set up the stand," she said.

"Perfect."

He waited for her to open the front door, and then he shook off the tree a little bit before lugging it up the porch steps and through the door. Halona directed him to her living room. After a few minutes and a little help from her, the tree was upright in its stand.

All three of them stood back for a moment. It was the perfect size for the room.

"I hope I have enough ornaments to cover it," Halona mused. Then she looked at Theo. "If not, I guess you can get busy making some, right?"

Theo nodded.

"Homemade ornaments are the best, in my opinion," Alex said. "Where's your box of ornaments and lights?"

"Still in the shed. I didn't have time to get those out earlier."

Alex headed toward the back door. "I'll get them."

"You don't have to," Halona called.

Alex turned. "No, but I want to," he said before stepping outside.

Halona reminded him of his grandmother in a way. They had that same strong, independent spirit that he admired.

He opened the shed and pulled the string for the light, illuminating the space. All the containers were labeled neatly. He easily located the one labeled CHRISTMAS DECORATIONS. Right next to the container that read TED'S THINGS.

Alex stared at it for a long moment as anger knotted his belly. He guessed Halona kept those things for Theo but Alex had a good mind to take them through the woods to the river and toss them in. Instead, he gave the box a firm kick before lifting the box of Christmas decorations. He'd always been good at managing his emotions, especially when it came to perps. Even though Halona's ex was deceased now, Alex still wanted to meet him in a dark alley just for a couple of minutes.

"Hey."

Alex turned to find Halona standing behind him.

"Just checking on you. You've been gone awhile. I was worried you couldn't find the box."

Alex tipped his chin at the box in his hands. "Found it. You keep things very organized in here. I can tell you that my grandmother's attic won't be as easy tomorrow."

Halona laughed as Alex stepped past her. She closed the shed door behind him and followed him back into the house. "I made hot apple cider. It's Theo's favorite."

Alex set the box of decorations on the floor next to the tree and turned to look at Halona.

"There's an extra mug for you already waiting on the table," she said.

"Well, it just so happens to be my favorite as well," Alex said. "Let me wash my hands, and I'll be right there."

Push-pull, push-pull, push-pull. As quick as his heartbeat when he was with her. In the bathroom, he let the hot water run over his hands and then changed the water to cold and splashed some on his face as well. He was letting her set the pace but all he wanted to do was *pull* her into his arms again tonight and have another kiss.

* * *

"So is it true?" Brenna looked at Halona over her coffee cup, a smile curling at the corners of her mouth.

"Is what true?" Halona asked. It was Monday morning, and the two women hadn't even officially planned on meeting up but both had come to the Sweetwater Café early hoping to find each other.

"You weren't going to even tell me about your date?" Brenna's mouth dropped open. "I thought we were friends."

Halona shook her head. "I still don't know what you're talking about."

"Your date with Chief Frisky!"

Now Halona's mouth was hanging wide open. "What?"

"People are talking, Halona. Starla Brinson said she saw you two getting cozy at Merry Mountain Farms."

Halona vaguely remembered waving to Starla as she'd followed Theo from tree to tree. "We weren't getting cozy. We were simply walking together."

"So you didn't go there together?" Brenna asked.

Halona wrapped her fingers around her coffee cup.

"Well, yes. We did but it wasn't like that. He's Theo's mentor, remember?"

"But not yours. The Mentor Match thing is just for the mentor and their mentee. Not the mentee's mom."

Halona lowered her face, hoping her friend wouldn't notice the flush that she could feel burning from her chest up to her cheeks. "Well, Alex offered to help us get our tree. Then he helped us set it up in the living room."

"Uh-huh. And did he stay a little later after doing that? Because Joanna Thomas said he did."

Halona looked back up at her friend. Joanna Thomas was Halona's neighbor, a quiet woman who ran a business out of her home. Apparently, she closely minded the business of others as well.

"She was in line behind me for coffee this morning. She said Alex stayed at your place until nine p.m."

"Really, Brenna, Alex and I are just friends." Halona took a sip of her coffee.

Brenna's wide smile faded. "You and Alex have never been just friends. I've always felt the heat between you two when you're together. That's why the town is talking."

"The people of Sweetwater Springs are talking because they have nothing better to talk about."

"Not true, and you know it. We're all talking because we've seen this coming for a long time. And now it's finally happening. The anticipation is so thick. It's like Christmas for the romantics around here."

Halona laughed. "Well, I hate to disappoint everyone in that simile because that fancy little present under the romantics' tree is just a package of socks. Boring white socks."

"Socks?" Brenna scrunched up her face.

"Yes. No exchanges, no returns."

"I was thinking more along the lines of lingerie." Brenna bounced her eyebrows a few times.

"You are crazy. And if anyone else fills you in on my love life today, please correct them for me."

"It's just socks. Got it. So, changing subjects. What are you doing tomorrow night?" Brenna asked. "The Ladies' Day Out group is getting together, and I want—*need*—you to come. As my BFF, it's your duty."

"We're BFFs?" Halona asked, finding the label heart-warming.

"I heard this through the grapevine as well. I think this bit of gossip might be true though." Brenna popped a piece of muffin into her mouth and grinned across the table from her.

"Well…"

"Come on. Please!" Brenna added. "It'll be fun."

"It's just, all the women I know who I might ask to watch Theo for me are part of the Ladies' Day Out group. You know that."

"Then don't ask a woman. Ask a man," Brenna suggested. "Alex Baker maybe."

"No, I can't ask him."

"Ask me what?" a deep voice said.

Both women turned to find the man himself standing there in all his glory. Badge shining, smile in place, and his eyes firmly pinned to Halona.

CHAPTER ELEVEN

$\mathcal{I}$ caught you talking about me," Alex said. "What is it you want to ask me?"

"Oh, it's nothing." Halona waved a hand and offered a laugh that sounded guilty even to her own ears.

"If you could watch Theo Friday night so Halona can come out with the Ladies' Day Out group," Brenna supplied. "I've been trying to get her to come with us for a while now. Everyone else has for years."

Halona started shaking her head. "It's fine. Theo needs me home. He'll need dinner and he always watches a movie on Friday night."

"I can do those things," Alex said. "And I don't mind."

"Really, you don't have to—"

"Officer Chew has been missing Theo anyway. He'll be happy for the playdate."

Halona wasn't sure whether to continue arguing or to say thank you. She hated asking for favors, and Alex was doing far too many for her these days. Watching the flower shop, mentoring Theo, helping them with the tree. He'd done more than that for her though.

"It's settled, then," Brenna said, filling the silence. "Finally, my favorite lady is going to have a Ladies' Day Out with us."

"Where is the group going this time?" Alex asked.

"Perfectly Pampered Salon is staying open late for all of us. We're getting holiday makeovers. Nails, toes, and Elsa has some kind of Christmas tinsel that she can weave into our hair. It lasts a few weeks and promises to make us eye-catching until then."

"Hair tinsel?" Halona asked on a laugh.

"Yes, and you're doing it with me. We need to make the most of our outing because I may never get you to join us again." Brenna cast Alex a meaningful look. "Unless Chief Baker here decides to start moonlighting as a baby-sitter. I know a few other women who'd like to join in the fun and have a child-free night."

Halona laughed. "We can try to rope Tuck into doing it too."

"Oh, your brother would love that, huh?" Brenna winked. Then she grabbed her coffee and scooted back from the table. "I better get to work. I have Doris Manchester coming in today to discuss a Christmas party she wants catered. Summer Rivera is also coming by later to discuss the Hope for the Holidays auction."

"She's already found me," Halona said. "I'm donating poinsettias again this year."

"And apparently, I'm baking cookies," Alex said. "Halona promised to find a recipe in her new cookbook to help me."

Halona nodded. "I ordered the *Two Peas & Their Pod Cookbook* the other night. It's from a blog."

"I'll have to check it out... And you two are baking these cookies together?" Brenna raised a brow. "Well, with the way the town is fluttering about seeing you two at Merry Mountain Farms over the weekend, selling homemade cookies from the budding couple might be profitable." Brenna waved and headed to the door before either Halona or Alex could respond to that.

"What was that about?" Alex asked.

Halona sighed as he took the seat where Brenna had been sitting. "According to Brenna, we've stirred up some excitement among those who have nothing better to do than talk about others."

"I guess that's better than them talking about me. Now Tony is telling anyone who'll listen that I threatened to take a swing at him."

Halona's stomach dropped. "Did you?"

"Of course not." He narrowed his eyes. "I'm not a violent kind of guy."

She nodded, feeling foolish about even questioning Alex. Halona wrapped her fingers around her cup of coffee, soaking in its warmth as a chill ran through her. "I can't believe Tony let you take his dog," she said.

"He didn't really have a choice. According to the vet, the puppy has been abused. There's no way it can return to Tony's care." Alex looked down at his coffee cup for a moment.

"Any breaks in your dad's case?" Halona asked.

"Not really. I have a few things to follow up on though. I'll never give up."

"I wouldn't expect anything less of you. You're a good man, Alex Baker. I'm really glad you were chosen as Theo's Mentor Match," she said.

"Me too." He reached across the table and touched her

arm, just for a moment, but long enough to fire electric shock waves through her body. And long enough for several people in the café to witness, no doubt. The most curious thing about that was that Halona didn't really care anymore if a few townsfolk thought that she and Alex were falling for one another.

* * *

On Wednesday at noon, Alex slid into a booth across from Mitch at a local burgers-and-fries joint. Mitch had come to work at the Sweetwater police station last year around this time, and he'd proven himself to be a good officer. Not that Alex was surprised. He and Mitch had grown up wanting to go into law enforcement. While Alex had gone to the police academy after high school, Mitch had joined the military and become a military policeman for a time.

"I already ordered for you," Mitch said, gesturing to Alex's sweet tea. "Cheeseburger and sweet potato fries are on their way."

"You deserve a raise," Alex joked.

Mitch laughed. "So how's your dad's case coming?"

"It's not," Alex said. "It's been eleven years. The leads have stopped, not that there were ever that many to begin with. No witnesses. No new evidence."

"Reopening the case every year is only opening old wounds," Mitch said with a frown. "Maybe it's time to..." He trailed off as Alex shook his head.

"I can't. I made a promise to my dad and Grandma Baker."

A waitress stepped up and slid a plate of food in front of each of them, creating a natural break in a conversation that Alex was already tired of. He knew that Mitch's advice made the most sense. As the chief of police, he had more pressing things to work on than dried-up leads.

Mitch picked up a fry and dipped it into a dollop of ketchup. "I know how much you'd love to get justice for your dad," he said, returning to where they left off.

"But the longer the case goes without being solved, the less likely it is that it ever will be." Alex nodded. "I know the numbers." He'd crunched them a million times. "I stopped by Steve Anderson's place again last week."

"Was he home this time?" Mitch asked.

Alex gave a nod. "Yep. Didn't let me come inside though."

"You surprised?"

"Nope." Alex reached for a fry. "Only people who have something to hide keep a visitor on the front porch."

"Right. Why not just let you in?" Mitch agreed. "It's suspicious."

"Well, we know the Anderson family aren't angels. I'm sure there's something to hide. I just want to know if it has to do with my dad. The only reason I have to think it might is because Steve's was an active case at the time of Dad's death."

"Bet he didn't enjoy having you sniffing around," Mitch offered as he continued to eat.

"He had a few choice words for me. He also wasn't happy about me hauling his nephew off to jail on animal cruelty charges the other week."

"He'll get over it."

"Doubtful. Let's talk about something more cheerful," Alex suggested, looking around the diner and its festive lights and red bows.

Mitch looked up from his food. "Okay. Like?"

"Your upcoming wedding."

This made Mitch smile wider than Alex had seen in a long time. Then Mitch started rattling off plans. "You bringing a date?" Mitch finally asked. "Because I hear you and Halona are getting cozy these days."

Alex took a sip of his soda to wash down his bite of burger before he choked on it. "I didn't realize you believed everything you heard."

"Kaitlyn keeps me informed, and I trust her as a source. I'm sure Josie is keeping Tuck informed as well."

Alex frowned. Tuck had always suspected that Alex had feelings for his sister, and he'd even encouraged Alex a few times. It was only a matter of time before Tuck came to see him and asked what was going on. It would probably be a good idea if Alex figured that out for himself before he had to have that discussion.

The problem was that Alex really wasn't sure what was going on. All he knew was he liked it.

* * *

"You have a callback list waiting for you," Tammy told Alex half an hour later as he walked into the station.

"I think you get a lot of satisfaction out of knowing my workload is piling up."

She shrugged. "A girl's gotta get her kicks somehow."

Alex froze as he headed down the hall to his office. Then he turned and approached Tammy's desk. "Can I ask you something?"

"Shoot." She started laughing. "That's cop humor," she said when Alex drew his brows together in question.

"Right. That's a step up from your usual humor, asking every day if I enjoyed my doughnuts."

Tammy cackled again. "What's your question, Chief?"

"The Ladies' Day Out group. You're one of the only women I know that isn't in it. Why? You're a woman. You're single." Not that being single was a requirement. "No kids. No outside responsibilities that I know of."

"Are you saying I don't have a life? Because you're wrong," she said with a touch of defensiveness. "You know how much I love to cook. When I'm off work, that's what I'm doing. Heating up the kitchen and feeding all my neighbors."

"That wouldn't keep you from joining the group every now and then though."

"Honestly?" Tammy leaned toward him over her desk. "I like men better. That's why I work here. You know how direct I can be. I've been known to hurt feelings because I don't like to sugarcoat things." She shrugged and leaned back in her chair. "That gets you talked about, and I don't like to be talked about."

"You'd rather be the one talking?" Alex asked.

"Exactly. I'm much happier in a group of men."

"Men's feelings can get hurt too, you know," Alex pointed out.

Tammy lifted a brow. "The rumor in town is that you don't have feelings. At least that *was* what everyone was saying." She cocked her head to one side.

"What's that supposed to mean?"

"The new talk in town is that you took Halona on a date this weekend and had breakfast with her this morning. I also hear that she's going to be joining the group while you watch her son this week. Sounds like you have a lot of feelings these days."

Alex pointed at Tammy. "This is why you're not a detective. Those facts are off. I took my mentee out this weekend, and his mom happened to come. I ran into said mom this morning, and we had coffee, not breakfast."

Tammy folded her arms over her chest, looking pleased with herself. "And you're caring for her son this week while she goes out."

"As a Mentor Match. How do you even know all this anyway?"

Tammy chuckled. "Good thing you're not an under-cover cop, because you aren't good at keeping things under wraps, Chief. Haven't you seen the news? You and Halona are the top story, picking out a tree at Merry Mountain Farms with all the other happy families."

Alex felt his heart drop. Is that the story that was spun on the news? Had he looked like he was there with Halona on a date along with her son? Doing a traditional family activity?

"I guess you haven't seen the segment." Tammy tsked. "So you're trying to tell me you don't have a thing for Halona Locklear? Because the camera doesn't lie, and I saw something there."

"I have no idea what you're talking about," he said before turning and heading back toward his office. He had a long callback list waiting for him but first he needed to pull up the SWS five o'clock news segment from last night and see exactly what had the town talking.

* * *

Halona had just gotten home and was about to start raiding the cabinets and fridge to figure out dinner when the doorbell rang. She hurried toward the front door and opened it.

"Mom!" Halona said as her mother breezed past with a

casserole dish in hand. If Lula Locklear wasn't doting on Tuck, Josie, and Maddie, then she was here with Halona and Theo. "You didn't tell me you were coming."

"Well, I was making succotash for Maddie because it's one of her favorites but as soon as I saw the news, I decided to carry it to you instead."

"What news?" Halona asked.

"I can't believe you didn't tell me." Lula placed the dish on the counter and spun to narrow her amber-colored eyes at Halona. "And now you're playing dumb? I'm your mother. When my daughter finally starts dating someone again, I should be the first to know. I certainly shouldn't be the last."

"Huh? I have no idea—"

"You and Alex," her mom said with a large smile. "Oh, I couldn't be happier."

"We aren't..." Halona shook her head quickly. "I don't know what you've heard but Alex and I aren't dating."

Her mom's large smile dwindled. "You're not? But I heard it from multiple people. And then I checked the news, and I saw the story myself. You two were picking out a tree, and you looked so happy together." Lula stepped into the living room and gestured at the tree. "There it is. You picked out a good one." She nodded approvingly.

"Alex took us to the farm but it was for Theo. Not me. I'm sorry to disappoint you but we're not dating, Mom." Halona actually did feel bad because her mom's spirit looked crushed.

"I see... Well, I just want you to be happy again."

Again. Halona had always tried to mask her fear and disappointment during that last year of marriage to Ted and then after her divorce. She'd always smiled and focused on the positive. She'd centered her universe around Theo so everyone else would too.

"I *am* happy, Mom. I don't need a guy for that."

"Alex is a good one though. I always thought so." Her mom gave her a long look. "I never told you so because you were always the daughter who dated the ones I warned you against and avoided the ones I liked."

Halona's mouth dropped open. "What?"

"It's true. I got your number, so I never told you what I thought of Ted," her mom said.

Halona shook her head. "Okay. What *did* you think?"

"No. I don't speak ill of the dead either."

"I'm shocked." Halona followed her mom back into the kitchen and watched as she lifted the dish. "Wait. What are you doing?"

"Well, this is Maddie's favorite meal. And your love life was a false alarm; I'll carry it to her instead."

"Theo loves that dish too," Halona pointed out.

Lula sighed softly and set the dish back down on the counter. "Okay. I'll just make Maddie a meal tomorrow night. Where is Theo anyway?"

"Reading in his bedroom."

"Head always in a book, just like you at that age. Except I couldn't get you to stop talking. Has he said anything yet?"

Halona started to shake her head but remembered when he'd said a word last week. "Actually, yes. One word."

"While he was awake?"

Halona's eyes stung just thinking about it. "Yes. We couldn't believe our ears."

Lula lifted a brow. "We? Who is we?"

"Oh, um…" Halona shrugged one shoulder. "Well, Alex and me. He was helping me at the community center and...well, Theo just adores him, and I'm not sure how or why but Theo spoke."

Lula's wide grin was back, and there was a knowing look in her eyes. "Well, that's incredible news. Better than the news story I saw of you and Alex on TV. This might turn out to be the best Christmas ever." Lula started walking toward the door.

"You can't stay?"

"No, your father would be lonely. I have dinner cooking for him in the oven. Tell Theo I said hello."

"I will." Halona walked her to the front entrance and gripped the side of the open door as she watched her mom slip out into the frigid night.

Lula turned at the bottom step. "Tell Alex I said the same if you should happen to see him."

Halona's mouth opened and closed but no sound came out.

"Good night, sweetheart!" Her mom's eyes held another knowing look. Apparently, the whole town knew something that Halona had only allowed herself to realize and accept now. She was the last to know about her own dating life.

CHAPTER TWELVE

"Here's a list of emergency contacts should something happen." Halona tapped her kitchen counter in front of Alex on Friday night.

He glanced at the list. At the top was 911 and the Sweetwater police station. Instead of pointing out that he *was* the emergency contact, he simply nodded. "I've got this. Go. Have fun."

"Theo has already eaten dinner. There's more than enough on the stove if you haven't yet."

"That's nice of you," Alex said, trying and failing not to notice Halona's formfitting clothes. She had on skinny jeans and a top that plunged an inch deeper than usual. Instead of being pulled back, her hair was down and falling around her shoulders, making his fingers itch to touch the silky softness of it. "We haven't talked about that news segment," he said as Halona continued fluttering around to make sure he had everything he needed for a couple of hours of being with Theo.

Halona froze and looked at him. "No, we haven't. Did you see it?"

"I did. After I heard about it from half a dozen people."

Halona's own fingers ran through her thick locks. "Same. To hear people talk, you'd think we were all over each other in the footage."

Maybe not their bodies but their eyes had been all over each other. Alex had looked at her beside him after every few words he'd said to Serena Gibbs, and Halona had watched him the entire time. He'd seen people look at each other like that before, with complete and utter admiration and affection. No one had ever looked at him in such a manner. It was no wonder it'd caused such a stir.

Had she always looked at him that way?

She stepped closer toward him, lowering her voice so that Theo wouldn't overhear whatever she said next. "Even my mom came by, wondering why I hadn't told her what was happening between us."

"What did you tell her?"

Halona was only a foot away now. Close enough to pull her in and touch those silky locks. "I told her that we were friends. And that you're Theo's mentor for the next couple of months. What did you tell people who asked?"

Alex shrugged a shoulder. "Pretty much the same. I'm sure the ladies will drill you on us tonight."

Us.

"Hopefully not. Honestly, can't a woman and a man spend any amount of time together and not be in a full-fledged relationship?"

"Not in Sweetwater Springs." Alex cracked a smile and shoved his hands in his pockets to solidify his shaky willpower. He had lots of women friends—Tammy was one of them—and none of them made him feel the way Halona did.

"I've been waiting for Tuck to come around and ask about us," Halona said.

There was that word again. *Us.*

"Me too, actually. I've been expecting him but he's been unusually quiet. Probably busy with work and family."

"And the horses he's added at Hope Cottage." Halona backed away, leaving a floral scent in her wake. "Anyway, call if you need me. I can be here in a jiff." She pointed out some snacks and Theo's DVDs, and then she headed toward the front door. "Thank you again for tonight," she said, her hand on the doorknob, keys in hand. "I guess I'll see what the fuss is about."

Alex laughed. "Just enjoy yourself and don't worry about us at home."

Us. Home. Those words felt a little too comfortable on his tongue tonight. "We'll be right here waiting for you."

Halona removed her hand from the doorknob and stepped toward him, her hair floating on the swoosh of air due to her quick movements. She went up on her tiptoes, and before he knew what was happening, she kissed his cheek. His hands reflexively braced her waist, holding on and never wanting to let her go.

Easy, Baker.

She returned to flat feet and stepped back. "See you later."

Alex watched her walk out, closing the door behind her and leaving him alone in her living room, his heart beating the way it did when he had a lead on a case. A noise came from the other side of the room. Alex turned to see Theo standing by the couch, notebook in one hand and a book in the other.

Officer Chew, who'd been sleeping on the hearth, got up and trotted over to get a head rub.

"Hey, buddy," Alex said, walking toward Theo, "it's you and me tonight. What do you want to do?"

Theo sat down and placed his notebook in his lap. Then he pulled his pencil out of his pocket and started to write.

Decorate the tree for Mom.

Alex looked back at the bare tree they'd chosen at Merry Mountain Farms. The box of ornaments he'd dragged out of the shed for Halona was pushed against the wall and waiting for someone to open it up. "Do you think your mom will mind if we do?"

Theo shook his head and then wrote.

She doesn't like decorating the tree. I heard her tell Elisi Lula.

Elisi must be the Cherokee word for grandmother. "Well then, let's do it."

An hour later, he and Theo stood back and looked at the decorated tree. They'd strung the lights and hung all the ornaments.

"Wow, buddy, we did it." Alex looked over at Theo whose eyes were wide in amazement. "Do you think your mom will like it?"

Theo nodded quickly and looked over at him. Alex

could read so much in Theo's dark eyes even without words being said.

"Did you and your dad decorate trees together?" he asked. He was probably talking out of turn because Halona and Theo never seemed to bring Ted up.

Theo hesitated and then looked down at his feet.

"If you don't want to talk about him, it's okay."

Theo grabbed his notebook and pencil and then started writing. *My dad did something bad, and you took him to jail.*

Alex felt like his heart had stopped. He hadn't thought Theo knew about that. How did he respond to this? "That's true, buddy."

Why?

Alex swallowed. "What did your mom tell you about that?"

Theo frowned and wrote some more. *She doesn't know that I saw what happened. You can't tell her I know.*

Alex grimaced. "I don't like keeping secrets, buddy. Especially from your mom."

Please. It'll just make her feel bad. I don't want her to cry.

Alex nodded. He had never liked seeing his mother cry as a boy either. Or as an adult. "I won't tell her right now but you should. She should know—that way you two can talk about what's bothering you."

Theo looked down at his feet again.

"Your mom cares a lot about you. If there's something on your mind, she'd want to hear about it."

Theo nodded, still not looking at him. Alex wasn't a shrink by any means, but a kid keeping things bottled up wasn't good and might be factoring into Theo's communication disorder. In Alex's experience, when things came out in the open, that's when the true healing could begin. "I think your mom is going to love how we decorated this tree," Alex said, directing the conversation back to something happy for Theo's sake. "Don't you?"

Theo lifted his gaze and nodded in agreement, the corners of his mouth turning up slightly. Alex wasn't fooled though. There was more going on inside this little boy than people knew.

⁎ ⁎ ⁎

"So...tell us all about Chief Frisky," Sophie Daniels said, seated across from Halona at the Perfectly Pampered Salon.

Halona had her feet soaking in a warm foot bath with lavender essential oils. Her fingers were spread on the table in front of her, and Elsa Woods was painting her nails a pale purple color to match the few pieces of tinsel that had already been woven into Halona's hair.

Overall, the night had been a lot of fun. Halona was chatting with lots of ladies who came in and out of the store throughout the year but that she never fully got to know. This was nice, and she thought she'd like to join the group again.

But now her chest felt tight at Sophie's inquiry. All the other ladies suddenly turned and zoned in on Halona's response. Halona stammered and stuttered. "I don't know what you mean," she finally said. She didn't think for a moment that anybody was buying it.

"Of course you do," Dawanda pooh-poohed. "You're among friends. You can tell us what's going on, and we won't tell a soul."

Of course they wouldn't tell a soul, because nearly all of the people that they would tell were already sitting right here.

Halona glanced over at Lula, who was smiling just a little bit too widely. Her mother wasn't buying Halona's story that there was nothing going on between her and Alex either. She'd made that very clear when she left the other night. "Well, he's Theo's Mentor Match, as you all probably know. And tonight he's watching Theo for me."

"I saw you on the news with him," Kaitlyn mentioned as she sat diagonally from Halona with her feet in a foot bath as well.

"We're friends," Halona said.

"Okay, I wasn't going to try and out you in front of the group," Janice Murphy said, "but I saw you two kissing at the Lights on Silver Lake event last weekend."

The collective group gasped and looked at Halona.

"Is that true?" Brenna asked. And if Halona wasn't mistaken, she seemed a little disappointed that she hadn't been privy to that piece of information before the rest of them.

Halona could feel her cheeks burning to a crisp, and she looked down at her nails even though Elsa was no longer painting them. Instead, like the rest of the group, Elsa was looking up at Halona and waiting expectantly. Halona couldn't outrightly lie to the women. If she did, she'd be calling Janice a liar instead, and she'd never climb out from under her guilty conscience.

"Yes," Halona finally admitted, "we kissed that night but it doesn't change the fact that we're just friends."

"How many other times have you kissed him recently?" Josie asked.

Oh, good grief. Halona took a breath. "Just that once," she said, sweeping a strand of hair from her cheek and locking it behind her ear.

The group stared at her. They were getting the biggest scoop in town tonight, and they looked like greedy kids under the Christmas tree awaiting more.

"Have you slept with him?" Janice had the gall to ask.

"What? No. We just kissed, and it's not going to happen again. There's nothing going on between Alex and me," Halona insisted. She hated telling a lie though, and this felt like a big, fat one. "I mean he's cute, of course," Halona said, backtracking on her little fib. "And he's nice and sweet, and great with Theo," she added.

"And he looks amazing in a uniform," Emma from the Sweetwater Café said. That got Halona's attention because she'd always thought that Emma had a little crush on Alex and vice versa.

All the women agreed about the uniform part.

"So what's the problem with dating him?" Claire Donovan wanted to know. "If he's Mr. Right, then you should be booking an event with me. I'm scheduling out at least six months these days for weddings, FYI."

Halona pulled her hand out from underneath Elsa's polish brush and covered her face. "I can't believe you guys. We're not getting married. We just kissed. We haven't had sex, and don't you dare spread any rumors otherwise," she warned the women. "Alex would be furious. He'll probably be upset that I even told you this much."

"Everything comes out eventually," Dawanda said, fanning out her own nails and looking at the sparkle that had been applied. "There are no secrets in Sweetwater Springs."

* * *

Alex had only closed his eyes for a moment. Theo was watching a movie on the couch beside him, and his lids had hung heavily. Just for a moment. The next thing Alex knew, he heard the front door open somewhere in his consciousness, and then he felt someone leaning over him.

"Alex?"

He jerked awake and blinked up at Halona. She was so beautiful. He must still be dreaming. Then he remembered where he was and why he was here. "Theo?" he said, whipping his head from right to left. There on the floor, Theo was curled around Officer Chew, both breathing heavily in their slumber.

"Looks like you two wore yourselves out," Halona said on a laugh.

He sat up and rubbed his eyes. "Am I fired?"

"What for?"

"A babysitter isn't supposed to fall asleep on the job."

Halona lowered her brow. "You were asleep?"

"Just resting my eyes, actually."

She tipped her head to the side, gesturing for him to follow her into the kitchen. "Don't want to wake Theo," she whispered as they walked. "The nights have been good lately. He needs all the sleep his body will allow to play catch-up for the last year."

Guilt knotted in Alex's belly as he remembered Theo

telling him about what he'd seen. Halona needed to know but he'd promised Theo he wouldn't tell. A secret. He was keeping a secret from a child's mother. That definitely didn't sit well in his gut. He was a man who loved the law, and there was probably some unwritten one somewhere about that.

"Want a cup of coffee?" she asked over her shoulder.

He noticed her hair now, and he stepped toward her. "You got that tinsel stuff. It looks exactly like Christmas tree tinsel. Is that what it is?"

"Not exactly. It's called fairy hair."

This made him smile. "Not something I would've pictured you wearing."

"Why not?" Halona poked her lower lip out. He had the not-so-fleeting desire to lean in and nip at it.

"You wear your hair back most days. You're a no-frills kind of woman."

"Maybe I'm looking for a little change."

"Oh?" He raised a brow. "I don't know. From where I'm standing, you're pretty perfect the way you are. Emphasis on *pretty.*"

"Are you flirting with me, Chief Frisky?" she asked.

He groaned softly. "I'll never escape that nickname, will I?"

"I think it's cute."

"Chiefs of police aren't supposed to be cute." But coming from her, he'd take it.

"You never answered about the coffee. Do you want some?"

He nodded. "That'd be great. Otherwise, I might not make it home tonight."

"That tired, huh?" she asked as she set the coffee maker to brew. "I hope Theo wasn't a lot of trouble."

"No, it wasn't him. There's a lot going on at the station."

"Anything on the graffiti artist in town?" Halona turned back to him while the coffee maker groaned in the background.

"Nothing. I think this guy is going to get off scot-free."

"Could be a woman," Halona said. "You never know."

He lifted a brow. "Are you confessing to a crime, Ms. Locklear?"

A giggle tumbled off her lips.

They were definitely both guilty of flirting.

"I don't wear guilt well. I hit a deer once and cried for a week. You'd know if it were me." She cast him a sheepish look with this tidbit of personal information. "I was seventeen. I called Tuck and he came and got the deer's body for me."

"I think I remember him telling me about that," Alex said. "I was with him that afternoon. I should've come to help too." But he'd already been resisting his crush on her for so long. "I should've been there for you," he said, meaning more than for just the deer accident.

"Hitting a deer is slightly traumatic but I got over it. Anyway, I hope you catch your perp before Sweetwater Springs is completely covered in graffiti."

"Me too." He looked down at her hands on the countertop and couldn't help reaching over and trailing his index finger along her skin. "Your nails look nice."

He watched her swallow, uncertainty playing in her eyes. "I have the toes to match," she said quietly.

His voice dropped a note too. "I'd love to see them."

Now he reached up and ran his finger along the surface of her hair, touching the glimmering strands of tinsel that had been added. He dropped his gaze, locked eyes with hers, and knew beyond a shadow of a doubt that they were going to kiss. All signals were a go.

It'd been a week since that first kiss, and he hadn't been able to stop thinking about it, wanting to do it again, wondering if the magic would still be there between them.

Unable to wait a second longer, he bent and brushed his lips against hers, disappearing in a kiss that had the power to erase every worry on his mind. Magic. That wasn't something that happened often so he was going to stay right here for as long as she'd let him. The rest of the night sounded good to him.

CHAPTER THIRTEEN

*H*alona sighed into the kiss, melting like a snowflake hitting the earth at the wrong temperature. This was right though, no matter what her intruding thoughts tried to argue. She'd been so focused on Theo's needs for so long that she'd neglected her own, which were screaming at her right now. She *needed* this kiss. She suddenly needed a whole lot more than that.

Alex's hands moved over the curve of her waist, anchoring at her hips heavily and grounding her. Her hands ran over his unshaven cheeks, savoring the bristly touch that was way more arousing than it should be.

"Theo's asleep in the living room," Alex said.

Halona pulled back for just a second and smiled against his mouth. "That's my line. He won't wake up. Not without making a lot of noise to warn us first."

Alex's body tensed against hers.

She leaned in and kissed his mouth again, satisfied when his body pressed into hers once more and his mouth covered hers in another hungry kiss. His hands didn't stay contained outside her clothing this time. Now they climbed below her top, running calloused skin over her stomach, reaching higher until he was at the band of her bra. A little gasp caught low in her throat as sensations tore through her body like hot pokers fresh from stoking the flames in a fireplace. His mouth dropped to the base of her throat as she moaned softly.

"I want you, Halona," he finally whispered. "I've always wanted you."

"I want you too," she admitted, her eyes closed as she absorbed the pleasure of the moment. "But if you give me half a second to think, I might consider this a bad idea."

Alex pulled away. "I would never do anything you didn't want," he said, searching her face.

Halona already knew this about Alex. He was law-abiding and honorable to his very core. He was as sweet as he was stern, sexy as he was intimidating. She fisted his shirt and tugged him back to her. "Then don't pull away from me again. Because what I want right now is *you*."

* * *

Sunlight splintered through Halona's bedroom blinds. She rolled to her side to avoid the harsh rays poking at her eyelids and let her mind wander before entering the real world. There was a smile on her lips that felt foreign in some way. Usually she woke with a start from one of Theo's nightmares. Not this morning. This morning she was waking at what felt like the right time of day. The aroma of coffee was thick in the air.

Coffee?

Theo had no idea how to make coffee—not that it was

rocket science—but he was seven. A sweet seven-year-old boy that she'd done her best last night to make sure didn't happen upon her and Alex as they'd kissed, groped, and stripped each other bare.

Halona's eyes popped open, and she flipped to her other side to see who she was sharing a bed with. It was empty. She pressed a hand to her chest as she remembered last night. They'd locked the door and done a lot more than kissing this time. Now he was gone. Was he still in the house?

She hurried out of bed and slid her feet into a pair of slippers. The last thing Theo needed was to wake up and find Alex half-naked in the kitchen. Her son may never talk again if that were the case. She shuffled down the hall and into the kitchen where she could smell freshly brewed coffee. Sure enough, the machine was on but Alex was nowhere to be seen. Neither was Theo.

She shuffled back down the hall toward his bedroom, and there her son was. Asleep with his little arm draped over Officer Chew. Alex had carried Theo to bed when they'd gotten up for a glass of water. Chew must've followed them into Theo's room.

But where was Alex now?

Heading back toward the coffee, Halona saw that there was a note beside the coffee maker. She picked it up and read Alex's neat penmanship.

Had to go to work. I'll call you later. I didn't want to wake Theo by getting Officer Chew. You can drop Chew off at the station or text me and I'll come get him later.

Alex

Halona prepared a cup of coffee and read the message again. And again. They'd just spent the night together and this was all he could manage? An empty bed while he rushed off to work. There was no *thanks* or *last night was wonderful*. Of course, Theo could've seen the note. He would've been careful to make sure there was nothing for Theo to see. And he *had* made coffee for her.

Halona lifted the mug to her face and breathed it in before taking a delicious sip. Then she replayed last night, moment by moment, touch by wonderful touch. It'd been amazing. Better than she'd ever dreamed it could be.

She carried her mug into the living room to turn on the morning news since it was early and Theo was still asleep. She stopped short at the sight of the decorated Christmas tree. Had it been like that when she'd gotten home? How had she missed it?

Someone tapped her arm, and she looked down at Theo.

"Did you and Alex do this?" she asked.

He nodded proudly. Alex wasn't just good for her; he was great for Theo. All her worries that dating someone might set Theo back seemed null where Alex was concerned. The more that Alex was around, the better, she decided for now. For both of them.

She looked up to admire the tree again. "Wow. Ornaments and lights. You two were busy. No wonder you and Chew fell asleep on the floor."

At the sound of his name, Chew came bounding over and nudged between them. Theo giggled, and Halona's hand instinctively moved to pat his head.

"Good morning, Officer Chew. Alex left you here last night so you could keep Theo company." Well, it hadn't exactly been last night. More like this morning. Just a white lie, which she seemed to be serving up a lot these days.

She met Theo's gaze to see if he knew the truth. Of course he didn't. No one else knew, and unlike that stolen kiss she'd told the ladies group about last night, she wasn't letting anyone else in on this little turn of events.

* * *

The house felt empty without Officer Chew as Alex sipped from a cup of coffee at his kitchen table. He'd woken several hours before and had slipped out of Halona's bed to return here. Hopefully, no one had seen his truck in her driveway past midnight. He couldn't explain that away with the Mentor Match program.

He finished off his cup of coffee and stood to prepare for a morning jog, hoping it would do its usual trick of organizing his thoughts. At the forefront of his mind was last night. He couldn't decide how to feel about what had happened with Halona. At least that was his mind's story. If he didn't think too hard though, he felt a kind of euphoria. There was a smile on his face that he couldn't wipe off even if he wanted to, which he didn't.

Alex walked out of his house and started jogging as he turned from the driveway heading toward the intersecting street. He lived only a mile from Halona's home on Cedar Trail. He could head in that direction and grab Officer Chew to run back with him. An added bonus was that he could face Halona and read how she felt about what they'd done. He hoped she felt as good as he did this morning. He also hoped last night didn't scare her off. This thing between them was a long time coming. He was ready to explore it, taking things at whatever pace she needed. Just as long as she didn't put the brakes on altogether.

He turned at the stop sign onto Elm Street, which was a winding road that fed into several neighborhoods in Sweetwater Springs. The weather was chilly this morning, cold enough for snow according to Serena Gibbs on the news earlier. Precipitation was forecast over the next week, and if conditions blended perfectly, Halona would get the white Christmas that Theo had told Alex she wanted.

Theo.

What was Alex going to do about what Theo had told him? He'd promised the boy that he wouldn't tell, but in the light of day and the clarity that came with it, that was a very irresponsible thing to do. Halona needed to know. Breaking Theo's trust could set him back in his progress, but breaking Halona's trust could end this thing between them. It was a dilemma that he needed to iron out, and soon. It'd be best if he could convince Theo to tell Halona on his own. Then Alex would be taken out of the equation.

A dog barked from someone's fenced backyard as Alex continued to ponder each thought that dipped and fluttered like a restless bird in his mind. Actual birds tweeted somewhere in the distance, probably regretting not flying south with the others right about now.

A car engine cranked to life in a driveway or garage somewhere behind him.

Alex became aware of the sound of his breathing, heavier as he pounded the pavement with his sneakers. Jogging was more fun with Officer Chew. Chew pushed him to go a little faster with his excitement for all the sights and smells and noises.

In the far distance, Alex heard a vehicle somewhere behind him, gaining speed as it approached.

His mind continued on its array of thoughts. Perhaps he could take Halona and Theo out tonight. Theo had enjoyed ice-skating the other day. Maybe Halona would enjoy it as well. He could pull Theo aside and convince him to use his voice in talking to Halona. Then maybe they could grab some hot chocolate or apple cider, and after Theo was tucked in bed, Alex and Halona could—

His thoughts were cut short as he felt the earth rumble beneath his feet. The vehicle's engine roared like a beast coming toward him. He ran on the outer white line and never worried that cars would strike him. They always slowed and swung out a safe distance. But instinctively Alex leaped and fell into the ditch this time, his gut not trusting whoever was behind the wheel.

He skidded on the slope of the ditch and whipped his head to look at the truck that rode with two wheels on the roadside and the other two on the street. It would've hit him. Alex stared after the truck as it righted itself and growled even louder, disappearing around the bend.

Had that truck tried to hit him?

Alex crawled forward to pick himself up and felt a splintering pain that shot up his wrist and forearm. He looked down at his left arm, which had taken the blow of his body weight as he'd leaped out of the truck's path. The skin was red and angry but he didn't see any obvious bones protruding. Instead of continuing to jog, he pulled his cell phone out of his pocket and called Mitch.

"I can't remember. Are you on duty this morning?" Alex asked, squinting under the rising sun and the pain throbbing in his forearm.

"Yep. Everything okay?"

"No," Alex said. "Can you come pick me up on Elm Street? I might need a ride to the urgent care as well."

"Are you hurt?" Mitch asked.

"I'm not sure. I took a fall on my left arm."

"Be there in five," Mitch told him.

Alex disconnected and shoved his phone back into his coat pocket with his right hand. Then he walked over and assessed the tire tracks in the dirt from where the truck had veered toward him. If Officer Chew had been with him, he might not have moved as fast. He might have stayed with Chew. Or Chew might have gotten hit.

Alex's gut twisted and turned like the street ahead. A couple of minutes later, he saw Mitch's police car racing toward him with its lights flashing. Alex gestured for Mitch to park on the other side of the street. He didn't want the tracks from the truck marred. They were evidence of what Alex suspected was attempted manslaughter.

* * *

Halona pulled her cell phone out of her pocket and checked it for the tenth time in the last twenty minutes. She'd texted Alex over an hour ago about Officer Chew, and he still hadn't responded. Now she was at her flower shop with Theo in the back room playing with Alex's dog.

Why wasn't Alex responding? Did he regret last night? She hadn't pegged Alex for the type to lose interest immediately after taking a woman to bed, but...

The bell above the front entrance jingled Halona out of her moment of panic. Kaitlyn Russo walked in and headed straight toward the counter.

"Hey, Kaitlyn. Something I can help you with today?"

"Just checking on my wedding details. I had a dream last night that you ran out of poinsettias, and I had to decorate the inn with just daisies. Daisies are lovely but they aren't the flower of choice for a wedding happening on the day after Christmas."

Halona laughed. "Agreed. And don't worry about anything. We have all the poinsettias you could possibly want and lots of garland. It will be a beautiful scene. The great thing about those choices is that the flowers should stay fresh well into the New Year."

"Claire has a heated tent being set up behind the inn, so no matter what the weather brings, we'll be warm. Then we'll move inside for dancing in the ballroom."

"It's going to be a wonderful day," Halona said. She was so happy for her friends, who'd met last fall. So much could happen in a year. Their lives had completely changed. They'd intertwined, and now Kaitlyn and Mitch were going to live it out happily ever after.

Halona swallowed past the memory of her own wedding day so long ago. It was only natural to think about it, but as soon as the thought entered, she pushed it away. Some circumstances were unforeseen. Some promises couldn't be kept.

"You're still coming, right?" Kaitlyn asked as Halona steered her thoughts back to the present.

"Right. Of course. I wouldn't miss it."

"And your plus-one?" Kaitlyn asked.

"Theo, of course."

"No, he's my ring bearer. He's not your plus-one. What about Alex?"

Halona was really going to regret telling the Ladies' Day Out group about that kiss. "He's one of Mitch's best men, right? He'll be there too."

Kaitlyn giggled. "I know. I'm just so excited about the possibility of you two."

Halona glanced over her shoulder toward the back room, hoping that Theo wasn't listening. "Don't get too excited. I'm not sure this thing between us is going anywhere."

"Well, that's what I thought last Christmas, and now I'm checking on flowers and catering. Speaking of which, I'm going to see Brenna at Taste of Heaven next. Mitch's mom offered to prepare the whole spread for the reception but she's already done so much."

"That's her way," Halona said.

"It is. Yesterday we made twelve gingerbread cheese-cakes for this week's Hope for the Holidays auction. It's such a busy month. What was I thinking planning my wedding to Mitch for the day after Christmas?"

"Christmas weddings are my favorite," Halona said. "It'll all be worth it. Do you know who the recipient is for the Hope for the Holidays auction this year?"

Each year, the town supported one member who was struggling. Last year, the town had picked Cassie Martin, a single mother who'd been diagnosed with cancer and couldn't afford the vast medical bills that came with it.

"Mary Beth Edwards, I think. We voted at the town council meeting earlier this week," Kaitlyn said. "Her hip fracture has put her out of work, which has been a financial strain on their family. You know she's raising her grandkids. Can't be easy for her."

"No, it can't. I need to go visit Mary Beth," Halona said. "She's always loved flowers. I'll make an arrangement and bring it over sometime."

"You are the sweetest and the best. Now, I need to go see Brenna. She's the best too, so I'm sure that there's no reason to even go check on the status of things but I can't help myself. I'm such a nervous bride."

"No cold feet though, right?" Halona teased.

"No way. Mitch is the one. I have no second thoughts." Kaitlyn practically glowed as she said so.

"That's great. And yes, I'll be there in two weeks. Less than that, actually. Your wedding day will be here before you know it."

"Ack. I know. So much to do." Kaitlyn reached across the counter and gave Halona's hand a little squeeze. "I'll see you soon!"

She let go, waved, and headed out the door.

Halona stared after her for a moment. Then she reached for her cell phone and checked to see if Alex had responded yet. No new texts. Her heart sank a notch. She pulled up Brenna's contact and fired off a text to warn her friend.

Kaitlyn Russo is on her way to see you. She's checking on wedding stuff this morning.

Brenna's response came a moment later.

Thanks for the heads-up! I always need extra coffee to prepare myself for nervous brides.

Ha-ha. Kaitlyn is calm in comparison to others we've had, Halona texted.

True! I missed you at the café this morning, btw.

Halona pulled her lower lip between her teeth. She'd

had coffee at home this morning. Coffee that Alex had brewed before slipping out after spending the night.

Sorry. Theo overslept, Halona said. That was true, and also very rare. We also had Alex's dog with us.

Oh? Alex's dog slept over? This sounds very interesting indeed!

Halona should really think before texting. Theo fell asleep on top of him, she explained. Alex didn't want to wake Theo when he left.

No need to mention that he didn't leave until dawn.

Gotcha. Coffee at the café next week? Brenna asked.

You're on.

Halona blinked at the phone, willing it to vibrate with another message. Not from Brenna, but from Alex. She startled as the back of her shirt tugged down.

Theo and Officer Chew were standing there, looking at her, neither much for words.

"Everything okay?" Halona asked.

Theo nodded. Then he held up his notebook.

Officer Chew needs to go outside. Can I take him?

"On your own?" Halona frowned. She couldn't leave the shop unattended. She could close for a few minutes or she could trust Theo to walk to the empty lot of grass next door. Usually that would be an easy choice but he'd disappeared at the tree farm the other day and had given her quite the scare.

"Okay, fine. But come straight back."

Theo nodded and then walked toward the back of the building. Halona sighed and then jumped as her phone buzzed in her hand. She lifted the screen to read.

Can you keep Chew a little while longer for me? Alex asked.

There it was. He was freaking out and trying to find a way to let her down easy before he saw her again. Maybe she should let him down first. It might be less awkward that way.

Sure, she responded.

Thanks. I'm a little busy this morning.

No problem, she texted back. Theo is happy to have him here with us.

I bet. I'll catch up with you later, okay?

She tapped out a quick response. Sure. If Alex was going to distance himself, she would too.

CHAPTER FOURTEEN

$\mathscr{A}$lex's jaw tightened as Dr. Ryan Miles manipulated his left arm on the examination table. Mitch had immediately taken Alex here to get checked out.

"It took the full impact of the fall?" Dr. Miles asked.

Alex nodded. "I jumped into the ditch and landed directly on it."

"Well, you're lucky you didn't break it."

"It's not broken?" Alex asked, relief flooding through him.

"Not unless it's a hairline fracture that we can't see yet. You sprained the wrist pretty good though. You're supposed to wait to do things like this until there's a thick blanket of snow on the ground, Chief," Dr. Miles said on a laugh.

That image immediately brought Alex's father to mind. His dad had several inches of white stuff to cushion his landing, and he'd still been killed right before Christmas eleven years ago.

"So I'm giving you a brace to immobilize the wrist while you're working and a prescription for pain medication in case you need it. Rest and ice are your two new best friends. I hear you have a puppy now, though, so you're allowed three best friends." Dr. Miles pulled a prescription pad out of his pocket and started writing.

"I don't have a puppy. I'm watching the little guy until I can find him a good home," Alex clarified. "You interested?"

Dr. Miles looked up. "In a dog? No." He didn't even offer an excuse like most of the people Alex had confronted.

"How long do I have to wear the brace?" Alex asked, changing the subject.

"A couple of weeks maybe. You can take it off every now and then and do some slow stretching. I'm going to have Tuck give you some physical therapy stretches and exercises to start next week. You can do them at your desk."

Alex nodded. "Great."

Mitch was waiting for Alex in the waiting room when he came out of Dr. Miles's office. "Let's grab breakfast. Then we can go to the station and file this report before I take you home."

"Sounds like a plan. But I want to be dropped off at Little Shop of Flowers when we're done."

Mitch gave Alex a curious look.

"I need to get my dog," he said, justifying his answer.

"Your dog? You keep slipping up on that, buddy," Mitch said as they walked outside and got into his vehicle. "Next thing I know, you'll begin calling Halona your woman. Then again, from what I hear, you already are." Mitch started the vehicle and pulled onto the road, heading toward a local diner for takeout.

Alex wasn't in the mood for Mitch's teasing. His left arm hurt but he'd never liked pain medication so he didn't plan on filling that prescription.

Mitch glanced over as Alex tried and failed not to grimace. "Did you see the vehicle that ran you into the ditch?"

Alex nodded. "It was a truck."

."Make and model?"

Alex tried to think. "A big one."

Mitch's gaze slid over for a brief second. "You're the chief of police. You know that's not helpful."

Alex massaged his forehead with his uninjured arm. "It happened so fast. All I know is that it was big and loud. Maybe a diesel engine."

"There you go. What color?"

Alex shook his head. "Possibly silver."

"That's a start. Any guesses on who was behind the wheel?"

Alex shrugged. "My guess is it was someone who isn't too happy with me."

"I doubt it was Janice Murphy," Mitch quipped.

"No. But it might be one of the Andersons."

Mitch nodded. "That thought has already crossed my mind. Along with the fact that this morning closely resembles what happened to your dad."

Alex nodded. He'd already made that connection too. "If I hadn't jumped, that truck would've hit me."

"You think it's the same guy?" Mitch watched the road ahead as he drove.

Mitch was a good cop with great instincts. If there was

anyone that Alex wanted to bounce ideas off of, it was him. "If it is, it means I'm getting close to solving my dad's case."

"Or you have a copycat who's upset that you stole his dog and have been sniffing around his wife."

"You think it's Tony?" Alex asked. He didn't like Tony. He had an anger problem but Alex wouldn't have pegged him as a killer.

"I don't know. I'd watch my back if I were you though, buddy."

And the backs of those he cared about, Alex mentally added.

* * *

It was just after noon when the front entrance to the flower shop opened, and Alex walked in.

Halona had used the past several hours to mentally build a wall around her heart when it came to him. It was so tall and thick that he'd never get through to her again. Ever. Then she saw him, and all those well-meaning bricks came tumbling down.

"What happened?" she said, rushing from the counter toward him.

Officer Chew beat her to it and propped his paws on Alex's thigh.

"Where did the brace come from? You have bruises," she said, reaching up to touch a goose egg on his head. He flinched under the pressure of her fingertips. "Did you get in a fight with Tony?"

Alex chuckled dryly. "If that were the case, I wouldn't have a scratch on me." He winked, and it felt like that guarded heart of hers, now exposed, melted into a puddle of goo. "Someone tried to hit me with their truck during this morning's jog."

"What?" Halona gasped.

Alex looked over at Theo, and Halona realized he was listening.

"Go back to the table in the back room, Theo. Officer Chew needs a snack. Get him a treat."

"You have bones at a flower shop?" Alex asked.

Halona nodded. "Tuck often brings Shadow in here with him."

"Right."

"Go on, Theo," Halona nudged.

Theo looked like he wanted to argue, but after a frustrated huff, he turned and did as she asked.

Halona lowered her voice to make sure he didn't overhear. "Why didn't you let me know when I texted you?"

"I didn't want you to worry. Mitch came and got me. He took me to see Dr. Miles."

"Dr. Miles? Is it broken?" Halona asked, a million questions circulating in her brain.

"Just sprained. Rest and ice. But I'm afraid I probably won't be baking any cookies for the Hope for the Holidays auction."

"You look a little pleased with yourself over that fact," Halona teased, still riddled with worry. "I told you to come to my place and Theo and I would help. It's for charity. No backing out."

"Well, as long as you're helping," he said, his voice dropping to a sultry note that she wasn't quite used to him having just yet.

"Who tried to hit you?" she asked.

"It's an ongoing investigation."

Halona nodded. "I think that's code for you're not going to tell me."

"There's not much to tell. But this is what I didn't want. You have enough on your plate without worrying about me."

"I'm a big girl," Halona said, half-serious, half-teasing.

Alex looked past her toward the back room. Then he brought his gaze back to her. "Theo's not watching. It's a good time for me to steal a kiss."

"Not if I steal one first." Halona stepped forward and pressed her mouth to his, the way she'd been dying to do since he walked in. So much for creating distance. His tongue tangled against hers just long enough to make her breath catch and her body temperature rise.

She pulled away, not wanting Theo to walk in and get confused. "I thought you were avoiding me," she said, taking a step backward.

"Why would I avoid you?" he asked.

"You know. Last night."

"Last night is a reason for me *not* to avoid you. You're all I've thought about all day. Lucky for me, my reflexes were working even if my brain was otherwise occupied."

Halona frowned. "You could've gotten seriously hurt. You could've…" She trailed off, not wanting to say her next thought. He could've been killed.

"I'm fine. Don't worry about me."

"Easier said than done. I'm glad you're okay," she said, her lips turning up in a smile.

Alex lifted a brow, his expression becoming playful. "Are you saying you would've missed me if I weren't?"

She tilted her head to one side. "Maybe."

"Sounds like you're getting used to having me around."

"Maybe," she said again.

"I could stop by tonight," he suggested, his tone dropping a notch.

"I think that's a great idea. And I already know exactly what I want to do with you." She nibbled on her lower lip, containing a giggle that threatened at the base of her throat. She could practically see the wheels in Alex's mind turning, and she knew exactly what he thought she was suggesting. "I've already bought the butter, flour, and chocolate chips."

Confusion settled along his brow.

Her giggles finally surfaced. "And I found a Christmas-themed apron for you to wear while we bake the cookie recipe."

"It's not nice to tease an injured man," he said.

Halona went up on her toes and gave him a quick kiss. "I'll make it up to you," she promised, returning to flat feet and catching the heat that ignited in his blue eyes.

* * *

Later that night, Halona and Alex both had flour dusted along their clothes, hair, and cheeks. They also had a seven-year-old boy and a puppy between them.

Alex let his good arm fall to his side dramatically and sighed. He looked at Theo. "My arm is tired. Wanna stir these ingredients for me, buddy?"

Theo nodded excitedly and went up on his tiptoes, taking the large spoon from Alex's hand. He struggled to move it through the thick mixture of flour, cocoa powder, sugar, eggs, and all the other ingredients listed for the Triple-Chip Chocolate Cookies.

"How about we do it together?" Alex offered, placing his hand over Theo's. "Teamwork."

Halona just watched as a gooey warmness spread all through her. They were just fulfilling their obligations for charity but, even so, baking cookies together felt like a family.

Slow down, Halona.

She and Alex hadn't even discussed the future. They'd only shared a bed once, and they hadn't even talked about that.

Halona pulled out her phone and snapped a picture of Alex and Theo together. "This will help the cookies bring in more money for charity," she said.

Alex smiled, looking as happy as she felt. "Okay. How does this work? Do we just plop a spoonful onto the cookie sheet?" he asked.

Halona let her mouth drop open. "You've never made cookies before?"

"If I have, it's been a while."

She looked at Theo and shook her head. "Theo, you need to teach Alex how it's done. Theo is an expert cookie dough scooper."

At the praise, Theo's eyes lit up. He took the spoon, looked at Alex, and then dipped it into the bowl. With care not to spill any, he brought the spoonful to the top corner of the cookie sheet and used his clean finger to swipe it off the spoon.

"Very good," Halona said. "Keep them an inch apart. They expand when they're baking."

"I think we can handle that," Alex said.

Theo handed him the spoon.

"My turn, huh?" He looked up at Halona and winked. Then he scooped three times as much dough as Theo had.

Theo shook his head and held up his hand. Then he

took the spoon once more, gave Alex a pointed look, and scooped the appropriate amount of dough.

When the first cookie sheet was full, they filled another. Then they slid both trays into the oven and cleaned up the kitchen together. Once the cookies were done, Alex did the honors of pulling them out and placing them on the stove top to cool. Then they retreated to the living room to watch *A Christmas Story* on TV. Halfway through, Theo fell asleep against a sleeping Alex. Halona watched them for a moment, her heart expanding and threatening to break through her ribs. Then she pulled out her phone again and snapped another picture. This one just for her.

Yeah, this was starting to feel like a family.

* * *

Alex felt like he'd been hit by a Mack truck as his eyelids resisted opening the next morning, the memory of yesterday surfacing in stark contrast to the dream he'd just been having. The dream was about Halona. The funny thing was his reality these days was even better than the fantasy.

He groaned out loud as he sat up and draped his legs off the side of his bed. Every inch of him ached. The other reality in his life right now was that someone had tried to hurt him yesterday. He'd seen the truck but now he had firsthand experience with misremembering the details of a traumatic situation. At first he could've sworn the truck he'd seen was silver. But then he'd seen a white truck on the road last night when he'd driven to Halona's house. Maybe it was white. Or pale blue. Maybe it was black, navy, or forest green. He had no idea. All he knew was that it was moving fast, and it'd taken all his attention and energy at the moment to dive into the ditch and save his own life.

Alex stood and headed down the hall, walking toward the kitchen where the coffee was. He didn't even like coffee. He drank it because his father had drunk it. He drank it because he'd grown up watching other cops drink it. In some way, it almost felt mandatory for a cop, especially the chief of police, to drink black coffee. Another reason was because the Sweetwater Café was right next to Halona's shop. All these years Alex had taken any excuse he could to walk by Little Shop of Flowers and glance inside the plate glass window.

After drinking a cup of dark brew, Alex headed back to his room to get dressed. It was Sunday, and as usual, Grandma Baker would be expecting him to pick her up for church. He considered calling her and telling her he couldn't today. He didn't want to use the excuse that he was sore because somebody tried to hit him with their truck. He didn't want to worry her any more than he wanted to worry his mom in Florida or Halona.

Did his attacker go to church with him? Would he be putting Grandma Baker in danger by going with her? His mind percolated new thoughts as he stepped into a pair of black trousers and slid a white button-down shirt over the brace on his arm. Thankfully it was long-sleeve weather. His grandmother might not even notice he had it on. He fumbled with the buttons on his shirt, taking twice as long to manipulate because of the swelling in his fingers. Once he was done, he picked up his cell phone and texted Halona.

Good morning.

He sat on the edge of the bed and awkwardly pulled on a pair of socks and shoes. Getting dressed with only one good arm was no easy task. His phone vibrated beside him.

Good morning yourself, **Halona** replied. How are you this morning?

Deciding that anything otherwise would be an obvious lie, he told her the truth. I hurt. But it hurts less when I think about you.

Are you taking your grandmother to church this morning?

I am, he responded. Hopefully, I'll see you there.

We'll be there, she texted back.

And now he was actually excited about heading out this morning.

An hour later, Alex walked into Sweetwater Chapel with Grandma Baker beside him.

"You're stiffer than I am this morning," she commented. "What's wrong with you?"

He'd hoped she wouldn't notice, and he was actually moving a lot better than when he'd first woken up. "Nothing, Grandma. Don't worry about me."

"Then don't lie to me," she shot back as they weaved through townsfolk and said hellos. His grandma liked to sit in the very front pew. Alex suspected she had a crush on Pastor Phillips, who was about the same age. On the days the assistant pastor preached, his grandma's attention was about as fleeting as his. On the days Pastor Phillips stood behind the podium, she hung on every word and went on and on about the sermon all the way home.

He smiled to himself as she sat down and made herself comfortable. Before sitting down, Alex looked back to see if Halona and Theo had arrived yet. The back pew was empty.

"Sit," Grandma Baker ordered, "and tell me the truth. You have a bruise on your forehead. Did you think I wouldn't see it? How's the other guy look?"

This made Alex chuckle. "The other guy was in a truck," he confessed.

His grandmother's face tightened, smoothing the folds of her cheeks but deepening those on her forehead. She was as smart as a whip and probably could've been a cop herself. No doubt she was already comparing the circumstances to her own son's accident.

"Stop worrying," Alex grumbled. "It won't help anything, and you know I have things under control."

"Horse manure!" Grandma Baker snapped.

Alex's eyes widened. This was his grandmother's idea of cursing. "Grandma, we're in church!"

"God can hear my swearing even when it's only in my mind so I might as well say it out loud. You only have things under control if the perp is behind bars. Is he?"

Alex frowned. "No."

"Do you know who it was?"

He clenched the muscles of his jaw. "I have a couple of guesses."

"Guesses aren't evidence. What do you have?" she asked.

"You know I can't tell you that," he said.

Grandma Baker frowned, and then she reached for his forearm. "I don't want to lose you too," she said in a quieter voice. "Just be careful, Alex."

"I always am."

She patted his knee. "So was your father."

CHAPTER FIFTEEN

Halona hated being late, but having a seven-year-old boy who tended to misplace shoes and who dragged his feet when it came to things like brushing his hair and teeth often put them walking in the door right on time, if not a few minutes after.

Halona held tightly to Theo's hand as she tried to quietly slip into the church. Pastor Phillips was discussing upcoming holiday events. Hope for the Holidays was at the top of the list because it happened this coming week. Halona's mom and dad looked over as she and Theo slid in beside them. Halona's dad didn't usually attend but it was this time of year when he was most likely to say yes to Lula's persistence. The happiest time of year when people reassessed the year they were leaving behind and looked forward to the one ahead. When people opened their hearts just a little wider and let others in.

Like Alex.

Halona looked toward the front pew, seeing the back

of his head. Grandma Baker was beside him, a good five inches shorter in the seated position. Halona continued to scan the congregation. Tuck and Josie were a few rows ahead with Tuck's daughter, Maddie. Claire Donovan and her boyfriend, Bo Matthews, were here. Sophie Daniels sat alone at the far end of the room. Halona always found that curious. Sophie was gorgeous, and when you spoke to her, she became even more beautiful. And yet she was single. She'd been set up with Tuck once before he'd met Josie. The way Tuck had described the date, it'd been more friendly than romantic. He was a widower getting back on his feet, and Sophie... well, she was holding back for a reason Halona couldn't pinpoint.

Halona should mind her own business. She had things she didn't want others to know too.

Dr. Charwood met Halona's roaming gaze on the other side of the room and offered a small wave, which Halona returned. Then Halona focused on Pastor Phillips. Or tried to. Her thoughts drifted in and out though, and before she knew it, the congregation had been dismissed.

Usually, Halona hugged her parents and made a quick exit to get Theo home. Today, however, she dragged her feet like Theo had earlier in the morning. She procrastinated and kept one eye on the handsome chief of police, waiting for him to come her way like she knew he would.

Lula glanced to the front of the room knowingly. "Tell Alex and Grandma Baker hello for me. I need to bring Edna a pot of my Three Sisters Stew. She loves it so much."

Halona nodded. "Theo probably wants to see Alex," she said, feeling a need to explain.

"Well, of course he does." Lula pulled Halona in for

a hug and did the same to Theo. Halona's father hugged her next.

"Santa is packing up his sleigh right about now," Tom Locklear told Theo.

Lula swatted him. "We're in church. We don't talk about Santa here."

"Why not?" Tom asked.

"You know why," Lula told him sternly.

Theo looked between his grandparents as they bickered. Halona suspected he already knew that it wasn't Santa who left him presents on Christmas morning but he didn't let on.

"I'll see you both at the Hope for the Holidays auction," Halona interjected.

"Yes. See you then." Lula smiled at Halona and then narrowed her gaze at her husband once more before exiting.

"Hey."

Halona snapped her attention forward, realizing that Alex and Grandma Baker had snuck up on her somehow. "Hey," she said, heart all aflutter.

"Hey, little man," Alex said, looking at Theo, who lit up. They did a secret handshake of sorts and then Grandma Baker pushed Alex aside and stepped in to give Halona a big hug.

"Good to see you, dear," Grandma Baker said.

"You as well. How are you?" Halona asked.

"Terrific." Grandma Baker pulled back and glanced over at Alex. "My grandson is not though."

"I told her my injuries are minor," Alex said.

"Anyway, we're having lunch at my house, Halona," Grandma Baker announced. "You and Theo are more than welcome to come. I put a ham in the oven this morning, and I have vegetables in my Crock-Pot. I even have a triple-decker chocolate cake," she said, looking down at Theo with a wink.

"We don't want to impose," Halona said, even though the invitation sounded nice. After all these years of avoiding Alex, now she was eager for any reason to spend time with him. Grandma Baker was the only family he had in town these days. She wouldn't mind getting to know her better as well.

"Don't be silly. I love company. You'd be making my day," Grandma Baker continued. "In fact, the more the merrier." She looked around the quickly emptying chapel. "Mitch!" she called out.

Mitch was standing with Kaitlyn on the far side of the room. He looked over and waved.

Grandma Baker gestured him over. "I'm serving up lunch," she told him when he and Kaitlyn had navigated through the crowd. "Will you and Kaitlyn come? I might not get to see as much of you after you marry. With the honeymoon and then all the babies I hope you'll have."

Kaitlyn laughed. "Those won't come for a while. And we'll always make time for you, Grandma Baker."

"Great. How about now? I always loved having Mitch and Tuck at my table when Alex was growing up. Such good boys. Where is Tuck anyway?" she asked.

"He's already slipped out with Josie and Maddie," Halona told her. "Now that my brother is in love, I don't see him as much."

"Ah. Well, that's what happens when you have a family. But you all will come, right?" Grandma Baker asked hopefully.

Halona looked up at Alex. His grandmother was asking but did *he* want her to come too? Spending time with each other's families somehow took things to a new level.

As if hearing her thoughts, Alex smiled, and there was no question in her mind. He wanted to be with her as much as she wanted to be with him, and he didn't mind who knew.

* * *

Alex looked around the dining room table. His grandmother had all six seats filled, which he imagined made her day. Once upon a time she'd hosted these lunches every Sunday. But, like she'd said, things changed as people grew up and got their own lives, complete with families. After his father died, his mom had stayed in Sweetwater Springs awhile but had then decided to begin anew in Florida where the sun always shined. That was probably best for her, but in some ways, it felt like he'd lost both parents. His only family nearby was Grandma Baker, which hadn't bothered him much until lately. Spending time with Halona and Theo and doing things that families did, like searching for the perfect tree, baking cookies, and watching Christmas movies together, felt nice. Having Halona and Theo beside him at Grandma Baker's dinner table was a welcome change too.

Bowls were passed to the left as each person served themselves. Alex took the pot of creamed corn, his fingers brushing over Halona's with the exchange. His body heated. He couldn't wait to get her alone again. And soon.

Once the meal was served, Grandma Baker looked at him from the far side of the table. "I have two

Sweetwater police officers at my table, and I raised a police officer myself," she said, talking about Alex's father. "I want the investigative facts. Tell me what happened."

Alex should've known she wouldn't let his injuries lie. "I told you already. A truck almost hit me while I was jogging. My arm is due to the fall."

"Mitch, I need you to watch after Alex until this reckless driver is found."

"I'm the chief of police. I don't need watching after," Alex said, stabbing his fork into a piece of ham.

"Everyone needs looking after."

Alex shook his head. "We're having a nice meal. Let's not ruin it."

"Fine." Grandma Baker pouted momentarily and then turned her attention to a happier subject. "Kaitlyn, I'm so excited about your upcoming wedding. I hear Pastor Phillips will be officiating."

Alex glanced up as he shoveled a spoonful of mashed potatoes into his mouth. His grandmother was a soft shade of pink now. His grandfather had been gone a long time so he guessed it was only natural that new attractions would develop, no matter her age.

Kaitlyn offered a wide grin. "Yes. You RSVP'd. You're still coming, right?" Kaitlyn asked.

"Wouldn't miss it, dear. I've attended so many of the weddings in Sweetwater Springs over my lifetime. I just love them. Your Grandma Mable loved them too," she told Kaitlyn. "We always sat together with a box of Kleenex between us, crying like old saps even when we were young like you. Love is the most magical thing of all." His grandma chuckled deeply and then reached for her glass of sweet tea.

There was no need for dessert when her tea was being served. Alex wasn't sure but he guessed the sugar-to-water ratio was two to one.

"I wish Grandma Mable could be at the wedding," Kaitlyn said with a wistful tone.

"Oh, trust me, dear. She'll be there in spirit. Not even death could keep her from coming," Grandma Baker said. "And I plan to keep that box of Kleenex next to me and an empty chair reserved just for her."

Kaitlyn looked over at Mitch, who'd grown up going to Mable's home. He'd thought of Mable Russo as a grandmother as well.

"And I'm sure that Halona is preparing the flowers for your wedding," Grandma Baker said.

"I am. Kaitlyn is keeping things simple so my job is easy," Halona told her.

"Simple is best. All the focus should be on the bride. It's her day," Grandma Baker agreed.

Mitch cleared his throat. "Um, what about the groom?" he asked. "It's my day too, right?"

They all laughed.

"The wedding is for the bride. The honeymoon is for the groom," Grandma Baker said.

The shock factor made everyone freeze momentarily. Alex looked at young Theo, who seemed clueless about that comment. *Good.*

"One of these days, my Alex will have a honeymoon," his grandmother added.

Alex choked on a bite of ham. Maybe he should've let his grandmother stick to the conversation about the investigation.

After lunch, Kaitlyn and Mitch left, leaving Alex and his grandmother with Halona and Theo.

"I'll watch young Theo," Grandma Baker offered. "You two go have fun. You're not working this afternoon, are you?" she asked Alex.

"No." He glanced over at Halona.

She hesitated and then turned to Theo. "Is that okay with you?"

Theo nodded quickly, no reluctance. Alex had noticed that his shyness around others had decreased the last few times he'd hung out with him. Theo offered a more confident smile and didn't lower his head whenever someone talked to him. Alex wasn't a therapist but that seemed like progress to him.

"Perfect! Theo can help me with my Hope for the Holidays donation," Grandma Baker said.

"What are you donating?" Halona asked.

"My time, for one. I'll be volunteering at the event this Wednesday night. I'm also jarring sweet pickles to auction off. Theo can be my assistant this afternoon."

"I can't remember the last time I had sweet pickles," Halona said.

"Well, you be sure to go on Wednesday night and bid on a couple of jars."

"I will. I'm bringing poinsettias as usual."

"Those are always a big hit. I'll be needing one myself," Grandma Baker told her. "And I hear that you helped Alex bake cookies for the auction. Those should pull in a lot of money for poor Mrs. Edwards. I wish there was more I could do for her."

Alex nodded. "We'll let you and Theo get started on those pickles," he said, eager to get Halona alone.

"Pickle making might take all afternoon," his grandmother warned. "Take your time."

"What will we do?" Halona asked as they stepped

outside of Grandma Baker's house and headed toward Alex's SUV.

"Well, I don't know about you but I need to finish my Christmas shopping," Alex suggested.

"That's a wonderful idea. My list has started haunting me in my sleep." Halona laughed.

Alex opened the passenger-side door and waited for her to step inside. *She* was the one haunting Alex these days, and even though he was trying to take things slow between them, *she* was the one topping his Christmas wish list.

* * *

After spending the rest of the afternoon shopping, Halona loaded her bags into Alex's vehicle.

"Care to join me for a walk around Silver Lake?" he asked.

"Don't you think we need to get back so that Theo doesn't completely drain Grandma Baker?"

Alex narrowed his eyes. "Have you met my grandmother? That woman never tires."

Halona laughed out loud. "You're right. I wish I had as much energy as she does."

"I wish I had as much as she does in just her pinky finger," Alex agreed. "She's fine, and I can assure you that Theo is having a wonderful time with her."

There was something romantic about the thought of walking around the lake at Christmastime with Alex.

He locked his vehicle with their bags inside and then placed a hand on the small of her back as he led her forward. There was something romantic about that gesture as well. She resisted the need to take that hand

and hold it in hers. They weren't at the PDA point in their relationship yet. *Yet?*

She knew better than to have thoughts like these but that wasn't stopping her.

"I wish I could be there to see Theo's face on Christmas morning when he unwraps that LEGO set."

Halona looked over, wishing the same thing. Her thoughts skipped to having Alex sitting there with them on Christmas morning. Last Christmas had been the first without Ted. Even though she and Ted were divorced, he'd still come over to celebrate with them. Last year, there'd been a void that couldn't be filled no matter how many presents she wrapped and placed under the tree for Theo.

Without thinking, she did what she'd already decided she couldn't. She reached for Alex's hand and held it in hers. He didn't pull away but instead glanced over with concern. "You okay?"

She sucked in a breath. "Last year was hard," she confessed, surprising even herself. "I just want this year to be better for Theo."

"And for you. You deserve a merry Christmas too."

Halona shrugged. "I guess when you're a mom, your Christmas is considered good if your child is happy. That's all I want this year."

She and Alex held gazes for a long moment. So long that she thought he was going to kiss her again. That's what she wanted. She'd been so focused on Theo and, before that, Ted's illness and the crumbling of their marriage. She'd been in survival mode for too long.

But now she had as many wants as needs, and Alex was falling into both of those categories.

"So," Alex began, averting his gaze and looking out on

Silver Lake, "you're going to the Hope for the Holidays auction this coming week?"

"Of course."

"And I'm going," he said.

Halona nodded. "And Theo. He never misses it."

"Seems a shame that we should all ride separately. Maybe I can pick you up and give you a ride?"

"You remember the fuss it caused the last time we all went out together to Merry Mountain Farms. It actually made the news," she reminded him. "Everyone was talking about us for days."

"I don't mind if you don't," Alex said, still holding her hand.

Halona's heart skipped around foolishly. "I don't mind at all."

"Good." He gave her hand a gentle squeeze. "I'll swing by and give you two a ride."

They'd traveled the perimeter of the lake; now it was time to head back. "Maybe it's time to go check on my grandma and Theo. Grandma Baker has a habit of sugaring kids up."

"Oh no." Halona laughed. "I'll have to find an outlet for his energy before bed."

"Sorry. Maybe I shouldn't have kept you so long."

Halona swallowed as she looked into his twinkling eyes again, no regrets in sight. "It was worth it."

CHAPTER SIXTEEN

*H*alona gazed at her reflection in the mirror, barely recognizing the woman who stared back. She looked happy and carefree, two things that had evaded her in the last couple of years.

Theo walked into her bedroom with a huge smile.

He seemed happier these days too. She hadn't been called to the school in the last two weeks, which was definite progress.

"Ready for the auction?" she asked.

He nodded. No words. She wished he'd make progress in that area as well.

"Great. Well, Alex should be here any minute." As if on cue, the doorbell rang. "And there he is."

Theo was on her heels as she walked to the front door, and for a moment, she wondered if he would race past her to answer first.

She opened the door and remembered to breathe. This was more than a casual fling between them. They weren't hiding anything from town members, which said a lot. Tonight, they were going out without pretenses. This wasn't a Mentor Match excursion. Even though Theo was in tow, tonight was a date.

"Hey," Alex said, locking eyes with hers. Then he lowered his gaze to Theo. "Hey, buddy."

There was a change in his voice. Deep and raspy for her. Upbeat for Theo.

"Thanks for taking us tonight," she said, grabbing her things and walking with Alex and Theo to his parked SUV. "You left Officer Chew at home?" she asked as she helped Theo into the back seat.

"He wasn't happy about it either. That puppy is getting a little spoiled."

Halona got into the passenger seat and buckled herself in. She watched Alex put the vehicle in motion. "I'd say he deserves a little spoiling after all he's been through."

"And I'd agree. As far as I'm concerned, the puppy should live out the rest of his days getting petted and offered dog bones." He glanced across the seat as he pulled out of her driveway and onto Cedar Trail. "So what are you bidding on tonight?"

"Hmm. Maybe some of Dawanda's fudge. You can never have enough."

"You'll never get rid of me if you're stocking her fudge in your fridge," he teased.

She held back from telling him that she may never *want* to get rid of him. How quickly her thought pattern could change from one extreme to another. "And what are you bidding on?" she asked.

He shrugged. "Lula's freezer dinners are tempting."

"Mmm. You'll have competition on that, you know."

"I suspected as much."

"The Springer kids usually donate dog-walking services," she suggested. "That might come in handy if you were to have a dog."

Alex slid his gaze over. "I have a temporary dog."

"So you keep saying."

They continued to chat easily. Halona was almost disappointed when Alex pulled into the community center where the auction was being held this year. Then they got out and walked with Theo between them.

"Well, don't you three look like the happy family?" Summer Rivera said as they approached. Summer's smile fell as she realized what she'd said. As much as it felt like they were these days, Halona, Alex, and Theo were not a family. Theo admired Alex but his Mentor Match didn't, couldn't, replace his dad.

Summer covered her mouth with one hand, calling even more attention to her slipup. "Oh, I didn't mean to say that. I only meant to comment on how happy and loving you all seem." She frowned sympathetically at Theo, who'd been smiling from ear to ear just a few moments before. Now he looked dejected, no doubt missing his father.

"Well, have fun!" Summer called in a cheerful voice as they continued walking past her and into the building.

Fun is very doubtful now.

They said hello to several other people and then took a seat near the back of the room where the auction was being held.

"You okay?" Halona asked Theo.

He looked up and nodded.

"No one can replace your dad, you know."

He nodded again. Then he looked around and pointed at Tuck, Josie, and his cousin Maddie nearby.

"Do you want to go sit with them?" Halona asked. "Go ahead." She watched as he headed over.

"Maybe that'll perk him up," Alex said, leaning toward her. "Summer Rivera sometimes blurts out whatever's on her mind."

Halona nodded. "No filter. Believe me, I know. Theo is resilient though. That's one thing I've learned. If only he would start talking again."

Alex looked away for a moment. "I'm sure he will soon."

"I wish I had your confidence. It's just been so long. I'm beginning to think this is just how it's going to be."

"You just said he was resilient. He's doing well for a kid who's been through so much. Time and love. That's the cure."

Halona swallowed past all the worry and fear that rose inside her so quickly. "Thank you. I know that, but sometimes I just need reminding." She looked at Alex, surprised at how deep her feelings for him were delving, plunging lower by the second.

"Watch it, now," Alex whispered. "Serena Gibbs and her camera crew are here tonight. We might make the news again."

Halona followed his gaze to the other side of the room.

"What do you think the headline would be this time?" he asked.

Halona looked at him and grinned wide. "Chief of Police Falls Victim to Sweetwater's Favorite Florist."

He smiled back at her. "I like that story."

"Me too," she said.

* * *

Alex was having such a good time tonight with Halona that he almost forgot about the cases he was working on. Almost. The brace on his left arm was a steady reminder though. Someone in town had tried to kill him, or at least seriously injure him.

And that someone might be looking for another chance to do just that.

Alex glanced around as Summer Rivera took to the stage and explained the charity auction's rules and what the cause was about. Money raised tonight was to help Mary Beth Edwards with her medical bills. There were bidding sheets with each silent-auction item placed on tables all around the room. People could walk around at their leisure, sign their names on the sheets, and raise their bids throughout the night. Some items would have multiple winners, like his grandma's pickles and Lula's frozen dinners.

After explaining, Summer gave the okay, and the auction began.

"Don't forget that there's hot chocolate and cookies in the back to eat while you walk around!" she called.

"Theo looks happy over there with Tuck and Josie. Looks like we're on our own," Alex said.

Halona followed his gaze to Theo and nodded. "Looks like it. I'm so glad. A while ago, that comment from Summer would've devastated him. I'm beginning to think this might just be one of our best Christmases." She looked up at him.

"I hope so." He looked around the room for a moment. He didn't usually find himself at these holiday events anymore unless he was working. "I'll admit it's not my favorite holiday," he said, looking at her again, "but you're making this one brighter than most."

She grabbed a hold of his hand, seeming to understand exactly what he meant. "I'm glad. You told me the other day that I deserved a merry Christmas too. Not just Theo."

He nodded. "I remember."

"Well, *you* deserve a merry one as well, Alex."

After his father's death the week of Christmas, he never thought he'd be able to celebrate again. It was too painful, and despite what others said, time didn't seem to temper that pain.

Halona did though. This year he was seeing the holiday through her and Theo's eyes, and he felt the hope this time of year was supposed to bring, instead of its usual despair.

He looked away and cleared his throat. "Cookies first?" he suggested before meeting her eyes again.

"You read my mind."

"That would be the first time I knew what a woman was thinking."

They headed over to the refreshments table, and Halona prepared them both cups of cocoa and a plate of cookies to share.

"I should be the one serving you," Alex said.

"You only have one good arm at the moment. I understand."

They started walking around the room and looking at the items up for auction. After a few tables, they walked up on Tuck, Josie, Maddie, and Theo.

"There's something we want that's not up for auction," Tuck told Halona.

She looked at her brother questioningly. "Okay?"

"We want Theo to spend tonight with us at Hope Cottage," Josie said.

Theo reached for his uncle Tuck's hand and looked at his mom as if to say, *Pleeease.*

Halona narrowed her eyes as she looked at Tuck. "You might need to wake up a few times. He's sleeping better these days but being at a new place might throw him off."

"I don't mind," he said. "And you will be guaranteed a night of beauty sleep."

"I don't think it's possible for her to get any more beautiful," Alex said, snagging a grin from Tuck.

"Uh-huh. It's about time you admit you like my sister."

Alex and Halona both looked down at Theo, who didn't seem upset by that notion at all. Of course, at his age, he probably didn't comprehend what "like" meant in reference to a man and a woman.

"I like your sister," Alex agreed, looking back up at Tuck. "Is that okay?"

"You know it is." Tuck laughed. "It always has been. So tonight?" he asked, looking at Halona again.

She nodded. "Okay. I guess I'm fine with Theo staying over."

"He has spare clothes at Hope Cottage already," Tuck said. "So Theo is ours until tomorrow evening."

"Evening?" Halona asked.

"I want to take the horses out for a ride once he gets out of school," Tuck said. "Relax, sis. You're looking at an expert dad now. We'll be fine."

She laughed softly and then nodded. "Okay. Be good for your uncle Tuck and Josie," she told Theo.

Josie leaned into Halona and Alex as they started to walk away. "You could catch up on sleep or maybe watch a movie," she suggested. "Or...who knows?"

Alex shook his head when they had gone. "People around here don't mind sticking their noses in other people's business, do they?"

"Not at all," Halona agreed on a laugh.

"I meant what I told your brother, by the way. I like you."

"I think you're pretty okay yourself, Chief Frisky," she said, casting him a sideward look.

After a few tables, Halona stopped at a display table for handmade jewelry.

"These are gorgeous," she said, admiring the beaded necklaces and earrings.

"They are," Alex agreed, paying no attention to the items. Instead, he watched her.

"So much detail. Wow. I had no idea that Penny Everson did this kind of thing."

"One thing I've learned as a cop is that you never know what's going on behind people's closed doors," Alex said, immediately regretting his words. He hadn't meant Halona but that brought her situation to his mind, and judging by the way she was looking at him, he didn't need to be a mind reader to know she thought he was talking about her.

Her expression pinched. "And something you might not have learned yet is that you can't judge a situation without all the facts."

What facts did she think he was missing? Ted had hit her. A neighbor had heard the commotion and dialed 911. When Alex arrived, Halona had bruises and red, swollen, tear-filled eyes. She hadn't denied that Ted had done it but she'd insisted it wasn't his fault.

Alex would never understand why some women protected their abusers. Halona was strong, tough, and smart. And she was still protecting Ted even though he was dead.

"Tell me, Hal. What facts am I missing?" he asked quietly, unable to help himself.

She whipped her face up to meet his, fire igniting behind the brown of her irises. "Are you kidding me? *Now* you want the facts? Why didn't you ask what happened *before* you arrested my husband?"

Alex kept his voice low but his temper went high. They were near the back exit of the community building so he grabbed her hand and led her outside into the cold. Then he turned her to face him. "I didn't need to ask. It was pretty obvious what happened."

She shivered in the night air, and her eyes welled with tears that pulled on every heart string he had. "You didn't have all the facts, and you still don't," she said, her voice cracking.

"So give them to me." Because he seriously doubted any new information would change his opinion on the matter.

"Ted was a gentle man who would never hurt a soul. Not intentionally."

"He hurt you."

She lifted her gaze and sucked in a shuddery breath. "Ted was sick, Alex. He didn't mean to hurt me. He was…sick." A lone tear streamed down her cheek. "My husband had a brain injury. We were trying to get him help, and you hauled him off to jail."

"He didn't look sick," Alex said. Although Ted had looked like a broken man when he'd been arrested. Alex had threatened that if Ted ever touched Halona again, he'd do more than take him to jail next time. It was the only time Alex had ever threatened violence on a perp.

Ted had only shaken his head. "I won't let it happen again." After making bond, he filed for divorce.

Halona hugged her arms around her body. "The doctors diagnosed him with post-concussion syndrome,

an unfortunate result of years of football-related head
injuries. I'm not sure if it was the cognitive changes
or the anxiety and stress that came with everything that
made him become violent, but he only...hurt me once.
The doctors and I were trying to make him better."

"Why didn't you say anything?"

She shook her head and looked down at her feet for
a moment. "Ted wanted people to continue to see him
as the football star and hometown hero. The one time I
pushed, he'd pushed back."

"That was when you fell and hit your head on the
countertop?" Alex asked.

She nodded as she looked up with fresh tears on her
cheeks. "He'd been sorry. What was I supposed to do? We
vowed to love each other in sickness and in health."

Alex stood there frozen. Had he made the wrong
choice in arresting Ted? "I wish I had known."

"No one knew. He made me swear to keep his secret."

"And you're still keeping it?" Alex asked. "Why?"

Halona wiped at her eyes. "Ted was always so proud
of his accomplishments. He didn't want his illness to
detract from everything he worked so hard for in his
football career. He was a proud, stubborn man but he
wasn't violent. One too many head injuries changed him.
He lost control of his emotions. He punched the walls,
broke things." White puffs of air escaped her mouth
as she released a ragged breath. "I wanted so badly to
help him, but..." She shrugged her shoulders slightly. "I
didn't know how. Even the doctors weren't sure if they
could relieve his symptoms. They only seemed to be getting worse, compounded by his fear and anxiety over the
situation."

"And you dealt with it all on your own." Alex reached

out for her, pulling her into his arms. "I'm so sorry for what you went through." Not for the part he'd played in it. If Ted was progressing, he would have only continued to hurt Halona, maybe even Theo.

"Please don't tell anyone else," she said, tipping her face to look at him. "I promised Ted."

"It's not my story to tell. But, Hal, if he was well, he wouldn't have expected you to carry something like this on your own...The skiing accident?" Alex asked.

Halona shrugged slightly. "He didn't just become anxious and angry. He became reckless and impulsive too. He shouldn't have been out on the slopes in those conditions. He wasn't thinking straight."

Everything was starting to make sense now.

"Alex, I know that you told him to leave me."

"Hal—"

"He was already talking about leaving us. For our protection," she said. "Ted never wanted to hurt us."

She pressed back into his body, shivering in his arms as he held her for a long moment.

"Sorry," she said, finally pulling away. "Was I crushing your arm?"

"My arm is fine. It's you I'm worried about." Alex glanced toward the light on the building. "I don't want to go back inside, do you?"

She shook her head. "Not really."

"Good. Why don't I take you home? We can watch that movie that Josie recommended."

She met his gaze, and it was all he could do not to kiss her right now. If he started kissing her here though, he might not be able to stop himself.

"Or..." she said, replaying Josie's suggestion, a soft twinkle in her eyes.

"Or…" he repeated, liking the sound of that unspoken option even better.

* * *

After leaving the Hope for the Holidays event, they swung by Alex's house and picked up Officer Chew and then continued toward her place. Halona's heart quickened as Alex turned his SUV onto Cedar Trail. Were they going to sleep together again tonight?

Yes. She didn't have any reservations. In fact, after sharing her story with Alex, she only felt closer to him. There were no more hidden truths, no secrets or ghosts lingering in her past. This thing between them was the foundation of a real relationship, something with long-lasting potential. Forever potential.

Slow down, heart. One step at a time.

They parked, and Alex went around to help her out of his SUV. Then they walked to her front door and went inside.

"Can I let Officer Chew in the backyard?" he asked.

"Of course."

She watched as Alex opened the sliding back door. Then he closed it and turned to her. "Alone at last."

She stood there awkwardly in front of him. "Do you want a drink?"

"Not really," he said, stepping toward her.

"A snack?" she asked, shivering despite the heat of the room and the space between them.

"Nope." He walked until he was standing right in front of her.

"Movie?"

He shook his head, eyes pinned on her.

They'd already slept together once but her feelings for this man were so much stronger now. Every caress, every kiss, every little act tied her heart to his in tiny, impossible knots. That made every act between them now a risk. She was still a mother, and her first priority had to be Theo and his health. Dating someone didn't seem like such a game ender anymore though. In fact, she was tired of carrying the weight of her own little world alone. Having someone else would be nice.

"I can leave if you want me to," Alex whispered.

"No. I'd rather you stay."

CHAPTER SEVENTEEN

*H*alona stirred. Sometime after making love, she and Alex had both fallen asleep. The house was quiet.

Where is Theo?

As quickly as fear had hit, relief flooded through her. With Tuck and Josie. It was just Alex and her tonight.

She turned to look at him, bare chested with one arm flung over his head, the other in its brace and down by his side. She'd wanted this man ever since she was a teenaged girl, which felt like forever ago. Her attraction to him had faded when she'd gotten married, but now...

She swallowed as her gaze trailed over his body, the bedsheet covering him from the waist down. Christmas was next week, and this was all she wanted every night next year. Okay, she also wanted Theo to talk. But those two things would make her a very contented woman.

"Hey," Alex said, his voice coated with sleep. He reached out for her, pulling her toward him. "What time is it?"

"Just after midnight. I woke up and wondered where Theo was momentarily."

He smiled softly and closed his eyes again. "The night is all yours. He's just fine with Tuck and Josie."

"I know." She curled into the crook of his arm, listening to his steady breathing until she thought he'd fallen asleep again. She couldn't return to sleep though. There were too many thoughts and questions floating around like helium balloons in her mind.

She stared up at the ceiling and the shadows dancing in the broken light coming through the window. Listened as the wind howled outside the house. Memorized every moment of the night, in case it all fell apart the way things tended to do.

A tiny spark of hope refused to be put out by her cynicism though. She'd had her chance at love with her late ex-husband. She'd always believed that there was just one special person for everyone. A soul mate. That had been proven wrong in her eyes when she'd watched her brother, Tuck, get a second chance at love with Josie this past spring. He was the happiest she'd ever seen him these days.

People did get second chances at happily ever afters. *She* could have a second chance. Lying in the dark, in Alex's arms, she made a wish that felt like it had already come true. She wanted this man in her life, in her son's life, from this moment on.

* * *

The next morning, Alex woke early, dressed, and kissed Halona softly.

Her eyes fluttered open.

"I have to go home and get ready to head to the station," he said. "Don't get up. Sleep in for once."

Her lips curled. "You speak the impossible. Besides, six a.m. *is* sleeping in around here." She sat up and pulled the bedsheet around her, watching as he collected his things.

Once he was done, he turned back to her. "I'll be back tonight."

Her mouth dropped open. "Oh. Um. Well, I don't think that's a good idea. Theo will be back, and I don't want to confuse him by . . . well, you know."

Alex chuckled softly. She was as adorable as she was gorgeous. "I thought we'd do our Mentor Match outing tonight and give you an opportunity for more time to yourself."

"Oh." She swiped a lock of dark hair from her face. "Right."

"And I agree," he said, bending to kiss her cheek. "We probably want to keep our hands to ourselves as much as possible around Theo. Even though I think he's starting to suspect the obvious."

She nodded. "He's a smart kid."

He kissed her one more time, this time staying longer and getting his fill because he didn't know when he'd catch her alone again. Then he straightened, waved, and headed into the kitchen to get Officer Chew.

As he drove home, his cell phone rang beside him. He tapped the speakerphone function so he could handle the wheel. The brace on his arm made everything clumsy. He was ready to dispense of it ASAP.

"You're late coming in," Tammy said.

Alex looked at the digital clock on his dash. "No, I'm

not." But he would be if he wanted a shower. "What's going on?"

"Mitch brought Tony Anderson in for a DUI. Thought you'd want to know in case, I don't know, you wanted to swing by and check on Sharlene at home."

Not a bad idea. "Thanks. I'll do that before heading in." Which really would put him late.

"You're welcome," she said.

"Anything else?" he asked, feeling her hesitation.

"I want to leave early today if you don't mind."

Alex pulled into his driveway and cut the engine. "Why is that?" he asked as he and Officer Chew got out and headed toward the house. Tammy was the only full-time secretary during the week. His part-time staff was out of town through the holidays.

"It's Christmas, Chief, and I've got things to do."

He grinned. "Fair enough. You've been working overtime this month. You deserve time off."

"I deserve an entire year off," she quipped.

"Can't afford to be without you for that long," he said, meaning it. "I'll be there in about an hour."

"Thanks. I'll hold down the fort as usual," Tammy said.

After showering and dressing, Alex got back into his SUV with Officer Chew at his side, his constant companion these days. Then he drove to Pine Cone Lane and pulled into Sharlene Anderson's driveway.

Officer Chew whined softly.

"Don't worry, pal. I'm not leaving you here ever again. We're just checking on the lady of the house. She was nice to you, right?"

Chew looked at him with expressive eyes, making Alex think of Theo.

"Come on, let's go." Alex got out of his vehicle,

headed up the porch steps, and rang the doorbell. When Sharlene didn't answer the first time, he rang it again.

Finally, the door opened, and Sharlene peeked out with the door covering half her face.

"Just me," Alex said. "I heard that Tony was locked up so I came to check on you."

"I'm fine," she said, and for a moment, he thought she was going to shut the door back in his face. Then Officer Chew barked at Alex's feet, and Sharlene looked down.

"Oh," she said, opening the door wider and bending to pet Chew's head. "There you are! I've missed you so much!" She rubbed Chew behind the ears for several moments before looking back up at Alex.

Alex swallowed painfully when she faced him. She had one black eye and a cut on the bridge of her nose.

His eyes connected with Sharlene's. "You can't keep living this way, Shar," he said, his words coming out harsh. He took a breath and softened his tone. He didn't want to sound like he was barking orders. He was just concerned. It was his job to protect the citizens in this town, and Halona was right. To do that, he needed to be seen as approachable. "You can trust me, Sharlene. Tell me the truth."

She shook her head as she continued to pet Officer Chew. For a long moment, she didn't say anything. "The truth is I'm scared."

"There are women's shelters. I could help you find one. I'll take you there myself. When he gets out, you could be long gone."

She looked at him, long and hard, her hand running over Officer Chew's fur in quick, nervous strokes. He could feel there was something more she wanted to tell him but wouldn't.

"All you have to say is yes," Alex said, willing the word from her mouth. "Please, let me help you."

* * *

Even the air seemed fresher this morning as Halona headed out of the house to get coffee and then go to work. Tuck was taking Theo to school. Halona had already called and held a one-sided conversation with Theo earlier, wishing him a good day.

Every day had been good lately though. And yesterday had been the best.

A little buzz zipped from her heart all the way to her toes.

"You seem to be in a good mood," Brenna observed after Halona got her cup of coffee from Emma and plopped down in front of her at what was becoming their usual table. "You're almost glowing." Brenna's eyes narrowed. "And I happen to know you left the auction with Chief Frisky last night sans Theo." She lifted a brow.

Halona laughed and shook her head. Not even the town's nosiness could ruin her good mood today. "I'm pleading the Fifth."

"Uh-huh. Well, speaking of pleading the Fifth, I hear Tony Anderson is in jail this morning."

"What?"

Brenna sipped from her coffee. "Yep. He was picked up for being drunk and disorderly."

"And you know this how?" Halona asked.

Brenna gave her a sheepish look. "Well, Emma told me. Dawanda told her. And who knows who told her?"

"Why am I not surprised?" Halona sipped her coffee. "Well, good. I hope Tony stays there for a long time."

"Me too, and I hope your new boyfriend throws away the key. They should've auctioned that off last night. I would've purchased it and taken the secret of where the key was hidden to my grave," Brenna said.

Halona's mood dropped a notch. She was supposed to take Ted's secret to her grave, and yet she'd told Alex the truth last night. It was a relief but some part of her felt like she'd also betrayed Ted's trust.

"Yoo-hoo. You okay?" Brenna asked. "You've stopped glowing."

Halona blinked, realizing there were tears stinging her eyes. "Yeah. Just…the thought of Tony's lawyer getting him out without any real consequence again is beyond frustrating."

"I hope that's not the case this time." They talked for a while longer, discussing Christmas and the items still on their shopping lists. Then Brenna stood. "I've had two cups of coffee and now duty calls. I'll see you tomorrow—same place, same time?"

Halona nodded. "Sounds good." She watched Brenna walk out and stayed seated for a few minutes longer, sipping her coffee until it was drained and trying to make herself feel okay about telling Ted's secret. She could trust Alex to keep it. She didn't need to worry about that. He was honorable and noble. She could trust him with anything, including her heart.

Halona stood and tossed her empty cup into the trash can. Then she headed next door to open her store. She freshened up the flowers, made a few calls, and completed some orders as they came in.

Around midday, her phone rang.

"Little Shop of Flowers," she answered.

"Ms. Locklear?"

Dread knotted low in Halona's belly. She recognized a call from Theo's school when she got one. "Yes?"

"This is Principal Nelson. I was wondering if you could come by the school at some point today. I'd like to talk to you about Theo."

"Is he okay?" she asked.

"Oh yes—he's fine. No need to rush over. I just think what I need to say should be told in person," the principal added.

Halona sucked in a breath. "I'll be there in just a few minutes," she said before disconnecting the call. Then she dialed up her mother. "Hey, Mom. I need a favor. Can you watch the shop for me right now?"

"Of course. I'm already on Main Street, matter of fact. I'll just head right over."

"Thanks." Halona grabbed her purse and keys and met Lula at the door not three minutes later.

"What's going on?" Lula asked as she walked in.

"I'm not sure," Halona answered. But being called to the school had never been positive news. So much for the rash of uneventful days. She should've known it was too good to be true.

* * *

Alex had been on the phone for the last hour talking to different representatives at various women's shelters. Now he was talking to the contact at a shelter three hours away.

Was that far enough?

"Chief Baker, we do a very good job of keeping women safe here. The biggest risk to a woman's safety is if she contacts her abuser after she's left home. We have therapists that offer daily counseling to make sure that doesn't happen. We also give our women the education and training they need to go out into the world and support themselves."

"That sounds like exactly what Sharlene needs," Alex said, feeling good about New Beginnings Women's Shelter.

"Unfortunately, we don't have a room open just yet," the woman told him.

"How long?" Alex asked.

"Well, it's Christmastime. Domestic situations increase this time of year so our rooms fill up fast."

It was the same story he'd already heard from other places. But the other places hadn't sounded like what Sharlene needed. This one did.

"It won't be until after Christmas," she told him.

"That's too long." Tony would be out of jail by then.

"I'm sorry. I wish there were more that I could do," the woman said. "We can put your friend's name on a waiting list, and I'll call you if anything changes."

Alex gave her his contact information so she could reach him directly. The last thing he needed was Tony intervening in the situation. After hanging up, he massaged his hands over his face. What was he supposed to do for Sharlene until after Christmas?

A knock on his office door drew his attention, and Tammy stood in front of him.

"I told you I was taking off early. Is it still okay?" she asked hesitantly, which wasn't like her.

"I didn't think I had a choice on the matter," he teased.

She shoved her hands on her hips. "No, but I like to let you think you do."

"Do what you need to, Tammy. I can handle the station. I'll see you tomorrow."

She started to turn and walk away but stopped. "Everything okay, Chief?"

He gave his head a shake. "There aren't any openings at the women's shelters for Sharlene. She's finally ready to leave, and I have nowhere to send her."

Tammy frowned. "You're one of the good guys, Chief Baker. You know that?"

"Depending on who you talk to."

Tammy laughed. "I hope you survive without me for the rest of the afternoon." She turned again and started walking down the hall.

"Won't be easy," he called after her, meaning it.

One of the good guys. He'd had his facts wrong in Halona's situation though. Ted hadn't been a monster; he'd been sick. Yeah, Halona had suffered, but if Alex hadn't stepped in, ignoring her pleas to look the other way, could Ted have gotten help? Would Ted have stayed with Halona and Theo? Would he still have been reckless on that mountain, skiing when he shouldn't have been? Would he be alive right now?

Alex's shoulders suddenly felt very heavy with the weight of responsibility for Sharlene and the past.

He heard Tammy leave the building and wondered briefly where she was going, not that it was any of his business. He had enough to concern himself with. The holidays weren't just busy at the women's shelter. The jail was full too, and he had a few too many cases to solve, his and his father's included. Then there was Halona.

He looked at the clock on his desk. Only four more hours until he got to see her. Already, she was distracting him and stripping away his focus. Already his priorities were reordering, and some of his cases were time sensitive, like Sharlene's. He needed to find a place for Sharlene before Tony was released. Alex needed to make sure she was long gone when her husband got home.

CHAPTER EIGHTEEN

Halona sat in the parking lot in front of the school for a long moment, readying herself to go in and meet with Principal Nelson. Theo was doing so much better these days. Everyone had setbacks though. This didn't mean he'd lost all the progress he'd made.

She took several deep, steadying breaths and then pushed her car door open and walked toward the building. Theo had his Mentor Match outing with Alex tonight and then after school tomorrow he had an appointment scheduled with Dr. Charwood.

"Good afternoon, Ms. Locklear," the office secretary said.

"Good afternoon. I'm meeting with Principal Nelson."

"Yes, he's expecting you." The secretary gave a cheerful smile and pulled the phone's receiver to her ear, dialing the principal. "Ms. Locklear is here...Yep. I'll send her right back." The secretary hung up and looked at Halona. "You know the way."

"All too well," Halona said on a sigh as she headed down the hall. She knocked lightly on the principal's door.

Principal Nelson looked up. "Ms. Locklear! Come in!"

Why was he smiling at her? Didn't he know that she hated these visits?

She sat in the chair across from him and smiled back—only because she felt like she had to. The only other option was to cry right now. "What did you want to discuss this afternoon?" she asked.

"Theo," Principal Nelson said.

She didn't find that humorous in the least but she laughed anyway.

Principal Nelson reached for a stack of papers on his desk and grabbed one. Then he placed it in front of her.

Halona leaned in to read what it was. It was a report in her son's handwriting entitled "All I Want for Christmas."

She held her breath as she read it.

All I want for Christmas is for my mom to be happy.

He backed the statement up with reasons why he wanted that and what might make that possible. He could try harder so that she wouldn't be called to the school. He could reverse time so his dad wouldn't die but he knew that wasn't possible. So maybe he just wanted his mom to have someone new to love, like Chief Baker, because Chief Baker seemed to make her smile more often. Lastly, Theo wrote that perhaps a dog would make his mom happy.

She laughed softly when she read that because Theo was the one who wanted a dog.

"It's a great, persuasive paper," Principal Nelson said when she finally looked up at him.

"It is. I'm not sure why you called me here though," she said.

Principal Nelson shrugged. "We've called you a few times this school year already. I imagine you're getting tired of hearing from us."

Halona reached for a Kleenex on his desk and dabbed under her eyes. "A little bit."

"Theo doesn't tell us much but he told us a whole lot with this paper. It appears that he worries about you just as much as you worry about him. And he loves you. Sometimes it's nice for us adults to know that. You're a good mom, Ms. Locklear. That's clear to me."

Sometimes it was nice to hear that too. She tried to be good but single parenting wasn't easy.

"Thank you. This report is wonderful. I'm not sure about getting a dog though. I have my hands full already." Getting an Alex was a different story. "I'm glad Theo is doing better in school," she said instead.

"He is. I stop by the classroom every day, and he seems a lot more upbeat. I've even seen him on the playground with other students. Whatever you're doing at home is working."

"He's still in counseling, and he's part of the Mentor Match program. Chief Baker is his mentor."

"What a lucky little boy. I would've loved to pal around with the chief of police as a kid. When I was Theo's age, it was Chief Baker's father heading up the police station. Another very honorable man."

Halona and Principal Nelson were about the same age. Alex's father had served while she was young too.

"Well, I just wanted to share some good news with

you for once. And hopefully more often," Principal Nelson said.

"Thank you."

Halona kept Theo's report as she left the building. She read it one more time before driving back to the flower shop to relieve Lula from duty.

"Everything okay?" Lula asked.

Halona nodded. "Long story short, Theo is doing better in school."

"That's great to hear," Lula said.

"It is." And if Halona thought about it too much, she'd start crying again.

"So...what's going on with you and Alex?" her mom asked, not budging from the stool behind the counter. "I saw you two together at the Hope for the Holidays auction last night. Looks like you're getting close."

Halona sucked in a breath as she put her purse under the register. "We are," she admitted.

"It's more than him just mentoring Theo, then?"

"I'm not exactly sure what we're doing yet, Mom." Halona shrugged.

"Well, I adore Alex—you know that. I saw the brace on his arm. What happened?"

"That's another long story. Someone ran him off the road and into a ditch while he was jogging."

Lula gasped. "You're kidding."

"I'm afraid not."

"That's so scary. And very similar to what happened to his father," she said. "Such a tragedy. I've always had my suspicions about who was behind the wheel that day."

Halona looked over with interest. "Who?"

"Steve Anderson."

"Why would he hurt Alex's dad?"

Lula shrugged. "I don't know. I always got a bad vibe from him though. Same with Tony but he was just a little boy when Alex's dad was killed. It was a long time ago but the pain of losing someone never really goes away. I'm sure you understand."

She was speaking of Ted.

Halona nodded. She understood all too well.

"This time of year, while happy, can be hard for those who've lost a loved one. Alex included."

Halona had already considered that. He'd lost his dad a couple of days before Christmas. No wonder he was working his dad's case and comparing it to his own. But there was no way the same person that killed his dad had tried to take him out too. Steve Anderson didn't even live in Sweetwater Springs anymore.

"Alex didn't win those frozen dinners I donated to the auction last night but I think I'll make him some anyway," Lula said. "It's Christmas, after all, and he's taking good care of my grandson. And my daughter." She winked and got up from her stool now. "Well, it looks like I have a lot of cooking in my future. I better go to the grocery store." She hugged Halona.

"Thank you for watching the store."

"You're welcome. Anytime," Lula said.

Halona waved goodbye and then took her place on the stool her mom had just occupied. She pulled Theo's report back in front of her and read it again, smiling through happy tears. All he wanted for Christmas was for her to be happy, and she was. Her son was doing better. Her store was thriving. And Alex had come into her life. She had everything she could possibly want right now. Her life was on an upward turn, and she intended to keep plowing forward. Looking backward wouldn't do anyone any good.

* * *

Safe Haven's Place was only thirty minutes away in Wild Blossom Bluffs. In Alex's mind, that wasn't nearly far enough but it was the only shelter he could find with immediate availability.

Sharlene wrung her hands nervously in the passenger seat beside him.

He reached out and briefly touched her forearm. "It's going to be okay. The shelter's whereabouts isn't public knowledge. He won't find you."

He pulled into the shelter's driveway, parked, and began unloading her bags. He'd told her to pack enough belongings to get her through the month. After that, he'd help her find a shelter even farther away if need be. She could file restraining orders and hopefully for divorce.

Sharlene hesitated as they climbed the steps toward the large two-story home.

Please don't back out now.

She looked up at him. "Thank you, Chief Baker."

His eyes burned, and he had to look down at the brick step he was on for a moment to rope in his emotions. "You're welcome," he said when he looked up.

"It took me a while to get here but I want you to know that I'm not going to go back to him." She lifted her chin a notch, her smile rounding at the corners of her mouth. "I'm a strong woman."

"I never doubted that, Sharlene."

She nodded. "I did. But I won't anymore. I might even go back to school."

"They have a program here that can help with that," he told her. The front door opened as they spoke.

"I thought I heard voices out here," a woman with long,

dark hair said. She looked between them. "You must be Chief Baker, and you must be Sharlene. I'm Carly." She stepped out onto the porch and shook their hands. "It's cold out here. Let's get you settled, Sharlene." Then she looked up at Alex regretfully. "If you don't mind, one of the women inside gets very upset when a male is in proximity."

Alex nodded. "I understand. Thank you for helping us."

"Anytime, Chief Baker." Carly smiled warmly.

Alex looked over at Sharlene. "I'll be in touch."

He stood there and watched the women go inside the house before turning back to his SUV. Then he drove home for a quick shower and a change of clothes. He also let Officer Chew out for a run. After that, he climbed back into his vehicle and headed to Cedar Trail for his Mentor Match outing with Theo.

Alex was flooded with relief over handling Sharlene's situation. Tony's lawyer was already doing his best to get him out on bail once more. Alex had no doubt that it was only a matter of time before he did. When Tony got home, however, Sharlene would be tucked away safely somewhere that Tony couldn't find her.

After all this time, Sharlene had let her guard down and trusted Alex. The way he interacted with people had changed since he'd started seeing Halona. He was softer, but by no means a softie. Would Sharlene have agreed to go to the women's shelter with him otherwise?

He was showing people the human side of himself. The side that had made his own father not only a respected chief of police, but one that the people here loved.

Alex breathed deeply as he pulled into Halona's driveway. Everything had changed in the last few weeks because of her, and he never wanted things to go back. He parked and got out, heading toward the porch. He took the steps two at a time, energized by the thought of seeing two of his favorite people, and rang the bell.

"Hey," Halona said when she opened the door.

"Hi." It was all he could do not to pull her into his arms and kiss her senseless. But Theo was standing right behind her, looking up at him with wide, excited eyes.

"Hey, buddy." Alex raised a hand for a high five.

Theo smacked his right hand with surprising force.

"Whoa! That's some arm you have. You might be on the force with me one day," he said with a laugh, lifting his gaze back up to meet Halona's. "Did you have a good day?" he asked her.

She gestured him inside and then closed the door, shutting out the winter cold. "We had a lovely day."

"Yeah? What happened?" Alex asked.

"Well, I got called to Theo's school today," she said.

Alex was tempted to frown about that piece of information except Halona seemed to be beaming. "What for?"

"Principal Nelson wanted to tell me in person what a wonderful job Theo is doing in school these days."

Alex felt himself grinning from ear to ear now too. "Wow," he said, looking down at Theo. "I'm really happy to hear that. Congratulations. I think that calls for a celebration," he said, making Theo's smile grow wider.

Halona hugged her arms around her body the way she tended to do. "That sounds wonderful. What are you two guys going to do tonight?"

Suddenly Alex had an idea. "Well," he said, "what are your plans for tonight?"

She shook her head. "I don't really have any. I just thought I'd stay here and maybe clean a little bit."

Alex looked down at Theo and hoped he wouldn't mind. "I'd say that, if I'm taking Theo out to celebrate, you should come with us. I know it's breaking the Mentor Match rules but this is an extenuating circumstance. What do you think, Theo?" Alex asked.

Theo nodded excitedly.

"Great." Alex looked at Halona, who was also smiling back at him.

"Are you sure? I don't want to intrude on your time together," she said.

"We want you to intrude," he told her. "We'll stay right here in the living room for you while you go get ready."

She looked between him and her son, and then, after only a moment's hesitation, she nodded. "Sounds like fun. I'll be right back."

Alex walked over and sat on the couch while they waited. He gestured for Theo to come sit beside him. "So?" He looked over at young Theo after several long minutes of silence. "Have you discussed what you told me with your mom yet?"

Theo's little brow rose.

"You know exactly what I'm talking about," Alex said.

Theo shook his head and looked away.

"I know you're worried about making her sad but I think she'd actually be happy about you sharing how you feel with her." Alex shrugged. "Just saying."

Before Alex could say anything more, Halona walked back into the room. She'd changed into a beautiful pink dress and wore a sweater over the top. Her hair, which had been pulled back moments before, was now down and cascading around her shoulders. For a moment, Alex understood Theo's position. Sometimes there were no words to convey exactly what was going through your mind. Or there were words but it wasn't appropriate to say them out loud.

"I'm all set," Halona said.

"That was fast." Alex stood.

"Where are we going for this celebration?" she asked.

He scratched his chin and looked at Theo. "Any suggestions?" He mentally willed Theo to use his words in answer. Instead, Theo grabbed his notepad from the table.

Ice cream?

Both Halona and Alex chuckled.

"For one," Halona said, "you haven't had dinner yet. And two, it's freezing outside. Ice cream probably isn't the best choice."

"Although, if you add hot fudge, it makes it a better choice," Alex countered. "Especially if we get it after dinner. What do you say, Hal?"

"Mmm." Halona licked her lips. "I say my mouth just started watering."

And for some reason, that drove his thoughts south. Maybe Theo would fall asleep on the way home, and he could get a little alone time with Halona.

* * *

Christmas music filled Alex's SUV as they drove downtown to Becky's Log Cabin, a nice restaurant that sat on Silver Lake. Halona could recall evenings just like this one with her own family as a child. Her dad would belt out the traditional songs on the radio, prompting her and Tuck to sing along with him. Her mom would always just smile and laugh. Sometimes Lula would sing a song in their native Cherokee language. They were great family memories.

Alex started singing and glanced over at her. "Come on. If a hard-nosed cop like me can sing, you can too."

"I'm an awful singer," she protested.

"Doubtful." He grinned over at her. "Please."

She nibbled softly on her lower lip. "Fine. But don't laugh."

"I wouldn't dream of it."

She felt a little foolish at first as they sang "Jingle Bell Rock" together. Then it felt natural, like two kids playing. She kept listening for Theo's little voice to join in from the back seat as well but he remained quiet. When she glanced in the passenger-side mirror, he was grinning though, and her heart soared into her throat, making it hard to sing for a moment. He really was doing so much better lately. He was happy and healthy; what more could she ask for this Christmas?

Theo had written that one of the things he wanted for Christmas was for her to find someone special like Chief Baker. Halona didn't want to get Theo's hopes up tonight, even though she was hopeful about what was happening between her and Alex. There was always a possibility that things could fizzle out between them, and she didn't want Theo to get disappointed if that happened. *She* should be the only one to get disappointed.

Ten minutes later, they pulled into the restaurant's parking lot.

"I've always loved this place," she said. "I haven't been here in ages."

Becky's Log Cabin looked like a house that someone

would live in. It was quaint and cozy. In the winters, there was always a fire burning in the fireplace and soft music playing. Sometimes Becky's husband, Jeremy, played the baby grand piano in the corner. Halona had recently heard that the couple was looking to sell the restaurant. They'd been running it for several decades, and it was time to retire.

"It's kind of fancy here though," Halona said. And expensive. Most of her spare income lately was going toward Theo's mounting Christmas list. Not that he got everything he asked for. That would break her bank for sure. "Maybe we should go to the diner down the street instead."

"Tonight is a special occasion," Alex insisted. "And this is my treat."

"You don't have to—" she began but froze when he laid a hand on her knee, sending a shock wave of heat right through her. So much for keeping their hands to themselves in front of Theo. "I want to," Alex said. "Let me."

She swallowed past the lump in her throat. "Okay, then. They might not have hot fudge sundaes though."

"Then we'll go somewhere else afterward." Alex casually removed his hand and turned to wink at Theo. Then he got out, walked around the vehicle, and opened the back passenger door for Theo and her door for her. When she stepped onto the pavement, she found herself standing very close to him. It was all she could do not to step a little closer but Theo wedged between them and took both her hand and Alex's.

Summer Rivera had been right. They probably did look like one happy, little family from the outside looking in. And from the inside looking out, it kind of felt that way too.

Alex held the restaurant's door open for them, and then a hostess seated them near a window overlooking Silver Lake.

"Look, Theo! You can even see the town square tree." She pointed to the town's main holiday attraction. "Speaking of which, I need to buy some gifts for the child's name I pulled at the Lights on Silver Lake event. Christmas will be here before I know it."

"The countdown begins," Alex said.

She watched his eyes dull for a moment and remembered what her mother had pointed out earlier. It was the happiest time of year for some, but not for everyone. She could certainly relate to that, even if this holiday was turning out so much happier than the last couple had been for her and Theo.

"Will you be spending the holidays with Grandma Baker?" she asked.

"A little bit. I'll probably work so the other officers can be home with those they love."

"What about your mom?" Halona asked.

Alex shrugged. "She likes Florida's warm weather. We'll chat on Skype. She'll ship me some presents, and I'll do the same."

"Sounds a little lonely."

He shrugged. "If Officer Chew is still around, I'll nab him a chew toy. Think he'd like that?" he asked Theo, pulling him into their conversation.

Theo nodded eagerly.

"Yeah, me too."

A waitress stepped up to their table. "Hi, guys. How are you all doing tonight?"

"Great," Alex answered. "We're celebrating a job well done at school," he told her.

"Oh?" The waitress looked at Theo. "Good job, little guy. I bet that'll earn you points with Santa too." The waitress then read off the night's specials, and they all ordered the house spaghetti and meatballs.

"I'll probably regret ordering that when it's all over my dress," Halona said as the waitress walked away. "I'll have to take it off as soon as I get home." She avoided meeting Alex's eyes because that had probably sounded unintentionally suggestive.

"Maybe they have bibs here," Alex teased.

Now she met his gaze. "A nice restaurant like this one? I don't think so. I'll just have to do my best to keep the food in my mouth."

"I won't say a word if you end up wearing it," Alex promised with a growing grin.

It was nice to see him relaxed and happy. She didn't like to think of him all alone on Christmas. It didn't seem right.

"You could spend the holidays with us, you know," she suggested, not giving herself time to think before tossing the idea out. She was doing her best to keep their romance out of Theo's sight right now, but Theo adored Alex. It could only make the holiday brighter.

Alex narrowed his eyes. "What do you mean?"

"Well, you know my parents. You've been over a thousand times growing up. We'll go over there on Christmas morning and have breakfast. My mom will lead us through some Cherokee songs, and then we'll open a few presents. There's always room for one more. My mom would be beside herself if you said yes."

Alex looked between her and Theo.

"Officer Chew can come too. Obviously," she added.

"I don't know—" Alex began.

"And Tuck and Josie will be there with Maddie. I think Maddie is even bringing her grandmother, Beverly Sanders. It'll be a lot of fun. Just think about it," she said before he could say no. She didn't let herself think about why she wanted so badly for him to say yes either.

"Okay. I'll think on it," he said. "Thanks."

"You're welcome."

The food arrived, and Halona did her best to eat it gracefully, which wasn't easy with elbow-deep noodles dripping in a rich marinara sauce. Alex seemed to have just as much difficulty as she did.

She looked up and laughed as he slurped one noodle up. "That's impressive."

Then Theo started slurping noodles just like his role model, and he didn't bother trying to keep the sauce from around his mouth and on his clothes.

Halona burst into laughter. *Best night ever.*

Toward the end of their meal, Becky, the restaurant's owner, stopped by their table. "I thought that was you, Chief Baker. Of all the restaurants in all of Sweetwater Springs, you choose mine." She laughed heartily, and then turned to Halona and Theo. "It's so nice to see you all in here too. Did you see where I placed the poinsettias I won at the auction on the front porch?"

"I did." Halona dabbed at her mouth with a napkin. "They looked beautiful, Becky."

"I outbid Dawanda on those. She threatened me, Chief," Becky said, turning back to Alex.

"Oh?"

Becky's petite frame shook with laughter. "I think you should have her arrested."

"I'm afraid the jail is full," Alex said.

"That's what Tammy told me too."

"Tammy?" Alex's teasing demeanor notably shifted at the mention of his office secretary.

Becky's bright mood seemed to dull as well. "Oh. Maybe I shouldn't have said anything just yet."

"Was she here this afternoon?" Alex asked. "Becky?" he prodded when the restaurant owner didn't immediately answer.

"Oh, you'll need to save your questions for Tammy, Chief," Becky said, looking flustered. "I shouldn't have said anything."

Alex narrowed his eyes momentarily, and then his shoulders lowered. "No worries, Becky. I won't even tell Tammy you mentioned her name," he promised.

Becky smiled gratefully and patted his shoulder. "Good man. Mayor Everson was in here just the other day, and I made sure to sing your praises. That way he keeps you appointed."

"I appreciate that," Alex said.

Becky nodded. "And I appreciate all you do for the town... Well, can I get my favorite customers any dessert?"

"Do you have hot fudge sundaes?" he asked.

Halona's gaze slid to Theo's. Half of his face was stained orange with marinara. He'd eaten all of it but the mention of ice cream seemed to have given him a renewed appetite.

"Matter of fact, I do. Three hot fudge sundaes?" she asked.

"I'm not sure I can eat another bite," Halona said. "I'm already full."

Alex shook his head. "Oh, no you don't. You're having some. How about we share one?"

There was something strangely sensual about that

offer. So much so that the only acceptable response was to say no. Even though she was failing so far tonight at her resolution to keep things platonic, Theo was a master observer, and she still needed to try.

Before she could respond though, Becky slid her pen behind her ear and nodded. "Two sundaes. One with two spoons for the lovebirds. Coming right up!"

CHAPTER NINETEEN

Alex glanced at Theo in his rearview mirror as they drove home. "Out like a light."

"I'm not surprised. This was pretty eventful for a school night," Halona said.

"Yeah, but tomorrow's the last day before Christmas break. Kids don't do anything in class except have parties and watch movies," Alex said.

"True." Halona laughed. "Thank you for tonight. It meant a lot to Theo. And to me."

"Just being a good mentor," he said, shrugging it off.

"Except you broke the Mentor Match rule. Parents aren't supposed to tag along," Halona pointed out.

"Confession: I was sweating bullets about the possibility that Jessica Everson was going to catch us tonight. I don't want to be fired."

"It's a volunteer job. You can't be fired."

Alex grinned. "I kind of like this mentor gig though. It's nice." They kept their voices quiet so they didn't wake

Theo. "Kids need someone to look up to. I had my dad
growing up but not every kid has that."

Foot, meet mouth.

Alex quickly looked at Halona. "Sorry. I wasn't
thinking."

"No, it's okay. You're right. That's one of the reasons
I agreed to put Theo in the program. He needs a good
role model."

"He already has one. He has you."

"But I'm only one person. Tuck is busy with his own
life. Spending time with you has been good for Theo."

Alex's chest tightened. His secret with Theo had been
sitting heavily with him. He'd made the boy a promise,
but in agreeing to be Theo's Mentor Match, he'd also
made a promise to Halona. He glanced in the rearview
mirror at Theo again. Still asleep. "I, uh, need to tell you
something." His gaze slid over.

He watched Halona subtly straighten. "Uh-oh. Judging
by the tone of your voice, I'm guessing I won't like it
very much."

"Maybe not." He sucked in a deep breath. Yeah, telling
Halona was the right thing to do.

"Well, are you going to keep me waiting all night?"
she asked when he took several more deep breaths and
stolen glances at Theo.

"Theo knows I arrested his dad," Alex said.

"What?" she asked quietly.

Alex glanced over. "He asked me about it last week
during our outing."

Halona just stared at him. "What did you tell him?"

"I told him he needed to talk to you. I didn't tell him
anything but he knows something happened between you
and Ted."

Halona's mouth fell open.

"He thought if you knew, it would make you sad."

"That doesn't make sense," Halona said.

"It does. You're his mom. He's worried about you," Alex said.

"That's not what doesn't make sense." The sharpness in her voice made him glance in her direction again. "What doesn't make sense is why you thought it was okay to keep this from me for an entire week. You know how much I worry about my son. You should've told me immediately." Her voice was growing louder with each word she spoke.

Alex glanced back at Theo again. "He asked me not to. I thought it was important to keep his trust."

"What about my trust? I'm his mother, Alex. I'm up every night with him, listening to the sound of his voice as he cries out, because that's all I ever get. I entrusted you with him, and that means knowing you'll keep my child safe and knowing that you'll tell me if there's something I need to know!"

"That's why I'm telling you now." He spoke softly, hoping to de-escalate the situation as he pulled into her driveway. This wasn't at all how he'd expected her to react to the news. "I realize I should've told you before now."

"Yeah, you should have."

Now that the SUV was stopped, he angled his body toward her, resisting his urge to reach out and lay a settling hand on her body. The fiery glint in her brown eyes told him she wasn't in the touchy-feely mood right now. He also knew, with one look, that she wasn't about to invite him inside the house.

"I'm sorry," he said again, feeling like a jerk.

Then he heard the back door open, and Theo got out. *When did he wake up?*

"Theo?" Halona said. "Honey, are you okay?"

Theo narrowed his eyes at Alex before slamming the vehicle door shut. *Crap.* Theo knew that he'd just told Halona the truth.

Alex massaged a hand over his face. Both Halona and Theo were mad at him now. When had this night taken such a downward turn? Oh, right. When Alex had decided to do the right thing. Couldn't he be satisfied with doing the wrong thing for once?

He stepped out of his SUV and stared across the hood as Halona got out as well.

"It's late," she said. "We can see ourselves inside. Thank you for tonight, Chief Baker," she said stiffly.

He nodded. Back to being Chief Baker. "Good night, Halona. Good night, Theo."

The boy wouldn't even look at him. Instead, Theo started walking to the front door with Halona trailing a few steps behind. Neither looked back as they let themselves in and closed the door behind them.

Well, the upside was that Alex didn't have to figure out how he was supposed to keep his hands to himself if he was invited inside tonight.

* * *

"Theo, honey?" Halona called after her son as he headed directly down the hall toward his bedroom. "Theo? Come back here, please." Halona sucked in a breath and waited to hear the sound of Theo's feet shuffling back toward her.

When he did, she sat on the couch and gestured for him

to sit beside her. "I guess you heard what Chief Baker told me," she said.

Theo nodded as he sat beside her but he didn't look at her. Instead, he reached for his notebook and his pencil.

Halona exhaled softly.

He said he wouldn't tell. He lied to me!

"Why wouldn't you want Alex to tell me? I just wish you had talked to me about what you saw," she said, keeping her voice soft and loving. "I'm not mad."

Tears burned in her eyes.

Theo looked up at her, and for a moment, she thought she saw his lips twitch and prepare to say something. Then he pinched the pencil between his fingers and started writing again.

I don't want to talk to you or Alex or anyone else.

Dr. Charwood had told Halona that she thought Theo was refusing to talk because he felt out of control with the loss of his father. Not talking gave him some of his control back. It made sense. What didn't make sense was why Theo had communicated with Alex instead of her. Halona supposed that was progress, and now that Theo was upset with Alex that momentum might be lost.

"One day, when you're ready, we can discuss any questions you have, okay?"

Theo looked at her again and then nodded. Then he set his notebook and pencil down on the coffee table, stood, and headed to his bedroom.

"I'll be down there in a minute to tuck you in," she called after him. She took a moment and sat with her thoughts. Some small part of her wished that Alex hadn't told her the truth tonight. Then Theo would still be a happy boy right now. And *she* would be happy. And maybe Alex would've come inside for a nightcap.

* * *

"What's wrong with you?" Brenna asked as Halona plopped down in the seat in front of her the next morning.

Halona sighed. "Long story," she said, pulling her cup of coffee to her.

"Uh-oh. Sounds like trouble in romance land."

Despite herself, Halona smiled. "Let's talk about you for a change. Still stalking your neighbor at his mailbox?"

Brenna rolled her eyes. "Luke Marini doesn't know I exist, which is just fine. I need a man nearly as bad as I need another bridezilla in my shop for her catering needs."

Halona laughed. "Bridezillas pay the bills so you actually do need those."

"Right. Exactly. And while dating might be fun, I'm swamped with business at A Taste of Heaven these days. Eve is still finishing up at the fire academy so we're shorthanded."

"You're still thinking she'll come back and work for the catering business when she's done?" Halona asked.

"More like hoping. Working at the fire department is dangerous. Why wouldn't she want to work with me?"

Halona sipped her coffee. "If she worked at the fire

department though, you'd have another reason to talk to your firefighter neighbor." She waggled her eyebrows and Brenna laughed. They talked for a few more minutes and then Brenna stood. "I have an appointment first thing this morning. We'll continue talking about your love life and my lacking one next week."

"Theo will be on Christmas break. I won't be coming in every morning for a while."

Brenna frowned. "Bah humbug. I've been looking forward to these daily coffees."

"Me too. When school starts back, we'll return to our routine."

Brenna nodded. "I'll see you at Mitch and Kaitlyn's wedding after Christmas."

"Yes, you will. Maybe you can invite Luke as your plus one," Halona teased.

Brenna tsked. "You have your own love life to worry about." She waved as she headed for the door.

Halona grabbed her coffee and headed in that direction as well.

What love life?

As if the world were her own personal Siri, she stepped out of the café and saw Alex standing in front of her shop's door. Oh right, *that* love life.

* * *

Alex didn't fancy himself a guy who was scared of much but he was a little afraid that Halona wasn't going to forgive him for keeping a secret about her son.

"What are you doing in front of my store?" she asked.

At least her tone of voice wasn't as hard as it'd been last night.

"You're the only flower shop in town, and I need a bouquet."

She stepped past him and unlocked her store door. Then she gestured for him to come inside. He watched as she turned the sign in the window from CLOSED to OPEN. "What kind do you need?" she asked, not bothering to make niceties.

"Something bright and cheerful. Like the last bouquet you made me."

"For Mary Beth?" She nodded. "That should be easy enough." She put her things down and got to work.

"About last night," Alex began.

"We really don't need to discuss it, Alex."

"We do. I feel really bad about everything. About not telling you, and then telling you and Theo overhearing. How was he this morning?"

Halona looked up from the flowers that she was collecting from the freezer. "I tried to get him to talk to me last night, and he wouldn't. He used his notebook to tell me that he didn't want to talk to me or you or anyone else."

Alex brought his right hand to his forehead and massaged the tension there. "I really screwed up. I don't have any business being someone's mentor."

"I wouldn't say that," Halona said hesitantly. She sighed and shook her head. "I screw up all the time. Kids are pretty forgiving. Next time you see him, he'll probably be over it."

"Somehow, I doubt that," Alex said, but Halona seemed to have softened with his groveling. "What about women? Are they forgiving too?"

She narrowed her eyes. "It depends on the woman."

Alex swallowed.

"But this one," she added, "is." A smile lifted her mouth as she shook her head and looked away. "I really want to stay mad at you but I know your heart was in the right place. You were honoring my son, loving him, and I can't blame you for that."

He hadn't thought it was possible to find her even more attractive than he already did, but apparently, it was. "Thank you. I tossed and turned all night hoping you wouldn't hate me forever."

"I never hated you, Alex."

"And hoping that the invitation to spend Christmas at your family's house was still open," he said.

Her mouth popped open.

"Unless you've changed your mind." He approached the counter where she was tying a ribbon around the flower arrangement.

She expertly secured the ribbon perfectly around the bundle that she'd collected. "No, of course not. The offer stands," she said, looking up.

"Do you think Theo will be okay with that?" Alex asked.

The corner of Halona's mouth quirked in the smallest of smiles. "Bribery is never the answer, but I admit that when Theo is really mad at me, I go see Greenlee Murphy at the toy store around the corner and buy him a LEGO set. The tactic won't work forever, and I'm sure Dr. Charwood would disapprove, but..." She shrugged.

Alex nodded. "A pro tip for kids. Thank you."

"You're welcome." She handed the bouquet of flowers to Alex across the counter. "Here you go. Just like the last bouquet."

"Perfect." He took it and handed Halona his debit card. She swiped it and handed it back to him. After putting his card in his wallet, he extended the flower arrangement back out to her.

"What are you doing?" she asked, pulling her brows together tightly. "They aren't what you wanted?"

"Oh, they are. I wanted them for you." He continued to hold the arrangement out. "I wasn't sure if it was good or bad etiquette to get flowers for a woman who owns her own flower shop. I guess it's only bad if you buy them from a competing flower shop."

Halona's lips parted as she took the arrangement. "No one has ever bought me flowers before."

"I guess because you have all the flowers you could ever want," Alex said. "Maybe it wasn't the smoothest idea."

A smile bloomed on her face prettier than any wildflower in the bunch. "No, they're perfect. I love them."

"Good...so I'll, uh, let you work. And I'll go to work too," he said, turning to walk away.

"Alex?"

"Yeah?" He turned back to look at her, suddenly a little breathless, like he'd been jogging for several miles. He was so relieved that she'd forgiven him. The thought of losing her had plagued him last night. This thing between them couldn't last forever though, could it?

"Theo has an appointment with Dr. Charwood after school today," Halona said, "but after that, we'll be home. I'm cooking spaghetti and meatballs. It's easy to make and one of Theo's favorite meals. He'll be in a good mood...if you want to come by."

Alex nodded. "Maybe I'll go see Greenlee Murphy and get a LEGO set before coming over. I can help Theo build it."

"Sounds perfect," Halona said.

Sounded pretty perfect to him as well. In fact, he couldn't think of a better way to spend a Friday night or two people he'd rather spend it with. "See you tonight."

The cool air hit his face as he stepped outside. Then his gut sounded off the alarm that he was being watched. On instinct, he looked across the street and met Tony Anderson's gaze. At that same moment, Alex's cell phone buzzed with an incoming text in his pocket. He pulled it out and looked at the screen.

The message was from Tammy.

Tony Anderson's lawyer just came in here with a court order. He's out.

Judging by the look he'd just gotten, Alex was pretty sure that Tony had already been home and figured out that his wife and her belongings were gone. And he blamed Alex.

CHAPTER TWENTY

Alex headed into the police station and straight to Tammy's desk.

She barely batted an eye as she looked up from the breakfast sandwich that she'd probably made herself. "There was nothing I could do to stop it," she said between bites.

"I know it's not your fault. I'm just glad that Sharlene is safe now."

"You sure about that, Chief? What makes you think she won't drop the charges? Or that Tony won't figure out where she is?"

"She won't, and he won't. I plan to keep a close eye on him."

"Tony isn't going to let this drop, you know. He was still muttering about you taking his dog when he walked out of here. Now you've taken his wife," she pointed out.

"Well, just give me a little time, and I'll take his

freedom too," Alex promised. "This time for good." He turned and walked toward his office.

"You got a breakfast sandwich waiting for you on your desk, Chief!" Tammy called down the hall. "Made it myself with love."

Despite his mounting frustration, he smiled. "What would I do without you, Tam?"

* * *

It was right around this time of day when Halona started to get excited about seeing Theo. Today had been the last day of school before winter break so hopefully Theo would be sugared up, excited about the upcoming holidays, and last night's ordeal would be a faint memory. That's what she wished, and it *was* the season of hope, after all.

The bell above her shop door rang, and Halona hurried out from the back room, expecting to see her mom and Theo. Instead, Tony Anderson stood there.

"Hello, Halona," he said, as he headed up to the counter.

She considered asking him to leave but it was easier to give him what he wanted than to get on his bad side. Everyone in town knew he had one. "Can I help you?" she asked, not bothering to smile.

"Yeah. I need flowers. That's what men give to women, right?"

"For what occasion?" she asked.

Tony lifted a nonchalant shoulder, the corners of his mouth curling slightly. "To say I love you. I'm sorry. I want to rock your world, baby. All of the above."

Halona wanted to throw up. What was Tony even doing out of jail? "Sure. I'll get you an arrangement.

You can come back for it in about ten to fifteen minutes."

Tony shook his head. "I think I'll just hang around right here. I saw Chief Baker coming out of your store this morning. You two friendly now?"

"We're friends, yes." Halona's heart rate picked up. Was Tony here for more than just flowers for his wife? Was he trying to get information about Alex?

"He took my dog, you know? You can't just go around taking other men's dogs. When I got home, my wife was missing too. You know anything about that?"

Halona glared at her customer. She held her tongue, holding back from telling him all the thoughts running through her mind right now.

As if reading her mind, Tony snickered. "I'm not too worried. She always comes back. And these flowers you're gonna prepare for her will make her see how wrong she was to listen to your boyfriend."

Ignoring him, Halona headed to the freezer. She picked a variety of lovely wildflowers, hoping Tony was wrong. Hoping Sharlene would never even see this arrangement.

"You think he was in the right, don't you? Why do you think your boyfriend was justified in stealing my dog and wife?" Tony asked.

Unable to help herself, Halona whipped around. "He didn't steal them. He rescued them both from you."

Tony's eyes narrowed. "Your boyfriend's a thief, and he's going to pay."

"Chief Baker isn't my boyfriend," she clarified, her voice shaking out of both anger and a little bit of fear.

"Not what I heard."

She grabbed the nearest ribbon, wrapped them around

the flowers, and shoved them toward Tony. "Free of charge. Just get out of my shop."

"Thanks." Tony tipped his ball cap at her and then turned around, passing Lula and Theo as they entered the store.

Lula looked at Halona. "Everything all right?"

"Yeah. I think so," Halona said, forcing a smile for Theo's benefit. "Good day at school?" she asked, desperately trying to normalize her breathing.

He nodded, looking a little more like himself this afternoon. At least that was positive.

"What was Tony doing here in your store?" Lula asked.

"The same thing everyone who comes in here is doing. He was buying flowers."

Lula made a sour face. "I don't like you in here alone with that man."

"Trust me. I got rid of him as fast as I could," Halona said. "Thanks for picking Theo up from school. And for closing up tonight."

"Of course. And you know I love to watch the store for you. It's so peaceful in here. Just like being in a garden."

Halona turned to Theo. "Grab a snack from the fridge. You can eat it on the way to your appointment. We don't want to be late."

He hurried into the back room.

"You need to tell Alex that Tony was here," Lula said quietly.

"Mom, Tony wasn't breaking the law by walking into my store." Although she *had* felt threatened just by his presence. "Alex has enough to worry about right now."

Your boyfriend's a thief, and he's going to pay.

Maybe she *did* need to tell Alex.

* * *

Halona looked at her watch. Theo had been in with Dr. Charwood for over an hour. Did he tell her about what he'd seen his father do and say too? Maybe he'd also sworn her to secrecy.

The door opened, and Theo ran out, all smiles as usual after he left one of these sessions.

"Looks like you enjoyed yourself," Halona said.

Theo nodded and then sat on one of the waiting room chairs and watched the TV mounted to the wall while Halona talked to Dr. Charwood.

"Did he, um, open up to you?" Halona asked. "About anything that might be bothering him from the past?"

Dr. Charwood raised her eyebrows. "No. Has he discussed things with you?"

Halona shook her head. "With his Mentor Match."

"Chief Baker? He seems to like him. He writes about him a lot in his notebook."

Halona glanced over to make sure Theo wasn't listening before continuing. "Well, he's a little upset with Chief Baker right now for telling me something they discussed. If he'll talk to someone else, why won't he talk to me?"

Dr. Charwood thought for a moment. "Sometimes, the more you want a kid to do something, the less inclined they are to do it. If you put too much focus on what you want, they dig their heels in harder."

Halona nodded. "I know exactly what you mean."

"So why don't we just back off? He'll communicate with us when he's ready."

"I guess that makes sense," Halona said, although it wasn't what she wanted to hear. She wanted the magic fix. She wanted to look into her son's eyes and hear his voice again, something she'd once taken for granted.

"Just relax and enjoy your holiday together. As you know, the office is closed until after the New Year, but you can call my cell phone for emergencies, of course."

"I doubt that'll be necessary. Enjoy your Christmas, Dr. Charwood," Halona said.

Dr. Charwood smiled warmly and then looked over at Theo and waved. "Bye, Theo. We'll see you next year."

Halona and Theo stepped outside. Halona could've sworn the temperature had dropped another ten degrees in the hour since they'd arrived. She hurried to open the back passenger door for Theo and then got behind the steering wheel. "Buckled up?" she asked him over her shoulder.

He gave her a thumbs-up from the back seat. No words. But that was okay. Dr. Charwood was right. She was just going to relax and stop worrying about him. Or, at least, she was going to try.

* * *

It felt good to leave the station on a Friday night with somewhere to go.

He'd been looking forward to dinner with Halona and Theo since he'd left Halona's shop this morning. But first, he needed to stop by the toy store for a little mom-approved bribe to win back Theo's smile.

It didn't feel right but he couldn't stand the idea of Theo being upset with him any longer.

"Good evening, Chief Baker," Greenlee Murphy said quietly as he walked into the little store just around the corner from Main Street. "I haven't seen you here in quite a while."

Greenlee was a petite woman with dark hair and a fleeting smile. She'd taken over the toy store after her aunt and uncle retired. She slipped under his radar in town for the most part. Greenlee was quiet, reserved, and she mostly kept to herself.

"Are you looking for a Christmas present?" she asked.

"Not exactly. More of an... 'I'm sorry' present."

"Ah." She nodded knowingly. "Do you know what you want?"

"A LEGO set."

Greenlee pointed at the far wall. "Right over there. The options have been picked over because of the holidays but there are still a few. The *Star Wars* ones are a hit every year."

"Thanks." Alex headed in that direction. He chose a *Star Wars* set at her suggestion and walked right back to the counter.

"That was easy enough." She offered another quick smile that didn't quite reach her eyes. He swiped his card in her card reader, and she slid the bag with his purchase toward him. "I bet it's been busy in here," he said.

"The week before Christmas always is."

"Do you have big holiday plans?" he asked, just trying to get to know one of his citizens a little better. Something he should've done before. Something he'd be sure to do from now on.

"Christmas Eve will be my first day off in weeks. I plan to stay home in my pajamas all day."

Alex looked at her more closely than he ever had. He recognized the loneliness behind her smile, even though he'd left his behind. "Well, enjoy it. If you get tired of your pj's, I hear there's a gathering at the community center on Christmas Eve."

Greenlee's eyes brightened a touch. "Good to know."

"Merry Christmas and happy New Year," he said, taking hold of his bag.

"You too, Chief Baker."

Bribe in hand, Alex headed out of the store, got into his SUV, and took the long way home to get ready for dinner. He wanted to drive by Tony's house just to check on things. Not that he had X-ray vision or would be able to see what was going on behind closed doors. If he had to guess, Tony was having himself an old-fashioned temper tantrum right about now.

He turned onto Pine Cone Lane and followed the road around the bend, slowing near the cul-de-sac. Tony's white pickup truck was in the driveway. Home when he should've been behind bars.

The blinds were closed. No sign of life inside. There wasn't even a tree flashing lights from the window.

Alex rounded the circle to head back out when the blurry image of the white pickup truck in his peripheral vision got his attention. Alex tapped the brakes and craned his neck to look at it, feeling a memory flash across his mind.

The truck that ran him off the road had been going so fast, and he'd only seen it for a split second. He really couldn't even recall any details about it. Not even the color.

Was it Tony's truck? Had Tony been the one to run him off the road and into the ditch?

No, Tony was a lot of things but he wasn't a killer. His uncle Steve, on the other hand, drove a similar truck. He also gave Alex a bad feeling.

Alex pressed the gas as he headed toward Cedar Trail. A bad feeling wasn't evidence though, and without ample proof, whoever was behind the wheel of that truck the other day would remain free to come after him again.

CHAPTER TWENTY-ONE

A little flurry of excitement fell over Halona as the doorbell rang that night. She hadn't told Theo that Alex was coming for dinner. She hoped it would be a pleasant surprise.

Theo gave her a questioning look as she passed from the kitchen to the front door.

She opened it to a blast of freezing-cold air and Alex, who warmed her from her toes all the way up. "You made it."

Officer Chew hurried past them toward Theo.

"Better not leave this door open for too long. Your living room will turn to ice," Alex said, stepping inside.

Halona closed and locked the door. "Just watched Serena Gibbs on the news. The forecast is predicting five to six inches of snow overnight."

"I heard." Alex removed his jacket and hung it on the coatrack near the door. "I hope I don't get snowed in while I'm here," he said, offering a wink.

That wouldn't be such a bad thing. In fact, she wouldn't mind one bit.

"I brought a little something for Theo," he said then.

Theo lifted his head at the mention. His usual greeting for Alex was to spring off the couch and give him a giant hug. Not tonight. Tonight, Theo didn't even have a smile to spare.

Alex tossed Halona a worried look. She patted his arm to reassure him but it only worked to fuel her attraction.

"You two look at what's in the bag. I'll finish dinner," she said, pulling her hand away.

"Sounds good." Alex headed over and sat down beside Theo while she went to check the food on the stove. She hoped they made up because she needed to discuss an urgent issue with Alex once Theo was out of earshot. She knew Alex could take care of himself but he needed to know about Tony's threat.

She drained the noodles and then poured the marinara sauce into the pot. It wasn't the most extravagant meal, and Lula would probably have a fit if she knew this was what Halona was preparing with Alex as their guest. Halona was pulling out all the stops for Theo tonight though.

She set the food on the dinner table, removed her apron, and then walked back into the living room. "Everything okay in here?"

Alex looked back with a wobbly smile. "I think so. I told Theo I'm sorry, and he took my peace offering. I think that means we're good, right?" He looked at Theo, who smiled at him.

"I think so," Halona agreed. "Dinner's ready. Go wash your hands, guys," she ordered. "And I have something very special for you, Officer Chew." She led the dog to a place mat on the floor where she'd set up a bowl of water, food, and a chew toy.

Alex stepped past her to wash his hands in the kitchen sink while Theo headed to the bathroom sink down the hall. "Spoiling the dog, huh? Maybe you've changed your mind about adopting him."

"Nope. I have my hands full right now," Halona said, "and I can't adopt a dog that's not available. Chew has a new owner whether the new owner wants to admit it or not."

Alex chuckled. "I'm not in the mood for an argument tonight. I'd probably lose after the day I had."

Halona angled herself and watched him dry his hands on the dishtowel. "Bad day?"

"Disappointing day. Tony is out of jail."

"I know," she said.

Alex's eyes narrowed.

"He came in my shop." She glanced to the hallway to make sure that Theo hadn't returned yet.

"What was he doing in your shop?"

Halona shook her head, causing a loose strand of hair to fall in her face. "Getting flowers to make up with Sharlene."

Alex's face soured. "Well, I hate to break it to him but Sharlene's not coming back to him this time. I've taken care of that."

"I know...but Alex, he said he was going to make you pay. I'm worried that it wasn't just an empty threat." Without thinking, she stepped closer to him, looking up into his eyes. "I don't want you to get hurt." She looked at his injured arm, still in its brace. "Again."

Alex reached out for her, brushing the loose hair behind her ear. "Don't worry about me."

"Can't help it," she whispered. "I kind of like having you around."

"Good, because I'm not going anywhere."

His hand was still curled at her jawline as he stood close. Halona almost forgot that they weren't alone. Then Officer Chew left his dog bowl to greet Theo, who was standing in the entryway and watching them.

Halona stepped back. "Did you wash your hands?" she asked.

Theo nodded, glancing between her and Alex.

She was mentally preparing her excuse for why she and his mentor were standing so close. Then Theo grinned wide, turned, and went to sit at the dinner table.

Halona looked at Alex. "I guess he approves."

"That's really good because I just told him on the couch that I didn't like hiding things. And I meant it."

Halona leaned in closer. "Me either."

"There's something else I've been hiding from you, Halona," Alex said then.

Her breath froze inside her. "What?"

"I've been hiding the fact that I like you quite a lot. I've liked you for a long time."

"Oh." She exhaled softly. "I guess I should confess, then, that I like you too. More than a little."

The corner of his mouth twitched. She wished she could kiss him right now but that was maybe a little too much for Theo to see.

Alex reached for her hand with his good one and started walking. "We don't want our dinner to get cold. We should eat."

"We should," she agreed, following him. Then they sat and ate their meal together.

* * *

Theo fell asleep before the Grinch even stole Christmas on the TV screen.

Alex looked over at Halona as they watched the movie, meeting her gaze and hoping she could read his mind as easily as she seemed to read her son's.

"I'll carry him to bed," she said.

"No, I got him."

Halona frowned. "You have one arm in a brace, Alex."

He glanced down. "Right. I just want to help."

"Are you always so heroic?" she asked with a small smile.

His intentions in wanting to help her get Theo into bed weren't noble right now. No, he wanted to get Halona alone.

Halona stood and scooped Theo up and then carried him down the hallway with Officer Chew following at her heels. A few minutes later, she reappeared. "Can I get you anything? Tea? Wine? Beer?"

"You," he said.

She walked around the couch and sat down beside him. "We probably shouldn't, you know. Theo is down the hall."

That hadn't stopped them the first time. But he understood, and he didn't mind.

"I don't need you to take me to your bed. There are a lot of other things that seem safe to do with him down the hall," Alex suggested.

She gave him a curious look. "Yeah? Like what?"

"Like this." He leaned over and brushed his mouth to hers, slowly, savoring the taste of her lips.

She sighed softly against him, making him wish he

had a full pass tonight. Who knew when he'd be able to get her alone? All he knew was that he would, and that was deeply satisfying.

"Why do you make me want you so much?" he asked.

"So it's my fault?" she asked, tilting her head to one side.

"Completely. I've worked hard all these years not to want you. It hasn't been easy, you know."

She scooted in closer to him. Not close enough in his opinion. "Then why didn't you just give in?"

"When I was a teenager, it was because you were my best friend's sister."

"You barely noticed me back then."

"Oh, I noticed. Believe me. It's not easy for a teen boy to ignore his attraction to the prettiest girl in his world. It was torture. I insisted that Tuck come to my house instead of me going to yours for a long time."

Halona laughed. "Liar."

"It's true." He trailed his kisses from her mouth to her neck as he spoke. She tipped her head back to give him access, which only worked to drive him even crazier.

"I had a little crush on you too, you know," she said on a sigh.

"Yeah?"

"Mm-hmm."

"Just a little one?" he asked, teasing her.

"Maybe a big one. Heart racing, palms sweating, dry throat."

"I know those symptoms." He pulled away and looked at her. "I've had a lot of them lately. When can I get you alone again? Really alone?"

She nibbled on her lower lip. "Well, Mom has been asking if Theo can come spend the night with her. She wants to make Christmas candy, and it's only a couple of days away. I'll set it up."

"Great." It took every ounce of strength he had to pull himself away from her. "Until then, I better get out of here before I lose all willpower."

She nodded. "Or before I do."

Alex swallowed, a serious note tempering all the positive emotions he felt when he was with Halona. "Tomorrow is the anniversary of Dad's death."

She frowned. "I know you miss him."

"Especially this time of year. I just want to do right by him and find the person who took his life."

"You will." She placed her hand on his knee. "I believe in you."

And he believed in himself a little more when she looked at him that way.

"Are you doing anything to honor him tomorrow?" she asked.

"I'll go to his grave. Then I'll spend the rest of the day at the station. Traditionally on the anniversary of his death, I work his case. I've already spoken to the driver of the last car my dad pulled over and interviewed Steve Anderson one more time. I've reviewed every piece of evidence, which never was much. It's nothing but dead ends."

"I wish I could help."

"Me too." He leaned in and kissed her mouth. "If you don't hear from me tomorrow, don't worry, okay? I just need space."

She nodded. "I'll see if Mom can take Theo the day after."

"Sounds good," he said, forcing himself to stand. "I'll look forward to it." Right after he was done dreading tomorrow.

* * *

The next day, Alex awoke in his bed to the sound of Officer Chew barking at the door. It took a moment for him to figure out the time and day. Saturday. The anniversary of his dad's death.

Woof.

Alex massaged his forehead. This was the hardest day of the year. Maybe just this once, he should sleep it away.

Woof. Woof.

"All right, all right." He sat up and swung his legs off the side of the bed. He reached for a T-shirt and pulled it over his head and then quickly pulled on a pair of jeans. He shuffled toward the front of the house where Officer Chew was going nuts at the door. Alex immediately grew alert when he saw the puppy's stance.

Chew had never woken him by barking before.

"Someone out there?" Alex asked. "It's okay." He put a hand on Chew's head, but Chew didn't relax.

Yeah, someone was outside, and Chew was worked up about it.

Alex reached for his keys and unlocked the desk drawer where he kept his gun. He put the weapon in the back waistband of his jeans just in case and looked through the door's peephole. He didn't see anyone out there but he or she could be hiding.

Or, after all these years of being a cop, he could've finally gone off the deep end with his paranoia.

He opened the door and looked in each direction, seeing nothing but a fresh coat of new snow that had fallen on the ground overnight. And fresh tracks as well.

Then he looked down at his feet where there was a

package waiting for him. Officer Chew gave it a few sniffs before Alex picked it up. No return address.

Woof!

"Who was here, Officer Chew?" he asked, turning to go back inside. He suspected that, whoever it was, Chew knew the person.

* * *

Halona was having the best dream. She was on the edge of waking but she didn't want to let her fantasy go. She was with Alex, walking hand in hand through Evergreen Park, several inches of frozen snow crunching beneath their feet. The air was cold and crisp, just right for hot chocolate—later. In her dream, she and Alex were on a mission to find somewhere private. And when they did, she couldn't wait to see what happened.

She wanted to kiss him without interruption.

Where is Theo?

Halona pulled away and blinked at Alex, trying to remember where her son had gone. She tried to make words but none came out.

"Halona? Everything okay?" The serenity of the dream was broken and quickly turning into a nightmare.

She yanked her hand away from Alex's and spun to scan her surroundings. *Where is he?* There was a set of small footsteps veering off onto another path. Halona took off running in that direction.

"Halona?"

She turned to look at Alex, struggling with her desire to run back into his arms. Her son was missing though; she had to go. Theo was her first priority.

"Theo!" she called out, finally finding her voice. "Theo, where are you?"

She broke through a clearing and was suddenly standing in Sweetwater Cemetery. There, standing in front of Ted's grave, was her son. She didn't move, didn't speak.

THEODORE "TED" MICHAEL BYRD
BELOVED SON AND FATHER

A half dozen bouquets of flowers lay scattered on the grave. She hadn't put them there. Who did?

Theo turned to look at her, snowflakes melting on his ruddy cheeks. Or were those tears?

She stepped forward to wipe them away and then whirled to the sound of Alex coming up behind her.

"Come back," Alex said.

She turned back to her son.

"Mommy?"

His voice!

"Mommy!...Mommy!"

Halona's eyes popped open, ripping her from her sleep as Theo's little voice rang out again. It was real.

"Mommy!"

"Theo?" Halona jumped out of bed and hurried across the hall to his bedroom in time to see his little body squirm and jerk under the covers.

"Mommy!"

"It's okay, sweetheart." She moved to sit on the edge of the bed and ran her hand across his forehead, some part of her wondering if Theo had gone to the same place in his dream that she'd just left. Was he standing there at Ted's grave too? In her dream, she'd been torn between him and Alex. Was Theo just as torn between staying with his father and coming back to her?

"What's going on in your little head?" she whispered, resisting the urge to wake him up. That was Dr. Charwood's advice too. If his subconscious was searching for answers, she wanted him to find them. Maybe Halona's subconscious had been doing the same this morning.

Theo rolled onto his side, his breathing slowed, and his face returned to one of a peacefully resting child. Was he torn between her and his father? After the divorce, she'd made sure Theo still got to see Ted. Supervised, of course, after Ted's explosive outburst with her. She'd had to beg Ted to come visit Theo that last year because he was so afraid of hurting his son. It had become harder and harder for him to control his anger. The slightest disappointment sent him into a rage.

Alex hadn't bought any of her excuses back then. He'd noticed the bruises wrapped around her wrist when he'd walked into her shop two years ago, and she hadn't been able to get rid of him. He was like a dog on a scent, determined to protect her. She'd insisted she didn't need protecting from her own husband but she had. She knew that now.

Ted's brain injury had changed everything about him—except his heart. He was still a good man deep down. That's why she'd been determined to help him. She'd made a vow to stick with him through sickness and health, and she took those vows seriously.

Evidently, Theo had seen and heard more than she knew. But how much?

His eyes opened, and he peered up at her.

"Hey. You okay?" she asked.

Theo blinked groggily.

"It's the first day of your Christmas break from school. I can get Elisi Lula to watch the flower shop if you want to do something together. I think there's even snow outside."

Theo's eyes widened as he nodded. He sat up in bed and wrapped his arms around her, giving her a huge hug. Exactly what she needed.

"Okay, then. I'll get you breakfast and call your grandmother." Lula loved to watch the flower shop so it shouldn't be a problem. Maybe she and Theo would finish up Christmas shopping and head over to Evergreen Park just like in her dream.

Or maybe they'd make a long overdue trip to Sweetwater Cemetery. She'd wondered if doing so would make Theo dwell on the loss of his father but maybe he needed to visit Ted's grave. Even as an adult, she still had difficulty processing all her emotions. How much harder was it for a seven-year-old boy?

"And tonight, we can make snow cream," she told Theo as she stood and led him down the hall toward the kitchen. He skipped ahead of her happily. They wouldn't be inviting Alex over for that though. He had his own ghosts to deal with today on the anniversary of his father's death.

CHAPTER TWENTY-TWO

Alex had been staring at the open file of his dad's cold case for over an hour. There was nothing new inside; he knew that. He glanced over at the package on his desk that had been left on his doorstep this morning. His gaze slid to Officer Chew on the floor beside him.

"Wish you could talk," he said. "Who was at my door this morning? Did you know him?"

Chew's eyes rolled upward.

"Talking to yourself?" Mitch asked as he stepped through the door.

Alex leaned back in his chair and shook his head. "To my partner in justice."

"Better than a partner in crime."

Alex looked up. "Speaking of which, Tony visited Halona at her shop yesterday. She said Tony made a blanket threat toward me."

Mitch raised a brow. "That's worth hauling him back

down here, don't you think? I mean, someone ran you off the road. Now Tony's making threats."

"Do you think it's him?" Alex asked.

"Not especially. If it were Tony, he would've bragged about it all over town by now. That's his way."

"What about his visit to Halona's flower shop? Do you think she's in danger with that kind of thinking?"

Mitch narrowed his eyes. "I don't want to say yes to that question but I can't say no either."

Yeah, Alex felt the same way. Tony was a loose cannon. He was quick-tempered, rash, and somehow, he got away with his crimes. At least so far.

Alex tipped his head at the package on his desk.

"What's that?" Mitch asked, stepping over and taking a better look. "No return address."

"It was dropped off on my doorstep this morning. Officer Chew was going crazy, but by the time I opened the door, whoever was there had already gone."

Mitch's brow furrowed. "You think there's something dangerous in there?"

"No way to know without opening it."

They both studied the package for a few moments.

"I tested for prints. There weren't any on the outside," Alex added.

"Which is suspicious in and of itself."

"I agree."

"Want me to do the honors?" Mitch asked.

Alex frowned. "Do you seriously think I would let you open a potentially dangerous package when it's mine to open?"

"You're the chief. The town needs you."

"And Kaitlyn needs you." Alex pulled the package closer to him and then grabbed a pair of scissors from his drawer. He slid the edge of the blade down where the tape secured the flaps closed and then sucked in a huge breath.

This day was already ominous as it was. A mysterious package wasn't helping.

Officer Chew stood on alert beside his chair.

"Might want to take a few steps back," Alex advised Mitch, who took a few steps forward instead. Figured.

Alex pulled open the flaps and looked inside. It wasn't a bomb. Not a weapon. Instead, he lifted out a man's shoe.

"A shoe?" Mitch said. "What the heck is that supposed to mean? Whose shoe is that?"

Alex knew exactly who the shoe belonged to. It was an important detail in his dad's hit-and-run case. His father had been found lying in the snow. Both shoes had been knocked off in the impact but the search of the surrounding area had yielded only one. The other shoe was nowhere to be found. That had always left Alex a little unsettled.

Had the person who'd hit his dad stopped and taken the shoe? There'd been tracks all around his father's body but numerous people were on the scene trying to revive his dad by the time the cops arrived. There'd been snow, mud, and blood everywhere. His dad had been rushed to the hospital, and a few hours later, he was dead. "It's my dad's," he said, looking up at Mitch.

"You sure?"

"Pretty sure, yeah."

"Well, that's great," Mitch said.

"Why is that?"

"Because it's a clue on a cold case. And you never know which clue is going to be the one to crack it."

* * *

Sweetwater Cemetery was covered in white snow, mostly untouched, as Halona and Theo made their way down the barely visible path toward the middle section where Ted was buried. His life was cut way too short, their marriage too, and Theo's father was taken from him far too soon.

She should've taken Theo here before now. She didn't like cemeteries, never had, but today, looking out on this one as they walked, it felt peaceful.

She glanced down at Theo, who was holding a bouquet of flowers that they'd stopped at Little Shop of Flowers to prepare before heading here. His expression was tight, pensive. Eyes wide, skin pale. Was he scared or just cold?

"Nothing to be afraid of," she told him. "We're going to visit your dad's grave. People leave flowers, talk to the headstones, or just stand quietly and offer up a silent prayer. You can do whatever you feel like, okay?"

Theo nodded, his dark eyes lifting to meet hers. She gave his little hand a squeeze and continued walking. She stopped in front of Theodore Michael Byrd's headstone. Beloved son and father.

"You can set the flowers down," Halona prompted.

Theo stepped up and laid the arrangement against the granite headstone and then returned to stand next to her. They stood there quietly. After a moment, Halona squeezed his hand and let go.

"I'm going to go sit on that bench over there so you can have some time alone with your dad. Okay?"

Theo's eyes widened, and she thought he was going to refuse, but then he nodded.

Maybe he wanted to talk to him but didn't want to

use his voice in front of her. That was okay. Whatever he needed was fine.

Halona sat on the bench and stared out at the new snow, sparkling against the high sun. It was supposed to snow even more before Christmas. The song "White Christmas" floated through her mind along with a memory of Ted before his brain injuries had become obvious.

He'd sung the song against her cheek as they'd stood against each other on a frozen Silver Lake. He'd just helped her up after she'd taken a fall but he hadn't let go. Instead, he'd pulled her close, and they'd slow danced awkwardly in ice skates. People passed by, leaving them alone in their own little world. That was the moment she knew she was going to marry Ted Byrd. There'd been no doubt in her mind. She wasn't dreaming of a white Christmas; she was dreaming of a lifetime of love and happiness, family and friends, laughter and joy.

But the life she'd thought they'd have had been snatched from her reach. The Ted she'd married had been a selfless man. He would've moved heaven and earth just to make her smile. If he could see her right now, she had no doubt that he'd be happy about her taking this second chance at a happy ending with Alex.

She blinked past her tears as Theo turned and headed toward her. "Ready?" she asked.

He nodded.

"Good." She stood up from the bench and they started back down the path toward her car. She noticed another set of footprints in the snow that hadn't been there before. She hadn't seen anyone here with them.

Halona looked around, scanning her surroundings and feeling more spooked than peaceful suddenly. Her gaze tracked the new footsteps to another bench nearby where a man was sitting and watching her and Theo.

Halona's breath froze as chill bumps traveled up her body, and not because of the biting cold.

Tony Anderson waved as she met his gaze. Had he followed them here?

Halona started walking a little faster, nearly dragging Theo in her wake. "It's freezing out here," she said. "Let's hurry and get to the car."

Halona's hands shook as she unlocked her car doors, got in, and reached for her phone in the middle console. She hesitated just for a moment and then dialed Alex's number.

"Hello?" he answered.

"Hi. I wish I didn't have to bother you." Alex had so many things to deal with today other than this. "I just didn't know what else to do or who else to call."

"It's okay. Something wrong?" he asked.

"I'm not sure," she said, putting the car in drive. She didn't want to stick around and wait for Tony to approach her. "I'm leaving Sweetwater Cemetery with Theo. I could just be paranoid but Tony was here. I think he's following us."

* * *

Alex grabbed his keys and coat and headed out the door before Halona had even finished explaining what was going on.

"Do you see Tony now?"

"No. I don't think so. There are no other cars in the rearview. The roads are slick," she added.

"Be careful."

"Should I go home? Maybe I'm just...I don't know. He was in my shop yesterday. Is it just a coincidence?"

Alex sighed heavily. "Could be, but I'm guessing that's not the case. I'll meet you at your house," Alex said. "You and Theo can pack some overnight bags. You shouldn't stay alone right now."

"What?" Halona asked in a shrill voice.

"It's just a precaution," he told her calmly. Alex pulled out of the station's parking lot and headed toward Cedar Trail. He was tempted to lay on the gas but the roads were as slick as Halona had said.

"Where will we go?" she asked.

"I'll call Mitch and see if there are any availabilities at the Sweetwater Bed and Breakfast."

"Oh, I don't think that's necessary. If we need to go somewhere, we can go to my parents' place. Or to Tuck and Josie's."

Alex considered her suggestions. "The inn is equipped with alarms, and Mitch lives there. Having a cop under the same roof will deter Tony."

"I don't think he'll do anything. He's just trying to scare us," Halona said.

"Maybe, but I'm not taking any chances. This is all my fault."

"No, it's not," she argued. "It's Tony's. You're the good guy, Alex."

So why did he feel like a criminal right now for needing to move Halona and Theo out of their home just before Christmas? They didn't deserve that. After all they'd been through, they deserved for this to be the best holiday ever, and because of him, they were possibly in danger.

"If you think the inn is the safest place for us, I won't argue."

Alex blew out a breath. "Good. Keep your phone on you. I'll call you right back," he said.

"Okay."

He disconnected the call and pulled up Mitch's contact.

"I need a favor," he said when Mitch answered. "It appears Tony is trying to get to me through Halona. I don't want her and Theo to be alone in their house right now. Can they stay at the inn for a couple of days?"

"Sure. A couple of guests that were scheduled canceled their reservations this morning because of the snow. The room is Halona's as long as she needs."

Alex hoped that Tony was just trying to intimidate her and send him a message. Then again, someone had tried to kill Alex last week. How much did that person still want to hurt him and how far were they willing to go to do it?

This morning's package and shoe had been sent to the lab for rushed prints, and Alex was crossing everything that there would be incriminating evidence to break his dad's case open once and for all. Maybe solving that case would solve his own too.

In the meantime, Alex's focus needed to be on protecting the ones he loved. *Loved?*

Yeah. He loved Halona. And he wasn't going to let anyone hurt her or Theo, no matter what.

"Thanks," Alex told Mitch before hanging up and calling Halona back. "You have a room at the B and B for as long as you need."

"Do you think we'll have to spend Christmas there?" she asked.

Alex directed his SUV toward Cedar Trail. "I hope not, but if you do, I can help you get the presents to the inn."

"Those will be at my parents' place anyway. We usually open everything there."

"Good." Alex nodded, gripping the steering wheel more tightly as he hit a patch of ice.

"Mom is so excited that you're joining us, by the way," Halona said.

Alex's grip on the wheel grew tighter still. "About that...I can't come. I'm, uh, sorry."

Halona hesitated. "Why?"

"We'll talk when I get to your place. I'm right down the road."

"Okay. I'll be waiting."

Alex's stomach knotted with the knowledge of what had to be done. In his mind, there was no choice. "Be there soon."

CHAPTER TWENTY-THREE

Halona pulled open two suitcases and started packing.

"This'll be fun," she told Theo with a smile. "You've always wanted to stay over at the B and B. And I hear that Kaitlyn makes amazing breakfasts."

Theo wasn't buying her enthusiasm. He pulled his notebook to his lap and started writing.

Someone's trying to hurt us?

Theo had been in the back seat on the ride home but she'd been careful about what she'd said to Alex.

"You're too smart for your own good, you know that?" She sat down beside him. "Some people just aren't nice. They're mean, like bullies."

Theo looked at her for a long moment. She could almost hear the wheels spinning in his little mind. What she wouldn't give to have free access to all his thoughts.

He lifted his pencil and wrote.

A bad man like Daddy?

Halona's lips parted as she read. "What? No. Your father was a good man. Why would you ask that?"

Theo looked away.

Halona touched his forearm. "Theo, talk to me. Why would you ask if your father was a bad man? He's nothing like the guy that Chief Baker is trying to protect us from."

Theo pinched his pencil between his fingers again, pressing his own lips tightly together. Then he started writing.

Because Daddy hurt you, and Chief Baker took him to jail.

Halona blinked past the sting in her eyes. She guessed it did seem like Alex had protected her and Theo from his dad. "It wasn't the same. Your dad wasn't healthy. He was sick, Theo."

Yes, she was breaking her promise to Ted who'd never wanted Theo to know...but Ted wouldn't have wanted Theo thinking he was a bad man either. "He had a brain injury. It made it hard for him to control his emotions. That's why he had to leave. He would never intentionally hurt us."

Theo was watching her closely.

Why couldn't the doctor fix him? he wrote.

"Well..." Halona wrapped an arm around his little shoulders. "They didn't know how. Your dad tried to get better, buddy. He really did." And she'd tried to help him. After Alex had arrested Ted, Ted had refused her help.

He told her that he was leaving for her own protection. "He loved you more than anything. I love you too. I will always protect you, okay?"

Theo nodded.

Her son had only been five at the height of Ted's illness. She'd tried to guard him as best she could but not enough apparently.

Halona reached for Theo's hand and gave it a squeeze. All that mattered was that he knew the truth now. The truth was that his dad, the real Ted Byrd that she'd fallen in love with, was a good man. And that Theo was loved and safe.

The doorbell rang at the front of the house.

"Oh, that must be Alex." She stood. "You keep packing, buddy. A few outfits and some books to keep you busy over the next few days. I'll go let him in."

Halona started down the hall. She didn't want to leave this house but she trusted Alex's instincts. If he thought this was best, then it was what she'd do.

She looked through the peephole before opening the door to Alex. "Hey. We're packing up. Come on in."

He stepped past her, and she waited for him to kiss her cheek but he didn't. He was in police chief mode—all business, no time for romance.

"Where's Theo?" he asked.

"In his room," she said. "He's not thrilled about the temporary displacement but he'll be okay. Are you...okay?"

Alex's face was practically grim. She knew today was hard for him already, and now he had her and her son to worry about. She hated putting any more stress on his already burdened shoulders.

"I just want to get you out of here so I can pay Tony a visit. I also have another development in my dad's case. Maybe."

Halona drew a hand to her chest. "That's great news, Alex. Is that why you can't come to Christmas?" She felt a little hurt that he'd changed his mind but she understood. He had a town to run and he took his role seriously. "It's okay," she said when he didn't answer immediately. "We can just have our own little celebration once you get off your shift. You can't work all day, after all. I'll bring some food home from my mom's. She'd insist on that anyway."

Alex averted his gaze, and Halona felt her smile go wobbly. There was a tension in the air between them, thick and uncomfortable, that made her wonder if Alex's demeanor wasn't about something other than the anniversary of his dad's death and Tony.

"We don't need to talk about this now," Alex finally said. "You should pack."

A thread of panic rippled through her. "Talk about what?"

His gaze slid to hers and locked. Her knees felt a little weak at the flicker of something regretful in his eyes. "Halona, I think we need to spend some time apart."

She swallowed hard. "For how long?" she asked, voice cracking under the pressure of her emotions.

"Until I get Tony in line. Maybe longer." He looked away and she understood what he wasn't saying. Maybe forever.

Was he breaking up with her?

Halona's emotions were already raw after her conversation with Theo. She pointed a finger at Alex's chest, forcing him to look at her again. "Oh, no you don't. You don't get to decide what's good for me and what isn't. *I* know what's good for me, and that's you, Alex."

"Tony is a threat to you right now, and that's because of me."

She offered a humorless laugh. "He's just trying to scare us. I don't mind going to the inn, but us not seeing each other because of him? That's what he wants, Alex. He wants to hurt you. To hurt me."

"If something happens to you or Theo—"

"Stop it," she snapped, cutting him off. She dropped her arm down by her side. "Just stop. You intervened in my marriage when you didn't have all the facts. You're the reason that Ted left us. I didn't have a say in that. You took it away from me, just like you're doing right now."

"It's not the same."

"Isn't it?" She paced in front of him. "You're the reason my husband wouldn't let me help him when he needed it the most, and why Theo was just asking me if his daddy was a bad man." Her voice cracked as all the emotion that Theo had just brought to the surface bubbled up along with the memories of that night two years ago when Alex had come to her door. She stopped walking and faced him. "Now you've decided that you're leaving us too, because you think that's what's best. What about what I think, Alex?"

"Halona," he said softly, reaching for her.

She stepped backward and shook her head. "Because I think that's not fair. You don't get to make me fall for you and then walk away."

"Keeping you safe is the most important thing. I'm sorry," he said softly. She wasn't sure if he was apologizing for the past or for what he was doing now.

"So am I." She kept her lips firmly pressed against one another, sensing that she'd break if she tried to say anything more. "So that's it?" she asked.

The regret in Alex's eyes was her answer. "Go get your things," he said finally. "I'll follow you to the Sweetwater Bed and Breakfast to make sure you get there okay."

Halona nodded. Then she turned and walked back down the hall to her bedroom, forcing slow, controlled breaths until she stood in the doorway. Theo was sitting on the bed. He looked at her and then wrote something in his notebook.

Are you upset?

She swallowed, wishing her eyes weren't welling with tears right now. She nodded, too full of her own emotions to speak. Theo walked over to her and opened his arms wide, wrapping them around her and squeezing. "Okay, sweetie," she said after a moment. "Done packing?"

Theo nodded.

"Good. Let me double-check. We don't want to have to come back here until we know it's safe." Or ask Alex for help. She didn't want to see or talk to Alex any more than she had to right now.

* * *

It was so quiet in the vehicle that Alex could practically hear the snow falling and hitting the windshield as he followed Halona's car. He wanted to make sure that they got to the inn safely and that Tony stayed away.

He hadn't realized that Halona was still so angry with him over what happened in the past. She still resented him, and during their fight just now, he realized that she always would.

He swallowed painfully. Would she ever fully forgive

him? Because even if this breakup was just temporary, they couldn't build a future on a foundation with fault lines.

He pulled into the driveway for the Sweetwater Bed and Breakfast. As soon as they came to a stop, Halona pushed open her car door and stepped out. Alex stepped out too, watching as she opened the back door for Theo.

"Come on, honey. We're here. Let's get inside to our room. I'm sure Chief Baker needs to get back to work." She popped the trunk and retrieved their bags.

"I'll carry those for you," he offered.

"No need. We got it." She didn't even look in his direction. Instead, she took the luggage up the steps with Theo at her side. No farewell or goodbye or *we can still be friends*.

Alex watched as Mitch opened the door and let them in.

He and Halona couldn't be friends. He'd tried that all these years while harboring feelings for her. Now that they'd crossed the line in their relationship, there was no going back. It was over between them.

"Hey, buddy. Coming inside?" Mitch asked as he approached Alex's vehicle.

Alex realized he'd just been standing there and staring at the inn's front door where Halona had disappeared. "No," he finally said. "I'm probably going to head back to the station and see if the lab has gotten any information on that package and its contents."

"Probably too soon," Mitch said.

"I asked them to put a rush on it. It was sent as a threat."

"Or just a cruel prank," Mitch said.

"Well, I'm not taking my chances."

Mitch's gaze trailed toward the inn. "Halona seemed upset just now. Is she freaked out about what's happening?"

"She doesn't think the move is necessary but she's okay with it."

"So what's going on, then?" Mitch asked. "You two have a fight?"

Alex's gaze slid from the front of the inn to Mitch. "You could say that." But the argument hadn't started this afternoon. It'd begun long before then. He just hadn't realized it was still going on. "I don't know that we were ever officially together."

"Sure seemed that way to me. What happened?" Mitch asked.

Alex shoved his hands into the pockets of his jeans. His fingers felt like icicles out here, and the cold was quickly making its way to his heart. "It doesn't matter. All that matters right now is that Halona and Theo are safe. I'm going back to the station."

"I'm going too," Mitch said.

Alex turned back to him. "You just got off shift."

"Yeah, but you need the extra help, and there's really no such thing as being off shift."

"True enough." Alex got into the driver's seat. "See you back at the station."

As he drove, he mentally reviewed his father's cold case again and the facts surrounding today's package. Ten minutes later, he walked into the station, and Tammy looked up from her desk.

"I wasn't sure if you'd return," she said.

"I'm here. Might be here awhile. Any messages?"

She nodded, her expression serious today. Everyone here knew the drill. It was the anniversary of his dad's death. There was no joking around. He might've felt better if things were normal, but probably not.

"Yeah. Gary at the lab called."

Alex's spirit lifted just a touch. "Thanks." He started walking down the hall toward his office but turned back to look at Tammy. "Not sure what I'd do without you, Tam," he told her for the millionth time. Then he continued walking to his office and sat behind his desk. He picked up his phone and dialed Gary right back.

"Hey, Chief," Gary said. "I have results for you."

Alex closed his eyes and inhaled deeply. "I'm listening."

"We lifted some prints off the shoe. Steve Anderson's prints were all over it along with one other person's."

"Let me guess. Tony's?" Alex asked.

"Oddly enough, no. The prints belong to Sharlene Anderson," Gary said.

Alex's eyes popped open. He'd fingerprinted Sharlene many years ago after she'd shoplifted. He figured that Tony had put her up to it, of course. "Sharlene? Are you sure?"

"Positive," Gary said.

* * *

The inn was the very image of a picture-perfect Christmas but that's not how Halona felt. She'd rather be home with Theo and looking at the tree that she and Alex had gotten at Merry Mountain Farms together. She'd rather be dreaming of spending the New Year with Alex like she'd done just this morning.

Now those dreams were crushed along with her Christmas spirit.

Kaitlyn slid a cup of peppermint tea in front of Halona and sat down across from her. Theo was in the kitchen with Mitch's mom, Gina Hargrove, who co-owned and operated the inn. "So, tell me what's going on."

Halona curled her fingers around the hot mug, soaking in its warmth. "Tony showed up at my shop yesterday and at the cemetery this morning when I took Theo to see Ted's grave. Alex thinks it's a threat."

"Why would Tony threaten you? Because you're dating Alex now?" Kaitlyn asked.

Halona looked up. "We were never exactly dating."

"I saw you two together at the Hope for the Holidays auction. You told the Ladies' Day Out group that you kissed. If not dating, what would you call it?"

Halona shook her head, not willing to mention that she and Alex had also shared a bed and feelings that ran deep. "Whatever we had, it's over. I just blew up at him."

Kaitlyn frowned. "Over what?"

Halona gave her friend a long, hard look. She was tired of keeping Ted's story a secret from everyone she cared about. She took a breath and then told Kaitlyn everything, finding that the more she told the story, the better she felt. "I know it's not Alex's fault but it's easier to blame him than blame a man who isn't here anymore. Ted should've stopped playing football after his first head injury. I told him that but he wouldn't hear it. He should've gotten help sooner. If he'd have been open about what was going on with him, Alex would've known the truth when he came to our door." Halona sighed heavily. "Ted and I still needed to live apart but I could've been there for him on the sidelines." The same way she always was when he played football.

"I can't believe you went through this all on your own," Kaitlyn said.

"I told Alex it was all his fault. I was upset and maybe a little scared about this whole Tony thing. And I was hurt that he was leaving us." Halona shrugged on a heavy sigh.

"Maybe this is for the best anyway. Theo is my priority. He's still in therapy. His nightmares are becoming less frequent but he still has them."

Kaitlyn sipped from her own mug of tea. "Alex is his Mentor Match, right?"

"Yeah. That's another reason I shouldn't have gotten involved with Alex to begin with. What if he doesn't want to mentor Theo anymore? Theo adores him. He'll be devastated."

"I don't think Alex would do that. But if he does, Theo will get through it."

"After Ted left us, Theo was inconsolable."

"Ted was his father though."

"But Alex is another male figure in his life. He won't take it well if Alex stops coming around altogether." Halona leaned forward, holding her head in her hands. "I've made a huge mess of my life."

"It was this time last year that I thought the same thing. Mitch and I had broken up, and I was wishing I'd never kissed him in the first place," Kaitlyn said.

Halona looked up. "And now you're getting married. I'm looking forward to that almost as much as I am to seeing Theo open his presents under the tree on Christmas morning."

"It's funny how things work out," Kaitlyn said.

Halona shook her head. "I don't think that's true in my and Alex's case."

"That's too bad. I really thought you two had forever potential."

Halona had begun to think so too. She never should've let her mind go there. Maybe she should've paid Dawanda a visit at the fudge shop and gotten one of her infamous cappuccino readings to tell her how things would end with Alex. Then she could've avoided this heartbreak.

"We have cookies!" Gina said, entering the dining room with Theo following her. She laid a plate down on the small table where Halona and Kaitlyn were sitting. "What a good helper Theo is. I might hire him to help me out sometimes."

"I'm sure he'd be okay with that." Halona's gaze fell on her son, whose mouth was outlined in crumbs. "Looks like he's already sampled the goods."

"Well, that's the fun of making them, isn't it?" Gina asked. "I sampled them as well. A good hostess always does."

Theo walked up to Halona and tapped her shoulder.

"What is it, honey?"

He frowned and made a gesture with his hands, pretending to use a pencil to write along his left palm.

"Your notebook? Where is it?" Halona asked.

He shrugged.

"Did you bring it with you?"

He shook his head.

Halona tried to remember when she'd last seen it. "It's at home?"

He hesitated and then nodded.

"Oh, well, that's okay. I have a notebook he can use," Kaitlyn offered.

Theo shook his head emphatically and turned pleading eyes to Halona. He wanted *his* notebook and pencil. Theo was a boy who liked the familiar. Change was stressful. Spending Christmas at a foreign place would no doubt turn his little world upside down.

Halona stood. "Can Theo stay here while I run home to get his notebook and pencil?"

"Alone?" Kaitlyn asked, her eyes rounding as if Halona had told her she was jumping off a bridge. "I thought the whole point of you being here was so that you wouldn't be alone."

"I'll be fine. It'll just be for a few minutes," Halona promised.

"Are you calling Alex?" Kaitlyn's expression was pinched with worry.

"No." Halona kept her tone of voice neutral for Theo's sake. The last thing she wanted right now was to come face-to-face with Alex. She'd either have to fight him or kiss him, and neither of those options were acceptable.

CHAPTER TWENTY-FOUR

Alex pulled his SUV up to the curb in front of Safe Haven's Place in Wild Blossom Bluffs and glanced over at Mitch, who'd come along for backup.

"I don't want to spook Sharlene. She's not under arrest."

Mitch nodded. "We're just questioning her. We don't even know if she's the one who sent the shoe. But why would her prints be on it? It doesn't make sense."

"That's what I hope to find out."

They got out of the SUV and headed toward the front door. He'd already called the director, and she was expecting them. She'd asked that they talk to Sharlene outside so they didn't worry the other women, and he'd agreed. Sharlene didn't know about the visit, just in case she decided to run. He didn't think that was likely though. In fact, Alex suspected that Sharlene was expecting him to come asking questions.

He approached the door and rang the doorbell. Within

a minute, Carly answered with a tight smile. "Chief Baker. Officer," she said in way of greeting to Mitch.

Mitch held out his hand. "Officer Hargrove."

She nodded. "I'm Carly." Then she looked over her shoulder. "Sharlene? You have some visitors outside. Nothing to be concerned about. It's just Chief Baker."

Carly turned back to them on the porch. "She'll grab her coat and be out shortly. Can I get you anything? I know it's freezing."

"It's not too bad," Alex said. "We're fine."

He and Mitch moved to the front porch swing to wait. A moment later, Sharlene stepped out.

Just as Alex suspected, she didn't seem a bit surprised.

"I got a package this morning," he told her, cutting to the chase.

"I know," she said, standing frozen to her spot on the porch.

"Why did you send it to me, Sharlene?"

"Because it was time."

"For who?" Alex asked.

"Well, you for one. How many years have you wanted to know who hit your father?" she asked.

"Eleven," he said without blinking. But who was counting? "And I'm not sure I know yet."

She narrowed her eyes. "No?"

"Sharlene, do you know that you can be charged for withholding information if you've known who hit my father and didn't come forward?"

Her frown deepened as she looked between the men. "I know a good lawyer, and you and I both know that I've been threatened with my life. Too many times. That's why it was time for me too." She looked away for a moment. "If you arrest Steve Anderson, he won't be around to threaten me anymore. I can handle Tony. He's never been the reason I stay. His uncle is crazy though. Steve will do anything to protect his family."

"Including threatening you if you leave Tony?" Alex asked.

She nodded. "And running you and your father down in the street for sniffing around his business. I've heard him brag about it." Her rigid posture softened. "I'm sorry I didn't tell you sooner. You've never been anything but nice to me. But I was scared."

"How did you know where to get the shoe?" Alex asked.

She fidgeted with her hands that needed gloves. "When Steve gets drunk, he likes to get cocky and show off the treasure in his trove."

"The shoe is his treasure?" Alex swallowed past the pain.

Sharlene started to say something, but seemed to hesitate.

"We're not arresting you, Sharlene. But you are going to the station for your own protection until Steve Anderson is under arrest."

Tears filled Sharlene's eyes, and her shoulders rounded in what appeared to be relief. Her nightmare would soon be over. She was about to break free.

Alex's nightmare was about to end too. He was finally, *finally*, going to bring his father justice after eleven long years.

"We've got coffee at the station. Or Tammy can get you a cup from the café," Alex told Sharlene.

Sharlene hugged her arms around her body. "You'll keep Steve away from me, won't you?"

Alex gave her a solemn look. "I promise to keep you safe."

"And I second that," Mitch said.

They spoke to Carly outside the house for a brief moment and then walked back to Alex's SUV and got in.

Thirty minutes later, as Alex pulled into the station parking lot, Mitch's cell phone dinged.

"Uh-oh," Mitch said as he read the text message on his screen.

Alex parked and glanced over, not liking the look on his friend's face. "What is it?"

"Kaitlyn says that Halona left the inn half an hour ago. She went home to get something and hasn't returned. Halona left her phone at the inn too. There's no way to reach her."

Alex's gut tripped. "Sharlene, go inside with Mitch. Tammy will get you that coffee."

"Call me if you need backup," Mitch said.

Alex nodded. As soon as Mitch and Sharlene stepped out of the vehicle and closed their doors, he pressed the gas and sped toward Halona's home on Cedar Trail.

* * *

Halona found Theo's notebook lying on the kitchen counter along with his favorite pencil. She picked it up and held it to her chest for a moment. Then she sat down on the stool. It wasn't often that she got a moment alone without Theo or her customers. Or Alex.

Alex wouldn't be in the picture anymore though, a result of both their mistakes. Talking with Kaitlyn about what happened had helped her work through some of her feelings. Her anger at Alex had mostly faded, and now she just felt a deep regret.

Halona stood and looked around her kitchen, making

sure she and Theo had everything they needed. Then she headed back to the front door and locked it behind her. Instead of driving directly back to the Sweetwater Bed and Breakfast though, she drove to the café. It was only a couple of minutes out of the way, and a coffee would re-energize her so she could keep up with Theo. Like any child his age, he was excited about Christmas. Add in their stay at the inn and all the festivities there, and his bedtime would no doubt be pushed back at least an hour.

Halona parked and walked inside the Sweetwater Café, and a bell chimed over her head followed by Emma's greeting from the counter.

"Hey, Halona! This isn't your usual time of day."

"No, but I needed a caffeine fix." Halona approached the counter with a smile.

"Your usual then?" Emma asked.

Halona nodded and then changed her mind. "Actually, all I need is a sugar fix. How about a hot chocolate with extra whipped cream?"

"Ohhh, I wish I could join you for that." Emma turned and started to work on the beverage. As she did, Halona looked around the café, her gaze snagging on a customer seated in the back corner. Halona's heart dropped into her stomach, and she looked away quickly. What was Tony doing here? He was the last person she wanted to run into right now. Halona looked at him again. His back was toward her, curved at the spine as he leaned heavily over the table.

"Here you go." Emma slid the drink in front of Halona. Halona handed over her debit card to pay. A moment later, Emma returned it. "Merry Christmas."

"Thank you. Merry Christmas to you too." Halona tipped her head toward Tony and lowered her voice. "What's he doing here?"

Emma followed Halona's gaze and shrugged. "He's been sitting like that for over an hour. I've checked on him a couple of times but he says he's fine."

Halona nodded and stepped out of the way so that the next customer could approach the counter. She turned toward the door but only made it a couple of steps before she stopped, took a breath, and turned back. This was a public place. There wasn't much risk in talking to Tony Anderson.

She walked toward the back corner and pulled out the chair across from him. "Hi, Tony."

He looked up at her, his eyes red, and she didn't think it was because he'd been drinking anything stronger than a coffee. "What do you want?"

Halona lifted a shoulder. "You look like you could use some company, and it's Christmas, so..."

"What does Christmas have to do with anything?"

Halona smiled. "It's the season of cheer, and you look like you could use some. I know Sharlene left you."

"No thanks to your boyfriend. I'm sure he put her up to it," Tony muttered.

"He's not my boyfriend."

Tony looked up. "I didn't believe you before, and I still don't."

Halona laughed softly. "Well, for your information, he broke up with me today. So, as much as I never thought I'd say this, you and I have something in common."

Tony's eyes narrowed, and then he shook his head. "Except I deserve to be left." He leaned his forehead on one hand. "I'm not a good husband. I make Sharlene promises that I'll do better, be better. And I mean it when I say it. But I fail."

"So you understand why she left?"

Tony nodded. "Of course I do. I also know she's not coming back this time," he said. "Even if she tried, I wouldn't let her. I'm no good for her. I'm no good for anyone."

Halona was surprised that she actually felt sorry for him right now. He'd done so many bad things. He'd brought all of this on himself. "Tony?" she asked.

He looked at her, his brown eyes dull and lifeless. "Yeah?"

"What were you doing at the cemetery this morning? I saw you there, watching me and Theo."

He chuckled. "As much as I'd love to take credit for ruining your day, I wasn't there because of you. My mother is buried there. I go see her this time of year."

Halona searched his face. He wasn't lying, and he wasn't a threat to her or her son. "We were visiting Theo's dad."

"I figured as much," Tony said. "I always thought Ted was a nice guy."

Halona nodded. "Thanks for saying so." She chewed her bottom lip for just a moment, wondering if she should say what was on her mind. "Maybe you won't get a second chance with Sharlene but you still have a chance to turn your life around, Tony. It's never too late for that." She reached into her purse, pulled out one of Dr. Charwood's business cards, and placed it in front of him.

Tony glanced at the card. "A shrink?"

Halona shrugged. "Everyone needs someone to talk to."

Tony took the card, pinching it between his fingers. "Why do you care?" he asked, looking up at her. "I'm pretty sure you don't like me much."

"I don't think you like yourself very much either. And

Christmas is also the season of hope. I *hope* you find a way to become the kind of man you want to be."

"You really think that's possible?" he asked. Something flickered in his gaze.

Halona nodded. "But you have to work on it." She tipped her head at the card. "And you need help."

He nodded. "Maybe I'll call. Thanks."

The sincerity in his voice made Halona's eyes burn. She hadn't taken a drink from her beverage yet, and she could get another one on the way out. She slid the cup toward him.

"What's this?"

The question made her smile. "Hot chocolate with extra whipped cream. For you." She pushed back from the table and stood. "Merry Christmas, Tony."

He gave a small nod.

She half expected him to respond with "bah humbug." That's what the Tony she knew would say. Maybe something had shifted inside him today, and like the Grinch, his heart had grown a few sizes.

"Merry Christmas to you too. And to that boy of yours."

Maybe he was fooling her but she believed he meant it.

* * *

Alex pulled into Halona's driveway and his heart dropped. Her car wasn't here. Where was she? He got out and jogged up the steps and then rang the doorbell to make sure. No answer. He returned to his vehicle, grabbed his cell phone, and hit Redial on Kaitlyn's number.

"Is she back yet?" he asked as soon as she answered.

"No, and I'm getting worried. It only should've taken

her thirty minutes to go home and come back. It's been over an hour."

"I'm at her place right now," Alex said. "She's not here." A sick feeling curled in his belly. This is exactly what he was trying to prevent. If Halona was in danger, it was all his fault. There was no sign of foul play though. No reason for his mind to jump to the worst-case scenario just yet. "Call me if she returns to the inn. I'm going to search downtown."

Kaitlyn agreed and he hung up the phone, heading toward the downtown area. On impulse, he turned down Pine Cone Lane and drove past Tony's house. His truck wasn't in the driveway. He wasn't home. Was he with Halona?

Fear gripped Alex's chest as he continued driving. He turned onto Main Street and his world righted when he saw Halona step out of the Sweetwater Café with a steaming cup in hand. He pulled into the parking lot and waited for her. When she saw him, she froze, her expression shifting subtly until it landed on indignation.

"What are you doing here?" she asked as he approached.

"Kaitlyn called me. She's starting to worry. I was worried too. You should've stayed at the inn where it's safe. Tony could've found you."

"I found him. He's inside that café realizing that he's lost his wife for good," Halona said. "He's broken, and I almost feel bad for him."

Alex gave a glance at the café. "He deserves whatever he gets."

Halona nodded. "I agree. But he's not a threat to me or Theo. I don't even think he's a threat to Sharlene anymore. I think he wants to change."

Alex stepped closer. He wanted to reach for her hand

and pull her to him. Wanted to kiss her until she melted in his arms. "Do you always see the best in people?"

"I try to."

And Alex loved that about her. "I still want you to stay at the bed and breakfast. Tony followed you to the cemetery and made threats."

"He was at the cemetery visiting his mother's grave."

Alex cocked his head. She believed the best in people but it was his job to be wary with people who had a history of lying and worse. "Even so, I'd feel better. He's a loose cannon right now, and a man who's lost everything has nothing to lose."

Halona frowned. "We'll stay tonight. Theo is actually excited about it. Speaking of, he's probably wondering where I am. And now that you know I'm safe...is there anything else to talk about?"

He shook his head, even though it was a lie. There was so much more to say. Like "I'm sorry. I wish things were different. I love you." Instead, he remained silent and watched her get into her car and drive away.

* * *

As Alex walked into the police station, Tammy looked up from her desk.

"Everything okay?" she asked.

"All's well that ends well," Alex said, stealing a quote from Grandma Baker. He needed to drop by and see her sometime before Christmas. He also needed to call his mom. They were long overdue for a chat, and she'd get comfort in knowing that his dad's killer was finally behind bars. Alex had put in a call to the WBB Police Department after speaking to Sharlene at the shelter. He'd requested that the officers in that jurisdiction arrest Steve, and Alex had already received word that the arrest was made. "Where's Sharlene?" Alex asked Tammy.

"Sleeping in the back room. Officer Chew is with her."

Alex nodded. "She's free to go home when she wakes up." Alex started to turn toward his office but Tammy called out to him.

"Chief?"

There was a note of trepidation in her voice that got Alex's attention. He turned back to look at her.

"I, um, wanted to tell you that I'm...leaving the police station."

"As in going home?" he asked, suspecting that wasn't what she meant.

She shook her head. "No. I've enjoyed working here, Chief Baker, but my dream is to own a restaurant. I've been saving every penny for years. This month's overtime has really helped the cause. I want to cook and make people happy."

"You make me happy," Alex offered, his heart sinking.

"Well, you can come to Becky's Log Cabin and get your fill of happy anytime you want. I'm changing that name to Tammy's Log Cabin after the New Year."

The pieces of information that Alex had already collected clicked into place. Becky was selling out, and Tammy was buying in.

"I'm happy for you, Tam," he said.

She lifted a wary brow. "Really?"

"Yeah. Sad for me, but happy for you. I don't know what I'll do without you around here at the station."

Tammy shrugged. "You'll find someone else."

"There'll never be another you." He stepped around the desk and gave her a long hug.

"You're not mad?" she asked when they pulled apart.

"Nah. Can't blame someone for following their dreams, can I? That would make me the biggest scrooge of all."

She laughed. "And you're already a pretty big one... You solved a cold case today. That's kind of making a dream of yours come true too. I think wherever he is right now, your dad is very proud of you, Alex."

Emotion swirled in his belly. He'd better get back to his office before he broke down, which wasn't like him at all. But he was at his breaking point right now. His personal life seemed to be crumbling all around him. "I'll be your first customer," he told Tammy as he took a few steps backward.

She pointed a finger. "Well, don't expect to be eating for free, Chief," she teased.

"Knowing you, I expect I'll be paying double."

"Payback." She grinned. "There's a container of home-made lasagna with your name on it on your desk."

He turned and started walking down the hall to his office. "What will I do without you, Tam?"

He was about to find out. He'd also be going forward without a cold case haunting him. And without Halona.

* * *

Halona stepped into their room at the bed and breakfast, feeling the weight of the day on her tired shoulders. When Theo smiled up at her from the bed though, everything lifted. Kaitlyn had brought in a cot for him but it appeared that he'd staked his claim. Halona didn't mind.

"Good night. Sleep tight." She kissed his forehead and walked over to the light switch and flipped it off.

"Mom?"

Her feet froze as she headed toward the cot.

"Mom?" Theo called again, making her turn and flip the light switch back on.

"What did you say?" Had she imagined his sweet little voice?

He looked at her and smiled, revealing the place where he'd lost his tooth a couple of weeks ago. "Mom, I'm glad you're okay."

"Me too, sweetie." Tears filled her eyes. "Me too."

"I love you," he said in a very small voice.

Her heart leaped at the sound. "I love you more than you'll ever know. I love you so much." She stepped over to the bed, sat down beside him, and pulled him into her arms. She didn't want to make a huge deal out of him talking. Dr. Charwood had said it was better to remain calm so that Theo didn't clam back up. Halona wiped her eyes and pulled away. "We better get our sleep."

He nodded and wriggled back down under his covers.

She turned the lights back off. As she walked to the cot, tears streamed down her cheeks. They were happy and sad and everything in between. Then she climbed under the blanket and quietly cried herself to sleep.

CHAPTER TWENTY-FIVE

Alex was still at the police station at nine p.m. when Sharlene woke up. She leaned in his doorway with Officer Chew at her side.

"You're free to go," he said. "Steve is somewhere that he'll never hurt you. And I spoke to Tony earlier. If he goes near you, I'll press charges on aiding and abetting his uncle in a crime and he'll spend the next several Christmases behind bars."

Relief washed over her expression, and a genuine smile lifted the corners of her mouth. "Thank you."

"I should say the same to you." He looked at the file for his father's case on his desk. Case closed. Mystery solved.

"I'm not sure I want to go back to my home though," she said, her hand petting Chew's head. "And if I don't have to, I'd rather not stay at the shelter. Another woman in need can have that spot."

Alex nodded. "Kaitlyn Russo has already offered you

a room at the Sweetwater Bed and Breakfast. You can stay there through Christmas if you want."

"Really?" Sharlene's smile deepened. "That's so thoughtful of her. It sounds nice, actually."

"I can grab your things from the shelter and swing them by sometime tomorrow if you'd like."

"You've already done so much. I don't know how I'll ever repay you."

"Just be happy, Sharlene. That's all I want."

Sharlene started to leave but then stopped and turned. "Chief? I know it's a lot to ask, and you've already given me so much. You've given me my life back," she said, continuing to rub Chew's head. The pup leaned into her, eyes closed and nose lifted slightly as if he were on the scent of complete joy.

"What do you need, Sharlene?" Alex asked as he sat back in his chair. Money? Food? Advice? He was ready to hand over anything that would help with her fresh start.

She looked down at Officer Chew beside her. "He was my dog," she said. "I brought him home because I thought it'd be nice to have unconditional love for once. Tony called him so many ugly things but his real name is Buddy."

Alex's heart sank. Was he really going to lose Halona, Tammy, and Officer Chew all in a day's time? "You want your dog back?"

Sharlene hesitated and then nodded.

Alex glanced down at Officer Chew—Buddy—assessing if his canine friend felt the same way. Chew melted into the side of Sharlene's leg, relaxed and happy.

Alex cleared his throat. He'd been trying to find Chew a good home all month, but even so, he'd become attached to the dog. Chew—Buddy—already had a good home though. He had no doubt that Sharlene would treat him well. "Of course, Sharlene. He's your dog."

"Thank you, Chief Baker," she said, voice cracking. "Merry Christmas."

"Merry Christmas." Alex stared after Sharlene as she and Buddy left. A friend of hers was waiting outside to drive her to the inn. Alex stood, grabbed his keys, and then drove home, completely exhausted from the day.

A package was waiting at his front door when he arrived. He didn't think this one was from any of the Andersons. No, that story was ending. He grabbed it, surprised by how light it was, and headed inside. It felt strange without a little puppy at his feet.

His mother's Florida address was in the left-hand corner. He frowned because he'd forgotten to get her a gift. There were still a couple of days before the holiday though. He pulled out his pocketknife and slid it through the tape and then opened the flaps to peer inside. There was a large candy cane like he used to get every year as a kid. There was also what appeared to be an online receipt.

Pulling the paper out, he read what his mother had purchased. A ticket from Florida to North Carolina. A smile tugged on the corners of his mouth. Well, there was some good news for the day. He pulled his cell phone out of his pocket, pondering whether or not to call her. He was drained though so instead he sent a text.

Looks like you're coming for a visit.

It took a moment for her to respond. More than a visit. It's a one-way ticket.

Alex looked at the receipt again. Seriously? Thought you loved the Sunshine State.

I do. Florida has been good for me. But my home is where my family is.

He hadn't expected that any good would come out of this day but this was something. His mom had needed the time away, to deal with the loss of his father, but maybe her coming home meant that she was healing. He had done some healing this year too, and now that his father's killer was in jail, he could do a lot more.

It won't be until late January but I couldn't wait to tell you, she texted.

This is a really good present, he told her. I'm not sure how I can top it.

A hug and a kiss are all I need, she texted back.

You got it.

As he began getting ready for bed, he looked around for Officer Chew before remembering that Sharlene had him. That stung a little. Then he remembered that Halona and Theo were also out of his life, and that stung a whole lot more.

* * *

On Christmas Eve, Alex closed the file on his desk and exhaled softly. It was over. After eleven years, his dad's case was solved.

Emotion burned at the back of his throat. He picked up the file and carried it over to a cabinet and then locked it up, never to be reopened. He'd thought he'd feel differently when he brought his dad's killer to justice but instead he felt a sort of numbness in his core that wouldn't be filled with ham or cranberry pie in the coming days. Maybe he'd skip Christmas altogether.

Grandma Baker needed him though, and he wouldn't let her down. He'd put on a happy demeanor even if that feeling felt too far away to reach. In reality, it was only a short drive away to Cedar Trail where Halona and Theo were. They made him happy but their little family had been threatened because of him.

Never again.

Alex grabbed his keys and walked down the hall. The secretary's desk was unoccupied. Tammy had told him she'd work through the New Year but he'd given her the next three days off to spend the holiday with her family. Until she returned, calls were being redirected to another office at the station. He left and climbed into his SUV and then cruised around town, looking for someone who might need his help. Looking for something to give him purpose today, because with his father's case closed, Sharlene Anderson safe, and Halona and Theo gone from his life, what was he supposed to do now?

Fresh snow reflected brightly on his windshield as he drove toward Main Street. He waved at people all bundled up for the cold. His mind retraced how everything had gone right this Christmas, and wrong. Somehow, after driving until his gas tank light lit up, he found himself parked outside of Sweetwater Cemetery where his father was put to rest. He pushed open his vehicle's door and stepped out. He felt empty-handed as he walked through the gate, thinking maybe he should've brought flowers, but that would involve seeing Halona. How the heck was he ever supposed to see Halona again without wanting to pull her into his arms and kiss her? Without wanting to drop to one knee and beg her to spend the rest of her life with him?

Crazy thoughts. Thoughts of a man who'd lost nearly everything.

Alex stopped in front of his dad's headstone, his hands shoved in his pockets. His breaths came out in white puffs against the winter air. "Hey, Dad, it's me."

The granite stone didn't answer back, not that he'd expected it to. If Grandma Baker was right, his dad had been at peace since the moment he'd been laid here. It was Alex who'd struggled. But it was over now. It felt like a weight had been lifted, and he could move on with his life without clinging to the past. Except Halona was now in his past, and he wasn't sure he could let her go.

* * *

"Mom!"

Halona's eyes flew open as she lay in bed. Sun splintered through the blinds. It was morning. Was Theo having a nightmare?

She flew up out of the comfort of her heavy quilt and slipped her feet into a pair of slippers. Then she hurried across the hall toward his room. His bed was empty. "Theo?"

"Mom, Mom, look!" She followed his voice to the dining room where he was looking out the window. Wide awake and talking!

She stood frozen in the entryway for a moment, heart swelling until it was hard to breathe. Ever since the night at the Sweetwater Bed and Breakfast, he'd been talking, little by little.

"It snowed more," he said, his voice strong and full of excitement. He looked back at her almost shyly, as if he knew she was on the verge of tears. She wouldn't cry in front of him though. She'd pretend like this was normal, and it was.

"Yes, it did," she said, finally walking over to stand beside him. There were at least two inches of fresh snow covering yesterday's footprints.

"Maybe Alex can come over and we can build a snowman," Theo said excitedly.

Her ballooned heart seemed to pop and deflate at the memories that weren't erased with a few inches of snow. She hadn't told Theo yet that Alex probably wouldn't be coming over as much. "How about after breakfast you and I go outside and build a snowman?" Halona suggested, turning toward the kitchen so Theo didn't notice the tears welling in her eyes.

"Yes!" he cheered.

Halona laughed as she opened the fridge and let the cool air dry her eyes. Then she pulled out the ingredients for pancakes.

She'd gotten the white Christmas she'd wanted. Today was also the start of her and Theo's new normal. Better in some ways and painful in others. They were strong though. She and Theo had proven that time after time. As long as they had each other, they could get through just about anything the day brought.

Tomorrow was Christmas. The day would bring laughter and love, gifts, delicious food, friends and family—but it wouldn't bring Alex back.

* * *

"Ho, ho, ho!" Alex called the next morning, letting himself into Grandma Baker's house. It'd been another restless night, and he was earlier than she was probably expecting. Still, he mustered a little holiday cheer for her sake. "Grandma?"

Usually, his grandmother would be at the stove on Christmas morning but the stove was clean. No pots. No delicious smells wafting in the air.

Adrenaline shot through his veins as he walked into the living room where his grandmother was sitting in her recliner and knitting.

"Grandma?"

She looked up with an inviting smile. "Oh, I didn't hear you come in. Merry Christmas, Alex."

"What are you doing?" he asked, as her hands continued to work on autopilot.

"What does it look like? I'm knitting, of course."

Alex glanced back at the kitchen. "Need me to get started on breakfast?"

She stopped knitting and looked at him. "Lula invited me to her home to eat. She said you were coming too."

Right. Alex scratched the side of his unshaven jaw. "I meant to tell you. There's been a change of plans. Halona and I are, um, taking some space."

Grandma Baker put her work in a basket beside her chair and stood, taking a few steps toward him. "You broke up?"

"Kind of."

Her expression became pained. "You broke up with her or vice versa?"

"What does that have to do with anything?"

She clucked her tongue. "So it was you? It won't be easy winning her back after breaking her heart at Christmastime."

"I'm not planning to try. She made it pretty clear that she doesn't want me in her life anyway."

His grandmother shook her head. "Alex, I'm old, and I don't have time to beat around the bush."

"Not that you ever have."

She chuckled. "True."

"Say what's on your mind, Grandma. You're going to anyway."

She smiled softly. Even though she was a good foot shorter than he was, she was no less tough. "You've always wanted to be just like your father. Even as a little boy. You couldn't wait to be a police officer just like him. A chief just like him. You wanted to be an expert marksman and go on long runs just like he did."

Alex felt his emotions rising, stretching the muscles along his jaw taut. "Not such a bad thing. Dad was the best man I've ever known."

"And you're just like him, Alex, in every way that counts...except one." She held up a finger.

Alex blinked past the sudden sting in his eyes. He felt his eyebrows pull together, questioning her without words. He feared that if he tried to speak right now, she'd hear the raw emotion in his voice.

"Your father was never afraid to love. He loved your mom, he loved you, he loved with every part of himself. The love he had for his job didn't even compare to what he had for his family. It couldn't. His life was short but it was full, Alex. Full."

Alex struggled to keep his composure.

"Do you love Halona?" she asked.

He took a breath. "A lot has happened between us. There are things you don't know about," he said. Things he wouldn't share. That was Halona's tale to tell, if and when she decided to.

Grandma Baker nodded. "That may be true but answer the question. Do you love her?"

Alex cleared his throat. He'd never been good at lying to his grandmother so why start? "Yes."

"Did you tell her so?"

He shook his head. "No. It doesn't change anything."

"Horse manure!" his grandmother said so forcefully that it surprised him. "Love changes everything. But only if you're brave enough to let it." She narrowed her eyes. "Love can tear us to pieces, yes, but it's also the only thing that can glue us back together. No matter how deep the break is. If you love her, Alex, tell her. Let her decide if what you have is worth fighting for."

Alex swallowed. That advice was right on the mark. Halona didn't have all the facts. She didn't know where he stood and how he felt. By not telling her, he was once again, unintentionally, not allowing her to decide for herself.

"You look like a man who knows what he wants," Grandma Baker said with a soft chuckle.

Alex nodded. He just hoped Halona wanted the same.

* * *

The snow reached Theo's midshin as he and Halona cut across her parents' yard on Christmas morning.

"Be careful," Halona said to Theo as he ran in the direction of the front door, tugging her forward.

"I can't wait to see what Grandma and Grandpa have for me under the tree," he said.

He was still talking. When she'd woken, she'd worried

that it'd all been a dream but it wasn't. It was real. Which meant all the other stuff that she'd hoped was just a dream was also real.

She and Alex were over.

The front door opened, and Lula appeared. "Merry Christmas! I'm so glad you could make it."

"Merry Christmas to you too, Mom," Halona said with a giant smile.

Lula pulled her into her arms and hugged her tightly. "I don't need any packages today, just you." She pulled away and looked at Theo. "And you."

"Merry Christmas, Elisi Lula," Theo said shyly.

Lula nearly leaped with joy. "What?" She looked at Halona. "Did you hear that? My grandson is talking again!"

Halona laughed. "I know. I know."

"It's a Christmas miracle." She pulled them both inside. "It's freezing out there. Come in. Is Alex on his way?" she asked, shutting the door and barring the cold.

News traveled fast along the grapevine in Sweetwater Springs, but apparently not that fast.

"Um, no. He's not coming. I'm sorry. I should've told you." Halona glanced over at Theo, not wanting him to hear more than she was ready to tell. "He's, um, busy."

"Oh." Lula frowned, seeming to sense the truth behind Halona's words. "I'm sorry to hear that. But we are going to have a wonderful day regardless," she said, looking at Theo. "I made all your favorites, and there are presents under my tree. They just mysteriously showed up this morning. Want to see?"

"Yes!" Theo cheered, his voice louder and stronger as he raced into the living room.

Halona laughed and watched her mother follow him. She stood there for a moment and took in a few deep breaths. Today would be wonderful, no matter what. She was here with family. Theo was talking again. It was everything she wanted. Almost.

The doorbell rang.

Halona turned and opened the door to an older woman with long white hair.

"Oh, hi, Beverly!" Halona said. Beverly Sanders was the maternal grandmother of Halona's niece, Maddie.

"Good morning and merry Christmas. Lula invited me over to celebrate with you all."

"Well, of course she did. Any family of Maddie's is our family as well." Halona gave Beverly a big hug. "You can hang your coat in the closet and leave your boots over there." Halona pointed to the rug nearby. She was just about to close the door when Gina Hargrove and her sister, Nettie, walked up.

"Mom invited you over too?" Halona asked with a laugh.

Gina nodded. "Kaitlyn and Mitch are tending the inn this morning so Nettie and I thought we'd take Lula up on her offer for Christmas breakfast."

"Come on in. The more the merrier." Halona double-checked outside before closing the front door and taking off her own boots. She headed into the living room where Theo was shaking his presents and talking up a storm as if he'd never spent time doing anything different. She plopped on the couch, laughing for a moment as she watched him.

The doorbell rang again.

Halona popped up. "I got it. I'll play hostess for all your many guests today, Mom," she said.

Lula looked at Halona's dad. "I don't think I invited anyone else. Did you?"

Halona's dad shrugged. "The whole town has a standing invitation when it comes to you, dear."

Lula blushed against her tanned skin and then turned back to Halona. "Thank you, sweetheart. I don't want whoever's standing out there to catch a cold."

Halona found herself actually smiling as she headed for the door. She opened it, a frigid blast of air blowing in and penetrating all the way to her bones and her heart as she stared back at the man on her parents' front stoop.

"What are you doing here?" Halona asked.

Alex shrugged. "You invited me, remember?"

Grandma Baker stood slightly behind him. She stepped up and gave Halona a hug. "And me. I never say no to Lula's cooking. Merry Christmas, Halona."

"To you as well."

"Go on in, Grandma. I'll be right there," Alex said.

As Grandma Baker stepped inside, Halona stepped onto the porch and closed the door behind her.

"You'll freeze out here without your jacket or boots," he said.

"I don't care. I don't want Theo to overhear us." She had so much she wanted to share with Alex. Theo was talking again, and not just to her. To everyone. He'd slept through the night for the last few days in a row too. And the gifts that Alex had helped her pick out before their walk around Silver Lake were perfect this morning. Theo had loved them all.

Instead, she blinked up against the brilliant white sunlight reflecting off the snow. "I'm glad you came."

"You are?" he asked, looking unsure.

She pressed her lips together. "I know I was a little

brief with you in the parking lot outside the café. I didn't mean to be. I was just embarrassed about the things I said to you when you came to our house."

"You don't have to be embarrassed. I deserved what you said."

"No, you didn't. I didn't mean any of it. I don't blame you for what happened, Alex. I've always known that you did what you thought was right. You always do what you think is right."

"Thank you. But you've taught me that there's a gray area between right and wrong. You added color to my world too."

"That's what a good florist does." She smiled back at him. "It might be awkward at first but I really hope we can still be friends. I'm willing to give it a shot if you are."

Alex kept his eyes trained on her for a long moment. "That's not possible. We can't be friends, Halona. We've tried that route and failed. Your brother is my friend, but you... I can't be just your friend."

Her lips parted. "You can't?"

"No. The way I see it, we have two choices. One: We ignore each other anytime we meet. We don't talk, don't wave, don't even think about the other."

Halona swallowed past the thick lump in her throat. "I hope the second option is a better one," she said.

He blew out a puff of white air that floated above her. "Option number two: We give this thing between us another shot."

"Is that really a choice?" she asked. "After all we've been through?"

"In my mind, it is. But you make your own decisions. I've learned my lesson," he said with a teasing look.

Halona laughed softly.

"All I know is I can't stop thinking about you or wanting you. I can't stop loving you even if I tried."

She shivered as she stood there in front of him but she wasn't the least bit cold. "What did you just say?"

"I said I love you, Halona Locklear."

Her breath caught in her throat.

"Are you going to say anything?" he finally asked, a worried look wrinkling his brow.

"I...I don't know what to say." Her heart thumped erratically against her rib cage.

"Do you need Theo's notebook? I can get it. It might be easier for you to tell me to get lost in writing."

Halona laughed again even as a tear escaped down her cheek. "That isn't what I'd write."

"No?"

She shook her head. "No. I'd write that I love you too, Alex Baker. I choose you." She stepped into his arms and looked up at him. He was right; there was no other choice but to love him with abandon. She couldn't stop even if she tried. They didn't have a past to overcome; instead, the past was part of what bound them together. It interweaved their lives until it only made sense to live them together.

"Seems like you and I both want the same thing," Alex said.

"So it seems."

"What do you think we should do about it?" He locked his arms around her waist.

"I guess we should go inside where it's warm and spend our very first Christmas together."

"I like the sound of that," he said. "First Christmas implies that there'll be more."

"Lots more, I hope," she said. "Then we can go back

to Cedar Trail and celebrate in private. Just you and me. Mom is keeping Theo tonight."

Alex tightened his hold on her, his blue eyes beaming with love. "That sounds like the perfect Christmas in my book. Looks like you got your Christmas wish," he said then.

Halona tilted her head in question.

"Snow. Theo told me a white Christmas was the only thing on your wish list."

Halona laughed and glanced at the scene around her. "Well, there was more than that," she said, thinking about Theo finally talking to her and telling her he loved her. She looked back up at Alex. She'd wanted him too. "But I got it all. Everything I could ever want."

Alex leaned in, hovering just an inch from her face, a kiss waiting to be had on his lips. "Me too," he whispered. "I got enough to make me happy for an entire lifetime of Christmases."

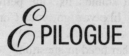

EPILOGUE

The snow still covered the ground one week after Christmas as a new year hung on the horizon.

"Mom?"

Halona turned to look at Theo over her shoulder. "Hmm?"

"Will Elisi Lula and Grandpa let me taste their champagne?"

Halona laughed. "You get white grape juice just like you do every year. It's just as good."

"Why can't I stay with you and Alex?"

Theo had been their constant shadow since Christmas. "Mommy and Alex need some time alone."

"Adult time?" Theo asked. "That's what Elisi Lula said."

"Yes, adult time. But tomorrow, we'll celebrate the New Year together. It's going to be an exciting one."

In fact, Halona couldn't remember the last time she'd been so hopeful and optimistic about the future. Theo was doing well. The flower shop was as busy as ever. And she and Alex were in love. It'd only been a week since they'd gotten back together but their relationship had deepened in that short time to something that spanned ahead like the new year, full of hope and promise.

The doorbell rang, and Halona turned to look at herself in the full-length mirror one last time before heading to the front of the house and answering the door.

"Hi," she said, feeling a little jolt in her heart as she looked at him.

"Ready for a night of fun?" Alex asked.

"Ready."

Halona and Theo followed Alex to his vehicle and then they drove to Halona's parents' house. After leaving Theo inside, Halona and Alex set out.

"Tammy reserved us a table at her new restaurant," Alex said.

"Nice to have friends in high places," Halona offered.

"I sure do miss her at the police station though. That's the one sure thing about life. Everything changes. Nothing stays the same."

"Sometimes change is for the better." Halona reached for Alex's hand.

He lifted her hand to his mouth and kissed it while glancing in her direction.

She shivered at the look in his eyes. She didn't doubt for a moment that he loved her. It was reflected in everything he said and did. "I hope Kaitlyn and Mitch are enjoying their honeymoon right now."

"I'm sure they are," Alex said. "It was a gorgeous wedding."

"Mmm. It really was." The food and all the decorations had been amazing, of course. Kaitlyn had been one of the most beautiful brides that Halona had ever seen but Halona's memories weren't tuned to those aspects. She and Alex had sat hand in hand during the ceremony and then had danced in each other's arms at the reception all night long. She hadn't wanted it to end. "Have you heard from Sharlene?" Halona asked.

"She and Buddy are doing really well," he said, looking over as he drove. "She's brought Buddy in to see me at the station. It's only been a week, but he's getting so big."

Halona grinned. "I bet. Puppies tend to do that."

Alex nodded. "I was thinking that you and I could take Theo on a trip tomorrow."

"Oh? Where to?"

"Well, Buddy apparently had a lot of brothers and sisters. The owner of the mama dog is a neighbor of Sharlene's and was never able to find a good home for the runt of the litter."

Halona's heart rate picked up. A dog? She'd insisted she wasn't ready for a pet but so many things had shifted in their lives in the last month.

"I really miss Buddy. Made me realize that maybe I was missing out. I was missing out on a lot of things."

He pulled up to a favorite lookout spot in Sweetwater Springs and cut the engine. At this point, you could see the entire town, covered in snow and lights. "Our reservation at Tammy's Log Cabin isn't for another twenty minutes. I thought we could wait here."

"Good choice." Halona looked over. "You know Theo is going to be demanding to see you even more if you plan on getting a dog."

"That's good." Alex lifted a hand and smoothed her hair behind her ear, giving her more spine-tingling shivers that quaked through her body. "In fact, I'm counting on it. I want you in my life until I'm old, with gray hair and wrinkled skin."

Halona's lips parted as she sucked in a startled breath.

"Too much too soon?" he asked.

She shook her head.

"Too little too late?" he asked then with a growing grin poking dimples in his cheeks.

She laughed out loud. "More than enough and right on time."

He stared at her for a long moment. "So next year?"

Halona lifted a brow. "What's the question?"

Alex looked out the windshield at the town. Halona followed his gaze. Covered in snow and lights, Sweetwater Springs was a sight to behold. It took her breath away, nearly as much as the man beside her.

Alex turned back to her, his expression serious. Then he shifted around in his seat and reached inside his jacket pocket, pulling out a small black box.

Halona's eyes met his.

"Too much too soon?" he asked again. "All I know is the past has taught me that we only have the moment that we're in. I love you, Halona. I love Theo." He lifted the lid and displayed a round diamond accented with small emeralds.

"Oh, Alex. It's beautiful," she whispered, unable to believe her eyes. This was not what she was expecting tonight. For anyone else, things might be moving too fast but, to her, it felt right. Perfect.

"Marry me?" he asked when she lifted her eyes to search his.

Halona didn't even need to think about it. She nodded and held out her trembling hand. "Nothing would make me happier."

Alex slid the ring on her finger. "I'll take that as a challenge," he finally said, his deep voice filling up the space between them. "I think I can make you a lot happier if given the chance. At least I'm planning to try."

Halona fanned her fingers, admiring the diamond momentarily. Then she looked up at him. "I love you."

"Ditto." Alex looked down at his watch. "Time to make our reservation at Tammy's Log Cabin. We have a lot to celebrate this year."

Halona sucked in a breath, excited and full of hope for all the things to come. She leaned in and whispered before kissing him. "And even more to look forward to in the next."

Triple-Chip Chocolate Cookies
from the *Two Peas & Their Pod Cookbook* by Maria Lichty

Chocolate lovers are in for a real treat with these rich cocoa cookies made with *three* kinds of chocolate chips: milk, semisweet, and white. It's the kind of cookie that technically will scratch the sweet-tooth itch after eating just one, but let's be honest: Who can stop there? Make sure you have a glass of cold milk nearby for dunking.

Prep: 15 minutes
Bake: 10 minutes per batch
Makes 33 cookies

Ingredients:

- 2⅓ cups all-purpose flour
- ¾ cup Dutch-process cocoa powder
- 1 teaspoon baking soda
- ½ teaspoon sea salt, plus more for sprinkling
- 1 cup (½ pound) unsalted butter, at room temperature
- 1 cup granulated sugar
- 1 cup packed light brown sugar
- 2 large eggs
- 1½ teaspoons pure vanilla extract
- ¾ cup milk chocolate chips, plus more for sprinkling
- ¾ cup semisweet chocolate chips, plus more for sprinkling
- ¾ cup white chocolate chips, plus more for sprinkling

Directions:

1. Preheat the oven to 350°F. Line a large baking sheet with a silicone baking mat or parchment paper. Set aside.

2. In a medium bowl, whisk together the flour, cocoa, baking soda, and sea salt. Set aside.

3. In the bowl of a stand mixer fitted with the paddle attachment, combine the butter and both sugars. Mix until smooth, 2 minutes. Add the eggs one at a time, mixing well between each addition. Add the vanilla and mix until combined.

4. Gradually add the flour mixture and beat on low speed until just combined. Use a spatula to stir in all the chocolate chips.

5. Drop the dough by the rounded tablespoon on the prepared baking sheet, about 2 inches apart. Not all the cookies will fit on the sheet for one batch. Bake for 10 minutes, until the cookies are set but still soft in the center. Don't overbake. Let the cookies cool on the baking sheet for 3 to 5 minutes before transferring to a cooling rack to cool completely. While the cookies are still soft, gently press the extra chocolate chips into the cookies to make them look pretty and sprinkle with the extra salt. Once the baking sheet has cooled completely, repeat with the remaining dough.

6. Store the cookies in an airtight container at room temperature for up to 4 days or in the freezer in a freezer-safe bag or container for up to 1 month.

About the Author

Annie Rains is a *USA Today* bestselling contemporary romance author who writes small-town love stories set in fictional places in her home state of North Carolina. When Annie isn't writing, she's living out her own happily ever after with her husband and three children.

Learn more at:

AnnieRains.com
Twitter @AnnieRainsBooks
Facebook.com/AnnieRainsBooks

Then There Was You
Miranda Liasson

Angel Falls is the last place Sara Langdon wants to be. Her hometown may be charming but it's also filled with memories of her "wedding-that-never-was." Yet Sara's grandmother needs her, and joining her dad at his medical practice gives Sara time to figure out what she wants for her future. But when her first patient turns out to be Colton Walker, the man who sabotaged her wedding, Sara starts to wonder if she'll ever be able to escape her past.

A bonus novel from award-winning author Miranda Liasson follows.

FOREVER

For anyone who must walk the
Alzheimer's journey with a loved one.

Sometimes the last person on earth you want to be with is the one person you can't be without.

—Tagline for the movie
Pride and Prejudice, 2005

Chapter 1

♥

Dr. Serafina Langdon stood in the Angel Falls Community Hospital ER before the door to exam room three, squeezing her eyes shut, struggling to be a better person. Clearly a higher power was telling her she'd made the wrong decision, returning to her hometown of Angel Falls, Ohio. Because the name on the sheet of paper in her hand said that the patient occupying the room in front of her was *Colton Bentley Walker*.

Not him. *Anyone* but him. She'd hoped to ease back into town, get herself established, and then confront— on her own terms—the man who'd helped ruin her engagement a year ago. Who'd been a burr in her side for years—since she was fourteen, really. She'd known this day would come; she just hadn't expected it during her first ER shift.

Sara sucked in a deep breath. She could handle this. She reminded herself again of the reason she'd returned to this sleepy small town to join her dad's medical practice after her high-powered Ivy League training at

Columbia. Her sweet, precious grandmother had recently been diagnosed with Alzheimer's disease, and Sara wanted to do all she could to help the woman who'd been her rock, her support, her unwavering cheerleader her whole life. She could face the demons of the past for Nonna's sake.

Sara opened her eyes. Slid the sheet of paper back into the metal pocket on the wall. She couldn't do it. Not today, and maybe not ever. She turned on the soles of her Dansko clogs and walked at a fast clip back to the nurses' station.

The ER was just as white bright at two on a Saturday morning as it was at high noon. And just as busy. Even the administrative assistant was on the phone. Sara peeked around the corner to find the doc she was sharing this shift with. Sara was a primary care doctor, but in a town as small as Angel Falls, the primary care docs worked alongside the ER docs to help staff the ER. Brian Graves, a guy from the next town over whom she knew from residency, was her partner this shift. He had one claim to fame: he'd bedded more women than an eighties rock star.

She hated to approach him, but what was worse? Asking a favor of a guy who wanted to get her in the sack or inflicting irreversible pain and suffering on the man she blamed for ruining her chance at happily ever after?

An unwanted flash of herself in her mother's wedding gown passed before her, pivoting slowly in front of the big mirror at Katie O'Hara's bridal shop, while her sisters and her grandmother and her stepmother oohed and aahed. Sorrow over the future that had come crashing down around her stabbed her in the gut, as it tended to do at the worst times. She didn't want to be reminded of all that pain, and she could *not* see Colton without wanting to kill him. All righty then. Brian it was.

She found him sauntering down the hall to an exam room, eyeing the butt of a nurse as she made the usual two a.m. pot of coffee.

"Trade me a patient?" Sara asked.

He reached out and took the electronic tablet she carried in her hand. "Oh, Chief Walker." He looked from the tablet to her. "You running away from the law or something?"

He chuckled at his own joke and trained his baby blues on her. Many women found them mesmerizing, but she was definitely immune to his slithery brand of charm.

Brian handed her back the tablet, but when she made to take it, he continued to hold on. "Can't do it. Sorry. Although it's an easy case, not sure why you're worried. A few stitches and a tetanus shot and you're done. Unless you're afraid you'll fall for the cop. You'd be better off with a hot doc like me. I love danger too, by the way, if that's what you're looking for."

She rolled her eyes. "I *know* it's an easy case, and I do *not* have a thing for him. What are you working on?"

"Potential cardiac arrest. Or maybe the guy just has bad heartburn from eating at that new Mexican place off Route 44. I already saw him and ordered tests, or I'd trade. Next time I'd be happy to accommodate." He let his gaze drag up and down, as if she were wearing

a boob-uplifting cocktail dress instead of blue scrubs,
a white coat, and a stethoscope adorned with a little
fuzzy koala bear. Her best friend Kaitlyn had given her
the koala as a welcome-home gift, so that the kids Sara
saw wouldn't be so afraid.

"Um, OK. Thanks." He was still eyeballing her with
that yucky I-want-you-babe look.

"Speaking of accommodating…"

"Not going to happen, Brian." She yanked hard on
the tablet. "Thanks, though," she called over her shoulder as she walked away.

Oh, what the hell. If she could handle horny Brian,
she could handle He-Who-Must-Not-Be-Named. So
she knocked on the exam room door and walked in.

There, lying on the gurney watching late-night
Spanish soccer, was Colton, his long lazy frame
sprawled out, one elbow behind his head as he inclined toward the wall-mounted television. The hospital gown fell away from his arm, revealing its sinewy,
tanned glory for all the world to see.

All that manly muscle distracted her momentarily
from his problem, which she now saw clearly. His left
arm was laid out straight, exposing the jagged edges of
a bloody wound that curved around his biceps.

His very toned biceps. He was a fit man, lean but
muscular. Not that she was noticing in any other manner but that of a physician evaluating her patient.

He would be handsome, if not for the fact that
he was the world's biggest jerk. That he was tall and
strong and broad shouldered only mattered from the
standpoint that if you had him with you in a dark

alley, you'd totally be covered. His hair used to be longish and thickly layered but was now cut in a no-nonsense buzz. He flicked his eyes—cool, devastatingly blue, with too-long eyelashes—from the TV to her. She saw the moment recognition set in, and hey, was that *fear*?

She certainly hoped so. After all, she would be the one wielding the needle. This was *her* territory. And Sara was not going to allow him to forget that, not for one second.

He looked her over in that bored, detached way he had, as if she were far beneath his notice. Before she could stop herself, her hand flew up to her glasses, which she suddenly remembered she was wearing for her middle-of-the-night shift. She caught herself from adjusting them in time. Reminded herself that high school was eons ago, that she wasn't that gawky, awkward girl with blazing-red frizzy hair he used to mercilessly call *Sara Jane the Brain*. Followed by more years of being mostly ignored and patiently tolerated, which made it especially awkward as he was her ex-fiancé Tagg's best friend.

Tagg was at the Cleveland Clinic an hour away, working as a neurologist, while she was back home in Angel Falls trying to carve out a life for herself that looked nothing like the one she'd envisioned a year ago. On the bright side, being back home with family reminded her of how much she'd missed them, although the fact that her dad was less than thrilled at having her as a partner at his practice still stung.

Sara had opened her mouth to utter what she hoped

would be a professional greeting when the door opened behind her. Brian stuck his head into the room.

"Hey, Colt, great to see you, buddy," he said. "Wish I could stitch you up myself, but I'm busy with a critically ill patient. You know how that goes."

"Yeah, he needs two Tums stat," Sara said. "Better hurry."

Brian laughed. "Very clever. I like my women with spunk."

"And I'd like to get going on my work." She held the door open and gestured for him to exit. Which he did, unfortunately winking at Colton first.

"I didn't know you and Brian were an item," Colton said. Of course his first words would raise her blood pressure, his favorite pastime.

"We are *not* an item," she said.

"Well, I just assumed. Judging by the lovey-dovey looks you two were exchanging just now."

Lovey-dovey looks? Was the man out of his mind? "I guess you don't need great powers of deduction to be the police chief in this town."

"Ouch," Colton said, pretending to be offended. "Well, excuse me for assuming. You're a little too wild for him anyway, huh, Red?"

Sara felt her cheeks heat, the curse of the redhead. No one called her that ridiculous nickname but him, and she hadn't heard it for years. No one poked fun at her for being buttoned up and uptight except for him, and he'd taken great pleasure in doing it ever since high school.

"Grow up, Chief." She washed her hands at the sink

and pulled suture materials from the drawers. "I just want to remind you that I'm going to be wielding a needle here shortly, so you might want to restrain your mouth. If you're capable."

He held up his good hand. "Hey, more than capable, Doc. You just do your job so I can get back to work, OK?"

She walked over to the exam table. "You also might want to pull a bullet out of your holster and bite on it while I'm stitching you up." He suddenly looked a little pale. She should have felt guilty, but instead she was just glad it shut him up for a minute. "So you got gashed by a rusty fence?"

"I was crawling under it to catch a perp."

"Did you catch him?" She forced her focus on the jagged bloody wound. And away from the biceps.

"I'm surprised a well-educated lady doc like you is so sexist," he said in a deep baritone that seemed to reverberate right through her. "How do you know it wasn't a *she*-criminal?"

"Because we sewed *him* up a half hour ago. What took *you* so long to get here?"

He grinned, but she remained totally unaffected by his bright, broad, and just-imperfect-enough-to-melt-panties smile. "Paperwork at the station."

"You were bleeding like this and you stopped to do *paperwork*?"

He leveled big blue eyes at her and shrugged. Which she interpreted as an "I can handle it all even if I am bleeding like a stuck pig" gesture. His arrogance didn't seem tempered even after all these years.

Her eyes flicked to his too-handsome face. Colton had been blessed with angel-kissed good looks that had been turning the heads of females since he was a boy. He'd been popular, a stellar athlete, and quarterback on the football team until an injury had sidelined him and caused him to lose his college scholarship. He was the guy who'd sat on homecoming and prom courts, and who'd always had his pick of women.

Bringing her focus back to the task at hand, she prepared a soapy solution by squirting a bottle of antiseptic scrub into a bowl and brought it over to his bedside.

"Maybe I should wait for the nurses to do that," he said, sounding a little nervous.

"They're all tied up," Sara said sweetly, holding the curved suture needle up so he got a good view of it. "Better if I do it all and get you out of here quicker. I'm going to soak your arm in the antiseptic now."

"Will it sting?"

"The last patient cried for ten minutes, but he was six. Since you're a tough guy, I'd anticipate you'd be fine in half that time."

His dark gaze met hers, his thick brows knit together. Under all that bravado, Mr. Arrogance did seem a little worried. Which made her unconscionably happy. To his credit, when she lowered his arm into the soapy tub, he didn't even flinch. Truthfully, he didn't have to, because the solution they used didn't sting at all.

As she irrigated and scrubbed, she felt his gaze on her, quiet and assessing. She didn't usually get unnerved when people watched her, but she didn't like being this close to him, smelling his spicy, woodsy smell, feeling his eyes drill a hole through her.

When she glanced at him, he steered his gaze quickly away. "Um, not to question your professional ability," he said, "but are you sure you can see out of those things? I mean, I wouldn't want you to screw up. My arm is one of my better features."

Her cheeks burned, and for an instant she was back in ninth grade, feeling the same acute anguish. *You ever think about getting contacts, Brain? There just might be a pretty girl under all that glass.*

He was the kind of man who used his charm and good looks to get away with acting like a jerk. *Still.*

She couldn't believe she'd ever expected him to have her back last year, when he'd failed to keep her fiancé from "celebrating" so hard he fell face-first into his bachelor party cake—*and* the woman in it. Valerie Blake had always had a thing for Tagg in high school, a fact everyone knew. Especially Colt, who'd hired her for the party.

Tagg had been Sara's first boyfriend, and he'd loved her despite her ugly duckling phase. He'd seen who she was and loved her for her brains, not despite them. She'd often wondered why someone as good-looking as Tagg would want her, and sometimes that had kept her up at night. But he'd proposed, and suddenly everything she'd ever wanted was about to come true—a great job, a loving husband, a home of her own.

Until Colton had gone and waved a half-naked Valerie in front of him. Colton had always had a way of knowing her deepest fear and shining a spotlight on it. And his actions last year hadn't just shone the spotlight, they'd blown up her entire life.

Yes, Tagg was to blame. She understood that. But Colton had lit the match. If he'd been a good best man and contained the party, Tagg would've gotten over his last-minute panic without incident. They'd be married now, all settled and enjoying life in the house they'd picked out in a pretty suburb of Cleveland. The one that Tagg was now living in with his girlfriend, aka Cake Girl.

Sara stood up straight. She couldn't afford to wallow in the past. "My glasses may not be attractive," she said, "but I can see twenty-twenty out of them. Of course, if I miss a stitch or two, the scar will just make you look a little tougher. Because you're kind of a pretty boy now."

He threw up his hand in defense. "Hey, no offense, Dr. Einstein. Just making a joke. I trust you."

He was looking at her oddly. For a moment she wondered if he felt bad for the glasses joke. Or maybe he'd made it on purpose to throw her off-kilter. It didn't matter.

Some people never grew up, never changed. Colton was obviously one of those people. But she had. And he couldn't hurt her anymore. She wouldn't let him.

* * *

Colton shouldn't have ribbed her about the glasses. He immediately saw that in her eyes. To be honest, he'd said it because he felt…uncomfortable. A little too close to Sara Langdon, who was all grown up and nothing like the shy, homely girl she'd been in high school. But to her he was still an emotionally stunted adolescent who needed to grow the hell up.

Surely Sara had to know how attractive she was now. All that thick hair the color of copper and those stunning green eyes. Not to mention her killer curves. She was Dr. Knockout, nothing like the Coke-bottle-bottom-glasses-wearing fourteen-year-old he'd known so long ago when he was a smart-mouthed hotshot and she was an easy target. Lest he soften, he reminded himself she was still the most type A personality he'd ever met. And Colt didn't do type A.

"Lie back," she said, flicking off the TV.

"Hey! Game's on," he said, but he hadn't really been paying attention to it. He knew he shouldn't be so difficult at every turn, but he couldn't seem to help himself. Irritating her was too much fun.

Warm soapy water flooded his arm and trickled into a basin she placed under it. She worked quickly and competently, and he felt his eyes closing. He was finally coming down from the adrenaline rush and it was, after all, the middle of the night. He even got pretty close to falling asleep, until he felt the sting of a needle.

He opened one eye and looked at her. "Warn a guy, will ya?"

She didn't respond, all concentration and focus. Whatever she'd injected had numbed him, so he watched her loop the needle in and out, suture and cut. Repeat. In and out, suture and cut.

"Is it bad?" he asked.

She turned her gaze on him. Even behind the big

glasses he could see the soft moss green of her eyes, just as pretty as he remembered. "I think you'll live. And I'm no plastic surgeon, but the scar will be minimal."

She worked in silence for a few minutes. The ticking of the old wall clock was the loudest thing in the room. Outside in the hallway there sounded a scattered symphony of beeps and alarms, intercom noises, and even the crackling fuzz of an EMS radio announcing another ambulance on its way.

When she bent her head he could smell her hair. *Lemons.* Nice. It made him recall a time, long ago, when things could've been different, when the animosity that gaped so large and wide between them might've turned into something else. But then Tagg had moved in and swept her off her feet.

Sara's life had been full of choices Colton had never had. After he'd busted up his knee in high school, he'd lost his football scholarship to Penn State. The policemen who'd worked with his dad—who'd started out as an Angel Falls cop before moving to Chicago, where he'd died in the line of duty—took him under their wing and helped him get to college. After college Colton had returned home to take care of his grandmother and sister, end of story. Whereas Sara had left town to conquer the world, attending Princeton on scholarship and medical school in New York City.

The opportunity for anything more between them had long passed, and the intervening years had cemented their relationship as antagonistic. He also understood she was furious at him. That ass Tagg had gotten drunk the night of the bachelor party despite

Colton's best efforts to cut him off. Colton had arranged for the cake stunt but had no idea the woman the company would send to pop out of the cake was someone Tagg had had the hots for in high school. And apparently still did.

Sara blamed Colton. After all, he'd been the best man. He was supposed to keep order and prevent things from getting out of control. What Sara didn't know was that Tagg had been nervous as a teenage shoplifter the entire week before the wedding. Colton had tried to quell his doubts and calm him down the best he could, had even driven Tagg home himself to keep him out of trouble the night of the bachelor party, but Tagg had still figured out a way to break Sara's heart.

Finally Sara was done, and he sat up, looking over her handiwork.

"Fifteen stitches," she announced, walking over to the counter.

"Thanks. Am I done?" He got ready to hop off the gurney.

"Not just yet," she said, coming to stand in front of him, blocking his exit. She pulled a syringe from her white coat pocket and uncapped it, displaying a needle that seemed to be the size of a quarter-inch drill bit. "Bend over and drop your drawers."

"No." As in, there was no way in hell he was going to drop trou in front of her.

She raised an elegant brow. "What do you mean, *no*?"

"I don't want it in my ass."

"Well, unless you want your arm to fall off, you

probably want to do as the doctor orders." She flicked
the syringe with her finger. Put her finger on the
plunger.

"I've never seen a needle that big for a shot. I'll just
wait until Monday when my *usual* doctor can see me."
She didn't have all the control here...did she?

"As you like. Except by then lockjaw will have set in
and you won't be able to swallow or breathe." She bit
back a smile. "Oh, and did I mention the drool? There
will be lots of it."

She was enjoying this way too much. But the picture
her words conjured was enough to keep him planted.
"You're serious, aren't you?"

Tapping the syringe with her finger, she said, "Dead
serious. Drop 'em, Officer Walker."

"*Chief* Walker," he mumbled as he stood up and
dropped his pants, leaning over the gurney.

He smelled the antiseptic scent of alcohol, felt the
rub of a cotton ball on his ass cheek.

That was when he decided not to let her get the best
of him. At the last minute, he cranked his head back
and gave her his most charming grin. Sara glanced up,
maybe even looked a little startled.

"You can turn around now," she said, cool as a cu-
cumber.

"I'd rather watch," he said, not backing down.

"Suit yourself," she said, drawing back and stabbing
the needle into his flesh.

Son of a bitch. Charm got him nowhere with her. It
never had.

The needle sliced through his muscle, burning and

stinging. It felt like an ice pick boring into his flesh. He bit down on the insides of his cheeks to take the pain.

Then she was talking again. "The most common side effect of a tetanus shot is pain at the injection site. You'll be fine in a week or two."

He pulled up and belted his pants before she could inflict more damage. Blew out the breath he'd been holding. "A *week* or two?"

"You just won't be able to sit comfortably for a while. Stitches come out in a week to ten days. Come back if anything looks red or swollen." She discarded the syringe in the red sharps container on the counter, pulled off her gloves with a snap, and tossed them in the trash. Then she wrote a few things down and handed him a clipboard. "Sign out here."

He took a step forward. His butt cheek hurt like he'd just been bitten by a yellow jacket. Still, he signed on the dotted line and managed a smile. "See you around, Doc."

She shot him a wide, innocent smile. "See you."

Chapter 2

♥

A light summer rain was pattering on Nonna's old slate roof when Sara awakened the next morning in her mom's old bedroom under the eaves of Nonna's little craftsman bungalow. The sound of the rain on the shingles above the sharply slanted ceiling brought her back to her childhood, when she used to snuggle and giggle with her sisters under this same patchwork quilt her grandmother had made when she was a young bride.

Desperate to know the mother they'd lost to cancer when Sara was just thirteen years old, her sisters and she used to carefully sift through her mother's childhood possessions—classic books like *Little Women* and *Gone With the Wind*, award ribbons for track and basketball, literary awards for writing and English. Air Supply and Journey posters pinned up on the closet door, endless balls of yarn and colorful handmade scarves. Every empty perfume bottle, every old notebook filled with notes and doodles was an endlessly fascinating clue to who their mother had been, a tiny piece of her to hold on to just a little bit longer.

But waking up in a shrine was lonely. She thought of Tagg, waking up under the eaves next to his girlfriend in the brand-new house he and Sara had meant to call home.

His rejection still hurt, but now her grief was more for the life she would've had rather than for Tagg himself. Being married, decorating their new home, planning a family...*that* was the life she mourned. After all, she was almost thirty-one years old. She'd wanted that life, dammit. A happy life with a partner she loved, settling down. Being able to do all the things she'd put off for years because she was too busy studying, working, and being broke while all her other friends already had great jobs and had started their real lives. She was tired of delayed gratification. And she wanted a dog.

For ten years she hadn't thought of her life as being any other way but with Tagg. And then suddenly...everything had changed. She'd gotten over the shock, yes. But she felt adrift, unmoored. Bobbing around in the middle of the ocean with no compass.

Her grandmother had always been her guide, and now Sara was losing her too. All the more reason to make every moment with Nonna count. To be there for Nonna the way her grandmother always had been for her.

Sara dug under the bed for her fuzzy purple slippers and tiptoed down the hall. The wooden floors creaked a little, but Sara wouldn't trade this old house for anything. She'd always dreamed of someday having a quirky house with a lot of charm, but Tagg had preferred a brand-new house in a cookie-cutter subdivision that looked like all its neighbors, and she'd gone along with it. How much else had she gone along with, not really wanting to?

It was definitely too early for soul-searching. Nonna wasn't up yet, which meant Sara had time to start the Sunday routine, one Nonna had followed without deviation for fifty years. First up was starting the coffee and homemade cinnamon rolls, then getting ready for Mass at St. Alfonso's, followed by coffee and doughnuts and socializing in the church hall, followed by a trip to the grocery store and an afternoon of cooking for Sunday dinner.

Sunday dinner was a tradition that had been going on for generations. During her years of medical school and residency, Sara had missed everything about it—the food, the easy camaraderie, the squabbling—typical family stuff that made anything else the world had to throw at you bearable. Gathering at Nonna's every week was nonnegotiable; unless you were overseas or serving a life sentence, you showed up, on pain of death.

Sara loved cooking alongside Nonna, spending time with her and learning to make the special Italian dishes that had brought her family together for generations. Not for the first time since she'd been back, it hit home hard that time with anyone was not an endless gift. Today would be the first time she'd see her entire family since she'd been back, and though her crazy family came with its own set of challenges, they loved each other a lot, and she never would've made it through the last year without them.

As Sara descended the stairs, she was greeted by the familiar clicking of Nonna's dog Rocket's toenails as he raced to her across the old pine floors. Rocket was a bull terrier with brown ears, a brown patch encompassing his left eye, and another on his right flank. A combination of pirate and Guernsey cow. His personality was definitely more on the pirate side; he was charming, sneaky, and a trickster.

"You got up early this morning, didn't you?" Rocket usually slept curled up against her back, since Nonna often shoved him out of her bed, claiming she couldn't sleep well. But he'd left her room sometime before dawn. Maybe he had insomnia too. Sara could relate. The events of the past year had kept her awake many a night.

"Oh, I bet you want some bacon, don't you?" she crooned as she scratched behind his ears. "Because it's Sunday, yes it is. Want to go get the paper?"

At the word *bacon*, the dog's ears perked up and he started jumping up and down, practically levitating with glee.

"OK, let's go."

She couldn't find a robe, but when she got to the front hall, she found Nonna's purple raincoat with a row of ducks along the bottom and slid it on over her pj boxers and T-shirt. Rocket, true to his name, darted out the front door into the wet morning to do his business.

The mid-June rain was steady but not pouring. The dark clouds and the fact that it was still quite early—

before seven—cast the day in gray. The smell of clean
fresh air mingled with the scent of roses in crazy, brilliant bloom along the driveway. Sara located the paper
in the grass near the road and, kicking off her slippers,
ran barefoot to where it lay, encased in bright-blue plastic. Just as she bent over to pick it up, Rocket swooped
in and grabbed it up in his mouth.

The dog was quick, but Sara was quicker. She
clamped on to one end of the paper and tugged. Unfortunately, Rocket seemed to think she was playing
his favorite game. As she tugged, he tugged harder.
Her hood fell off, sending a cascade of cold rainwater
spilling down her back.

With one wrenching pull, the dog sidestepped away,
bolting for the yew hedge that separated her grandma's
property from the street. Sara ran through the wet grass
after the dog. He teased her by showing her the paper,
an arm's length away, but as soon as she reached for it,
he dashed into the hedge.

He emerged a few seconds later, wet and leaf
covered...without the paper.

Oh, bollocks.

There it was, lying in the mud under the hedge, surrounded by prickly branches that rivaled Sleeping
Beauty's briar patch. Sara walked around to the road
side, having no choice but to get down on her hands and
knees and dig out the paper. Ugh, and all this before
coffee. She stuck her arm into the tangle of branches
and was trying to capture the bag with her fingers when
she heard a car idling behind her. And something that
sounded suspiciously like a whistle.

Sara immediately popped her head up and turned around. A spotlight with the wattage of the noontime sun beamed on her. Through the glare she could make out a police cruiser. There sat Colton behind the wheel, his arm sticking out the window. The arm that she'd stitched up just a few hours ago. Clearly healing well, due to her excellent care, thank you very much.

"You can turn the floodlight off," she said. "And did you just whistle? Because that would be completely unprofessional."

"Of course not." But he was biting down on his cheeks to keep from laughing. "I just happened to be driving home, minding my own business, when suddenly there it was... plain as day."

"There *what* was?" Sara asked, lifting a brow. He'd better not mention anything about her behind. That would be... inappropriate. But, she couldn't help thinking, completely par for the course as far as their relationship went.

He swept his hand in her direction to demonstrate. "A roadside distraction."

She rolled her eyes.

"Need some help?"

"Thanks, but I'm fine. I was just fishing the paper out of the hedge." Rocket sat next to the cruiser at full attention. Colton reached under his seat and tossed him a dog biscuit. Clearly something he'd done before, judging by Rocket's expectant look and the fact that his tail was wagging faster than the speed limit.

As if on cue, the front door of the house opened and her little gray-haired grandmother stepped out on the porch. She was wearing a bright flowered apron and waving excitedly. "Colton! Yoo-hoo, Colton!"

Yoo-hoo, Colton?

"Hey there, Rose," he called back. "I'll be right up."

Sara shot him a startled glance. *Right up?*

"Hurry up, dear," Nonna said. "I'm just going to put some cinnamon rolls in."

The thought of Nonna baking sent a stab of fear through her. Dad and her stepmom, Rachel, had already gently and painstakingly taken away Nonna's car…Surely operating an oven was just as dangerous as driving.

Colton gave Sara a satisfied grin and backed up the cruiser, pulling it into the driveway while she dug around in the hedge and rescued the soggy paper. They walked silently to the house, the dog trailing happily at Sara's heels. She felt aware of Colton in an uncomfortable way—a way that prickled the hairs at the back of her neck. Extreme irritation could do that to you, she supposed. It had nothing to do with that white, just-short-of-perfect smile that lit up his face and made little crinkles appear around his striking blue eyes, which were filled with amusement. These traits might make him seem like a warm and caring person, yet she reminded herself he was not. "After you," he said, holding open the door.

It took the willpower of the ages not to roll her eyes again. Once they were inside, she took off her grandma's rain jacket and shook it, then hung it on a hook in the foyer to dry. When she turned around, she saw Colton quickly avert his eyes.

Realization dawned, sending heat blazing to her cheeks. She was wearing pj boxers and a black T-shirt with a rib cage on it that read "I Got an 'A' in Anatomy." She grabbed Nonna's long gray sweater off a hanger and tugged it on, along with the purple slippers she'd left on the foyer floor.

Nonna appeared in the doorway. "Come in, you two. I just put coffee on."

Sometimes Nonna amazed her and seemed completely unaffected by the disease that had crept up so insidiously. It was a cruel thing, the dementia. Even though Sara was a doctor and knew the course, the moments Nonna acted exactly like herself made hope soar, as if this whole thing were a nightmare and she would wake up and Nonna would be... Nonna again. Then the next moment her grandmother would repeat a thought for the tenth time, and hope would come crashing down.

"Here you go," Colton said, handing her grandmother a nice dry newspaper. Sara looked at the soggy blue bag in her hand, pierced with multiple fang marks.

Ass kiss, she mouthed behind Nonna's back.

"Oh, you are a dear," Nonna said, patting Colton's hand. "I bet you worked all night too."

"I did have the night shift, yes, ma'am," Colton said, grinning widely. His charm knew no bounds, affecting women of all ages. And dogs, as Rocket had no reservations about accepting Colton's friendly scratch behind the ears as an invitation to glue himself to his side.

"You must be starving then."

Was this what had been going on while she'd been

gone? Colton had insinuated himself into her grand-mother's good graces. For free meals and other grandmotherly services, no doubt. Like socks-darned, buttons-sewed, shirts-ironed kinds of things.

In the kitchen Sara was surprised to see her younger brother Rafe sitting at the heavy oak table, still in his firefighter uniform. He rose, walked over, and kissed Nonna. "I let myself in," he said, gesturing to the back door. "I see I'm just in time for breakfast. Hey, Colton. Hi, Sis." Sara hugged her baby brother, who was around three years younger than she but was also a broad-shouldered, muscular six two, so *baby* probably wasn't quite the right term. Colton and Rafe shared some kind of complicated handshake that made it clear they were on friendly—*fist-bumping*—terms.

"Tough night?" Colton asked, sitting down with Rafe at the table. Rocket flopped down at his feet and promptly fell asleep.

"Big three-alarm blaze in the next county. Took us most of the night to put it out. Fortunately it was an abandoned warehouse, so no one was hurt." Rafe spoke animatedly with his hands, and his whole face lit up.

"You firefighters can't wait to rush to a great fire, can you?" Colton said.

Rafe laughed. "At least no one's shooting at me. Or making me chase them under barbed wire fences. Your arm OK?"

Sara helped Nonna put the rolls in the oven, then watched Nonna disappear into the dining room to fetch a platter. She sneaked a glance at Colton, whose response to Rafe was a shrug and a smile. Today, as in the ER, he seemed to take pains to downplay the danger of his job. She wasn't sure if he was just cavalier or if maybe time had humbled him a little. Probably the former. He always had been Mr. No Big Deal.

He sat there talking shop with her brother, looking the picture of masculinity in his navy-blue uniform, his hands grasping his coffee mug. Sara couldn't help but notice the sinewy muscle that ran the length of his tanned arms, and the elegant, long fingers curled casually around his cup.

"I heard you were in the ER," Rafe said. "Hopefully your doctor did a nice job fixing you up." Rafe gave Sara a wink.

"Yeah," Colton said, "my doctor did a nice job but also gave me a nice pain in the ass. But I guess that's OK, because she also complimented me on it."

Sara dropped the mixing bowl she was carrying into the sink. "I did *not* compliment you on your ass." There was no way she was going to let him get away with that in front of her brother.

"Maybe not, but I could tell you wanted to."

What an ass. Literally. "That is the most ridiculous—"

Nonna shuffled back into the kitchen. "Sara, be a dear and pour Colton some coffee, would you?" Nonna asked.

"Can I put arsenic in it?" she mumbled as she took the coffeepot out of its holder.

"I heard that," Colton said quietly as Nonna proceeded to wipe off the counters. "So much for the Hippocratic oath."

"That only applies to patients," Sara said.

Colton slid his cup toward her as she approached the table. "You did sew up my arm, so I guess you *are* my doctor."

"A one-time visit to the ER does *not* make me your doctor."

"You're right. I'm not a one-night stand kind of guy."

Rafe laughed. "That's not what I heard."

Colton's face turned red. Sara was surprised he was capable of a good strong blush. "I could tell stories about you, Rafe," Colton said, "but out of respect for your grandma I'll refrain. Besides, you're listening to too many rumors."

Rafe patted Colton on the back. "They're not rumors, Colt my man, they're legend."

Sara made an involuntary gagging noise.

"Sara, are you choking on something?" Nonna asked.

"Just the thought of all those poor women," Sara said so only the men could hear. "I'm fine, Nonna," she said louder.

"Don't feel bad for those women," Rafe said. "They were all very…happy."

Colton gave Rafe a cease-and-desist look. "Rafe, so help me God, if you do not shut up, I'm going to tell everyone about the time we all went out for your birthday and you decided it would be fun to take a little dive into the river buck naked with that—"

"Hey, Nonna," Rafe said loudly, "those rolls ready yet? I sure am hungry."

These guys and their fish stories. Sara found it interesting that Colton seemed so eager to downplay his reputation. Rafe had told her once that the firemen and the town's one deputy police officer jokingly referred to Colton as the Revolver, and it wasn't because of his gun.

"Oh, you boys go out and have fun together, do you?" Nonna asked, bringing the sugar bowl to the table.

"Yes, Grandma," Rafe said. "Colt and I go out all the time."

Sara was happy to take a seat at the far end of the old oak table and tune out their banter. Since she'd been gone, it seemed Colton had become part of the family. She hadn't counted on negotiating that now that she was home to stay.

A big bay window overlooked her gran's backyard and a giant old oak tree that she and her siblings used to climb. In the years when her grandpa was alive, they used to swing on a swing he'd hung from the lowest branch, which was now much higher than she remembered. The swing was long gone. Even the dirt patch underneath, worn by little feet pushing higher and skidding to a stop, had filled in with grass.

Sara supposed she'd have to get used to such change. After all, this was not the world of her childhood, or even the world she'd left behind when she left town for college and med school. Or, for that matter, the world she'd left last year when her engagement went bust.

"I can't find that darn pot holder," Nonna said, rummaging through a drawer.

Sara got up to help, found the pot holder on top of the toaster, and pulled the rolls out of the oven.

"Would you like some cream, Colton?" Nonna asked.

"No, thanks, Mrs. Faranaccio. I take it black," he said.

Sara helped Nonna ice the cinnamon rolls. When she returned to the table, she noticed a full, steaming cup of coffee sitting at her place.

Nonna couldn't have poured it. Rafe was at the other end of the table, near the back door. That left Colton.

She must have looked a little puzzled. He passed her the cream, chatting to Rafe about some kind of potluck the police and fire departments were going to host.

How did he know she took cream?

"Colton, would you like cream, dear?" Nonna asked again as she brought the rolls to the table and sat down.

"I'm good, thanks, Mrs. F," Colton said politely.

Sara caught his gaze across the table. He hadn't embarrassed Nonna or pointed out that she'd asked twice. Still, Sara got busy stirring her coffee, unwilling to let him see her concern.

Every little slip-up Nonna made caused a little trickle of dread to churn in her stomach and gave her a tip-of-the-iceberg kind of feeling. Nonna, however, was in a great mood, laughing and joking with the guys.

After polishing off half the cinnamon rolls, Rafe said, "I gotta run."

"I'll walk you out," Sara said, following him out the front door and closing it behind her.

"What's the deal with you and Colton?" he asked as soon as they were out of earshot. "You were busting his chops."

"You *know* what the deal is."

Rafe's brows pulled down as he frowned. "He's a good guy."

Sara crossed her arms. "Legends? Antics with women? And you pal around with him."

"You certainly seemed amused about his dating history," Rafe said. "Maybe you're a little jealous?"

"Jealous? Of the Revolver? You're . . . you're nuts!"

"Right. Well, you know how I feel about things," Rafe said. "Tagg got his just deserts, if you pardon the cake pun. All he thought about was himself. Good riddance."

"God, Rafe, I wish you'd have more conviction about things," Sara said, smiling. He'd always been a straight shooter, and he'd always been quick to stand up for her, even when they were kids. She had to admit it felt really good to have her grown-up little brother defend her. But that didn't mean she was going to agree with him about Colton.

"Anyway," Rafe said, "give Colton a chance. He might surprise you."

"Um, last time I checked you were my *much* younger brother, and therefore it goes against natural sibling order for you to offer me advice. You're forgetting I've known Colton longer than I've known Tagg. Once a jerk, always a jerk."

"Geez, give the guy a break, OK? People can change."

"Dad swears most of his patients still have the same personality they had when they were thirteen."

"That's fatalistic," Rafe said.

"So is dating a different girl every week," Sara said, tossing him a pointed look.

"I said people can change—if they want to. I, how-ever, have no reason to, seeing as I'm in my sexual prime. See you tonight for Sunday dinner?"

"Yeah." She kissed her brother on the cheek. "See you." Sara couldn't be too critical of her brother's dating habits. His longtime girlfriend had died in an accident when he was just twenty-one, and for years he'd barely dated at all. She supposed the fact that he was dating now and joking about it was a big improvement. She just wasn't sure how much of his attitude was bravado.

She watched from the front porch as Rafe got into his shiny black F-150 with custom chrome rims and drove away. Colton came out of the house carrying two rolls in a baggie. No one ever left Nonna's house with-out a full doggie bag.

"Thanks for letting me stay for breakfast," he said.

She shrugged, although she was secretly surprised he'd bothered with a thank-you. "Not my choice. It was Nonna's."

Colton was standing very close. So close she couldn't help noticing the vibrant blue of his eyes, a cross between summer sky and Caribbean ocean. Man, the guy had been kissed by the gods in looks. A real heart-stopper.

Not that he stopped *her* heart or anything.

"Bye, Mrs. Faranaccio," he called to her grandmother, who was still in the house. "See ya, Red." His gaze flicked quickly up and down Sara. "I tend to agree with your shirt. You do get an A in Anatomy. But it's a shame, because the rest of you is a little salty." He gave Sara one last sweeping look, put on his hat, and headed out into the rain.

Chapter 3

♥

At four forty-five p.m., Nonna's kitchen smelled like spaghetti sauce and freshly baked bread. As Sara pulled the homemade rolls out of the oven, she silently declared Nonna's house ready for Sunday dinner.

"Nonna, where's Gabby?" she called to her grandmother, who was in the dining room setting the table.

"Oh, I don't know, dear," she said as she set two forks by one plate. Before Sara could intervene, Gabby's voice called from afar.

"I'm up here!"

"I'll grab Gabby and be right back to help you finish setting the table," Sara said.

"Take your time," Nonna said, lining up yet a third fork near the other two.

"Here" turned out to be the attic, up the pull-down ladder at the top of the stairs to a space under the dormers lined by old crossbeams and layers of fluffy pink insulation. A solitary light bulb hung on a chain from the central roof beam.

Sara climbed halfway up the ladder, her head at floor level, debating going the rest of the way up. "Hey, Gabs, dinner's in fifteen minutes. Can you come down and help? Nonna needs some help setting the table."

"Oh, sure," Gabby said, crinkling up her cute nose. Gabby was Sara's closest sister, in age and in bonding. They were only fifteen months apart, and they told each other nearly everything. Gabby was one of the big reasons being back home was tolerable.

"Come up here, I'm scared," Gabby said, exuberantly holding out her arms. Did Sara mention she was the dramatic sister as well as the imaginative one? "I need my big sister. Especially since I've barely seen you since you've been home. Besides, Nonna sent me up here to look for those pretty dessert plates with the white scalloped edges, and I can't find them. Remember those?"

Sara hauled herself up the remaining rungs and sat down near Gabby on a couple of stacked wooden crates.

"This place always creeped me out," said Gabby, who was sitting in the middle of the wooden floor surrounded by open boxes. "Rafe used to tell me terrible stories about families forced to live in the attic—like in those novels everyone was reading years ago, remember?—and I believed every word. I never wanted to come up here as a kid."

"You always had the biggest imagination too," Sara said.

Despite being a wills and trusts attorney, Gabby was a dreamer, and Sara wouldn't be surprised at all if she'd gotten caught up in rifling through Nonna's stuff, completely losing track of time.

Sara took a glance around under the dim light of the solitary bulb. For an attic it was pretty meticulous: Boxes lined up and tidy. Rolls of fabric propped in one corner, covered in plastic. An old wooden rocker and a baby bassinet hanging from hooks, plastic zipper bags containing old curtains, an old aluminum washtub that they used to wash their dog in.

"Maybe while you're at it you can find my thirteenth-birthday present."

"You still haven't given up on that, have you? God, we looked everywhere for that."

Sara shrugged. Her mom had been very sick on her thirteenth birthday and had died just a week later. "Mom was really good about that. She never forgot a birthday. Maybe she just hid it so well we never found it."

"Well, I'm happy to keep looking. And while we're at it, you can help me find Mom's journals." Gabby dug into a nearby box and took out something wrapped in yellowed newspaper. "Wow, look at this." She held up a ceramic flamingo standing on one pink foot. "Fabulous. I might need this for my apartment."

"Nice," Sara said. "Mom had journals?"

"She was always writing in spiral notebooks, do you remember that?" Gabby said. "They have to be here somewhere." She pulled out another box. Also filled with newspaper-wrapped objects.

Sara reached in and unwrapped one. "Oh, Nonna's Fiestaware!" She dug through the box. "In all colors of the rainbow. I remember this stuff!" A thought suddenly occurred to her. "Does Dad know where Mom's journals are? Maybe he'd have them instead of Nonna."

Gabby shook her head. "I'm checking here first. I mean, when Dad married Rachel, he probably gave most of Mom's stuff to Nonna. That makes sense, doesn't it? You wouldn't keep your dead wife's personal belongings in your attic, would you?"

Sara had no idea. What she did know was that even now, her dad said very little about their mother. He never talked freely, and when questioned gave the briefest answers possible.

Sometimes she longed to sit down with him and have a heart-to-heart. Ask him about their mom, their childhood, happy memories. With Nonna's memory fading, she wished her dad would share more about her mother.

Actually, she wished her dad would share more, period. With her mother gone, her dad had turned into a man who was very involved in guiding and shaping their life decisions as he saw fit. Without their mother's more relaxed and intuitive attitude, her father sometimes pushed for things he felt strongly were right but weren't necessarily so.

"Have you asked Nonna?" Sara asked.

"All she says is, 'Your mother was always scribbling in those notebooks of hers.'"

"Maybe someone got rid of them. Jane Austen's sister burned two-thirds of her letters, did you know that? Presented to the world only a certain scrubbed version of events. Some people claim she ruined her sister's legacy."

"I'd call that a good sister," Gabby said.

Sara laughed. "Maybe so. But Gabby, journals are private. Maybe Mom wouldn't want us reading them."

"I need them," Gabby insisted. "Don't you ever feel you wished you knew her? Not how we knew her as children, but how she was as an adult?"

Sara got up and hugged her sister. It was a relief to know she had as many questions about their mom as Sara did. "I wish that all the time." She sat down next to her on the floor, pushing aside a box of recipe clippings. "I wish Dad would talk to us more about her."

"Dad has a different life now. He hates talking about Mom, and I always feel uncomfortable bringing it up in front of Rachel."

"Well, I think looking for her journals is a great idea, and of course I'll help." Sara examined the old box of cut-out recipes, for sure Nonna's doing. "So, everything going OK with Malcolm?" Gabby had reconnected with her college sweetheart, who was a hedge fund manager they'd all been very relieved she'd stopped dating years ago. At the time he'd spent more time exercising than being with Gabby, and that about said it all.

Gabby flashed a bright smile. A little too bright, but maybe that was just Sara's imagination. "Things couldn't be better. Malcolm is awesome. He showers me with gifts and never fails to tell me how much he loves me. In fact, he's planning to come out to dinner with the whole family sometime soon. Are you free some Friday or Saturday?"

"For you, I'm free anytime."

"Great. You know, we've gotten pretty serious."

Sara raised a brow and tried hard to put a nonjudgmental expression on her face. "Really?"

Gabby nodded. "I know you didn't like him that much, but he's changed. Grown up. I think you're going to really like him."

Sara's recollection of Malcolm was that he was always into *things*. Bigger, better, more expensive things. One look at Gabby's face and Sara realized her sister was waiting expectantly for her to say something. Screaming *Get out while you can!* probably wasn't what she wanted to hear.

"Gabby, my main objection to Malcolm back then was that he was really into himself. He spent a ton of money on you, but it seemed like that was all part of his image. I hope that's changed."

"Malcolm's very ambitious. Dad would love that. He's a hard worker but he still finds time for me. He doesn't beat children or kill cats. Plus I'm twenty-nine. He's not perfect, but who is? Maybe he's as close as I'm going to come."

"Oh, Gabby." Sara hated the idea that Gabby seemed to be talking herself into believing how great this guy was. "You're not over the hill yet."

She shrugged. "Not yet. But it's getting really hard to meet nice guys who aren't already taken, going through nasty breakups, or who aren't just plain weird." She paused. "Oh, and who also meet Dad's criteria for a good spouse: educated, makes good money, worthy of his daughters."

Sara laughed but had to admit Gabby was right

about their father. He definitely had certain expectations about the men he wanted them to marry.

"Also, I have one more bit of news: I just got promoted to partner, but that's less thrilling. Overall, life is great!" Gabby worked for a law firm in downtown Cleveland and had a gorgeous loft apartment there.

"How come you didn't tell us about the partnership? That's fantastic! Another reason to celebrate."

"The money's good, but it's dullsville, Sara. I'm working eighty hours a week, and every single minute, I feel like pulling all my hair out one strand at a time."

"God, Gabby."

"I know. Please don't tell Dad, but I'm working on an exit plan. Besides, for now, Malcolm makes up for how crappy I feel about my job."

Worry riffled through Sara like a good strong wind before a storm. Their father had urged Gabby, wonderful, artistic, creative Gabby, to go to law school. It had probably saved her from becoming a hippie. It also appeared to have made her very unhappy.

Despite the bad vibes, Sara put on a cheery smile. "Well, we can't wait to see him again." She pulled something out of a box. "Oh, look what I found!"

"Is it the dessert plates?" Gabby asked.

"No, it's my beat-up old copy of *Pride and Prejudice*. Look." She held up the battered book with curled edges and yellowed pages, which looked as if it had definitely seen better days. The first thing she did was to put it to her nose and sniff it. God, she loved the smell of real books. Especially old and beloved ones, and this one had been—and still was—her favorite.

"Oh, you carried that thing around for years," Gabby said.

Sara grinned. "I love it. I just never thought *Pride and Prejudice* would become my life."

"What are you talking about?"

"Oh, just Tagg. I mean, I thought he was my Darcy." She sighed.

Gabby sat down beside her and gave her a squeeze. "Tagg would definitely play the role of the perfidious Wickham in your life. But then who would be Darcy?" She tapped a finger against her lips. "Oh, I know. Colton!"

"I was just going to tell you how much I missed you and how happy I am to be home because you're here. But after that comment I can't." Sara paused. "And besides, Colton would have to be Mr. Collins," she said, pulling a face.

"First of all, he can't be Mr. Collins because he's not our cousin." Gabby laughed. "Plus he's nowhere near hideous."

"Not in looks, but in personality he is." Sara rose and headed to the stairs. "Come down and help me fix Nonna's creative table setting before everyone gets here." There were definitely no Mr. Darcys on her horizon. She certainly hoped for Gabby's sake that Malcolm had transformed during the intervening years from a Wickham to a Darcy, but she seriously doubted it.

Chapter 4

♥

When Sara and Gabby returned from the attic, Sara helped Nonna set the old Duncan Phyfe dining room table with the pretty floral bone china passed down from Nonna's grandmother, quietly subtracting extra forks as necessary.

Sara took a plate from Nonna. "I've always loved these," she said, smoothing her finger over the intricate pattern of pink roses intertwined with English ivy. They reminded her of being a child, sitting at this very table with her mom and dad. She used to study the flowers and the twists and turns of the ivy as she waited impatiently for all the big Italian dinners they'd eaten every Sunday, every holiday. She always called them the rose plates, not just because they had roses on them but because that was her grandmother's name too.

"My mother's mother brought these dishes from Italy," Nonna said. "They were a gift from her parents for her wedding. Then my mother gave them to me for my wedding." They were beautiful and old-fashioned and delicate, yet they'd withstood many years of wear.

Although Sara loved them for another reason too. "Remember the bullies?" It had never been easy being the fair redhead among a bevy of dark-eyed, dark-haired siblings: her older sister Evangeline, her younger sister Gabriella, and Raphael, their baby brother. Kids at school loved to tease them for having all been named after angels. The story went that after Evie, their mom couldn't get pregnant, and prayed and prayed for a child. Four years later, she found herself pregnant with Sara, then Gabby was born just fifteen months later, and Rafe came along two years after that. "I'm the luckiest mother in the world to have four beautiful angels," her mom had said. Sara loved the story, and her name, but it was just one of the many things that had made her a target at school.

It didn't help that their parents had chosen their names despite the fact that Angel Falls had an angel legend of its own. The centerpiece of downtown, beautiful cascading falls that used to power paper mills in the 1800s, were flanked by a quaint bridge guarded by a bronze statue of two angels. Any couple who kissed in front of the angels (and had their picture taken) was supposed to have true love forever. People came from all over to see the falls, shop along the quaint Main Street, and of course get their photo taken in front of the angels.

Despite being the only redhead, Sara was also the only sibling with glasses, which she'd worn from the age of four. Every year it seemed they got thicker and thicker. One afternoon in fourth grade, after she'd been made fun of by some kids on the playground, her mother had sat her down at this very table and told her how special she was, and how loved. "We wouldn't want any of you kids to be the same as anyone else. You're all unique, on the inside and out," her mom had said.

Nonna had pushed a glass of milk and one of these very plates, full of warm chocolate chip cookies, in front of her. Sara hadn't been hungry until she'd smelled the cookies. Nonna had sat down beside her and put an arm around her. "My little Serafina, the ivy is very different from the roses, yet they're still wrapped around each other tight. They still belong together. That's how families are."

That's exactly how her family was, thank God. In some ways she and her siblings couldn't be more different, but they were all bound by an unalterable I've-got-your-back mentality.

And that family bond had been in full force over the last year after Sara's wedding imploded and she'd taken a position as a temporary physician out west, getting as far from Angel Falls—and Tagg—as she could. Nearly every day that she'd been gone, one of her siblings, Nonna, her stepmother Rachel, or even her father had called her to tell her crazy stories about their days, to entertain or amuse her, or just to ask how she was. They must've had a rotating schedule, and she'd worried that she was becoming yet another to-do item in their already busy lives. But those calls had gotten her through a really rough time, and the knowledge that her family stood behind her had helped give her the courage to come back to a town with a long memory for mistakes.

Sara ran her finger around the delicate pattern on the plate before her. She could almost see her mom sitting here. What would she say about the state of Sara's life now? The humiliation of an embarrassing failed engagement with no romantic prospects in sight, and going AWOL from academia to work in their tiny town?

All of Nonna's memories connected her to her mother. Now Nonna was unable to offer her usual loving advice, but she still had a great reserve of memories. If Nonna lost that thread, would Sara lose it as well?

"You always did love these plates."

"They're very special, Nonna," Sara said.

"That's why I'm leaving them to you. Because you're very special too, Sara Jane." Her grandmother's voice cracked with emotion as she wrapped her arms around Sara.

Sara spoke past a tangle in her throat. "Nonna, please—let's not talk about that. I don't need the dishes."

Nonna grasped Sara's hand and pierced her with vivid blue eyes. "It's important. I've got something special for each of you girls. But the china is yours. Now that's that."

That's that. One of Nonna's favorite sayings, and an excellent way of cutting off all further discussion.

"Is Tagg coming for dinner, dear?" Nonna asked.

Sara's stomach seized up. The comforting smell that

had made her so hungry a moment ago now made it churn sickly. "Tagg and I broke up, Nonna," she said quietly. "He won't be coming."

"Oh yes, of course!" Nonna said, nearly dropping one of the dishes. "I meant to say *Rafe*. Is Rafe coming?"

"He'll definitely be here," Sara said just as they heard the front door bang open.

Rafe walked into the dining room, placed a big white ceramic bowl and a brown paper bakery bag on the sideboard, and immediately wrapped up their tiny grandmother in his big arms. Gabby came out of the kitchen to greet him carrying a giant bouquet of orange tiger lilies and set them in the center of the table. Rocket, never good at being ignored, leaped up and down until Gabby broke down and petted him.

"Those are beautiful, sweetheart," Nonna said to Gabby.

"Thanks, Nonnie," Gabby said. "I picked them in the field next to the grade school this morning."

"You're not supposed to pick the flowers at the school," Evie said, walking in behind them. She was the oldest and the stickler of the family, the only one married or with kids, whom she'd quit her job as a pottery artist to stay home with. In practical mom style, she'd brought a bagful of paper plates and cups for easy cleanup. Sara took them and hid them in Nonna's pantry. They'd be using the rose plates, even if she had to stay up until midnight doing the dishes.

Gabby shrugged. "I just took a few of them. No one will notice."

"You look extra beautiful tonight, Nonna," Rafe said, grinning his handsome smile. He looked around at the food that was already spread out on the table—pork tenderloin, antipasto salad, rolls wrapped in a linen towel to stay warm, some prosciutto and cantaloupe sliced thin, a pasta dish with chicken, and the massive bowl of pasta waiting for Nonna's favorite sauce front and center.

"What, only five courses today, not six?" Rafe asked.

"I'm glad you're hungry," Nonna said, patting Rafe's stomach. "We missed you last week." Funny how Nonna could be forgetful about a lot of things but certainly remembered dinner attendance.

"There was a fire last Sunday, Nonna."

"Fire, schmire. You have to eat, don't you?"

"Yes, and I'm very hungry now." He sneaked an olive.

"Where's that nice girl you bring sometimes? The one who owns the coffee shop?"

"Kaitlyn?" he asked. "We're just friends, Grandma. And she's busy baking this afternoon. Oh, I almost forgot. She wanted you to have something." He walked over to the sideboard, picked up the white bowl, and set it on the table, then presented Nonna with the brown bakery bag.

"Rafe, you made salad!" Evie said, inspecting it. Romaine, cut-up veggies, grated cheese, croutons. And a cruet of homemade dressing to boot.

"Hey, I can cook now," he said. "Have to at the station."

Gabby pinched his cheek. "Some little woman is going to be so happy because of those culinary skills."

Rafe gave her a little push on the shoulder. "Number one, I have many other skills that women would find far more appealing than cooking, and number two, only Nonna's allowed to pinch my cheeks."

"Kaitlyn sent something with you?" Sara asked.

"Yeah. I ran into her at the coffee shop and she handed me this."

Sara made a mental note to call Kaitlyn ASAP. Between Sara's getting settled at Nonna's and starting work and Kaitlyn's busy schedule as owner of the Bean, the coffee shop downtown, they hadn't had a moment to sit down and catch up. Sara and Kaitlyn had been best friends since third grade, and yet it was surprising to hear Kaitlyn had been coming to Sunday dinner, something Sara would have thought her friend might have mentioned. The fact that she hadn't made Sara wonder if Kaitlyn still harbored her long-standing crush on Rafe, which, given Rafe's theories on "dating," could only end in disaster.

Nonna peeked inside the bag Rafe handed her. "Blueberry muffins. My favorite. Tell Kaitlyn I'll enjoy them with my coffee tomorrow morning." She pinched Rafe's cheek. "Sara and I baked brownies and made extra for you to take to the station. I have them all wrapped up for you already."

"Thank you, Gram," he said, kissing her on the cheek and shooting his sisters the I'm-her-favorite look.

Rafe walked over and made Sara the next object of his
bear-hug affection. "Anything else exciting happen last
night in the ER besides stitching up our heroic police
chief?"

"You stitched up Colton?" Gabby asked, unwrap-
ping a plate of some kind of orange-colored dip and
chips and placing it on the table. "And he made it out
alive?"

Sara made a face. "I'm a professional, Gabby. I'm
capable of doing my job, no matter what my personal
feelings are."

"Yeah," Rafe said, chuckling. "You did a nice job
with the fifteen stitches, but the tetanus shot in the butt
was a little over the top."

"What do you mean over the top?" Sara asked, then
regretted not changing the subject entirely when she felt
her face heating up.

Gabby's mouth fell open. "You saw Colton's *ass*?
How'd it look?"

"Gabby! He needed a tetanus shot. I gave him one.
End of story."

Rafe gave her a look. She tried to signal him with
her eyes to please shut the hell up. "I'm a paramedic,
remember?" he said, clearly not taking the hint. "You
don't usually give tetanus shots in people's butts."

Busted. "Well, I did, OK? His left arm was all
messed up and bloody and he's right-handed. So that
left giving it to him in his butt." *Or his leg*, but she
didn't have to say that.

The door opened again, thank God, bringing Dad
and Rachel and Evie's husband Joe with their two

little kids, Julia, who was five, and Michael, who was three.

The kids ran over to their mom—or tried to, until Rafe scooped them up and ran around the living room with them, eventually tossing them onto the couch, where they landed laughing and squealing. Rocket, never one to miss out on the action, ran over to join the fun.

Julia tumbled off the couch and came running over. "Aunt Sara," she said, holding up a pink furry purse, "I brought barrettes. I'm going to fix your hair after dinner."

Julia loved Sara's long red hair, and Sara had missed playing hair salon this last year. "Can I fix yours too?" she asked, bending down to kiss and hug her niece.

"Mine too," Michael said. "I want my hair fixed too."

Joe looked a little wary.

"Don't worry," Evie said, patting her husband's arm. "It's all right."

"Sara, you're a doctor," Joe said. "Your sister thinks it's fine if he plays with Barbies and baby dolls. I just don't like it."

"Oh," Sara said. Evie was drilling her with a look, as if she'd better be on Evie's side *or else*. "Well, of course it's fine. I mean, boys and girls should be able to play with anything they want."

"Sometimes Julia dresses him up in Disney princess skirts," Joe said.

Sara laughed. "Once we made Rafe wear ballet tights. And then Mom took pictures."

"Hey, someone better have burned those photos," Rafe said.

"You had nice legs, Rafe," Evie said. "That's what Mom said, anyway."

"The point is," Sara said, "Mom wasn't too concerned. I wouldn't be either."

Just then her dad, a tall, soft-spoken man with gray hair and glasses, walked over and hugged Sara. "Hey, sweetheart," he said.

"Hey, Dad," she said.

"The girls are very excited to see you tomorrow at the office."

Sara tried not to cringe. Or notice that her father hadn't said *he* was excited. "The girls," as her father called them, were actually two women close to retirement age who'd been working in her father's office since before she was born. They were both really sweet, but she had a feeling they, like her father, were very set in their ways.

Rachel placed a pie on the sideboard. This made Sara feel a little bit bad. Cake had been a part of every Sunday dinner since forever, but her stepmother knew that after the bachelor party incident, the sight of cake—any cake—still made Sara sick to her stomach.

"Hey, Daddy," Gabby said, giving him a hug. "Sara gave Colton a tetanus shot in the butt. I think he could have a case for malpractice."

Their dad raised a brow, and Sara glared at her sister. Gabby had always been the sister she told her secrets to first. Perhaps she should start rethinking that policy.

"Colton's such a nice young man," Nonna said. "He takes out my trash every week."

"He's also really arrogant," Sara said. "Still a first-class jerk. Some people never change, you know?"

"I always liked Colton," Gabby said. "I know he had a tough upbringing, and maybe he wasn't all that nice when you knew him in high school, but he comes in sometimes to testify in the hearings for family court and always sticks up for the kids."

Rachel scooped up some of Gabby's dip. "When UPS leaves my shipments at the door of the antique shop, he always helps me carry them in. Plus he's a great police chief. Everyone in town loves him. And he's very kind to the library ladies. Always hauling books back and forth every month for the sale. He tells them that's how he keeps himself in shape."

"All the ladies love him, Rach," Evie said. "And he loves them back. That's the problem—he goes on more dates than Rafe. I'm with you, sweetie," Evie said to Sara. "Avoid him and all men like him like the plague."

"I don't know," Gabby said. "I'm sort of liking this enemies vibe. Lots of sexual tension. It's like watching a rom-com."

"One that will end like a Stephen King novel," Sara said darkly.

"Well, don't forget your blind date next Friday," Gabby said.

"Gabby, we've gone through this. I don't think now's the time—"

"Sure it is. There's no better way to show everyone in town you've moved on."

Sara'd had a few dates in the past year, but nothing serious. She just hadn't had the heart.

"I'm so happy you're back, honey, and joining your father at the practice. I think it's going to be a wonderful partnership," Rachel said, clapping her hands together. As always, her stepmother was quick to jump to her rescue. "And maybe now your dad will be able to slow down just a little and enjoy some golf and more time with me."

"Now, Rachel," her dad interjected, "you know it's only temporary. Sara's going to reapply for her infectious disease fellowship next year." Sara had given up her spot in the prestigious program at the Cleveland Clinic after the wedding that never was. Tagg had gotten a position there as well, and there was no way in hell she could have seen him every day. Not without losing her mind, anyway.

"Well, maybe she'll fall in love with Angel Falls and stay."

Rachel was endlessly optimistic. And her dad clearly hadn't changed his expectations about the kind of future he saw for Sara, and it wasn't as a hometown family doctor.

"Honey, are you all set to start tomorrow?" her dad asked.

No. Absolutely not. The thought of working side by side with her dad brought on as much trepidation and dread as excitement.

She tried to channel a bit of Rachel's optimism. "I think so, Dad."

"How about we meet over at the office later and I'll go over how I run the practice?"

Disappointment riffled through her. Her father had agreed to their working together to placate her need to be near Nonna. He didn't want to hear her ideas about improving his office, of bringing it into the millennium. He didn't want her as a *partner*. "Sounds great."

"We can talk about your fellowship applications. Maybe you should go more Ivy League again, what do you think?" Sara's heart fell. Her dad had always wanted her to be an academic, a nationally recognized expert in her field, and it didn't seem he was going to stop pushing until she accomplished that. And at one time she'd wanted that too. The problem was, Sara wasn't exactly sure what she wanted anymore. All she knew was she was happy to be back home and looking forward to things in a way she hadn't in a long time, since even before the wedding disaster.

Gabby tapped their father on the shoulder. "Dad, your grandson wants a pony ride and he's requested you be the pony. Career decisions can wait till after dinner, OK?"

When he left to do his grandfatherly duty, Rachel turned to Gabby. "How's that boy you said you're dating?" she asked. "I want to hear more."

"You remember Malcolm, don't you? From college?" Sara didn't miss the sudden look of concern that appeared on Rachel's face. "The hedge fund guy?"

Oh God. They all remembered Malcolm, an egomaniacal, self-absorbed guy. Even the fact that he had a job her dad approved of could not save him.

"We reconnected," Gabby said, and her smile said it all. "He wants to take us all out to celebrate my promotion, so you'll all get a chance to see him again next weekend."

"Is this the guy with the Bugatti that he wrecked the same day he got it?" Rafe asked.

"That wasn't his fault," Gabby said. "The car was just really…fast. I'm going to check on the brownies," she said cheerily, escaping into the kitchen.

All this and dinner hadn't even begun yet. Yep, it was great to be home.

Just then the doorbell rang. Nonna rushed to get it, Rocket zooming at her heels. Sara followed them, just in case.

But it wasn't Nonna who was at a loss for words when she opened the door. Standing there with an enormous package in her hands was Claire Milhouse, Tagg's mother.

"Hello, Rose," Claire said, smiling her practiced doctor's wife smile. Her stylish blonde hair was perfectly in place, and she was dressed as if she'd just walked out of a Talbots window, in a cute navy sailor's dress and pumps. Sara had not seen her for a year, this woman who had been just shy of two days from being her mother-in-law. And yet she'd not heard a word in all this time. Nada.

"Sara, you look wonderful," Claire said, giving her an air kiss on the cheek. "Taggart told me you were back in town. How are you doing, dear?"

"She's doing great," Rose said. "She's a doctor now. Going into practice right here in Angel Falls with her father." Nonna patted Sara's shoulder, and she shot her grandmother a grateful look.

"Is that right, dear?" Claire asked. "Taggart didn't mention that to me."

Sara bit back the urge to ask how Tagg was. She wondered how he'd known she was back, if he missed Sara, and if he felt any remorse at all. Not that she would take him back, of course. But still it was odd, how one day your life could be sailing along as usual, and the next, the person you'd talked to every day for ten years was simply…gone forever. Cut out like a friend on the edge of a cropped photo.

"Anyway," Claire said pleasantly. "This box arrived from Australia. It's a wedding gift. I thought I would bring it over so you could mail it back to whoever sent it."

"Mail it back?" Nonna said. "That son of yours is so smart, Claire. It's a pity you never taught him to mail a package."

Sara took the package, but Nonna lifted it right from her hands and took it into the kitchen.

"Sorry, Claire, you'll have to excuse Nonna," Sara said, but didn't really mean it. Last summer, after the wedding that wasn't, it had taken her an entire week to ship all the gifts back. Tagg couldn't take care of one gift? And who lived in Australia? Not anyone from her side, that was for sure.

Claire lowered her voice to a whisper. "It's the dementia, isn't it?"

"Yes, yes, of course," Sara said. "Well, thanks for stopping. Have a nice day."

As soon as she closed the door, Nonna was back. "That box rattles. It's something cheap, I can tell," she said and made a gesture as if she were dusting off her hands in good riddance. "Imagine the nerve. Asking you to return more wedding gifts after her son was the one to call the wedding off."

"Hey, Sara," Gabby called from the kitchen. "Could you come help?"

"Coming!" Sara called and gave Nonna a kiss on the cheek.

In the kitchen Gabby was frantically opening cabinet doors. The box that Claire had brought was sticking conspicuously out of the trash can. The dementia or not? Sara wondered. She liked to think not. At least she wouldn't be returning anything to Australia.

"What's going on?" Sara asked.

"I snuck some icing," Gabby said. Nonna's homemade brownies sat stacked on an old-fashioned milk glass cake holder, looking pretty and perfect.

"So what else is new? You've been doing that since you were three."

"Sara, the icing tastes terrible. I'm no baker, but it tastes like Nonna must've put flour in it instead of powdered sugar." She gestured to the bag of flour sitting next to the icing bowl. "I'm looking for the powdered sugar so we can make more really quick."

Sara swiped her finger into the bowl and tasted it. "Oh my God," she said, making a face.

Then she joined her sister in the search.

The powdered sugar was not in the cabinet reserved for baking supplies. They finally found it shoved on top of some canned goods in the pantry.

"Do you remember the recipe?" Gabby asked, then pulled out her phone. "We can Google it."

"I remember it. Powdered sugar, cocoa, butter, vanilla, and a little milk." Sara whipped up another batch while Gabby scraped all the bad stuff off each brownie. They'd just finished re-icing and restacking every brownie when Nonna walked in.

"I came in for the sauce. Oh, I thought I iced those already."

"Gabby licked one and so we just repaired it a little," Sara said. "Right, Gabby?"

Gabby shot Sara a dark look.

"Gabby! My goodness, dear," Nonna said. "Poor thing, you must be starving. Dinner's ready. Come eat some real food." Nonna linked elbows with Gabby and tugged her toward the dining room. "Bring the sauce, Sara, sweetie. It's time to eat."

Sara took a deep breath. She thought about a hospitalist position in New York City she'd been offered by one of her mentors. She could've been very happy taking that and telling her family it was too good an offer to pass up. She could have avoided her opinionated dad and the fact that her sisters, even Gabby now, seemed settled in relationships. She'd never have had to face Colton or Tagg's parents or even Tagg himself, or the fact that she'd never find anyone in this one-horse town.

Yet she loved Nonna fiercely. And Nonna needed her help. Her gut told her in a way she'd never experienced before that she'd made a difficult decision, but the right decision.

As she carried the old aluminum pot into the dining room she realized it was the first decision she'd made for herself in a very long time.

Chapter 5

♥

It was early evening when Colton pulled up the driveway of the little pale blue cape where his grandmother and eighteen-year-old sister Hannah lived. The teenage boy he'd hired to paint the house, Aiden Cross, was still here, judging by the once-red-but-now-faded-to-rose, somewhat rusty Toyota Corolla parked in the driveway. A ladder leaned against the side of the detached garage, which Colton could see was already half-scraped. The kid was a good worker, and apparently still hard at it on a Sunday evening at seven p.m.

Colton parked his police cruiser in the driveway and walked toward the garden. On his approach, Cookie, his paternal grandmother, rose from where she was kneeling, tying up a row of tomato plants, a bright-red fisherman's hat over her gray hair, matching red garden clogs on her feet. "Hello, sweetheart," she said, kissing him on the cheek. "I'm sorry about not fixing dinner tonight. Hannah's in the kitchen grabbing something between her waitress shift and dance class. Did you eat?"

"Hannah and I are capable of fending for ourselves, Cook." Cookie deserved a break after caring for him and his sister all these years, and he didn't want her to feel guilty for going to lunch with her friends. "I grabbed a pizza with a couple of the kids at Lou's, and there's leftovers for Hannah if she wants them."

Colton believed in keeping a heavy presence at Lou's, a local pizza joint with a couple of pool and Ping-Pong tables that tended to attract a lot of teens. It was a fun place where the kids could hang out and stay out of trouble, and he wanted to keep it that way. It also happened to be where Hannah worked, so he was able to pop in and keep an eye on his little sister too. Which she didn't much appreciate, but hey, curse of the big brother.

"You need to get off the clock some too," Cookie said. "It's Sunday."

"Yeah, yeah."

"Don't tell me, young man." She gave him a shrewd once-over, noting his ball cap, his sweaty appearance, and his grass-stained clothes. "You spent the afternoon clearing that plot of land, didn't you?"

"I've got plans for it, Granny," he said, smiling. "Besides, it's not work. It's...fun."

"I wish you'd just move into our house, Colton, once I move to the condo and Hannah leaves for college," Cookie said. "It's a nice house, and the yard is fantastic. Isn't that better than living in that apartment all by yourself?"

   Colton had moved into his own place after he'd gotten the chief job a year ago. Not that he didn't love Cookie and Hannah, and he did try to spend nights off with his grandmother as often as he could, but he was thirty, and he didn't want to have to explain his comings and goings to either one of them. But even the idea of living in Cookie's house alone didn't appeal. The house was dated in a seventies-ranch sort of way. He didn't mind that it needed work but the seventies vibe just wasn't his thing. Even if the yard was great and had played host to many a ball game when he was younger.

   "I'm sorry, Cookie." They'd been through this before. The land he'd bought six months before was in the middle of town, next to the park, surrounded by woods, and it had become available when the grandchildren of an elderly couple had decided to sell off a couple of parcels of a twenty-acre allotment. The adjacent plot, which was also for sale, held a dilapidated century-old colonial that looked like something out of *Hoarders*. He had no use for the disaster of a house but for a guy with a job that sometimes made him feel like he was living in a fishbowl, that hidden plot of land seemed like a magic oasis. Even if it was a wild mess.

   "Well, OK, but don't say I didn't offer," she said.

   "You're not going to be thinking much of this place in January when you're basking in the sun in Palm Beach while we're up to our butts in snow here." That was her plan. A little condo across town, snowbirding in Florida for the cold and icy months. No one deserved it more.

"So Sara Langdon's back in town. Have you run into her yet?"

Of course it had taken Cookie about ten seconds to change the subject and mention Sara. "Sure did. She's the one who stitched me up last night." He stuck out his arm, which he was keeping wrapped with gauze, just like Sara had instructed him. As far as he could tell, things were healing up pretty well. Unlike their relationship, which was just as prickly as ever.

Cookie glanced at the bandage. "So did you ask her out on a date while she was stitching you up?" His grandmother would never give up on this topic. She'd always had it in her head that Sara was the one for him. He would never understand the vagaries of granny matchmaking.

"No, Grandma, I did not. That would be a little awkward, seeing as the woman can't stand me." He called her "Grandma" when he was a little irritated, and "Granny" as an endearment. Other than that, even though her name was Charlotte, she was Cookie. To everybody.

"Oh, pish," Cookie said, waving a hand dismissively. "Now that she's free of that idiot, you'll make her see what a real man is like."

For once he didn't jump to defend Tagg. Which said a lot, because Tagg and his family had taken Colton under their wing when he was an unruly teenager and shown him that he could succeed despite his messed-up past. Tagg had helped him study in high school and catch up after the years when he'd lived with his mom and school had been hit or miss. His family had taken Colton places like amusement parks and on vacations that Cookie could never have afforded, plus Dr. Milhouse, Tagg's dad, had counseled him about college and helped him apply for the police officers' scholarship after he'd busted up his knee and his football scholarship fell through.

He'd always be grateful for all of that, even though as adults, Tagg and he lived very different lives. Besides, in the last year, Colton had truly come to believe the idiot remark was accurate. He'd only talked to Tagg a few times, and had gone out with him even less, making excuses when he could. "Thanks for the encouragement, but I'm not looking for a relationship."

"Nonsense. Everyone's looking for love, and you're not immune. Sara may be a little angry right now, but you've got to make her understand what really happened. Sometimes it's hard to believe people you love are dumb enough to do stupid things like that all on their own. It's easier to blame someone else."

"Do we really have to talk about this now?" If Sara needed to take her wrath out on Colton, so be it. It wouldn't be the first time.

He'd been a smart-ass with a chip on his shoulder for anyone who'd had all the benefits and opportunities he'd never had. Yes, he'd called her Brain and teased her for being smart and nerdy and uncool. But once when one of his football buddies tripped her on purpose and her glasses went flying, he'd rescued them. And noticed for the first time she had the most vivid green eyes, even if she had turned as red as the town's new fire truck when he handed her glasses back. But after she'd thanked him, in typical Sara fashion she then delivered a lecture on why he shouldn't hang around with assholes.

That's how it had always been with them. She'd always been able to grind down to the raw bone to irritate him. That hadn't changed in all these years.

But she'd certainly looked good in those boxers this morning.

Cookie was still talking. "I want to see you settled. You and Sara would make such a nice couple. And I want to see great-grandchildren before I die. It's my right as your substitute mother. And your grandmother. Double reasons to get going on that."

Cookie had taken them in a few years after Colton's father, a Chicago city cop, had died in a gunfight during a bank robbery when Colton was eight years old. His mom hadn't done well without his father, going from bad job to bad job and from bad to worse men. Hannah had come along when he was twelve—they'd never known who her father was—but by then his mother was on a downward spiral. She needed a new liver after four years of pickling hers in alcohol, but despite three bouts of rehab, she couldn't stop drinking long enough to get one.

By the time his mother passed and Cookie brought them to Angel Falls, Colton had become his sister's protector. He was determined to do anything to give her the future he didn't get to pick for himself. And he was determined to give Cookie the break she'd never had because she'd spent her time raising them.

Suddenly Hannah ran out of the house, dressed in

yoga pants and a T-shirt, ready for her job as an assistant dance instructor at the ballet studio downtown.

"Thanks for the eggs, Cookie," Hannah said. "I washed up the pan. Hey, Colton, I'll see you later if you're around, OK? Or maybe not. A few of us are going out for pizza and a movie after class." She gave them both quick kisses on their cheeks, then let her gaze trail to the detached garage at the side of the house. "And wow, how long's the hottie here for?"

Colton steered her from her position staring at a shirtless Aiden's wide, tattooed shoulders as he stood on the ladder scraping paint off the side of the garage.

"His name is Aiden," Colton said, "and he's earning some extra money by helping me out." Note to self: Aiden had to put a shirt on. ASAP.

Hannah rolled her eyes in a way Colton knew only too well. As a much older sibling, he often straddled the line between big brother (which was cool) and parental figure (which was absolutely not). "I know his name, and he's very nice, and he just graduated, just like me. Not to mention he's gorgeous. And a bad boy, even hotter. But you must like him to bring him here to work, huh?"

"It doesn't matter if I like him. He's here to work and stay out of trouble. That means no fraternizing. This one's got 'Stay away from me' written all over him." As soon as the words left his mouth, he regretted them.

"Hmm," she said with a smile. "Intriguing."

"Don't you have to get going to work?" he asked, steering Hannah along the driveway to her car.

"Geez, you're such a killjoy. I'm allowed to look at

boys. Maybe someday I can even date them like normal girls whose brothers don't do background checks on them before they can come within a five-mile radius."

Colton frowned. As was so often the case with his sister, words failed him. He owed her parental guidance because a) he was responsible for her and b) he didn't think Cookie would be blunt enough. But every time he tried, his tongue got tied up in knots. "I want you to be safe. Date someone nice." Actually, not dating at all would be his preference.

"Geez, Colt, do you think I'm going to be a virgin forever?"

He blanched. "Maybe just until you're thirty." He tried to smile, but to him it wasn't really a joke. "Have a nice day at work. Don't talk to any boys."

She saluted. "Aye, aye, Chief." But her eyes slid back to Aiden.

Aiden was ripped, he'd give him that. He was tanned and muscled, and he wore a ball cap backward as he worked. Exotic tattoos covered his shirtless chest, back, and arms and disappeared beneath the waistband of his jeans. He was also destined for trouble unless someone intervened. He'd been busted for smoking pot with his deadbeat buddies, most of whom already had criminal records. His dad was a drunk and his mother was gone. Colton had first noticed him doing his community service hours at the park, picking up litter. The kid had filled five large trash bags in a half hour while the other kids were whining and complaining it was too hot.

Colton had decided to give him a chance, just as Chief McGregor, the former police chief, had given

Colton a chance when he was an insolent, angry kid all those years ago. He'd taken a parked car for a joyride on a dare and gotten busted for it. The chief had made him do a hundred community service hours, but more than that, he'd taken Colton under his wing.

"Run along, Hannah," he said, giving his sister a gentle tug toward her car.

"No fair, Colton." She pushed out her lower lip like she'd done when she was three. "I'm enjoying the view."

"Time to go teach those little girls how to do pirouettes," Colton said, opening her car door. *And to stop noticing ripped guys with tattoos.*

"Bye, Cookie." She waved to her grandmother and blew Colton a kiss. "Love you both!" she called as she drove down the driveway.

"That girl's going to be the death of me," he said, clutching his stomach. Judging from the little jabs of pain he was experiencing, maybe he was getting an ulcer.

"You've got to let her grow up, Colton," his grandmother said. "She's going to be living on her own in just a few months." Hannah would be starting college at Ohio State in the fall. Wasn't it yesterday that she'd been a sweet, big-eyed toddler with chocolate ice cream dripping all down her chin?

"How do you know she's going to make good decisions?"

"You don't. You just pray a lot and hope what we've taught her sticks."

He cracked a little smile. "Did you worry about me like that?"

Cookie shook her head and laughed. "A thousand times worse."

He wrapped his grandmother up in a hug. It couldn't have been easy, taking in a thirteen-year-old boy and a one-year-old baby. He'd been argumentative. Disrespectful. And so angry over his mother's succumbing to the addiction that had taken over her life after his father was killed. How had his grandmother ever dealt with him?

Cookie patted him on the back. "But look how far you've come. Your father would be so proud, do you know that?"

He drew back from his grandmother's embrace. "I don't know what my father would think about me being a small-town cop. Maybe he'd be disappointed." Aw hell, he shouldn't have said that. Cookie would think he was fishing for praise.

"Nonsense. Don't even think like that." Of course she would say that. Cookie was Colton's biggest fan.

"Have I ever thanked you for everything you did for me?" he asked.

"Sweetheart, you thank me every day by letting me see what a good man you've become. And as far as your job, no person should ever underestimate their influence. You'll know if you're in the right place. Your heart will tell you. Just like it will when you've found the right girl."

"Yada, yada," Colton said, starting to walk toward the house.

"Where are you going?"

"I'm going to go tell this kid to get a shirt on. Especially when Hannah's around."

"I'm off to book club. If you're hungry, there are bagels on the counter."

He gave a wave to his grandmother and approached Aiden, who was down from the ladder and taking a swig from his water bottle. "How's it going?" he asked the kid, extending his hand for a fist bump.

"Great," Aiden said. "I've been here since eight, but it was raining, so I went and bought the paint. And I've got most of this side scraped."

"Looks great. Hey, why don't you pack it up for the night? It's already seven."

"I want to get a little more done before it starts to get dark. I've got to work at the discount warehouse tonight so I might not get back here until noon tomorrow."

Colt knew Aiden stocked shelves at night and parked cars on the weekends for events at a big hotel in downtown Cleveland. The kid was a worker, he'd give him that.

"So, have you given any thought to your plans for the fall?" Colton asked.

"If you mean college, it's not for me."

"I thought you wanted to be an electrician." He owed it to the kid to press him, just as Chief McGregor had gotten on Colton's case when he was a kid. The chief had been his dad's best friend, and his investment in Colton had made all the difference.

"I missed the deadline for applying to the program at the technical college."

"No excuses." Colt crossed his arms, knowing it made him look a little intimidating.

"Give me a break, Chief," Aiden said. "The deadline was around the time I got in trouble last spring." He glanced downward. "Plus I don't have money for school."

"Well, there's loans and scholarships and—"

"Those are for people with better grades than me. I'm not—"

"Good enough? Look, you're not going to get anywhere if you talk like that. And I actually made a call to the technical college. They admit people if someone drops out. So get your application in so you can get on the waiting list. You never know what can happen." Plus Colt had a buddy who taught at the college and said he'd look into what he could do for the kid. Colt didn't tell Aiden that, though.

"It was easier for you because you came from a good family."

Colton sighed. He really hated telling his story, because it was still painful in a way. But this kid needed to hear it. "My parents both died before I went to high school. I was an all-state wide receiver with a full ride to a D1 school until I blew my ACL in the last game of the season. I had to give up my scholarship and my dream of playing football. Even though I rehabbed that knee for a year, I never got back to my prior form. But people lent me a hand and I got through it. You can too."

He'd become a cop because his dream had gotten shot all to hell, and because the Angel Falls force, who had known his father well when he'd worked here as a rookie cop, took care of their own.

Not that he'd deserved their help. He'd been an arrogant SOB and hadn't wanted anyone's help. But they'd offered him a job cleaning toilets and emptying the city's trash cans, then helping out at different events like the traffic camp for little kids, and they'd shown him a cop's life. It had changed his outlook, given him another purpose, and he'd discovered he wanted to be a cop.

After college and the police academy, Chief McGregor offered him a job, and he came home to take care of Cookie and Hannah. He might've had grander dreams, but family was family, and Angel Falls was where he'd ended up, for better or for worse. Not that he didn't like his job—he did, a lot. He just wondered sometimes if he should be somewhere he could make a real difference instead of rescuing people's dogs and giving out parking tickets.

"The way I see it, you can accept you're not going to get anywhere and have a shitty life or fight like hell to pull yourself up." He slapped Aiden on the back. "Bring your application by the station and I'll go over it with you."

"Yes, sir," Aiden said.

"And Aiden?"

"Yes, Chief?"

"You should put your shirt on so you don't sunburn and get skin cancer."

"Aw, don't worry about me, Chief. I'm wearing sunblock."

"I'm sure you are. But my grandmother can see you and it might be too much excitement for her."

"Aw, Chief, your grandmother's not going to care if…"

Colt interrupted. "It's not just my grandma I'm worried about, if you get my meaning."

Aiden rubbed the back of his neck.

"Just keep the shirt on, got it?"

"Yes, sir," he said cautiously.

Colton nodded. As he turned to walk to the house, a dog bounded over to them from across the grass.

A bull terrier with brown ears and a big pirate patch over his left eye.

Rocket.

As he looked up from petting the dog, sure enough, there was Sara's grandmother coming up the driveway, a little out of breath. She was dressed in turquoise pants, a sweater, and white orthopedic walking shoes, and she was carrying Rocket's leash. She didn't look disheveled at all, but he recognized a certain look of panic in her eyes.

"Oh, Colton, I'm so glad to see you!" she said, clutching his arm. "Hello," she said politely to Aiden.

Colton patted her hand. "Is something wrong, Rose? How can I help you?"

"Oh, you're a dear. Maybe you can help me. This isn't my street. I—can you tell me where Glenwillow Lane is? I was taking Rocket for a walk, but I was so busy daydreaming I wandered off course a little bit."

Wandered off course. Ever since her dementia diagnosis, he'd been keeping an extra eye out, but she'd never done this before. His cell phone went off at his hip before he could reach for it to call Rafe.

"Hey, Colty, you big hunk of love," said Carmen, his dispatcher, the pleasant lilt of her Puerto Rican accent familiar and friendly. She was sassy and flirty and really good at her job. Plus at sixty, she didn't take crap from anyone, even him.

"Hey, Carmen, what's up?" Worry instantly pricked Colton's neck. Carmen fiercely guarded his time off. She never called unless it was important.

"I know you're off duty, but I just got a call from Sara Langdon that her sweet old *abuela*'s gone missing. I thought I'd catch you on your cell because you might be somewhere around the 'hood. Unless you're with a lady friend or something, in which case I do *not* want to know."

Colton ignored the lady comment. Carmen was always trying to find out details about his love life. "You have great instincts, because Rose just walked into my grandmother's yard."

"I always have great instincts as far as you're concerned, babe." Carmen paused. "Sara's worried about Rocket too. You got Rocket there?"

Colton bent down to scratch the dog behind the ears. He promptly went belly up for more. "Rocket's present and accounted for. Thanks, Carmen." Rocket started bathing his hand with his tongue in a gesture of gratitude. Colton stood up. He and Rocket were pals, but he drew the line at being coated with doggy saliva. "Hey, will you call Sara right away and tell her everything's under control? And will you give me her number, please?"

He'd call her and tell her he was driving Rose home. As a public service, of course.

"Bold move, Chief. How much is it worth to you?" his smart-ass dispatcher said.

Oh, for God's sake. "Just text me the number, Carmen."

"Okeydokey, Colty. And you show that girl what a gem you are, baby. Make her forget all about that no-good ex-fiancé of hers."

"Bye already, Carmen."

He guided Rose up to the back patio. She wound her arm through his, placing her thin, veined hand on his forearm as they walked through the grass. "Come sit down a minute, and then I'll drive you home." He wanted to make sure she was all right. Offer her some water or something. And call Sara.

"It was the strangest thing, Colton. All of a sudden I looked around and I didn't see anything I recognized. Until I saw you." She patted his hand. The fear in her eyes twisted his gut. What kind of disease was this that hijacked a person's life, made someone who'd lived here her whole life forget her own damn neighborhood? He felt bad for Rose. And for Sara, who must be panicking.

Speaking of Sara, suddenly there she was, running down the sidewalk, waving.

Just then Cookie came out the back door. She was dressed for book club in white pants and pumps and a bright floral blouse, but when she saw him sitting with Sara's grandmother, she tossed her purse on a chair and walked over.

"Hi, Rose, dear," Cookie said, giving her a hug, then stooping to pet Rocket. "I just made some lemonade. Can you stay and chat for a few minutes?" She looked over at Aiden, who was carrying a bucket to the hose. "Aiden, you too. Come have a drink." She winked at Colton, and he nodded. Thirty years as a kindergarten teacher had made Cookie an excellent multitasker, always ready to jump into action.

Colton met Sara halfway down the driveway, took her by the elbow, and guided her to his cruiser. She was clutching a hand to her chest, a look of alarm on her face.

"She's fine," he said, holding on to her arms and looking her in the eye until he was certain that registered. Her eyes instantly filled with tears, and she clamped a hand over her mouth.

"Oh, Colton. Thank God. Carmen called me, and I just took off running down here."

He rubbed her arms, which wasn't very professional, but she was clearly upset. "You OK?"

"Just upset with myself. I told Nonna I'd go for a walk with her and went up to find shoes and then she was just ... gone. Like she'd forgotten I was coming with her, maybe? Anyway, I panicked and called the station."

"You did the right thing," he said in the most calming voice he could muster. "Rose saw me out in the yard and walked over. She was a little panicked. Said she didn't know how to get back to her street."

"Oh God." She took a step toward her grandmother, but Colton stopped her.

"I don't think it would help her if you're upset. Maybe take another minute before you go over there."

She nodded. "I was supposed to be keeping an eye

on her. That's the whole point of my coming back home to live with her."

Ah. He'd wondered why Sara had come back home. "Don't blame yourself. Everything's fine. She didn't go far, and she knew to ask for help."

Sara nodded, but he could tell by her expression it wasn't fine at all.

She turned those piercing green eyes on him, and he nearly melted. "Thank you for taking care of her."

"Not a problem. I'm happy to help anytime you need me." And, strangely enough, he meant it.

He released her, and together they walked over to the back patio. Aiden was standing with the older women, giving them a tour of the numerous tattoos inked all over his arms and chest while they watched, enraptured. "This one is the Chinese symbol for 'gentle but strong' and this is my dog's name, Sparky. He died last year."

Colton made sure not to roll his eyes. He wasn't sure if he should be horrified or pleased. The kid was certainly friendly. But he still had his damn shirt off.

Rose saw Sara and broke into a smile. "Oh, there you are, dear." She held out her hand, which Sara immediately grabbed. To Sara's credit, she didn't get emotional or freak out. "I was just taking Rocket out for a walk," Rose said, "and look who we ran into. Colton and Cookie invited me to sit down for a drink, wasn't that nice?"

"Help yourself to a brownie, dear," Cookie said, pointing to the table. "And some lemonade."

Sara hugged Cookie and thanked her, then sat next to her grandmother and made small talk. Rocket came and sprawled at her feet, resting his head on her tennis shoe.

Colton sat down too. Sara was telling a story that made the ladies laugh about a kid she'd treated in her residency. She was animated, using her hands, her eyes lighting up with laughter.

That started Cookie off telling school stories. At one point Colton caught Sara looking at him. Or maybe she caught him looking at her, he wasn't sure which. But she shot him a grateful look and mouthed *Thank you.*

It was strange seeing this side of her. He was used to the wound-too-tight Sara, the one who was a perfectionist above all else and expected the same from everyone else around her. When she chatted and laughed, she looked like a normal person. A pretty person. One whose phone number he had in his phone.

Where had *that* thought come from? He'd never call her. No way. Out of the question.

His thoughts were distracted, fortunately, by Hannah's car pulling back up the driveway. She got out, clearly in a hurry, not bothering to close her car door. "I forgot my dance bag!" she called in their direction, waving to everyone gathered on the porch.

She stopped suddenly on her way into the house. "Oh my gosh, Sara, what are you doing here? Hi, Mrs. F. Rocket! There's my good boy! How are you?" Rocket came bounding over, thumping his tail against the patio stone and leaning against Sara's leg in admiration. "Oh, I've missed you so much," she crooned, petting him. "My mean brother took Champ with him when he moved out and I'm totally doggy deprived." She looked up at Sara. "What's going on?"

"We were just passing by on a walk," Sara said. Hannah stole a look at Colt as if to say, *What alternate universe is this?* But Colt kept his expression neutral.

"I'm glad you're back in town," Hannah said to Sara. "Talk to you soon, K?"

"Let's have coffee and catch up," Sara said.

"Sounds great. I gotta go!" She bolted into the house. A few seconds later she ran out the door with more quick waves.

"Hey, no rushing," Colton said in his cop voice. "Wouldn't want you getting in an accident."

"I won't. Bye!" she said, running back to her car. But not before she took a long hard look at tattoo boy.

Even worse, Aiden turned as she passed and unabashedly checked out her ass.

As a cop Colton was trained to notice things, but he sure wished he hadn't noticed that.

Chapter 6

♥

Good morning," Sara said cheerfully, walking into her father's office bright and early Monday morning. His two longtime employees, Leonore and Glinda, were already there. She could see them through the big glass window that separated the reception area from the waiting room. Opening the door and walking into the back office, she placed a coffee cake on the Formica counter.

Yes, a coffee cake. She'd sucked up her aversion and made one as a gesture to get started on the right foot.

"Good morning, sweetheart," Leonore said, getting up from her workstation, where she had been leafing through a *People* magazine and drinking from an Eddie Redmayne coffee mug. Leonore looked like the world's most perfect grandma—plump and pleasant looking, with nearly white hair and boxy glasses that magnified her eyes and always made her look a little surprised. She was also a hardcore knitter and every item on her desk was enclosed in cases of all colors of the rainbow she'd made herself—a cup cosy, a cylindrical holder for pens, a rectangular one for her iPhone.

"Oh, here, I made you something," she said, thrusting a tiny brightly wrapped square in Sara's direction.

"Oh, Leonore, you shouldn't have." Sara was a little nervous, as the last gift from Leonore had been a winter hat with floppy dog ears on it, a little embarrassing to wear in public. She ripped open the package. It contained a multicolored knit pouch with a long string attached in a big loop. Hmm. Something to wear around your neck for loose change? Breath mints? Emergency tampon?

"It's a little case for your phone or whatever that you can wear around your neck," Leonore said. "It'll be convenient for the office."

"They're so handy," Glinda called from the exam room hallway, holding up a white version that she wore around her own neck, no doubt to match the starched white nursing uniform she wore every single day. "Especially on the days when you don't have pockets."

Indeed. "Thank you," Sara said, walking through the little half door that separated the behind-the-desk area from the rest of the office to give Leonore a hug. She placed the bright knit square around her neck. "I can't wait to use it." Come to think of it, she hated wearing a white coat. They made kids cry and always had to be laundered and pressed, even if they did have tons of pockets. So maybe the pouch wasn't such a bad idea after all. Especially the emergency tampon part. Besides, she was constantly misplacing her pens. Was it scary that she was already thinking of so many uses for this thing?

Glinda approached the reception counter. "Oh, coffee cake! What a treat from our new doctor. Did you make it from scratch? Come have a piece too." Glinda adjusted her vintage nurse cap over her blonde hair that she'd been teasing into a bouffant since 1960 at least.

Yes, Sara had made it from scratch, because she knew they loved coffee cake. Even though it looked really good, she couldn't bear to have a bite herself.

Leonore brought over the coffeepot and some ceramic mugs, each of which bore a different drug company's slogan. "Of course she did, Glinda. Would you expect anything less from our little Sara? We're so proud of you, sweetie. You've come such a long way since we caught you in the back studying your father's anatomy books."

Sara felt the first blush of the day spreading across her cheekbones. She'd been thirteen, and they'd found her reading one of her dad's heavy illustrated anatomy atlases—the one about the reproductive system. Well, a girl's got to learn somehow, right? Those years between her mom's death and her dad's marriage to Rachel had been a little short on trusted womanly influence, so she'd filled in the gaps in her knowledge by doing her own research.

Glinda patted her back. "And you've come a long way since your marriage mishap last year."

Here came blush number two. And it wasn't even eight o'clock yet.

"I never liked that Taggart," Leonore said, cutting a large slice of cake. "He always struck me as hoity-toity, you know why? Whenever I ran into him around town and had my grandkids with me, he never even so much as said hi to them. What kind of father would a man like that make?"

"Seriously," Glinda agreed, putting her much smaller piece on a paper plate. "Doctor told us you won't eat cake anymore. Does that include coffee cake too?"

Sara waved her hand dismissively. "Oh, it's not a problem, really. I mean, it's not the cake's fault, right?" She'd never admit it, but it *was* a problem, and it was all cake. Coffee cake, ice cream cake, any cake in the world.

"I was the one who took your beautiful wedding cake to the homeless shelter," Leonore said solemnly.

Sara's stomach churned. It was getting really difficult to keep this smile plastered on her face. Just then the office door opened, and Mr. Humphries, the bank manager, walked in. "Ladies, good morning," he said, waving through the glass partition and taking a seat in the waiting room. At seven forty-five, he was early for the first appointment of the day, which typically began at eight thirty.

No one jumped to get him signed in and ready. "Yep," Leonore continued. "Doctor called me and said, 'Leonore, would you mind getting this thing the heck out of my house because it's making my

daughter cry' and I said 'No problem, boss, I'll
be right over.' It was a Saturday, and I was still
dressed in my pj's." Ah yes. The cake had been delivered to her parents' house by accident, after the
wedding was called off. Bless her dad, thinking of
the shelter. At least someone had gotten some pleasure out of it.

"I'm so excited to be working here, ladies," Sara
said, smiling her cheeriest smile and hoping to leave
the topic of her beautiful failed wedding in the dust.
"I know my dad will teach me so much, but I'm also
hoping to help the office make some adjustments to
move us more into state-of-the-art patient care." At
least she *prayed* she could do that, but she knew it
wasn't going to be easy.

"Well, we're all about state-of-the-art patient care,"
Glinda said. "Your father's the best doc in town, but
let's face it, this place needs a face-lift." She straightened the frame on the iconic Norman Rockwell print
of the doctor giving the little boy a shot in the butt. It
made Sara think instantly of Colton. She wondered if
he'd been cute with a buzz cut like the boy in the painting. Actually, he was cute with a buzz cut *now*, in a
whole different way.

Ugh, why had she just thought that?

"What kinds of adjustments, dear?" Leonore asked,
the slightest furrow forming between her brows.

"My dad's going to get penalized by Medicare if
he doesn't turn his charts electronic, so I said I'd
get us started on that. Plus we talked about getting
new computers for the reception desk and electronic

tablets to bring into the exam rooms. And painting the office. Getting a new EKG machine. That kind of stuff."

"I like everything but the electronic records," Leonore said. "That sounds a little scary."

"Don't be afraid, Leonore," Glinda said. "It means a better computer. You'll be able to play Words with Friends even faster."

"Well, we'll all be learning together," Sara said. "I also had some ideas about streamlining the day so we can get out of here earlier."

Leonore patted her on the back. "You do that, honey. All my grandkids play sports, and I never get out of here on time."

"I'm sure Sara will have kids one day too," Glinda said. "I mean, when you meet someone, that is." She blushed, knowing the topic was a sensitive one. "And when you do, you'll want to get home too."

"Glinda, I want to get home before seven now, even though I don't have a boyfriend *or* kids."

"Look, we love your dad," Leonore said. "He's a kind man and a wonderful doctor. But the man can talk. He knows everyone and he'll help anyone with any problem. But sometimes you just need to get to business and get home, you know what I mean?"

Sara knew her dad loved to talk to people. It was what made him beloved in the community and also what made him chronically behind schedule. It would improve everyone's life to make a few changes.

Just then her dad walked in, gave her a quick squeeze, and went for a piece of coffee cake. "Welcome to your first day," he said. "Did you see what's on your office door?"

"What? No, I-I haven't been back there yet." A few weeks ago, Sara had helped clean out a little room down the hall that had been used for supplies but was now her office. When she walked back, she saw a wooden engraved plaque attached to her door that read "Sara Langdon, MD."

"Oh, Dad," she said, getting teary.

Leonore slipped her iPhone out of its vibrant multi-colored case as Sara rejoined them. "OK, you two, smile now. First-day picture!"

Her father wrapped his arm around Sara and pressed his cheek against hers, grinning widely. She couldn't help but grin too. "That's my girl," he said proudly as he let go. "Glad to have you here, sweetheart."

"Aw, that's so sweet," Leonore said, looking at the picture. "I'm going to frame this and hang it next to the picture behind your desk of Sara running around the Christmas tree in her diaper. Won't that be so cute?"

Sara pretended not to hear that. She was still smiling at what her dad had said. For a moment her heart reached out to grab everything in its path—his approval, the fact that he'd just basically said that he wanted her here with him, as his partner. That maybe it was all right not to be in an academic fellowship far away from family, doing research and presenting papers at Harvard. That she might belong right here at home after all.

Leonore showed her the photo. "We should put this on the practice website, Dad," Sara said.

"Do we have a website?" Glinda asked.

"Well, we probably should have one," her dad said. "But by the time we get it up there, Sara will probably be gone."

Sara tried not to let her expression fall. *Gone?* Despite the plaque and his kind words, her dad clearly still expected her to move on to bigger and better things.

"I can see Mr. Humphries," she offered. Best to get busy. Show her dad she was gung ho about starting and that she believed in efficiency.

Glinda checked her watch. "It's only eight-oh-five, sweetie," she said. "We don't start with the patients until eight thirty."

But he'd been here for twenty minutes, and Sara could use a distraction. "Well, maybe we could see him early today so he could get back to work." And keep traffic in the office flowing, which seemed to be a novel idea.

"Oh, all right," Glinda said. "Sure. I can put him in a room."

Leonore took her dad aside a moment to confer about something before she returned to her desk. Sara had just moved to pick up the patient's chart when her dad appeared at her side, clearing his throat and putting a hand on her arm. "Um, I'll see George," he said. "Longtime patient, you know?" He lowered his voice. "It will be a lot easier for me to just take this one."

Sara frowned. "Did he—did he insist on seeing you?"

"Well, you know how it is, sweetheart . . . people have their certain problems and they feel most comfortable with who's been listening to them for years. You understand that, don't you?"

"Right. Of course." She forced a smile.

"Don't worry," her dad said, giving her another squeeze. "You'll be plenty busy all day. It's not even eight thirty yet."

Sara fought against the awful sinking feeling in her abdomen. Her dad had a personal relationship with *all* his patients. He truly cared about them, and they adored him in return. It looked like neither her dad nor the patients were going to be able to give that up easily.

Resolutely she walked back to her office to stare at her blank white walls and her too-tidy desk. She stuck a pack of gum and a pen into her new knit kangaroo pouch. It was early yet…the first hour. But she had a feeling it was going to be a long day.

* * *

"So what are you doing here so late anyway?" Sara asked her best friend, Kaitlyn, that evening at the Bean, the coffee shop Kaitlyn had inherited from her grandfather. "Don't you have something to do with that hunky high school football coach you're dating?"

Kaitlyn was scrubbing coffee carafes in the big industrial sink while Sara sat at the steel kitchen counter sorting sugar and Splenda packets. "You may as well know," Kaitlyn said, "I broke up with him."

Sara looked up. "You broke up with Steve? Why didn't you tell me?"

"You've had a lot on your mind, what with moving back and starting work…and flirting with Colton." Kaitlyn attempted a smile.

Sara chose to ignore the Colton remark. On second thought, she would address it immediately. "You mean fighting, not flirting. And have I been that unavailable that you couldn't even tell me that? If I have been, I'm a shitty friend and I'm sorry."

Kaitlyn pushed back a strand of hair that had fallen out of her ponytail and kept scrubbing a carafe. Steam drifted up, curling Kaitlyn's already wavy blonde hair. She turned off the water and pulled off her rubber gloves. "Truthfully, Sara, I haven't felt like talking about it. I'd really rather talk about your life. It's more exciting. Speaking of which, how'd your first day working with your dad go?"

Sara smiled. "Hardly exciting. And speaking of not wanting to talk about it..." She laughed. "Seriously, it was all right. I'm optimistic. And more importantly, I'm really glad I took this time to come home and be with my nonna. And closer to you. I've really regretted being so far away. Come sit down and talk with me."

"OK, fine. I'm done here anyway." Her smile was genuine this time as she gestured for Sara to follow her as she took a seat at one of the cute tables in the coffee shop proper. "What can I get you to drink? Or I have leftover muffins if you're hungry."

"My dad and Rachel are having Nonna for dinner tonight, so I'm free. Want to order a pizza?" Sara asked. "Like the old days?"

"Anchovies and onions? I don't think so."

"Oh, come on. I'll even splurge for the Cherry Coke."

"Blech, you're making me sick. I can do a veggie

pizza with a two-liter of Diet. And a salad. If you make the call."

"Deal." Sara ordered the pizza from Lou's, their favorite local pizza restaurant and bar. "Twenty minutes until pickup," she announced.

Kaitlyn got them each a glass of water and sat down. "I'm tired."

"You must be. You start at like four a.m., don't you? And you're still here. That's worse than my dad's hours."

"The business is going great. What I mean is, I'm tired of pretending I'm in love. Steve's a great guy, but I don't love him. That's why I broke it off. I tried my best, but it just didn't happen."

"Oh, Kaitlyn. I'm sorry." Sara squeezed her hand. She worried about Kaitlyn, who kept dating guys but none of them stuck. When they were younger Sara had blamed that on Kaitlyn's having a hopeless crush on Rafe. Now she wasn't so sure.

"There's no reason to be sorry. Now Steve has the chance to meet and fall in love with someone he really loves. And I do too."

Well, that sounded positive, but Kaitlyn didn't look like she felt very positive. "You've dated a lot of guys," Sara said. "At least you've got the experience of knowing what you want."

"Well, mostly what I don't want." She played with a Splenda packet in the center of the table. "My mother would say I'm too picky. Is it too picky to want a gentleman, someone who's polite and considerate, has a good job, is kind to animals, and can cook?"

Oh well, Rafe definitely couldn't cook...much. So maybe Kaitlyn was safe. Plus she did look sad about Steve. So hopefully Rafe was out of the picture. On second thought, Rafe had brought a really good salad to dinner last weekend.

There was a sudden knock at the big plate glass window. Sara turned to see her brother's face plastered against it. Kaitlyn laughed, suddenly animated at seeing Rafe.

Rafe popped his head in the door. "Hey, Sara, Katesters." Sara didn't miss that Rafe's glance lingered on her best friend. Or that he called her that goofy name. "Anything new in coffee world? Hey, I need another bag of that Red Bull coffee you sold me a couple of weeks ago."

"You mean the Himalayan high altitude mix?" Kaitlyn asked.

"Yeah, that's it. The guys at the station love that stuff for when we're up all night."

"Rafe, did you really come by to buy coffee now?" Sara asked. "We're having girl talk. Besides, the Bean is closed and Kaitlyn is off the clock."

"Want to know the truth?" Rafe asked. "I figured if I offered to pick up your pizza, maybe you'd let me stay and eat a slice."

"Or ten," Kaitlyn added. "How did you know we just ordered?"

"Because I just called for one too, and Lou told me. I'll be back in a few."

"Here, let me get some money," Kaitlyn said, already halfway out of her chair.

"Don't bother," Rafe said with a killer smile. "You

get it next time, Katie Scarlett." Then he was gone, disappearing back onto Main Street, the bell above the door tinkling in his wake and Kaitlyn's face as crimson as the nickname Rafe had just called her.

Katie Scarlett? As in *O'Hara*? What was going on with the cute little endearments? "Since when did you get so chummy with my brother?" Sara asked.

Kaitlyn shrugged. "We've always been friends." She paused a long time. "That's the problem."

"No, Kaitlyn! Not Rafe. He's the worst kind of commitmentphobe. He will break your heart. Guaranteed. Do you hear me? *Guaranteed.*"

"It's my heart to break, Sara. I want it all, the whole package—the rapid pulse, the swoony kisses, the feeling that you know when he's in the room because your whole body reacts to his presence. That's how I feel around Rafe."

Sara disguised her horror because Kaitlyn looked so...passionate. "Are you going to tell him?"

"I don't know what I'm going to do. Because right now we *are* friends. We hang out sometimes."

"I heard you've been to Nonna's for dinner."

"A couple of times. Her lasagna is *amazing.*" She rubbed her stomach. "One day, your brother is going to wake up and discover he's in love with me too. I just know it."

Kaitlyn got up from the table before Sara could roll her eyes. "Where are you going?" Sara asked, holding back her panic.

"I have leftover muffins for Rafe to bring to the guys at the station."

"No. Do not give my brother your muffins!"

"He can have my muffins if he wants them."

Oh God, were they really talking about muffins? "You're too kind and generous. He will stomp all over your muffins and break your heart, because that's what Rafe does, without even knowing it."

"Someone's going to get through to him, Sara. Maybe it could be me."

"I just care about you. I want you to be happy."

"And I appreciate it. Not to change the subject, but...Gabby and I want you to be happy too. So we've, um...found you a date."

"No, Kaitlyn." This was going from bad to worse. "I'm not ready yet."

"You said yourself you're sick of everyone talking about last year. People will forget all about it if you get back on the horse. Besides, the guy is a doctor, and he's cute. My aunt Millie tried to set him up with me, but he's not my type."

"Of course not. Because you think Rafe is your type."

Kaitlyn shrugged. Then she looked up, a huge grin spreading across her face. Sara turned around to see that Rafe had entered through the back way, carrying a big pizza box. Geez, she had it bad.

"I haven't been on a first date for thirteen years," Sara mumbled, mostly to herself because Kaitlyn was so preoccupied.

Kaitlyn tore her gaze from Rafe long enough to flash Sara a smile. "Well, that's going to change on Friday. And Gabby and I are going to help you."

Chapter 7

♥

The next Friday night, Sara walked into Lou's Pizza only to find Hannah working the hostess stand. She hadn't been to Lou's in ages, but it felt the same—crowded red booths with people talking and laughing, black-and-white photos all over the walls of Lou's family making pizzas in Italy in the very old days, and the smell of the best pizza this side of Cleveland. The smack of pool balls resonated from the pool and Ping-Pong tables in the back, where the teenagers usually hung out. Not the most romantic place to meet a blind date, but definitely a popular one.

"Hi, sweetie," Sara said, giving Hannah a hug. "You look pretty tonight." Since their grandmothers were friends, she'd known Hannah since she was a baby. And she'd been Hannah's counselor at the local day camp during her summers in college. Hannah had been one of her favorite campers, notwithstanding the fact that Colton was her brother.

"Hi, Sara," Hannah said, pulling out a menu from

behind a wooden stand. "Your sister and Kaitlyn are already here."

Sara scanned the restaurant until she caught sight of Gabby and Kaitlyn sitting together in a booth near the windows.

Hannah looked her over, no doubt noticing that she was dressed up and had makeup on. "You look really nice. Do you have a date?"

"Actually yeah, I do." She held out her hands. "I even got my nails done." Gabby's idea. It had taken a whole hour, but it had been kind of fun. Sara fingered a blue stone Hannah wore on a leather cord around her neck. "Cute."

"I made it in a jewelry-making class at the community center. Want me to make you one? Better yet, you should come to class with me. It's on Monday nights."

Sara tried hard to imagine herself taking a Monday night off to make jewelry. Yet this was her new life, and she was determined to make an effort to do normal things, for Nonna's sake and, tonight, thanks to Gabby, for her own sake. Hence the blind date. And the nails. And the fact that she was wearing Gabby's top. It was part of the new Sara. Open to new experiences, not working all the time. Moving on from Tagg, which in this town was a feat, as her patients mentioned her breakup multiple times a day. "That sounds like fun," Sara said.

Hannah seemed to genuinely brighten at that. She had the same striking eyes as Colton, only hers were hazel, not blue. Dark-brown hair like his too, but hers was straight and shiny and pulled back in a ponytail.

"Hey, congrats on OSU," Sara said. "Is your summer going OK?"

"It would be better if my brother didn't hang out here." She gestured toward the back. "He's lurking over there."

Oh no. Colton was *here*? Sure enough, there he was in the back, holding a pool cue and leaning his long frame against the wall, talking to a couple of guys she hadn't seen since high school. As Hannah led her to the table, she made certain not to look in his direction, focusing on not tripping in her high-heeled sandals (also Gabby's).

"I don't think this is a good place to meet a date," Sara said to Gabby and Kaitlyn as she sat down. "Too noisy," she added, nodding toward the back. And too close to Colton.

"Wow," Kaitlyn said. "Is that you?"

"Gee, thanks for the vote of confidence," Sara said.

"No, I mean—wow. You look different. Kind of... hot." Easy for Kaitlyn to say. She was blonde and blue-eyed, with a sweet smile and all kinds of guys drooling at her feet.

"OK, that's it. I'm leaving," Sara said, moving to escape the booth.

"Don't let the fact that Colton's here bother you," Gabby said, reaching out to pull her back. "Besides, you said he was really good about everything last Sunday when Nonna got lost."

"Yes, he was. Like a normal compassionate human." She knew she wasn't exactly being fair. He'd seemed genuinely concerned and... kind.

"You're just meeting Ken here for a drink," Kaitlyn said. "He's a nice guy, a microbiologist, and really smart, according to my aunt Millie." Yes, it had taken Kaitlyn's aunt Millie, a medical technologist, to find her a date in this town. That should've said it all. "Then you're going to a nice restaurant."

Sara rolled her eyes. "I'm really grateful to you both for setting this up and supporting me, but I don't need date coaching. I'm thirty years old!" They'd insisted she meet them here so they could help her relax before her date.

"You've been with the same guy for a hundred years," Gabby said. "Trust me, you need date coaching."

Why had she agreed to this? The sound of pool balls breaking made her turn. Colton had just made a shot and happened to glance up at the same time she happened to be looking at him. He did a double take. Oh God. She looked quickly away and nervously pulled up the halter part of her blouse. It was cute, but her boobs just didn't fill it out like Gabby's.

"Stop fidgeting," Gabby said. "Your boobs look great."

Sara took a sip of Gabby's drink. What was he even doing here on a Friday night? Shouldn't he be out revolving some poor unsuspecting female? Oh, why hadn't she insisted on meeting her date anywhere but in Angel Falls?

"You're out of practice," Gabby said. "We just want to go over a few things." She pulled out a list.

"You have a *list*?" How pathetic was she?

"Yes. First, you look very nice." She was wearing the outfit Gabby had told her to wear, a black V-neck sleeveless top that had a halter back and showed some skin and a little black skirt and heels.

"You look terrific," Kaitlyn said. "Girly."

She didn't want to look girly. She wanted to be curled up with a good book on Nonna's couch in her flannel pj's.

"We should be fixing *you* up, Kaitlyn," Sara said. If only to get Kaitlyn's mind off Rafe.

"Don't try to distract us," Gabby said. "Rule number one. Don't talk about work."

Sara frowned. "This guy is a doctor too, right? Maybe he won't mind that."

"Don't do it," Kaitlyn said. "Show him you've got other interests." She paused. "You *do* have interests outside of work, don't you?"

Sara swallowed hard. She used to—but lately? Hmmm.

"What shows have you binge watched lately?" Gabby asked.

"Seen any movies?" Kaitlyn asked.

"What's the last book you've read?"

"Volunteer work. Done any of that?"

Sara bit down on her lip. "Um, I've been busy?" she said.

Her friends stared at her.

"All right, I haven't been that busy. I guess I mostly did what Tagg wanted. And this past year... was hard. I was a little off balance." She had managed to watch all ten seasons of *Friends*. Did that count?

"OK," Gabby said. "You're going to have to make some stuff up until you get a life."

"At least she got her nails done today," Kaitlyn said. "That's a start."

Sara looked at her nails. They were a shiny dark maroon. She had to admit they were pretty. "Look, you guys," she said. "I just want you to know how much I appreciate this. I really want to start over with a fresh slate. Give people other things to talk about than my sad past, you know what I mean?"

"That's exactly what we're going to help you to do. Don't forget to sit up straight. Good posture. Think sexy." Gabby rattled off more items from her list.

Sara missed her comfy scrubs and beloved Danskos. She was worried that her skirt was too short and her heels were a little on the slutty side. But when Gabby telegraphed her the evil eye, she threw her shoulders back and sat up straight just to get her off her case.

"The important thing is to be relaxed. And show him you've got a great sense of humor," Kaitlyn said. "Don't forget to smile. And let's order you a glass of wine while you're waiting. We'll celebrate your making it through your first week." Kaitlyn signaled the waiter while Sara racked her brain to think of a humorous anecdote she could relay in a relaxed, smiling way.

The last funny thing had happened today in the office when her father got down on the floor of the waiting room to read a story to a toddler while his mom was with Sara for her annual gynecologic exam. Sara walked past the waiting room to see her dad and the toddler eating cookies and leafing through a picture book. Her dad was unconventional and sometimes old-fashioned, but he was a great doctor. But that didn't seem like the kind of story that would exactly have a new date rolling on the floor.

Oh God, she was out of practice and in trouble. Panic welled up to lodge in her throat. Her hands felt cold and clammy. She choked down a few sips of wine. Not much help. She hadn't had a new boyfriend since she was *eighteen*. That was almost thirteen years ago! She didn't even remember what to say on a first date—the last time it had been things like "Algebra sucks" and "I hope I pass my driver's test."

Gabby glanced at her watch. "Rachel's picking Nonna up from the senior center, so I've got to go. I've got Nonna covered tonight. Just have fun. Let loose a little. Everything will be fine."

"Don't do anything I wouldn't do," Kaitlyn said, squeezing Sara's arm.

Gabby kissed her cheek. "See ya later," she said with a wink.

OK, there was no reason to panic. Sara fiddled with the stem of her wineglass. It was just a date. She could handle it. And she would get herself a life. Her friends were right, she spent too much time working. Now that she was out of residency, she'd have time to do the things she used to enjoy. Funny she couldn't quite remember what those were. When she was dating Tagg, they used to see artsy films, go to lacrosse games, have dinner at expensive restaurants. She'd gone along with what he wanted. Where had she lost herself in the process?

She must've been deep in thought, because she looked up to suddenly find Colton standing next to her booth. "Hey, Red. What brings you here tonight?" he asked, leaning casually on his pool stick. He took in her sexy black top, her nails, her makeup.

Sara felt a hot blush creep into her cheeks.

"I have a date," she said.

"Is that right?" The corner of his mouth twitched a little. "Funny, because this restaurant is only rated four stars, not five."

"I'm sure it'll be just fine."

"Well, I'm glad to see you can let your hair down. A bit of advice—just be sure not to scare the guy with a bunch of talk about work. I know you probably think it's a turn-on, but... not so much."

He was still needling her, just like back in the day, when he'd teased her mercilessly. What was his deal, anyway? "Colton, why don't you just go back there and play pool like you've been doing every Friday night since high school? Geez." Apparently the nice cop who'd been kind to her grandmother had left town.

Suddenly a teenager with a crew cut barreled into Colton, wrapping his arms around him. It was Stevie Cox, one of her Down syndrome patients, whom she'd just seen in the office that morning. "Hi, Chief!" he said exuberantly. "Are you ready to play Ping-Pong with us? I'm going to win tonight." Stevie looked around and saw Sara. Pointing at her, he said, "She's my doctor. Hi, Dr. Sara."

Before she could respond, he engulfed her in a Stevie-size hug too. Looking over his shoulders, she saw a group of gangly teenage boys gathering near the pool tables.

"I didn't know you played Ping-Pong," she said to Stevie.

"I'm really good at it too. I'm going to beat Chief. Right, Colton?"

"Oh, I don't know about that, Steve. I feel pretty lucky tonight." Colton rotated his arm at the shoulder like he was seriously warming it up and smiled.

And that smile. Sincere, not laced with sarcasm— just a simple, honest smile. And you know what? Seeing it wrecked her, down to her toes. It showed the countenance of a decent man. A man capable of spending time hanging out with teenage boys who probably needed a good influence, and it was in sharp contrast to the smart-mouthed wise guy he seemed to reserve only for her.

"The guys are waiting," Stevie said, pointing a thumb toward the back.

"Why don't you start warming up?" Colton said. "I'll be right over."

"OK. I'll tell everybody you're coming." Stevie turned to Sara before taking off. "Bye, Dr. Sara!"

"Bye, Stevie," she said. "Have fun."

"See ya around, Red," Colton said to Sara, turning to go himself. "Gotta get back to my lame Friday night. Enjoy your date."

That was it? Before she knew what she was doing, she got up from the booth and followed him a few feet. "Look. I—I'm sorry I made fun of you." He stopped in his tracks. "But you don't always have to be so insulting."

He turned back to her slowly. "How am I insulting?" His stare burned a hole through her.

She swallowed. "You treat me like I'm...a snob. Unable to let loose. Like I'm...frigid. And you seem to thrive on making me think you're a jerk until I suddenly find out you're...not. I was wrong about you. Maybe you're wrong about me too." Oh, why had she even bothered going after him? What was the point?

His gaze drifted downward, to the hem of her short skirt, to her bare legs and heels, then swept back up to her face. The intensity of the look he shot her made her suck in a quick breath. A memory, jogged into the present, suddenly hit her full force. He'd kissed her once, long ago. Back in college, during the one and only time she and Tagg had broken up.

She squeezed her eyes shut, not wanting to remember, but the memory surfaced anyway.

Spring of freshman year, they'd shared a ride home from school—he'd driven, and for the first time things had been...different. For one thing, Tagg wasn't with them, and his absence seemed to have unleashed a completely different Colton.

They'd laughed and joked and actually talked for the first time. She'd ended up going with him that evening to his sister's dance recital, where she'd sat between him and Cookie. It was odd to see him act fun and teasing to Cookie, and be a loving and supportive brother to seven-year-old Hannah. And it was clear by Hannah's adoring looks that he was the moon and the stars to her.

Sara begged off before the family pictures. She was

glad to leave the stuffy auditorium and clear her head of thoughts she shouldn't be having. With that dark, too-long hair hanging over his collar and falling adorably over his forehead, Colton was handsome in a dangerous way. *Too* handsome.

Besides, she was still upset over the breakup with Tagg. After over a year of dating, she still hadn't slept with him. Oh, they'd done plenty of other stuff, but as for sex—real sex—she'd held off. And he was getting upset with her. She didn't know why she was so hesitant—she loved him. She'd known him a long time. But something held her back. Maybe it was that falling-in-love feeling that she missed, which had faded since the time he'd first noticed her, the first boy who thought she was pretty and appreciated her smarts and ambition.

But those feelings weren't supposed to last, were they? What was important was the fact that they had similar interests, similar goals and backgrounds. That was the stuff that made for a lasting relationship, right?

But Tagg was getting irritated, frustrated. Looking at other girls. And they'd broken up. *Fine*, she'd said. *Go date someone else.*

She'd gotten a quarter of a block away from the high school auditorium when she heard steps beating on the pavement.

"Hey," Colton said, catching up with her, barely out of breath, "how about some company?"

Her pulse skipped again at the sight of him. Tall, just as recklessly teen-idol handsome, yet... different. Edgier. And very, very appealing.

It was a gorgeous spring evening, unseasonably warm. It had rained earlier, so the smell of rain on top of growing things and spring blossoms was heady and fresh. Tiny pink petals and helicopters from the maple trees were stuck to the pavement as they walked along the old uneven sidewalks. The clouds were clearing, revealing a big yellow three-quarters-full moon, like a big peach with a bite out of it.

Soon they approached the bridge, the showcase of the main street of town. At its entrance was a large brass sculpture of two angels leaning toward one another so that their bodies and arms together formed a heart. An endless photo opportunity for people who spent the day in town shopping, or came for one of the art shows or programs on the green below the bridge, or to attend the local theater or a speaker program at the popular independent bookstore downtown.

Colton slowed his pace at the center of the bridge. Old-fashioned iron streetlamps flanked its sides. In summer the city hung baskets of flowers from them, but now, in early spring, they were bare. He fingered the decorative iron safety railing that rose up from the concrete. There were three padlocks attached to one of the iron posts. They had names written on them in permanent marker: Jon and Allison, Christopher and Heather, Matthew and Sigrid.

"People are always doing weird shit like that," he said.

"What do you mean?"

"They hook locks all over the bridge, then the fire department saws them off and tosses them."

"Why don't they just let them be? It's a cute idea."

"In Paris they had to saw all the locks off because they weighed more than forty-five tons. They made the bridge too heavy. Love is dangerous," he said. Then he looked at her.

Oh God, *he* was dangerous. The shadows of the setting sun brought out the strong lines of his face—his square jaw, his strong cheekbones. She'd always thought his looks were raw in a hard, mean way, but lately...lately he seemed different. Softer. Gentler.

"And then there's the stuff they throw into the river," Colton said, curling his fingers around the rails and leaning over.

"You mean like coins?"

He laughed. "When I worked for the police department last summer, I had to put on a diving suit and scoop them all out. Three hundred fifty dollars' worth. But you wouldn't believe the other stuff I found down there."

"Like what?"

"Boots. A stuffed animal. A muddy wedding dress. But the best thing was a time capsule."

"What was in it?"

"A love letter."

"No!"

"To a lost love. Someone who died fifty years earlier. People think this angel stuff is magic."

"Angel Falls needs a museum."

"You could be the curator. Every year you can dive in and find new exhibits."

"Ha ha. Very funny."

"That would be a different job."

"Well, I guess I've always been a little different." Oh God, she'd said that out loud. *How dumb.*

"That's a good thing," he was quick to say.

OK, now she felt like she was living in an alternate universe. "Colton, I'm surprised you'd say that. Because for as long as I can remember, you've been giving me shit for just about everything."

"I used to think you were spoiled. That you grew up having everything you wanted, didn't have to struggle for things."

She knew his father had died on the police force in Chicago. The rumor was that his mother had drunk herself to death, but who knew. He never talked about that.

"Do you want me to apologize for my family?"

"No." He'd turned and was staring at her. A slow steady hum buzzed through her limbs like an electrical current, making her weak and unsteady. All her senses were telling her to flee, but she couldn't seem to move, so she just stood there and stared back at him.

"I was an idiot in high school," he said.

His gaze dropped to her lips. Wait—was he going to—oh no.

"For what it's worth, I don't think you're an idiot now." Her voice sounded funny. Hoarse. A whisper.

He turned back to the falls. The cheery sound of water splashed in the background, like nothing was amiss. Like Colton Walker hadn't just apologized.

"What will you do—after college?" he asked.

"Go to med school, hopefully. And after that...I don't know."

"You could go anywhere. Do anything you want."

"So could you."

He shook his head. "My knee ruined any chance of that."

"I'm sorry." She was sorry. What else could she say?

He tossed her a brief glance. To see if she meant it? But then he was back to looking at the water. "Don't be. I'll be coming back to take care of my grandma and Hannah. Maybe on the police force. If I can time it right and get a job in town, that is."

He had burdens she couldn't even fathom. And he was right, her freedom was limitless compared to his. She'd once thought he was shallow, but she was coming to understand things were far more complex.

"So I guess I'll be a townie forever."

"I love our town. That's not necessarily a bad thing."

She looked down at the falls too but suddenly felt his gaze on her, intense and as palpable as a touch.

Then he leaned over and kissed her. His lips were soft and careful on hers, the pressure gentle but steady. That simple, chaste kiss made her heart squeeze, her breath catch. The world spun dizzily as her knees threatened to collapse beneath her, making her grasp his arms to steady herself.

Colton pulled back, an unspoken question in his eyes. She answered it by standing on tiptoe, curling her hand around his neck, and kissing him back, her lips moving against his, feeling the softness of his mouth, the contrasting rasp of stubble. He cupped her face in his hand, tangled his fingers in her hair, and tugged her against his hard body.

She went hot and cold. A noise squeaked out from her throat. She opened to him, their tongues tangling together, their mouths fitting together perfectly. That kiss, it was the most erotic thing she'd ever experienced. The way his mouth moved over hers, the way he held her tight against him, the way she could feel he trembled too.

He tasted...wonderful. He smelled like plain soap and leftover sunshine from the warm day. And he kissed like...like no one had ever kissed her before. Like she'd imagined being kissed in a dream.

Suddenly there was a flashlight shining on them, even though the sun hadn't yet set. The first thing Sara thought was, *What if it's the cops?* Then her family would know, Tagg would know...

Tagg. Oh, what was she doing? She'd forgotten all about him. About *them*.

The flashlight belonged to old Mrs. Mulligan, who was walking her dachshund Georgie.

"Oh, just look at you two kids," she said. "So cute. How about a picture?"

That was the thing. Everyone was always taking pictures in front of the angels. Couples especially. Rumor had it that if you had your picture taken there and tossed money into the water, your love would last forever.

"For good luck," she said.

Surprisingly, Colton got ready to pose. "Thanks, Mrs. M.," he said.

The old lady snapped the picture while Colton held on to Sara's waist, her panic climbing the mercury scale, high and higher.

Mrs. Mulligan moved on, Colton let go. He still had that dreamy look in his eyes, like he would've been perfectly happy to get back to whatever it was they were doing before they were interrupted.

"I-I have to go," she said. Guilt tore at her conscience.

He held her back with his arm. "Wait." His gaze locked on to her like a tractor beam, forcing her to stare into the pure, deep blue of his eyes. "Come with me to the art museum next Friday. They always have music in the courtyard. It'll be a nice break from studying for exams."

She was speechless. She should say no, but the words wouldn't form.

"Give me your phone."

She did, God knew why, and he punched in his number. "Promise me you'll think about it."

"Colton," she said, and it was as if she'd said his name for the first time.

He raised his head. He had a look on his face. Hopeful. Anticipatory.

"OK," she found herself saying. "I'll do it. I'll see you Friday."

He broke into a smile. Held her hand and insisted on walking her home. But not before he reached into his pocket and tossed some coins into the falls.

Guilt and confusion warred within her. As well as shock that Colton Walker had given her the most amazing kiss of her life. He was so different from the cool, standoffish persona he projected so well. She'd had him pegged all wrong.

In the back of the restaurant, the sound of kids cheering jolted Sara back to reality. Stevie had won a point or a game, she wasn't sure which, but he was holding up two Ping-Pong paddles with a triumphant expression on his face while the other boys slapped him on the back.

Her date with Colton so long ago had never happened because he'd stood her up. When she'd sought him out at his dorm room, he'd answered the door shirtless, female laughter echoing in the background. At that moment she'd known everything had been a joke. All these years later, that thought *still* made her sick to her stomach. She'd learned unequivocally from that experience that Colton couldn't be trusted, and he'd proven over and over through the years that that was the case.

She warned herself to heed that advice now. Colton stood there, not speaking, that same blue gaze drilling through her with an intensity that caused gooseflesh to rise on her arms. She wasn't sure if she'd stunned him by her confrontation or if he simply intended not to say anything. Just as he opened his mouth to finally speak, a tall, thin man appeared at her side.

"Are you Sara Langdon? I'm Ken. Dr. Ken Houseman, from the microbiology lab at the hospital. I'm sorry I was running a bit late. Lots going on at work, you know?" He glanced at Colton. "Am I interrupting something?"

"No. Not at all," Colton said, still staring. "See you

around, Doctors." He gave Sara a little salute and walked back to join the kids.

Her date sat down across from her and ordered a scotch. She downed the rest of her wine. It was difficult to concentrate on the small talk he was making. "You're Ivy League trained, aren't you? So am I. Princeton. I study mutant bacteria. Ones that aren't susceptible to any antibiotics. I always wonder what would happen if we accidentally poured some down the sewer and started a killer epidemic, you know?"

Sara tried to focus on what he was saying, but frankly, she wasn't into killer germs or the creepy way he'd just casually mentioned the possibility of a deadly epidemic. Honestly, he could've announced he'd found a cure for cancer for all she would've cared. Out of the corner of her eye, she watched Colton play Ping-Pong, laughing and joking with the boys.

Thing was, she was seeing a completely different side to Colton. First with her grandmother, and now with these boys. Heck, even in the way he'd treated her when she was distraught the other day. But every time they had an opportunity to get closer, he seemed to draw a line in the sand, doing something to push her away.

Chapter 8

♥

At eleven a.m. the next Friday, Colton pulled up in Cookie's driveway. This was Cookie's morning to volunteer at the Salvation Army store downtown, and he knew Hannah wasn't scheduled to work until the dinner shift today, so he was hoping she'd be home...sort of. Meaning he needed to talk with her but was dreading it about as much as a testicular exam.

He walked into the kitchen to find her sitting at the breakfast bar in a T-shirt and pj bottoms, her long hair pulled up in that complicated messy bun only girls knew how to do with a few flicks of the wrist and a rubber band. She was doing something on her phone and eating a bowl of Cap'n Crunch, her favorite cereal since she was three.

Dammit, he *wished* she were three. Then he wouldn't have to have this discussion with her. "Do you have something you want to tell me?" he asked, instantly realizing that he'd started this off all wrong. He hated being a quasi parent. He didn't know what the hell he was doing.

"Good morning?" She had no makeup on, and she looked so young and innocent his stomach hurt.

He crossed his arms, more to make himself believe he was tough than because he felt that way. "Anything else?"

"No, Colton, nothing else. I'm just a normal teenage girl trying to lead a normal teenage life, if my brother would just get off my case." She let go of her spoon, which clattered against the side of her cereal bowl. He'd done it now, managed to irritate her with two sentences. Fuck.

"I had coffee with Lou this morning."

She bit her cuticle, her usual tell, and glanced at her phone again, which was buzzing with texts from her million friends. So, she *was* a little nervous about what he was about to say.

"I haven't missed a shift since I started working there. What's the problem?"

"You were there past midnight last Saturday night."

"I'm allowed to go out with my friends."

"Not this particular friend."

Her phone dropped, and she bent to pick it up. When she popped her head up again, he could tell she was biting the insides of her cheeks, but still she didn't say anything.

She looked so much like their mother. Slight build, pretty heart-shaped face. But where their mother had had blue eyes like Colton, Hannah had big hazel eyes that he'd always thought were honest with him. Until now. Where his mother had been flighty, whimsical, and anxious, Hannah was in general calm and even-keeled.

But she had her moments. Moments that made him worry. He didn't want her going down the same pathway as their mother. It was his job to ensure that. But first he'd have to stop pissing her off as soon as he walked through the door.

He tried a different tack, sitting down across from her on a stool. It was her turn to cross her arms and give him the evil eye. "Why didn't you tell me you were seeing Aiden?"

"It was a little hard considering the first words out of your mouth about him were *Stay away*."

Colton sighed. "I said that for a reason. The guy has a troubled past. His family life sucks. He's already been in trouble once with the law."

"But you're trying to help him. He deserves a chance, Colton."

Suddenly a weird thing happened. Colt heard Sara's voice in his head. He saw an image of her in Lou's the other night when she'd run after him. *I was wrong about you. Maybe you're wrong about me too.*

Maybe he did tend to leap to conclusions about people. But this kid…He was bad news. He didn't want Aiden anywhere near his sister.

"Look, Hannah. You're bright and smart and beautiful. Your future is in front of you, and it's a great one. I don't want anything to derail that, do you understand?"

He had to say things that he did not want to say. That were his obligation to say. But the back of his neck and his palms were starting to sweat. He wanted her to have a good life. A *great* life. He didn't want her to get dragged down like their mother after his father died—

with bad men, one after another. Hannah was compassionate like their mother. She saw the best in people. That had been part of their mother's downfall. She'd trusted people who didn't deserve her trust.

He couldn't lose Hannah like they'd lost their mother. He *had* to make sure she made the right choices. But he was at a complete loss as to how to do that.

Hannah looked at him as if he were speaking Greek. As if he were the most clueless person on the planet.

He decided to try one more time. "The people you hang out with impact your life and your future. You've got to pick your friends wisely. You can't let yourself get dragged down by other people's problems."

Aiden's family was a train wreck. He'd had a terrible childhood. Colton had no idea how that neglect and chaos had imprinted itself upon his personality, but with everything he saw daily, he could believe it had had some bad effects. Effects he did not want his sister hanging around.

"Look," Colton said. "Lou saw you and Aiden making out, and from the looks of it, you two were just getting started."

Hannah glared at him like he'd just crawled out of a sewer. But he held his ground. If, God forbid, Hannah and Aiden were having sex, he needed to make sure that she was protected against an unplanned pregnancy. Hannah wasn't saying a thing, but she didn't have to— her hostile stare said it all. He opened his mouth to say something, but nothing came out. "Don't have sex" didn't sound like a good opening. Or the more gentle

"Abstinence is important," or the more blunt "Are you having sex?"

"Are we done here?" Hannah asked, sliding off the bar stool and grabbing her phone. "Because I have to take a shower before work."

"We're done," he said, putting up his arms in surrender.

That went well. They were done, for now, but he knew he had to do something to make sure Hannah was safe. He wasn't about to let her future get screwed up or her choices get taken away like his had been.

* * *

Colton walked into the Bean around noon, and the first thing he saw was Sara with her forehead pressed against the glass bakery cabinet, rolling her head back and forth.

"Take a deep breath," Kaitlyn said, working the espresso machine. "Your coffee'll be ready in a sec. Breathe."

"Remind me why I came back here again."

Kaitlyn took a rag and wiped down the counter. "Because your nonna needs you. She's what matters the most."

"My father is so set in his ways. He doesn't want any change. He watches over me like I'm a med student and questions every test I order. And every patient but one this morning mentioned my wedding. Or lack of one, that is."

"Which one didn't?"

"His name was James Pollard, and he was a new-born. And his mom was too nervous about bringing him in to care about my love life. But everyone else did."

Colton edged a little closer to the door. He didn't want to open it or the bell would go off and out him for sure.

"Don't make me go back there," Sara said.

"Sara," Kaitlyn said, "this is only your second week. It's a big adjustment for everyone. Give it some time. A little bit of caffeine and you'll feel like a million bucks."

"Now I know why my father didn't have a partner all these years. He doesn't *want* a partner. He doesn't want an interloper in his practice."

"Your dad's got to know you're an awesome doctor." Kaitlyn banged something around behind the counter that indicated she was making some kind of fancy drink. "You even got that fancy award last year for being the most outstanding resident before you grad-uated. What was that called again? The Doppelganger Award or something?"

"Hopplebauer Award. And it doesn't matter. No award in the world can prove my worth to my father."

"So melodramatic," Kaitlyn said. She looked over Sara's shoulder. "Oh, hi, Colton," Kaitlyn said brightly, outing him for good. "Your usual?"

Sara's head bolted upright.

"The usual's great, thanks," he said. No use pretend-ing he hadn't just heard everything. He turned to Sara. "Rough morning?"

"Go on. Just...say it," she said. "Hit me with it."

"With what?"

"Some snide remark. Some snippy comment. Remind me of all my faults and inadequacies. I'm ready."

"I was just going to say that you're a good doctor and . . . and it's going to be OK."

"No advice? Platitudes? An I-told-you-so or a You-better-go-back-to-your-Ivy-League-world?"

He wasn't going to do that. Or do something to get her spine prickled, like ask her how that loser date had been last weekend. Because he already knew. Rafe had told him all about the microbiologist and his fascination with killer bacteria.

This time, Colton dug down deep and tried to be something he hadn't been so far. A friend. Call him crazy, but when she'd come after him at Lou's and accused him of being insulting . . . Well. Maybe she was right. He could tone it down a little.

"Your dad's really respected around here. People say he takes the time to talk to them, unlike all the docs who are watching the clock and try to get in and out like seeing patients is some kind of race. It's just that anyone who's been at a job for that long is going to have certain . . . ideas that are resistant to change."

"Like ingrown toenails," Kaitlyn said. "Completely embedded."

"Thanks for the gross visual," Sara said.

"Hey, you're the doctor," Kaitlyn said, passing Colton a big cup of coffee with a lid on it. "I was just trying to use an example you can relate to."

Sara threw up her hands. "My dad's still using paper records. And manual blood pressure cuffs. The EKG machine has one strip, like a grocery store cash register receipt. And they might still be killing rabbits for the pregnancy tests for all I know."

Kaitlyn's eyes went wide. "They used to do that?"

"Yeah. In 1960," Sara said.

"Here you go," Kaitlyn said, handing Sara her coffee. "I put an extra shot of espresso in that, by the way."

"I love you," Sara said. Her phone went off with a text, and she set down her cup on the counter to pull it out of her purse. "I have to run. See you later. Thanks for the help. I think." Sara blew Kaitlyn a kiss, gave Colton a quick wave, and left.

Well. The first interaction in a week where she hadn't threatened to kill him. Things were looking up.

"It'll get better," Kaitlyn said, pulling a big tray of freshly iced cinnamon buns off a shelf behind her.

He leaned his arm against the bakery case. "Yeah. New-job problems."

Kaitlyn held out the tray of cinnamon buns. "Actually, I was talking about you, Colty. These are still warm, by the way. Want one?"

The scent of warm cinnamon rolls was already permeating the whole shop, making his mouth water. Colton took one. "If you don't call me that, sure, I'd love one. But I'm not sure I'm following you."

Kaitlyn shrugged. "Any bad blood between you two is none of my business. But don't think I can't see that I-want-to-eat-you-for-breakfast way you look at her. Plus it's getting exhausting pretending I hate you too."

Colton narrowed his eyes. "Why are you suddenly on my side?"

"I happen to know you're a nice guy. Not that you

used to be, though. Of course, Sara hasn't forgotten that."

No, she hadn't. He wasn't the same jerk he'd been in high school, but she still thought he was, and it seemed at times he couldn't help feeding into that. It was just that Sara seemed to be able to push all his buttons. Remind him that he was a small-town cop in the same town where he'd lived for half his life. He didn't have her grand aspirations and dreams—mostly because he'd had an obligation to do what was right, take care of his family. Work to give Hannah the choices he'd never gotten. But it niggled—had he settled?

"Oh, look. It's your lucky day," Kaitlyn said, nudging her head toward the top of the bakery case.

"Why's that?"

"Sara forgot her coffee. And if anyone needs coffee today, it's her, right?"

He took the cup. "I'm going that way anyway. See you around, Kaitlyn."

"Hey, ladies," Colton said a few minutes later, resting his elbows on the windowsill in the Langdons' office and peering at Leonore and Glinda through the glass. "How's it going?" No sign of Sara. Looked like she was already back at work. He should just leave the cup and go, but that perverse part of him that seemed to totally enjoy getting himself into trouble spoke up.

"How's Sara getting along?"

"Oh, hello, Chief," Glinda said, sliding open the window. "Well, she's a sweetheart, always has been. But Doctor's set in his ways. It's hard for him, after working alone all these years."

Leonore pulled off her giant earphones. "Whew-y! That Sara sure talks a lot when she dictates her charts. Lord, my fingers are going to fall off from all this transcribing."

Glinda laughed. "That's because Doctor barely says anything at all, just 'normal exam.'"

"Well, Dr. Sara includes every body part in her physicals. And the tests she orders! I haven't heard of half of 'em!"

Colton smiled. "Sounds like Sara's just what this office needs. Like getting a big gust of fresh air in here."

"Why Chief Walker, are you sweet on her?" Leonore asked.

"Absolutely not." He shoved the coffee cup closer to the window. "Sara forgot this at the Bean. And I'm—um—here to get my stitches out. Sara told me I could just stop by sometime and I've been so busy I keep forgetting. But if now's not a good time—" Oh, hell, what was he doing? He hadn't intended to get his stitches out right now. Guess he'd panicked a little. He certainly didn't want them to think he'd gone out of his way on Sara's account.

Glinda immediately disappeared into the back, then reappeared a minute later to open the door to the waiting room. "Come on back, sweetie. Doctor can see you now. He said no need to wait for Sara. He's got a couple of minutes."

A strange wave of disappointment washed over Colton, which he quickly brushed off as he made his way to an exam room. Had he actually been looking forward to sparring with her over his suture removal?

Her father would be the saner choice. Plus he wouldn't have to worry about getting another shot in the ass.

"Well, hello there, son." Dr. Langdon said, pulling his bifocals down his nose and rolling a stool up to the exam table where Colton sat. "Let's have a look." The older doctor inspected his arm. "Sara did a nice job with these. Everything looks well healed."

"Yes, sir." As the doctor tore open the suture removal kit, Colton asked, "What's it like having your daughter here working with you?" *Why don't you just keep your mouth shut and get your sutures out?* a voice in his head said. He was never good at listening to voices of authority anyway.

"Oh, it's fantastic. I'm so proud of her," Dr. Langdon said as he snipped a suture. "I just fear we may not have her here with us for very long. She's destined for things more prestigious than a family medical practice in a tiny town like ours."

Tiny town. Right. Sara wouldn't be hanging around here for very long, that was for sure. "You ever tell her that—how proud you are of her?"

He paused with his instruments in midair. "Excuse me, son?"

Oh boy, he was really overstepping now, yet he couldn't seem to stop his mouth. "Oh, just that maybe she needs to hear that. I mean, I imagine working with your dad is a great thing, but it can be a little stressful too, especially in the beginning. Everyone has to be a little flexible, which is hard after doing things the same way for so long—and everybody needs to know they're wanted, right?"

Dr. Langdon raised a thick gray brow. "Yes, well, sure. Are you implying that my daughter doesn't feel that she's wanted here?"

"No, sir, I'm not saying that. It's just that I could understand how she might feel you might not want a partner to interfere with your way of doing things."

Dr. Langdon chuckled. "Sara's made a decision I don't necessarily agree with. I respect her wanting to come back home to be with her grandmother, but I disagree with her delaying her fellowship training to do it. She's meant to do greater things than Angel Falls can offer."

The doctor sat back and cleared away his instruments. "There you go, Chief, good as new."

"Thank you." OK, this discussion was done and Colton had clearly overstepped his bounds. Plus Dr. Langdon had just echoed what he'd known all along—Sara wasn't here to stay. This town was just a tiny pit stop in a life full of bigger things. Harvard, Mayo Clinic—who knew what would be next? He jumped down off the table, inspecting his arm. "Oh, I was talking to the firefighters," he said. "We'd like to have a medical person come in and talk to both departments about our protocols for Narcan use during our drug overdose runs. Would you be able to help us out?"

They walked together out of the room, stopping beside the reception area. "I think that might be something Sara would jump at the chance to do."

"Did you just sign me up for something?" Sara asked as she flew by. She halted in her tracks just in front of Colton. "Colton! What are you doing here?"

"He brought your coffee," Leonore said, putting her cup up on the counter. "Wasn't that a sweet gesture?"

"Sweet," Sara said, looking at him with a puzzled expression. She was standing close enough that he could see the light smattering of freckles she'd tried to cover with makeup but hadn't quite succeeded. Her scent wafted over to him, a fresh, light vanilla, like a cupcake straight from the oven. All that wondrous hair of hers was pulled back in a no-nonsense ponytail, which left an expanse of creamy white skin exposed on her neck. Pretty. He had a sudden urge to reach over and place his lips on it.

No, no, no. "You forgot it," he said. "At the coffee shop."

"Oh, thank you." She took a sip and smiled. He must've been an idiot all these years, making her frown instead of flash that smile.

"Your dad took my stitches out," he said, holding out his arm. "All healed." Now he was acting like an idiot. "Anyway, have a nice day."

"Thanks. You too." As Colton turned to leave, he heard Sara ask, "What happened to Larry Crosby, Leonore? I swear he was in the waiting room a minute ago."

"Oh, we were a little backed up, so I told him he could run and get his hair cut, as long as he came back in about a half hour."

Sara's gaze drifted over to his. He caught her incredulous look and worked hard to suppress a chuckle. She grabbed her coffee and took a big swig. When she looked up, her mouth was turned up in the tiniest smile, like they'd just shared a private joke. "Thanks again for the coffee, Colton," she said.

"Hey, no problem," he said. But inside he had a growing feeling that it was.

* * *

Yep, she'd really needed that coffee. And Colton had delivered it, with a smile. Without a gotcha. Yet.

Sara realized she'd been standing near the reception desk, staring at the closed door.

Leonore cleared her throat, making Sara snap to attention.

Glinda inclined her head toward the exam rooms. "I heard Chief Walker in there just now talking to your father. He was *defending* you."

"Defending me?" What on earth . . . ?

"Yeah. He said your dad should tell you how proud he is of you because people need to hear that. Isn't that sweet?"

Sara blanched. What was worse, she wondered, the fact that the staff was eavesdropping on private patient conversations or the fact that Colton had felt a need to intervene with her father? She wasn't going to earn her father's respect by having someone else fight her battles.

And why on earth would Colton suddenly stick up for her, anyway? It was unnatural. Like just now, when he hadn't even drilled her with his usual smart-ass comment. Just grinned that unholy grin and sauntered out. Leaving her with cappuccino and a dumb smile on her face.

"I hate to say it," Leonore said solemnly, "but I think Chief's got a crush on you."

"What?" Sara said. "No way. That's ridiculous."

"Yep," Leonore said. "He brought your coffee. And he didn't even have an appointment to get those stitches out."

"He's like the boy in grade school who pulls the little girl's braids," Glinda said. "She thinks he doesn't like her, but it's just the opposite."

"It had better *not* be the opposite," Sara's father said, suddenly materializing at the counter. "That boy's a good police chief, but he's not marriage material. Now don't we have some patients to see, ladies?"

Sara winced for what felt like the thirtieth time that day. She had enough problems—she could not let runaway speculation about Colton or her personal life be one of them. Grabbing a chart and heading to a room, she was more than happy to get back to work.

Several hours later, she felt a hand on her shoulder—her dad's. "Hey, pumpkin, it's quitting time. You've officially made it through your first two weeks."

Sara looked at the clock. Nearly seven. Seven o'clock! No one here seemed to think an eleven-hour workday was unusual.

"Rachel just called," her dad said. "Gabby's friend Malcolm is in town. She wants us all to meet for dinner at Giuseppe's. Can you come? Say around eight-ish? You can ride with us."

Giuseppe's was the world's most wonderful restaurant, the place where the family often celebrated big events, but Sara was dead on her feet. "I'm going to stop at home," she told her dad. "I'll meet you at the restaurant." She said good night to the ladies and walked out into the golden summer evening. Except her steps didn't walk her toward home.

She couldn't have the ladies in the office gossiping about the possibility of a romance between her and Colton. People would overhear and it would be all around town faster than you could say *happy hour specials at Lou's*. And she didn't want Colton interfering in her business with her father—no matter that he was actually being nice for once, for God's sake.

There was no time like the present to shut this rumor mill down quick. The irony was not lost on her that now that Colton had finally done something nice, she was going to tell him to back off.

Chapter 9

♥

Sara walked into the main room of the tidy white-brick police station where the full-time deputy, Evan Marshall, was talking on the phone. "Chief Walker's off duty now, Mrs. Robertson, but I'm happy to come by. So Mr. Clinton's dog pooped on your lawn again?"

Evan looked up and waved. He was an eager twenty-three-year-old, but to her he still looked like the freckled little kid she used to babysit. Except he never had outgrown that gun fetish of his. He was sitting behind one of three desks and a console with more blinking lights than the starship *Enterprise*. She made out a police radio, two printers, and a big black scanner with red lights scrolling maniacally back and forth.

Just then Colton leaned into the room, stretching his arms over his head on the door frame between the main room and his office and suppressing a yawn. He had dark circles under his eyes. His gray uniform shirt was a little rumpled, and there was a giant grass stain on the thigh of his uniform pants. (How did a person even get a grass stain there?) All of which led her to believe maybe he'd had sort of a not-great day too. Which suddenly made her feel awful about coming here to give him grief about being *nice* to her.

Evan covered the phone receiver with his palm and spoke to Colton. "Louise Robertson's insisting on talking with you."

"Tell her I'll stop by on my way home," Colton said.

"I can take care of this, Chief. It's just dog poop, and you were supposed to be out of here an hour and a half ago."

Colton shook his head. "Harry Clinton needs to step up his game. When's he going to learn that having his dog poop in the yard of the widow he wants to ask out on a date isn't going to get him anywhere?"

He chuckled. That small bit of laughter changed his entire face, took it from simply ho-hum handsome to please-be-the-father-of-my-children devastating. Sara's stomach catapulted. Heat spread through her abdomen, rushed into her cheeks, weakened her knees.

Settle down, ovaries. It was just the Colton Effect. Which was impacting her due to the fact that it had been a year since she'd had any physical contact with a man. So there.

The moment he saw her, his hands dropped from the door frame and he stood up straight, cracking his knuckles—nervously? Nah, Colton Walker didn't do nervous. She was the one who was struggling to keep it together right now.

"Sara, what are you doing here? Is something wrong?" He sounded—concerned.

In fact, he'd sounded concerned a lot lately. Starting when her grandmother got lost and continuing through today at the coffee shop. And again at the office.

A ball of guilt suddenly lodged in her throat.

She swallowed it down. Reminded herself that he was the same person who'd sat in speech class sophomore year during her inspirational speech on finding your passion and mimicked everything she'd said; who'd been kissing Stacey Prescott in the hallway and said to Sara, who must've been staring, "Like what you see, Langdon?" And laughed. Who'd kissed her one time—*once*—and never spoken of it again. And literally looked at her in annoyance and disgust for years afterward.

Why was she even thinking about that now?

She had to get things straight with him if they were going to coexist in the same town. She wasn't going to back down now.

"No, I just—I wondered if we could have a word in private?" she said.

"Sure," he said, waving a hand toward his office.

She walked in, and what she saw surprised her. He'd clearly inherited Chief McGregor's massive glass-topped desk, and it was covered with stacks of papers. But in the deep windowsill behind the desk there were…plants. A philodendron climbing all around the window frame and headed to a nearby bookshelf. Palms and other houseplants and even a cactus.

A blue-and-black-striped rug sat tidily under his

desk and the walls were painted a light blue. A cluster of framed photos hung on the wall near the desk, including one of Chief McGregor linking arms with three smiling cop buddies, arms around each other's shoulders. A German shepherd lying in a dog bed in the corner perked up his ears as soon as she walked in.

"Police dog?" she asked.

He nodded. "Champ's working," he said, his mouth lifting at the corners.

"I see." She nodded as the dog trotted over for affection. "Can I—pet him?" The dog nudged his nose against her palm until she did, taking that decision off the table.

"Actually, he fell a little short of passing the K9 exams as a puppy," Colton said. "He's my dog now. I bring him to work with me most days."

"You're a handsome boy," Sara said as she scratched behind the dog's dark ears. The dog sniffed her hair and licked her face. "And ferocious, I see." She took a seat in one of the simple navy upholstered chairs on the other side of his desk. "Look, I came here to get something straight between us. Leonore overheard what you said to my dad this afternoon about—about maybe being a little more—flexible—and I—maybe you were trying to help, but..."

Well, she was quite articulate, wasn't she? She thought of all those years when Colton had definitely not ever tried to help her. Why on earth he'd be interested in doing so now she couldn't fathom. The Colton Walker she'd seen over the past two weeks seemed like someone she'd never met before.

She tried again. "I appreciate what you were trying to do, but I have to handle my dad on my own. If it looks like I need help to do that, I'll never gain anyone's respect. Plus Leonore and Glinda are convinced you're sweet on me, and that is not only insane but the last thing I need to contend with in the office—or in town, because if that gets around, neither of us will have any peace."

When she'd been a teenager with braces and pimples, she'd had no words. She'd been completely and utterly tongue-tied in front of him, intimidated by both his good looks and by whatever mean things he could utter. But now the playing field between them had been leveled. And Tagg was no longer in the middle. It was just the two of them.

A peculiar feeling slid through her. That they were both different people now. That this was a completely different ball game, and she wasn't sure of the rules.

He leaned forward a little. A desk lamp was on, shining a blue-white beam over all the paperwork and the dozen sticky notes marching in a neat row down his desk. It also highlighted his great bone structure— his strong jaw, that five o'clock shadow already well on its way to becoming a full beard. He stared at her, mulling over his reply.

"For what it's worth, *I* respect you." He paused to let that sink in. "Since I've been chief, I've become a problem solver. It's what I do. I was just trying to be helpful. I'm sorry if I did the wrong thing." He tapped a pencil on his desk, which worked his forearm muscles, which were...impressive. Plus he was tanned. And he had nice hands. He used to have great hair too, but it was short now, no nonsense. Like he'd shaved all his vanity off.

Sara sucked in a breath. That was it? She'd expected...resistance. Anger. At least sarcasm. But an apology?

She was completely thrown.

"Another thing, Red, I know you're eager to get your dad's office up to snuff and running efficiently but you might just want to...relax a little. This isn't Columbia. Not that some things don't need changing around here but big adjustments take time, you know what I mean? Just my two cents." He didn't say it in a know-it-all way. In fact, he sounded concerned. Like a friend. Except the feelings coursing around inside her right now weren't exactly giving off a friends vibe.

"I get it. Rome wasn't built in a day and all that." She cringed. God, could she babble any worse?

He leaned back in his chair. "I have something else to ask you too, while you're here."

"OK, what is it?" He seemed so calm. When it felt like a flock of geese had suddenly overtaken her stomach.

"It's my sister. She needs a physical before she starts college."

A simple enough request. "Oh, sure, of course. There's still time to get her scheduled for that."

He cleared his throat. "I want to make sure she has...all the facts. Before she goes off to school."

"Facts?" What he was really asking suddenly dawned. He wanted her to make sure Hannah was informed about sex. "Oh, *facts*. Of course. Sure, I'd be happy to see Hannah. Just have her call the office."

"Great. Thanks. Anything else we have to talk about?"

He stood and walked around his desk until he was mere feet away. She stood too, but she still had to look up—way up—to see him, a definite disadvantage. And God, he was tall. Even though he was a little disheveled at the end of the day, he looked devastatingly handsome. And—something she'd never noticed before—he had beautiful, full lips. Plus he smelled good, a light, barely there scent that reminded her of the woods after a rain. She took a step back, trying to escape his pheromone field, but he moved a step closer, spearing her with that deep-blue gaze. She opened her mouth to speak, but the words got stuck somewhere. Hot and cold flushed through her, and her heart suddenly felt like it was trying to beat itself right out of her chest. "Colton, I—"

That was all she managed. His mouth turned up in the slightest quirk. He was amused! Oh God, who would've known a simple apology could be so... arousing?

She shook her head. Swallowed hard and backed up with a step so big she knocked into one of the navy chairs.

How could she allow herself to be so flummoxed over him? It suddenly dawned on her that maybe all his nice behavior was a reaction to something else—his behavior last year. The bachelor party. "Look, you don't have to make up for—"

He frowned. "For what?"

All those years of torment? Culminating in that awful bachelor party that got so, so out of control? Maybe his trying to help her out today had been a result of his guilt over that.

"For the past."

His eyes narrowed a little. "What about the past?" he asked.

"Maybe you're trying to help me because you feel bad about things that have happened."

"What are you talking about?" He looked completely clueless.

She sighed. Might as well come out with it. "The bachelor party."

"Wait a minute." He stepped back, almost as if startled. "You think I'm being nice to you because I feel bad about the bachelor party?"

Sara put her hands up in defense. "I don't blame you for what happened. But maybe you're trying to make up for that by trying to . . . help me."

"I think you *do* blame me for what happened, if you think I'm trying to make up for something."

"Well, things clearly got out of control. And maybe you feel guilty for that." She slid her gaze over to his, which was lit up with anger.

"Guilty? You think I feel guilty for Tagg acting like an idiot? Maybe you need to ask him what happened instead of always assuming the worst about me."

Fine. Except Tagg, that bastard, had never had the courage to explain his behavior. He'd just done this desperate, severing act to get out of their marriage. What other explanation did she really need? So Colton was technically right, Tagg was the idiot. Except now

Colton was pissed, and he wasn't going to tell her anything either. And maybe Tagg was a nitwit, but it sure seemed that Colton was still loyal to him. "Looks like you and I are back to square one, Chief Walker." Sara turned to go, but Colton held her back.

"No. No, we're not. I want you to know." He took a deep breath, and she had no idea what he could possibly say next. "I took Tagg home after the bachelor party and put him to bed. That's how I left him. I should've stayed with him. Made sure he was OK. Made sure *you'd* be OK. I am sorry for that. And I never hired Val. She came with the cake. I had no idea."

Her eyes filled with tears, even though she willed them not to. Took Tagg home? Put him to bed? And he'd still found Val. Sara closed her eyes. This shouldn't be painful anymore, but the hard truth always was.

"I'm sorry, Sara."

"You're right," she said, "I did assume the worst about you. I didn't think you took anything seriously. I figured you sat by and watched things get out of control."

"I should've cut him off. I wish I would have."

She shook her head. "It wasn't a bachelor party mistake. He didn't want to marry me. I knew as much. But thank you for telling me the truth." She took a big breath and swiped at her eyes. "I'm late for dinner out with my family. I'd better be going." She had no idea what time it was; all she knew was she had to get out of there.

"Let me give you a ride home."

She shrugged away from his touch. "No, I—walking

will be good, thanks." Which made no sense if she was really late. She headed for the door, and frankly, she couldn't get out of there fast enough.

* * *

"How's work going, sweetheart?" Rachel asked as the family settled around a large table on the patio at Giuseppe's, where Sara's family celebrated every graduation, birthday, and family event. Tagg and Sara had announced their engagement here, right on this very patio under the lovely wooden arbor covered with grapevines. The fact that he'd stood up to make a toast and smacked his head on a low-hanging branch should have been a sign that things would not go well for them.

Sara took a sip of her wine. "It's going great," she said. "Thanks for asking."

Sara had learned long ago with Rachel to simply say things were just fine. While Rachel was kind, and they always got along, their relationship had never really deepened into something more. Maybe because of the simple fact that Rachel was not her mother. By the time her dad remarried, Sara was eighteen, and she and her sisters had become a tight network of support, together mothering Rafe. They'd learned not to need a mother anymore.

"Oh, that's wonderful," Rachel said with her usual enthusiasm. "Your dad is so thrilled to have you in the office." And did she mention that Rachel also tended to speak for her father?

"We had a pretty good day today, eh, Dad?" She elbowed her dad playfully.

Sara decided to make the best of the evening. She was with family (except for Rafe, who was working, and Nonna, who was at her twice-monthly bingo night with her girlfriends), and it was a gorgeous night, the summer evening sweet smelling and warm, flowers overflowing from boxes rimming the patio, and tiny white lights twinkling everywhere.

Funny, though. She wasn't really fretting about all the office issues she wanted to work on that had been at the forefront of her mind. Instead she had an image stuck in her mind of Colton in his cop uniform, bending down to pet his dog. That navy uniform showing off those baby blues, that muscle peeking out from his sleeves, those competent-looking hands.

Dear God, he'd taken Tagg home and put him to bed and still felt guilty he hadn't done more. Yet she'd accused him of inciting things, riling things up. She'd thought the worst of him.

She rubbed her chest. It suddenly felt funny in there. Oh, Rachel was looking at her strangely. Probably wondering why she was staring off into space.

"Rachel, how's the shop lately?" Sara asked. "One of these days we'll have to have lunch." If there was ever time for lunch. By noon the office was already backlogged, and today, like most days, she and her dad had both worked straight through the lunch hour.

"Oh, I'd love that. The shop is great. In fact, it's going to be featured in the Lifestyle section of the *Plain*

Dealer next month. Because of my trip to Italy and all the Renaissance antiques I brought back."

"That's really cool, Rach," her sister Evie said. "I'm glad the shop's doing so well." She looked at Joe. "I love being home with the kids, but I miss working sometimes." The fact that the rent on her studio at the art space had gone up too high for her to justify the expense of a sitter had factored into her decision to stay home with the kids, but Sara knew Evie really missed her pottery wheel.

Joe grabbed his wife's hand. "I was thinking maybe we should turn the garage into a little studio for you."

"A kiln is expensive," she said.

"You should do it, Evie," Sara said. "You're so talented. Plus it would be good stress relief." Evie threw everything she had into being an amazing mom, and Sara knew she loved being home with her kids. But she'd really loved being an artist too.

"I'm plenty busy with the kids right now, but…maybe." She smiled at her husband and he winked back. Aww. They always were the perfect couple.

Which reminded her. "Don't forget I'm babysitting next week for the Fourth," Sara said.

"Oh, thank you," Evie said. "The kids are already getting excited for the fireworks."

"I am too."

"OK, just so you know, Michael sometimes pees his pants when he gets excited, so nothing too thrilling."

"Gotcha," she said. Now that she was back home, she was really looking forward to being able to spend more time with her niece and nephew. She couldn't wait to spoil them rotten.

Just then Gabby arrived with Malcolm, who looked like he just stepped off the cover of a Billionaire romance novel. Sara smiled politely and greeted them. It was obviously important to Gabby that he meet the family, so Sara owed it to her sister to try and keep an open mind.

"You all remember Malcolm, right?" Gabby said. "He's a partner at his hedge fund group now."

It was no accident Gabby shot a look at their father. That Malcolm was a hedge fund manager was sure to press a couple of acceptable-spouse buttons in their father's mind. Seemed Sara wasn't the only one of them to seek their father's approval.

"Tell us, son, what kinds of funds do you manage?" her dad asked as he got up and leaned across the table to shake Malcolm's hand.

"Only the lucrative kind, sir," Malcolm said, slicking his hair back in a gesture that bespoke vanity. "I work for Wernor and Vescott downtown. We're doing quite well. So rest assured, I can keep Gabriella in the style to which she's accustomed."

Sara took another sip of her wine. What the hell did that mean? Her sister made a great income on her own. Plus she hung out in sweats and flip-flops. She wasn't "accustomed" to a life of wealth or leisure. Sara had forgotten a lot about Malcolm in the years since Gabby had broken up with him, but she was beginning to remember why she'd disliked him so much.

After the waiter brought more wine and poured

some into everyone's glass, Gabby cleared her throat.
"Now that our drinks are finally here, I can tell you all
the good news." She paused. "We're getting married."

Sara choked on her wine, which promptly spilled
down the front of her brand new cream-colored romper.
She hurriedly dipped her napkin in water to try to flood
the stain as exclamations went up around the table.

Gabby hadn't even hinted about this to Sara in their
conversations, which created a new wave of guilt.
Maybe Sara had been too wrapped up with her own
problems lately to really listen.

"How long have you two been dating?" her father
asked, frowning. Rachel gently put her hand over his.

"We reconnected six weeks ago, Dad," Gabby said.
"But you only knew our mom that long, right?" She
beamed at Malcolm. "We knew right away it was love."

Malcolm beamed right back, which was a little reas-
suring. He was very Italian looking, tanned and toned,
with a head of hair whose thickness rivaled John
Stamos's. His custom-tailored suit clung to his muscular frame like a wet suit, and his very nice haircut had
probably cost more than their dinner. Sara could understand lust, maybe. But *love*?

She tried to reconcile this Malcolm with the guy
she dimly remembered from Gabby's college years. That
Malcolm had worn seersucker pants and brightly colored polos with the collars lifted up. This Malcolm
dressed better but was still showing signs of trying too
hard to flaunt his wealth and status. But wait—just
then he took Gabby's hand and stared lovingly into
her eyes before he addressed her father and Rachel. If

Sara wasn't mistaken, his eyes were a little teary. "I love your daughter, Dr. and Mrs. Langdon. More than anything." Gabby blushed prettily.

"Well," her father said judiciously, "congratulations." Turning to Malcolm, he said, "If my daughter loves you, we will too. Welcome to our family."

As everyone hugged and congratulated the happy couple, Sara thought it was a good thing Rafe wasn't there. He wouldn't be as accepting, at least outwardly, as their father. But she couldn't help thinking their father was right. They owed it to Gabby to give him a chance.

"Let's show them your ring, honey," Malcolm said, holding up Gabby's hand, which she'd been subtly hiding under the table. A diamond the size of a small snow globe gleamed and sparkled on her ring finger. Gabby had never wanted a snow globe. She'd wanted something out of the box, unique. Vintage, maybe. But flashy and enormous? Sara just couldn't see it.

Sara chided herself. Maybe she was just being bitter and envious because of her own broken plans. She'd never been jealous of her sister, but maybe being back home was stirring up all her own conflicted emotions—and, let's face it, loneliness. She could do better. Be more positive. For Gabby's sake. Still, she couldn't shake the unsettled feeling that shifted through her.

"I bought it at Tiffany's," Malcolm said. In case they had any doubt it wasn't the best.

While everyone was oohing and aahing over the ring, Malcolm's phone went off. "Excuse me. I have to move my Tesla. I'll be right back."

As soon as he left, Evie, never one to stay silent, spoke. "Gabby, six weeks? That's not very much time."

"It's not like we just met," Gabby countered. "Really, Evie, can't you just be happy for me for once?"

"We are happy for you, Gabs," Sara said quickly. "We just don't want you to rush into anything, you know?"

"I'm not rushing. I love Malcolm. And I'm old enough to know this time. I wish you all would have faith in me." *He's not perfect, but maybe he's as close as I'm going to come.* Gabby's words from the attic echoed in Sara's brain. Her stomach churned sickly.

"We do," Rachel said, ever the peacemaker. "Now, we want to hear all about the proposal, right, girls?"

Malcolm returned, and talk turned to his proposal on the observation deck of the Empire State Building with a violin quartet nearby. "Because Gabby loves *Sleepless in Seattle*," Malcolm said.

That seemed very thoughtful. Maybe he *had* changed. Maybe he did love her sister. That thought, and the fact that everyone in the entire restaurant seemed to be paired up over candlelit tables on this beautiful summer evening, made Sara feel a little weepy. A picture invaded her brain of Colton on such a night, sitting across from her at a candlelit table. Laughing, casually taking her hand and bringing it slowly to his lips, where he would plant a tiny lingering kiss, promises of many more to come, while looking sexy as sin.

Wait, what was she doing? How had she made that leap from annoying and awful to a decent man, and then suddenly to this? The Revolver didn't do candlelit dinners or monogamy. Maybe he *was* a decent guy, but he was *not* boyfriend material, as even her own father had noted.

After the main course was finished, Sara headed to the ladies' room. Under the bright fluorescent lights, the stain down the front of her brand-new romper looked hideous, like she'd spilled an entire bottle of pinot noir instead of a small sip. In a stall she had to unzip one zipper on the back and another on the side and shimmy out of the entire garment. She usually didn't wear such complicated clothing, but the romper had a crocheted neckline and was summery and cute.

She *was* feeling a little weepy, and she wasn't sure exactly why. She was happy for Gabby…but also worried. Was she a little jealous? Definitely not of the Tesla. Or the ring…Well, on second thought, maybe a snow globe wasn't such a bad thing after all.

But still Sara couldn't help but reflect upon her own situation. She'd chosen unwisely, and look where she was now, back in a town where everyone knew everyone's business, and where there were no eligible men for miles. Except for Colton, and he didn't count.

With that she stood and shimmied the romper back up, then threaded her arms through the arm holes. The back zipper went up just fine, but the side zipper got stuck halfway up. She yanked and pulled in vain. Sara left the stall and went out into the main part of the bathroom where there was more light and tried to tug the zipper down and then back up. No luck.

Exposed to the air conditioning was a good hunk of pale white flesh over her left hip and—horrors—more than a little of her granny panties. Why had she worn the comfortable undies today? On second thought, maybe she should be grateful that she had extra material to stretch upward to cover her exposed skin.

A stall door opened. "Oh, hi, Sara," came a voice from behind her.

Sara stopped wrestling with her zipper and turned. There, striking and beautiful, her lips coated with a bold sheen of red lipstick, was Valerie Blake, aka Cake Girl. Tagg's girlfriend. She wore a flowing, sleeveless black maxi dress and jeweled black sandals. No jelly roll around her waist to get skirt zippers stuck in, no sirree.

Sara yanked up on the zipper so hard she heard a rip. Oh God. One glance down told her the fabric had separated from the zipper. That was strike three for the poor romper. She covered the gaping hole with her hand. "Valerie! Hi! How are you?"

Frankly, she didn't care how Valerie was. She just did not want Tagg to see her like this. She was certain he was out there somewhere, looking like his usual handsome self, while she was literally falling apart at the seams.

Why did she always think of really bad jokes at the worst times?

"Oh, I'm great. Tagg and I just got back from Greece." Val smiled a blinding white smile and flipped back her long, silky hair. "You can probably tell from my tan."

She did look beautiful. In fact, she looked like a Grecian goddess, wearing that beautiful black dress with beads that sparkled from the fringe at the hem. She had some kind of smoky eye thing going on, and dangly earrings, and her neckline was low and showcased her perfect boobs. She was hot, she was sexy, and Tagg *loved* her.

And that thought made tears burn behind Sara's eyes.

"Tagg and I are so happy," Val said. "It was like it was meant to be. I wanted you to know that—that it's not some quick thing with us. It's *forever*."

Sara forced a smile, but words seemed to get caught in the sudden clog that had lodged in her throat. Forever. With Tagg, her boyfriend of ten-plus years, whom Sara'd thought she'd known inside and out. True love initiated by a sudden pitch face forward into a cake, while she'd been oblivious at home, carefully laying out her wedding clothes and dreaming of her future. Maybe Colton was right. Maybe she needed to start placing blame where blame was due. "Is Tagg—here?" *Please God, say no. Please please please. Not tonight.* Not when she was bursting out of her clothing and looked like a sad drunk on a binge.

"He's meeting me here in a little bit. We'll come find you, OK?" Val at long last made her way to the door, while Sara kept smiling her frozen smile and tried to keep herself covered. "I'm sure he'd love to say hi." Did this woman have no clue at all that Sara might possibly be affected by the fact that Valerie had *stolen her fiancé*? Did she really believe that they could all visit like civilized people when Sara hadn't seen or spoken to Tagg since *last summer*?

Sara lurched out of the bathroom like she had a bad hip, because keeping both hands plastered over her wardrobe malfunction took work. Finally she made it outside to the table. "Family, I love you, but I've got a migraine coming on and I think I'm going to say goodbye." She kissed Gabby, hugged her new future brother-in-law awkwardly with one arm, and blew kisses to everyone else.

"Sara, what's wrong?" Rachel asked, trailing behind her to the door.

Rachel looked so concerned, she decided to tell her the truth. "I ran into Val in the bathroom. My zipper got stuck and when I tried to fix it, it ripped." She flashed Rachel a bit of skin, as well as more than a little of her granny panties. "And Tagg's here somewhere and I *really* don't want to run into him like this."

"How about I drive you home?" she offered. "You've had a long day."

"Rachel, they need you at dinner. I feel awful leaving, but...God, Rachel, what is Gabby thinking? Or am I just a bitter old hag, jealous of my sister's happiness?"

Rachel shook her head. "I think you're more of a good sister with legitimate concerns. But Gabby's grown up a lot since college. We can give him a chance, for her sake."

"Right." Sara thought about her dad's philosophy about people, having watched most of the town grow up as they came and went through his office. Personality was part of who you were, and most people didn't change much over time. Fatalistic, perhaps, as Rafe would say, but true? She wasn't sure.

Sara kissed Rachel goodbye and hobbled out to her car. She'd had enough of this day. She couldn't wait to get home and go to bed and let it end.

Chapter 10

♥

"Hannah, you can't go out to the lake now with a bunch of idiots. It's too late." Colton glanced at his watch, which was lit up by his dashboard. Ten p.m. on a Friday night, and he'd been driving around for hours, Champ snoozing in the back seat of his cruiser. He'd even helped Mrs. Jennings get her cat out of a tree, which Champ hadn't exactly appreciated. Not the usual way he'd spend an evening off. But he couldn't relax. Couldn't get thoughts of Sara out of his mind. And now he was back to dealing with Hannah and walking on thin ice to try not to mess up, but he was going to fall through anyway.

"I knew I shouldn't have even told you what I was doing," she said, the familiar tone of irritation evident in her voice.

"I'm glad you did, but you still can't go." *Be calm*, Colt's inner voice said. *Be reasonable.* Both things he was not feeling.

"I'm going to be in college in less than a month, doing whatever I want." He winced. "You can't boss me. You're not our mom or dad."

Colton bent his head and pinched the bridge of his nose. No, he certainly was not. He was just a guy who'd had a long workweek who wanted some peace and quiet. Except he kept seeing visions of a certain redhead in front of him. One who'd always assumed the worst about him and still did, despite his efforts to prove her wrong. And that irritated the hell out of him.

"Colton. Colton, did you just hear me?"

"Sorry, what did you say?"

"I said I promise to be back by midnight. It's just the lake. All my friends are going."

"Hannah, the lake on a Friday night this late means nothing but trouble." Kids smoking weed, drinking, doing God knows what else. She was not. Going. "Don't you have to work in the morning?"

"Yeah, but I told you, I won't stay long. It's summer, Colton. My friends and I don't have much time to be together before we all leave and go off in separate directions. Don't you trust me?"

Of course he didn't, because he was a teenager once himself. Plus what if she was sneaking around with Aiden? But he didn't even get a chance to formulate a response.

"I don't have to listen to you. You're just my brother." The line went dead. Colton tossed his cell onto the passenger seat and stared at it until the lights went out like it was a living thing. What was it with women in his life steamrollering him before he could even get his thoughts across? Wait. Since when was Sara a "woman in his life"? Jesus.

She thought he was an arrogant ass and a know-it-all. He'd encouraged her to believe the worst about him. He wanted to believe she was ultra type A, Dr. High Achiever, hell-bent on changing the world, but the thing was, she was so much more than that. She adored her grandmother. She was hardworking. She had a vulnerable side. His sister loved her. She had amazing legs.

When she'd grabbed his arm that night in Lou's and told him, *You don't always have to be insulting*, she'd been right. He *had* been insulting through much of their teenage years, yes, but that was because he'd been an idiot. Now he knew better.

How much of his teasing now was because he hated that she'd accomplished so much and he was stuck here, leading a small-town life? A life he hadn't really chosen? She was destined for bigger things. Why did that rankle him so much? Why did he use the teasing to push her away, keep her at arm's length? And why was all of this bothering him so much?

He should have spoken to her, not about the bachelor party but about *them*. What it was that made him act like an idiot. About how he didn't want it to be like that anymore between them.

A Honda Civic with a taillight out passed him and pulled him out of his thoughts. His heart rate accelerated a little. Because Sara had a Civic, and Evan had stopped her a few days ago about the light. Without having a clue what he was about to do, he started his car and pulled out onto the road.

* * *

Sara left the restaurant in her old but reliable Honda Civic and had just reached the Angel Falls town limits when she saw a flash of red and blue lights in her rearview mirror. A glance at her dash showed she was going thirty-five in a thirty-five zone. There were no other cars on the deserted road that wound through a dark stretch of wooded park.

The police vehicle accelerated until it was directly behind her. No question it was on her tail. She had no choice but to pull over. Being on the border of Angel Falls and Richardson, she had no idea which police department was responding. It brought her a sense of relief to know it wouldn't be Colton, who'd definitely be off duty by now.

The relief was short lived. Her heart tripped as she considered she was alone in the middle of the woods. What if she was about to be maimed and beaten by a cop poser? It was pitch-black, and the opportunities to stow a body would be endless.

Footsteps fell on gravel, and a bright light shone in her face. "Your taillight is out, ma'am," said a too-familiar voice.

Colton. What was worse—a cop-posing killer or him?

Lord, would this day never end? Hadn't she had enough of him for one day?

She held her hands in front of her face to shield her eyes. "I thought you were off tonight," she said.

"Technically, I am," he said.

"So you're out in your car during your time off cruising around, looking for trouble?"

"And it looks like I've found her."

He put his hands on the car window and bent over close enough that she could smell the zingy scent of that woodsy cologne he wore. And feel his body heat—and the intensity of his gaze as it swept over her. She shivered a little—but it was just from the evening air. Surely.

"So. The taillight," he said, pulling out his tablet to write her up.

With everything else going on this week, she'd forgotten all about it. Surely he wasn't really going to write her up, was he? Well, it was Colton, so anything was possible. "I'll get it fixed this weekend, OK?"

"This is your second warning," he said. "Evan told me he stopped you a couple days ago."

"You must be really bored tonight if you're lying in wait in the woods for people on your night off. Why don't you go pull some cats out of trees or something?"

"The law's the law. And actually, I just spent an hour doing just that."

"Well, I'm sure you have to go write up a report about it. So how about letting me go home?"

He inhaled deeply. His mouth twitched. "Have you been drinking?"

He shone his beam into the car. His gaze flickered from her bare legs to her wine-stained cleavage. Suddenly remembering the gaping patch of flesh on her side, she slid her hand down to cover it.

"I had one glass of wine, and most of it's on my top."

"Are you sure you didn't have more than one glass

and that's why you spilled it? With your rough first couple of weeks and all, I wouldn't want you drinking and driving."

"I'm a doctor. I don't drink and drive." What was with this guy?

"Calm down, I believe you. Hey, I need to ask you something. Will you come sit in my car for a minute?"

"Because you're going to write me up for a ticket? Your grandma would be ashamed. Absolutely ashamed."

"I'm not going to write you up for a ticket." He leaned over the driver's window, his arm muscles taut, and stared directly at her. "Champ's in my back seat and he's getting all worked up. But the real reason is I just need to talk with you. Please."

Oh. Just like that, her anger deflated. The fact that Champ was there would've probably gotten her to move, but the *please* definitely did it. "OK, I'll come," she said, then opened her car door. Because maybe it was finally time to stop assuming the worst about Colton Walker.

* * *

Colton knew he should stop this and allow her to go on her way and go back to his calm, quiet life. But he couldn't. Because it seemed to him that since she'd come back, calm and quiet had fled on foot screaming. Plus he had things to say that were sitting there festering, especially since their conversation earlier. Things he couldn't stop thinking about.

He opened the passenger door of his cruiser and waited for her to get in. His gaze flicked quickly up and down her. Her hair was down, and her outfit and heels showcased her pretty legs. She stirred him, as always, against his will.

"Why are you walking like that?" he asked.

"Like what?" she asked. She held both hands over her left hip and lurched a little in her heels. "Not used to the heels," she mumbled.

She sat down in the seat. Champ stuck his nose through the bars. She rubbed his snuff with her index finger, which made him push against the bars even more and bark. Even the dog wanted more of her attention.

Sara looked nervous, glancing up and down the street for traffic. "No one can see us talking," Colton said, "if that's what you're worried about."

"Colton, you've lived in this town a long time, just like I have. When has anyone not seen everything?"

"That time I kissed you," he said quietly. "No one saw that."

That quieted her fast. He could hardly believe he'd said it himself. The silence hung over them, palpable as a heartbeat.

Sara leaned closer, close enough that he could see the little golden flecks in her green eyes. Her eyes had always fascinated him, but he'd never given in to the temptation to look for too long, first because of Tagg and now... well, she'd mostly been too angry at him for any civilized discussion.

"No, no one saw, except Mrs. Mulligan." She shifted

her weight. "But even that turned out to be a big joke to you. Like everything else."

He tightened his hands on the steering wheel. "Let's get one thing straight. That kiss wasn't a joke."

"Oh yes, it was." She pointed a finger at him accusingly. "You never even showed for our date the next week."

He shook his head adamantly. "You don't even remember that *you're* the one who stood *me* up."

"I didn't stand you up! I waited at the museum in the dark until eight that night. Then I came to your dorm." She shook her head back and forth, like she was trying to fling the memory out of her head.

His heart lurched. Jolted. He stared at her in disbelief. "You went to the museum?"

"Of course I went. I-I was excited about it. I thought you meant it. I didn't know you were just playing a joke on me."

He gazed out the windshield, breathing heavily. Trying to get his shit together. Gripping the wheel like it was his last hold on reality. Because what she'd said...It couldn't be true. Because that would change...everything.

He finally turned to face her. "Tagg told me you'd gotten back together. That's why I didn't show. When you knocked on my door that night, I figured you were just coming to tell me what I already knew, that you were back with him."

"Tagg told you..."

"Tagg was my best friend. I'd felt guilty enough for kissing you. But when he said you two had made up…there was nothing I could do but accept that. So I got drunk and slept with Tiffany Downing." Because he'd been nineteen and stupid and heartsick.

Silence filled his cruiser, thick and dense, like an invisible fog. Even Champ lay quietly on the back seat, surely sensing that something grave was going on. Colt had done it now. Spilled his guts. What had he been thinking, pulling her over like this? And how the hell had he never known that they could've actually had a chance together?

Jesus.

Sara rubbed her temple. She looked…upset.

Oh God. One kiss. One lie. One missed opportunity from ten years ago.

"I stayed away after that." He'd pretended it didn't matter, that there were plenty of other fish in the sea, and a hell of a lot of them wanted him.

He tried to push his feelings down, somewhere deep and dark where he'd pushed everything regarding Sara for years. "I told myself I hated you. You chose Tagg. He was everything I wasn't."

She was sitting forward now, hands resting on the armrest between the seats. Champ had given up on getting any attention and had fallen asleep with his paws up in the air. Colton had an urge to curl his hand over one of hers, but he didn't dare. He'd already crossed enough lines tonight.

Her face was tilted upward, her eyes big and round. She looked stunned and upset, things he had little idea how to deal with in the context of relationships. He understood sex. Wanting. Desire. But not this.

He sat back in his seat and blew out a breath. Closed his eyes.

After all this time, he couldn't deny his feelings. He could tell himself she was the most annoying woman on the planet, that she was uptight and anal. But she was so much more in ways he was just beginning to discover. Truth was, those long-buried feelings from years ago still mattered. They still fucking mattered.

* * *

Sara was aware of Colton's big body, ramrod straight, the tension rolling off him in waves, his long fingers curled around the steering wheel. For a moment their gazes locked, and for the first time she wondered if there had been a toll for him all these years.

Had it hurt him when Tagg and she got back together? Had he thought of her, of what could have been? Or had he simply moved on over time? Everything about him suggested the latter, except the way he was looking at her now.

His gaze was...piercing. Electrifying. As if he saw straight through her. And it did things to her, made heat flare through her in big, unwelcome waves.

"You're nothing like Tagg," she whispered. She was coming to believe Colton wasn't anything like what she'd thought he was.

He cracked a little smile. "I take it that's a good thing?"

"Tagg and I weren't right for each other. What happened was for the better."

For the first time in a year, she was able to say that. It still hurt, but not the way it had.

"You're still pretty torn up about it? Your breakup with him? I mean, it's only been a year, and that would be natural after all those years together..."

"I'm not in love with Tagg anymore, if that's what you're asking."

She wasn't sure exactly what he was asking, but he seemed to look relieved.

She should be focused on what he was saying, but she didn't want to talk about Tagg. Instead her mind went back to their past. She'd known he'd slept with Tiffany What's-Her-Name that long-ago night, and she'd been repulsed. Angry. She'd stood there humiliated, feeling again like that nerdy teenage girl he'd poked fun at. She'd vowed never to trust him again. Instead she'd gone back to Tagg, accepted his assurances that he loved her and believed his promises of a happily ever after.

Yet Tagg had been the one who'd lied. Not Colton. Tagg.

Colton got out of the car and opened her door. Watched her walk out in silence, his gaze drilling into her back.

She felt like she should do *something*...Say thank you? Or run the hell out of here as fast as her legs could carry her?

Should she tell him she was sorry for misjudging him all these years? It hadn't really sunk in, any of it. That the wild, carefree persona he played so well was not who he was at all.

Things suddenly got awkward. For one thing he was still staring at her, and God knew what he was thinking. Hopefully not about the gaping hole in her clothing, which she'd forgotten to cover, which she tried to rectify now.

"How about we start again," he said, his jaw so tight she could bounce a quarter off it. He didn't seem to be focused on the zipper at all, thank goodness. What a gentleman.

"Start again?"

"Yeah. A fresh start. A new beginning." He extended his hand for her to shake. "Friends," he tacked on.

Friends? A handshake? Not what she'd been expecting. But what *had* she been expecting? She glanced from his face to his hand. He looked...hopeful. Or maybe she was just imagining that. After all these years of his I-don't-give-a-shit attitude, how could he look like he cared what she thought? What she did?

Finally she awkwardly stuck out her hand. To be polite, of course.

He wrapped his big hand around hers. It was warm, and his grip was strong and no nonsense. The grip of a man you could count on. She stared at him incredulously—suddenly the impassive eyes, the perfect posture had returned, and she realized he'd gone back to being the cop on duty.

She was beginning to see how he was able to wear a mask to hide his feelings. It occurred to her that he might be waiting for a sign from her.

But she was still shocked by what he'd said. Still trying to reconcile who the real Colton Walker was.

Their hands were still locked together, and had been for far longer than a normal handshake. His nearness was making her shaky, giddy, confused.

She broke away and walked to her car, but he jogged ahead and got there first to open the door. She moved to get in, then stopped. Impulsively she stood on tiptoe and kissed him on the cheek. It was rough and raspy in a very sensual, masculine way.

For a second he didn't move or look at her. She was kicking herself for the reckless gesture when his radio went off.

"Hey, sweet pea," Carmen the dispatcher said. "You big hunk of love, we've got a 314 on Elm Street."

Colton pulled his radio off his belt. "I'm sorry Pete's exposing himself again, Carmen, but I'm off duty."

"Evan has a migraine, and besides, I know where you are from the Find My Friends app on my cell. You want me to call him or you want to take the call?"

"I'll take it, Carmen," he said into his radio, but his gaze had swung to Sara. "Tell Pete to keep his pants on." Sara ducked down into the car, not wanting to keep him from his work. And anxious to get the hell out of there.

"Hey," he said. The tiniest smile turned up his lips. "You OK?"

His voice was low, easy, rough at the edges, and it reverberated clear through her taut nerves. "Yeah. I'm fine." She smiled. "Thanks for not giving me a ticket."

"I won't give you a ticket, but I hope you don't mind my giving a bit of advice."

"Sure. What is it?"

"Next time a cop pulls you over, don't pull your zipper down to try and get out of the ticket."

"I would *never* do that. My zipper broke!"

He winked. "And those high-waisted white bloomers. Really sexy."

Now she was going to die. She knocked her head against the steering wheel.

He placed his hand over hers on the steering wheel. Just covered it lightly, giving it a small squeeze. She looked up in time to see him nod, close her door, then head off to do his job.

And despite herself, hope, dangerous and headstrong, bloomed within her.

Chapter 11

♥

"OK, Nonna, I've got everything ready," Sara said, standing in her grandmother's kitchen after work the next Friday. Strawberries, raspberries, blueberries, blackberries, check. Lemon juice, check. Butter, check. Vanilla ice cream, double check.

She was making pie. Not just any pie, her mother's mixed berry pie, though the recipe had come originally from Nonna. She was killing two birds with one stone with this one. Nonna was showing her how to make it, so she would learn her mom's secrets, and...she was making it for Colton's birthday.

She'd found out from Carmen, whom she'd seen at the Bean today, that he was on duty until ten tonight, so that didn't leave much time for celebrating. But she thought she'd call him over for a piece of pie. A gesture of friendship. Except maybe she should've made cake...yes, maybe she should've. But her mother's berry pie was the bomb.

"Put that butter back in the fridge until just before

you're ready for it," Nonna said in a commanding grandma tone, and Sara instantly obeyed. "Everything's got to stay as cold as possible for a good crust."

"Yes, ma'am," Sara said.

"Who are you making this for?" Nonna asked, looking her over carefully.

"I'm just really craving pie," she said. "Doesn't that sound delicious tonight before bed? Warm berry pie with ice cream melting all over it?"

Nonna had just taken a pitcher of sun tea from the yard and was making lemonade to mix with it for her favorite summertime drink. She narrowed her eyes and gave Sara the once-over. "Yes, but you hate baking, Sara Jane. I know you."

"Fine, it's for Colton's birthday."

Nonna clapped her hands. "Oh, you're making him pie for his birthday. This is serious. You know what your grandfather always used to say."

"Um, you find your way to a man's heart through cooking?"

"No. Of course not. 'Kissin' don't last, but cookin' does.' And truthfully, the kissin' can last too. But it sure helps if you can cook." Nonna chuckled at her own joke.

"OK, Nonna, what next?" Sara asked, waving the measuring cup to bring her grandmother's attention back to the recipe. Actually, it was a relief to have her make bad jokes. "How much flour?"

"Four cups," she said. Four seemed like a lot, but Sara dutifully dumped that amount in a large bowl. "Got it. Now what?"

"Put some of this in," Nonna said, shoving the sugar bag over. "You know how to do it."

Sugar, in the crust? Sara was no expert, but that didn't seem right. She'd just pulled out her phone to Google how to make a piecrust when Nonna thrust a tin of Crisco on the counter.

"Oh, I've already got the two sticks of butter ready," Sara said.

"But it needs Crisco," Nonna said. "That's the secret ingredient."

"I did want to kill Colton, Nonna, but not by giving him a heart attack."

Just then there was a rap on the back door, and Rachel walked in.

"Hi, Sara, hi, Nonna," she said, giving them both a kiss. "What's cooking?"

"We're making a berry pie my mom used to make a lot," Sara said. "Nonna's teaching me." Sara hugged her grandma. Although she was convinced the piecrust was a bust. Maybe Evie knew the recipe. Or maybe she should dump everything and just go buy a pie at the bakery. She tried not to be disappointed that her grandmother could no longer make the family recipe she loved so much, and cursed herself for having been gone for so many years. She'd been so wrapped up in her own life. She hadn't cared about piecrusts at all, and now it was too late.

"You finish now, dear," Nonna said, patting her arm. "I'm going to take my drink and sit down. Rachel, how about some tea and lemonade?"

"Thanks, Nonna, I'd love some." Rachel came to

stand next to Sara at the counter and surveyed the work in progress.

She hoped Rachel didn't see the sadness in her eyes. No, not disappointment. Heavyheartedness. First off, Nonna never sat down. Ever. She was a powerhouse of energy. The old Nonna would've snatched the ingredients up and had them all blended and mixed and would be champing at the bit to show her *exactly* how it was done.

Rachel gave her a squeeze and smiled and was her usual undaunted self. "So you cut the butter into the flour"—she looked into the bowl—"except that looks like a lot. There shouldn't be more than two cups in there. And you add ice water by the tablespoon until it turns into dough. And there's a secret ingredient— lemon juice. Got any of that?" Rachel began moving things on the counter and rustling around for a new bowl.

Sara stepped back while Rachel became a whirlwind of reorganization. She'd never even thought Rachel would know how to make this recipe. Never even thought to ask her. And that shook her to her core.

"What's with the sudden urge to make pie?" Rachel asked, as Nonna sat outside the back door on her little deck watching the birds at the feeder.

"It's for Colton's birthday." Maybe she shouldn't've said that, but frankly it was a relief to tell someone.

"Oh," Rachel said judiciously. Her careful tone spoke volumes.

"We're just friends," Sara added hurriedly.

"I see."

"We had a talk. Got a few things straightened out."

"Is that right." Rachel cut the butter into the flour with a fork.

"I would never want to do him—I mean *date* him. *Date* him!" *Oh my God.* "It's just that he's working late on his birthday today and I thought he might like some pie. A gesture of friendship, you know?"

Rachel stopped and looked at her until Sara met her gaze. "Sara. Sweetheart. It's OK. It's just pie."

The *sweetheart* kind of melted her.

"I mean, I'm totally not ready to start anything with anybody. Especially someone who lives in the same town. After all those years with Tagg, I mean, come on. I need to meet lots of different men, right? Nothing serious for me, no sirree. And let's face it, Colton would never get serious about anyone. He's not that kind of guy. In fact, he's the kind of man most sensible women stay away from."

Ramble, ramble, ramble. She needed to shut up already.

Rachel's mouth twitched. "Oh, I don't know about that. Maybe he just hasn't found the right one."

Sara got busy collecting dirty dishes and wiping the flour off the counter.

Rachel touched her shoulder. "Sara, it's OK to explore your feelings. Besides, I like Colton. It's Malcolm we have to worry about."

Sara looked up. "He's still awful, isn't he?"

This time Rachel outright laughed. "Why are we the only ones who know this?"

"What are we going to do?"

"I don't know. But something pretty quick."

As Sara considered that, she put dishes in the sink and started washing them. Rachel added tablespoons of ice water to the flour mixture. It was actually starting to look like dough. "Nonna used to be able to make pie crust in her sleep," Sara said.

"I'm sorry, sweetie. You know, I've got her signed up at the senior center for some activities there."

"You mean senior day care?"

"Yes. The director is your dad's patient. Apparently it's quite a nice community, and they offer lots of options. We're going to check it out next week. And remember Claudia Gaines? Her husband died recently and she said she can come be with Nonna a few days each week. Take her places, grocery shopping, to get her hair done, that kind of thing."

Sara nodded, although her heart was twisting. Her grandmother couldn't be alone anymore. They'd talked about all these things, but it was so hard to accept.

"We've all agreed to keep her at home for as long as we can. I think between all of us, we can make it work. One day at a time, right?"

"Girls, come out here, quickly!" Nonna said. "There's the cutest little chipmunk and he's eating all the birdseed. I wish I had a camera!"

Rachel guided Sara toward the door. "Don't miss the chipmunk. Oh, one more thing. Over the years, Nonna's given me a lot of your mom's recipes. I'm working on assembling them all for you girls and making keepsake books. So if you need anything, just ask me, OK?"

"Oh. Thank you, Rachel." She hugged her stepmother, tears gathering in her eyes. In part from relief that the recipes weren't lost. But mostly over Rachel's thoughtfulness. Somehow it had never occurred to Sara that Rachel would want to be a protector of her mother's legacy.

Sara walked outside to see Nonna enraptured by the antics of two chipmunks who were chasing each other around the patio near the bird feeder.

"Aren't they the cutest things?" she said, chuckling.

Sara sat down next to Nonna. She remembered all the times her grandmother had gotten excited about little things like birds, or the color of one of her roses, or some little anecdote she'd heard. She had a simple excitement about things that had always been contagious.

Somewhere along the line, Sara feared she herself had lost the ability to enjoy—or even notice—simple things. When was the last time she'd sat like this on a porch? Or taken time to notice the flowers? She couldn't even remember. Life had gotten too busy.

But not today. Today she would hold her Nonna's hand and sip iced tea and lemonade, and watch the chipmunks chase each other across the lawn.

* * *

Colton had just spent the past two hours settling a domestic dispute. Elias Riegler, who lived in a rental whose front yard resembled a garage sale in progress, had thrown a bottle that barely missed his wife's head. His fist, however, made contact just fine. The man wasn't drunk, and being an idiot wasn't good enough reason to bring him in when his wife refused to press charges.

She'd said it was her fault she made him mad.

Elias was the family's only income source, so with five kids, the woman was terrified to toss him in jail. Or maybe she was afraid of what he'd do to her once he got out. So Colton left without an arrest. It wasn't the first time he'd been called out there either.

Colton had no problem with his job when he could help people, but when his hands were tied...Well. Let's just say it wasn't exactly the kind of call he wanted to respond to on his birthday. Or any day, for that matter.

Thinking about Sara on his drive back to the station was far more pleasant, but a little uncomfortable too. He hadn't spoken to her since last weekend, just waved to her across the street one time while he was helping ninety-year-old Moira Perkins navigate the curb on her way into the library and Sara was walking out of the antique shop.

It wasn't like him to avoid anyone. In this town it wasn't possible to do that. But Sara...something had shifted between them. And he wasn't quite sure what to do about it.

Thing was, he couldn't stop thinking about their talk last weekend. The part, specifically, when she'd stood on tiptoe and kissed him on the cheek.

Her hands had rested for that brief moment on his chest, and he'd wondered if she could feel his heart practically beating out of it like a trapped bird. Or the sudden way his breath caught. Because it was all he could do to keep himself from wrapping his arms around her and pulling her flush against him, turning his head so that his lips met hers, not his damn cheek.

Instead he'd stood still as a statue while her lips made contact. While her pretty scent surrounded him and her hair tickled his neck. She'd worn it down for once, all that thick red hair spun through with gold. He'd never in his life seen hair like that, and the urge to drag his fingers through it and pull her lips to his had him fisting his hands at his sides.

He'd be a fool to read anything more into that kiss besides a truce, a gesture of friendship. They'd spent ten years nearly despising each other. Why couldn't he just be grateful that was over? After all, he'd been the one who'd stuck his hand out like an idiot and suggested friendship in the first place. *Good one, Einstein.* He could no more be her friend than he could be her enemy anymore.

Ten years of crossed wires. Who knew what could've happened between them if it weren't for one simple lie? Who knew what still could?

That kiss had opened a floodgate of possibility. Thing was, he had no idea what to do next. Pray the attraction would pass? Hope it was just temporary insanity brought on by an old memory best left forgotten? Certainly getting involved with her was a bad idea in a small town where they had to face each other nearly every day. Not to mention how that would complicate his relationship with Tagg.

Besides, he didn't really do relationships. He liked keeping things casual and fun, without attachments.

He'd had a few steady girlfriends—none of them from town—but he didn't want to be shackled to anyone. Yes, his buddies called him the Revolver in jest, but it was true in that he didn't care to have any of them stick.

Colton checked his watch. One more hour on duty, then it was the weekend. The Fourth of July was tomorrow, and besides some paperwork in the morning, he was finally getting some time off.

His phone buzzed just as he finished his last cruise through town for the night.

Can u stop by on your way home? the text read. It was from Sara. How had she gotten his number? He'd wager from Carmen.

Sure, he typed back. Everything OK? His first thought was that maybe something had happened with her grandmother.

Nothing wrong. See u soon.

Those last three words triggered a flurry of emotions. Puzzlement. A little trepidation. And yes, excitement. He'd missed her. Although he wasn't quite sure what to do after that heart-to-heart. Maybe he needed a good run-in with her to show him how annoying she was and prove to him why thinking of her romantically was a very bad idea.

When Colton pulled up to her grandma's little bungalow, Sara was sitting on the swing, the porch lit only by a couple of outdoor candles—the kind that kept the bugs away. She motioned for him to hurry up.

As he got out of his car and climbed up to the porch, he saw a solitary birthday candle planted in the middle of a pie sitting on the low table. She sat there in a gray Indians T-shirt and cutoffs, smiling. The candle-light flickered on her hair and her face, casting all her features in a warm glow that nearly stopped him in his tracks.

Rocket was cuddled close to her side, snoring.

"Nonna believes in recycling candles," Sara said with a sheepish smile. "This is the only one in the house, and it's down to a stub. Make a wish fast."

His brain finally put two and two together. How had she remembered? "You got me a pie for my birthday?" Suddenly the simple act of drawing in air became complicated, like he'd somehow forgotten how to do it. He dragged his gaze from her to the pie so she wouldn't see what was surely on his face.

How touched he was.

"Nope." She shook her head. "I didn't get you a pie. I *made* you a pie."

Words clogged up in his throat. Her eyes were dancing in the low light, and he could see the golden highlights in her hair. Forget the damn pie. He wanted to taste *her*.

Whoa there, Colton. Friends, friends, friends, he repeated to himself. What had happened to all that animosity between them? The desire to tease her, to make her blush? To keep her at a distance, which was what all that bickering had done. Now he found he did want to make her blush. But for a completely different reason.

"Did you celebrate today?" she asked.

"Carmen made cupcakes. I'll have dinner with Cookie and Hannah this weekend."

She patted the swing beside her and he took her up on the invitation, staking out a spot on the other side of

Rocket, who sniffed him discerningly, then leaned back against Sara. His uniform grazed her leg, and his gun banged awkwardly against the swing.

"Better hurry and wish before it fizzles," she said, gesturing to the candle, which really did seem to be on its way to flickering out.

Oh, he wished all right, while she did a speedy rendition of "Happy Birthday." She couldn't hold a tune to save her life, but he loved it just the same. Then he blew out the candle.

As it sat there smoldering, a thin wisp of smoke curling elegantly into the wooden slats of the porch ceiling, Sara jumped up. "Do you like warm pie? I'm going to nuke some pieces and put ice cream on them, is that OK? I've been waiting for this all ni—"

Before he knew what he was doing he reached up for her arm, tugged her back down beside him, and planted his lips on hers. Then he curled his hand around her neck and pulled her in deeper.

Her lips were soft, and she tasted amazing, sweet like the pie, and sure enough, she was kissing him back, parting her lips, resting her hand lightly against his chest. Over his heart, where he was certain she could feel its wild rhythm as his entire body responded to the thunder of that kiss.

Caught up in the feel of her, soft and warm in his arms, he lost track of time and his sense, and for once he didn't even care if half the damn town drove by and saw their chief not being chiefly.

When he finally wrenched himself back, he was shaking a little.

"You're awfully grateful for birthday pie," she said. She was breathless too, he was pleased to note. Her hair was mussed, and she looked a little stunned. And so beautiful he knew he'd remember this moment forever.

"I am so grateful," he said. God, he sounded like an idiot. Before he could think better of it, he kissed her again. She made a sweet little noise deep in her throat. Her hands slid up his back, curving around his shoulders, and she grabbed on, tugging herself flush against him.

The woman was driving him mad. She wasn't uptight or tense or any of the type A adjectives he'd once accused her of being. She was just soft and lovely, and she fit perfectly in his arms.

The dog, clearly offended at being left out, insinuated himself between them and started licking his arm. At the same time, a voice calling out from the house made them suddenly break apart.

"Is that Colton's car parked in the driveway?" Nonna asked.

"I was just wishing Colton a happy birthday," Sara said, her lips curved into a little smile.

"Well, happy birthday, Colton," Nonna said. "I'd come out, but I've got my curlers in."

"Thanks, Mrs. Faranaccio," Colton said, but he was looking at Sara. Her pretty blush. Her slightly dazed expression. All he knew was that he wanted to kiss her again.

"Come have some pie with us," Sara called out. "We don't mind the curlers."

"Thanks, sweetie, but I'm headed to bed. Happy birthday again, Colton."

Nonna waved from the screen door and disappeared into the house. "I'll be right back," Sara said as she got up, scooped up the pie, and disappeared into the house, leaving him with the dog, who stretched out on the swing and went belly up for more love.

Best. Birthday. Ever.

* * *

Oh my God. She'd kissed Colton. Well, technically he'd started it, but she'd fully taken part. Why had she done that, kissed someone she used to hate—well, OK, *hate* was a strong word—disliked intensely up until a few days ago? And she'd liked it. So, so much. She reached up to touch her lips. Dear God, he was a fantastic kisser.

Sara never remembered having this feeling of being electrified, on fire, hot and cold, weak and ready to dissolve into a boneless pile, panting and restless.

"Need help in there?" Colton called from the porch.

She was standing at the kitchen counter, staring at the fridge, panic surging through her veins. Kissing Colton Walker? What had she been thinking? *Well, that's what happens when you bake a man a birthday pie. He gets ideas.* Well, and she clearly had ideas too. Friendship ideas, like he'd suggested. Friends she could handle. Then where had that lip lock come from?

They were opposites in every way. He was chill, she was high-strung. He laughed easily and was beloved by everyone. She…Well, she wasn't sure where she quite fit in, but she knew she definitely didn't have the type of personality that made teachers forget their reprimands and every woman within fifty yards feel faint and giddy. And she didn't have dimples. Definitely no dimples.

Most important of all, he was Tagg's friend. And that reason, above all, was enough to warn a sensible person away forever. And yes, Sara reminded herself, she was a sensible person. She had to handle this…attraction. It was there, but she could rein it in. She didn't have to act on it. Plus he was the Revolver. God, what was she thinking!

She was back outside a few minutes later, handing him a warm bowl loaded with berry pie, ice cream sliding down over the top like the snow atop a mountain. "Here you go, Colton. Happy birthday." She cleared her throat, which suddenly felt like it was stuffed with a massive ball of cat hair. She nudged Rocket down off the swing and scooted a healthy distance away from Colton. The dog gave her an offended look and crawled beneath the swing.

Colton took a healthy bite. "Amazing," he said, but he was looking at her.

"My mom's recipe," she said, dropping her gaze to the table, the floor, anywhere not to make contact with those blue eyes that were signaling something very, very dangerous. Blatant desire. Wanting. She took a small bite, but it caught in her throat. She put down her fork, forcing a swallow. "You don't mind pie, do you?"

"Why would I? It's terrific." He looked confused. Understandably, since cake was her issue, not his.

She fidgeted her fingers in her lap, suddenly not

knowing where to put them. "I really haven't had cake since before... the wedding."

"Sorry to hear that," he said.

"The bakery delivered the cake to our house, did you know that? This gorgeous thing, covered with perfect fondant icing and tiny edible pearls. I was the one who opened the door."

He shook his head. "I'm sorry, Sara." That was two *sorrys* in under a minute. She had to signal to him in no uncertain terms that there would be no. More. Kissing. Kissing was bad. Off-limits. Too dangerous.

"It's OK." She smiled stiffly. She barely knew what to say, but from the expression on his face, she could see he'd gotten the hint.

He set down his bowl. They both stood up, awkward now.

"No one's ever baked me a pie before. I mean, besides Cookie." He assessed her in that thorough way of his, a slight frown forming.

"Listen, Colton," she said, suddenly looking straight at him. "I—don't think anything more than being friends is a good idea for us. I'm totally not ready for a relationship and—um, well, we both work in the same town and all. Things could just get really... awkward, you know?"

Something flickered in his eyes. Disappointment, maybe? She couldn't tell. He was very quiet.

"I hope you understand it's nothing personal," she said. "Just that I think it's better for us to keep it platonic, you know?"

Not better. *Safer.* Much, much safer.

"Well," he said quietly. He looked confused, maybe even a little stunned. "All right then. Thanks again for the pie. It was delicious."

"Have a great birthday celebration," she said, too cheerily.

She watched him walk down the driveway at last, carrying the pie she'd made him take.

The pie that she'd been so excited about. Well, that had certainly taken a bad turn.

She could not start something with him. She could not subject herself to that awful scrutiny again—the embarrassment, the humiliation, which surely would happen once things ended because, you know, it was *Colton.* She would chalk this up to temporary insanity. Rework things in her mind to adjust to their being friends, and be a lot more careful about doing things that might send him the wrong signals. Starting with no more kissing!

It would be all right. She could do this. She would be cordial and friendly and carry on as they'd planned, as friends. It was the right thing to do.

As he drove off, he waved. She stood there for a long time, watching his car disappear, touching her lips.

Chapter 12

♥

The next day was the Fourth of July. Colton had spent the morning catching up on paperwork and now sat on the freshly painted bench outside the police station having lunch with Rafe. He'd packed a turkey-and-cheese sandwich with an apple. Rafe was eating spaghetti and meatballs, and his lunch looked a lot better.

"You make that?" Colton asked.

"Yep. Made the sauce from scratch too."

Colton scowled. What with Cookie planning to snowbird in Florida come winter and Hannah leaving for college, he was going to be in trouble. "You taught yourself to cook like that?"

"I've learned a few things at the station." He leaned over to check out the contents of a plastic Tupperware container. "What's in there?"

Colton had packed a healthy slab of his birthday pie. He took a plastic knife and cut it in half, then slid it onto a plastic lid near Rafe. "I brought extra. Have some."

Rafe took a bite. "Oh, wow. This tastes just like my mom's berry pie."

"It *is* your mom's berry pie," Colton said. Rafe raised a brow. "Your sister made it." He and Rafe were good friends. He wasn't about to lie.

"Evie made you pie?" Rafe asked. "Wow, what'd you do, rescue her cat or one of her kids or something?"

"Sara made it." There, it was out. Rafe would be touchy if he knew Colton had kissed his sister, and he saw no reason to discuss that, but the truth was the truth. Not like there was anything scandalous in making someone a pie, anyway.

Rafe looked him over carefully. "Is there something you're not telling me?"

Colton snorted. "No." Rafe telegraphed him a glare. "Not at all," he said more adamantly.

Apparently Rafe didn't buy that. "Wait…no…not you and Sara. She hates you, man."

Colton suppressed a groan. What had he been thinking? He definitely should've lied about the pie. "She doesn't hate me," he said, a little irritated. "She just doesn't more than like me."

He'd kissed a lot of women, but none of them had affected him like Sara. None of them had the ability to piss him off like she could either, that was for sure. But last night he'd barely slept, and his mind kept circling back to how amazing it had been to kiss her again. Even better than he'd remembered from way back when, and that was saying a lot. Those soft lips, those little sounds she made in the back of her throat as she kissed him back, the way her body melted into his. He could swear she'd been as eager as he'd been.

He hadn't meant to kiss her. It had just…happened. Then she'd pulled the friend card on him and shut him down, just like that. To be fair, he'd been the one who'd played that card first. Idiot.

"She must like you plenty if she's baking you pie," Rafe said, brows pulled down in a staunch frown. "My sister hates to cook." He took another bite. "Wait a minute. What about the bachelor party? You two come to terms with that?"

"What happened after that bachelor party was not my fault. You *know* that. Geez." He stuffed his half-eaten sandwich back in his bag.

Rafe studied him. "Look, Colton, I mean, Sara's had a rough year. I love you, bro, but you're not exactly a relationship kind of guy. And I don't want you thinking you can use my sister as—"

"Forget I said anything, Rafe, OK? And it's not like that. At all. Besides, I have a date tonight."

Colton had asked Hannah if she'd like to go to the fireworks in the park with him, but she'd said she was going with some friends. Even Cookie was going with the book club ladies. So when Everly Peterson, who was in charge of the little theater company in town, had asked him this morning if he'd like to go with her, he'd been just peeved enough at Sara to say yes. Going out on a rare night off would be a distraction. It would remind him in case he was in danger of forgetting that he was single and it was never a good idea to get stuck on one woman. Especially a woman like Sara who wouldn't be hanging around Angel Falls for long. Besides, Everly had been trying to get him to go out all summer.

"Here. Have the rest," Colton said, handing the container over to Rafe.

He was done with the pie. He was going to move on. Starting tonight.

* * *

"I want cotton candy," Sara's five-year-old niece Julia said as they walked across the green in the middle of downtown, where everyone was setting up chairs and spreading blankets for the Fourth of July fireworks. It was nine thirty, the horizon still glowing with a rim of deep indigo where the sun had just set. "Can we get some, Aunt Sara? Please?"

"Of course we can," Sara said, eager to finally get the opportunity to spoil Julia and her three-year-old brother Michael. Gabby, minus Malcolm, who was working, was holding Michael's hand as they walked across the grass. Kaitlyn brought up the back of their little group, carrying a giant waterproof blanket. She'd decided at the last minute to tag along instead of staying home and fretting about her breakup, which Sara thought was a positive thing. Sara was hoping to find some time to really talk to her about it, because so far she'd been avoiding the topic.

"How about here, ladies? And boy," Sara said, bending to plant a kiss on the top of her nephew's sweet blond head. She'd found an empty space in the middle of the green, which was dotted with a veritable patchwork quilt of multicolored blankets, each occupied by a little cluster of family or friends.

She loved the town's Fourth of July celebrations. The parade, the picnics, the fireworks—yet today she couldn't help but feel that something—someone—was missing. Every dark-haired, broad-shouldered guy who walked with a noticeably confident stride made her think of Colton.

She hadn't heard from him since last night, which was hardly cause for alarm, but she knew deep down that he wasn't going to call or text her. She'd given him a message, and he'd gotten it, loud and clear.

In her mind she kept seeing the expression on his face when she'd handed him that pie. He'd seemed truly touched.

She'd be out of her mind to even consider getting involved with him. As far as she knew, he'd never had a girlfriend for longer than a lunar cycle. It would be crazy to think that someone like her, Sara Jane the Brain, could break that streak.

He'd always been the cocky, too-handsome boy who was completely out of her league. Yet she didn't feel like that nerdy high school girl around him anymore. When he looked at her, she felt the absolute heat of his gaze. The way his eyes lingered on her told her he wanted her. The way he'd kissed her, so suddenly and unexpectedly, had taken her completely by surprise, but the way they'd fit together, and the heat of their kisses, wild and unrestrained, told her a lot more could've happened between them if she hadn't put on the brakes.

Not that she'd kissed a lot of guys, but she knew what it was like to have a kiss travel south so fast it made your toes curl. And heat up other places along the way.

"Here come Colton and Rafe," Gabby said, and Sara almost choked on the lemonade she was sipping.

Sure enough, the two guys were walking toward them, both of them out of uniform. Colton was wearing a black short-sleeved polo and gray shorts. He looked tanned and lean, his biceps flexing under his shirt. It was disconcerting to see him dressed like a normal person. And to find he looked just as hot out of uniform as in it.

Rafe said hi to Kaitlyn and tossed his niece and nephew up in the air, his usual riling-up activity that would leave them totally wired for at least the next half hour.

"Hi," Sara said, avoiding Colton's gaze. He wore a dark expression, his brows knit down low, adding to his sexy vibe but also disconcerting her even more. She had to steel herself not to look at him because…muscles. Serious ones. And really nice legs. He was wearing athletic flip-flops and even his toes were really nice. Geez. She needed help.

"Excuse me a second," Colton said before Sara could get her head back on straight. He called after a boy of around ten who was running past with another boy. Curious, Sara watched Colton out of the corner of her eye while Gabby and Kaitlyn made small talk with Rafe. Colton reached for his wallet and handed a bill to one of the boys. "Go to the concessions and grab a hot dog, OK?" she heard him say.

"Their dad's sick and their mom's working two jobs," Rafe said quietly to Sara. "Colton tries to make sure they get to do something fun once in a while."

Sara looked up at her brother and blushed. Not so much because he'd caught her eavesdropping as because she'd just witnessed another example of Colton's proving that she'd been completely wrong about him.

"Want to join us?" she asked Rafe casually as Colton jogged back to the group. There went those fine, fine muscles again.

"We can't," he said. "I've got to get to work soon and Colty here has a date." He gave Colton a playful slap on the back.

"A date?" Sara echoed. Her gaze wandered over to Colton, who suddenly seemed to find the grass really fascinating.

Just then a pretty blonde walked up, threw her arms around him, and gave him a big kiss on the cheek. "There you are," she said. "It's so crowded I was afraid I'd never find you."

Well, Colton certainly hadn't wasted any time fretting over Sara's rejection, had he? She recognized the woman as Everly Peterson, from their high school class. She'd moved to New York to become an actress. Evie had told her she'd returned last year divorced from her plastic surgeon husband, but with boobs three times their previous size. Sara didn't like to make judgments about anybody, especially since high school had been a long time ago. Everly had come back to run the town's little nonprofit theater. Maybe she'd changed and wasn't the attention-seeking drama queen she'd been back then.

"Oh, cute kids!" Everly said, tugging down her already low-cut T-shirt so it showcased her boobs. She checked out Julia and Michael, who were currently running around Rafe's legs as he pretended to be a monster, growling and moaning and tickling them as they passed. "They yours, Sara?"

"My sister's. I promised them cotton candy before the fireworks start." With that she turned to Kaitlyn and Gabby. "Want anything from the concessions?"

"Oh, I'd love some cotton candy!" Everly said.

"No problem," Colton said. "Sara, I'm happy to get your stuff too."

"No thanks," she said. She could get the kids their cotton candy herself, thank you very much. He went off, and she grabbed her purse from the blanket.

"Hurry up," Gabby said. "Fireworks are going to start any minute."

Of course she ended up in the line right behind Colton. She tapped her foot anxiously against the grass. There was no reason to be angry. She was going to be calm and dignified about this. Everly was beautiful in a way Sara would never be. More importantly, Everly was Colton's type of woman—beautiful and buxom. She even had this giddy little laugh. Clearly she was fun.

In line, three separate people said hi to Colton. An elderly woman thanked him for hauling her Christmas tree down from the attic for her Christmas-in-July celebration, a father thanked him for talking to his son after he'd gotten caught spray painting graffiti under the bridge, and Mr. Langotti, who owned one of the cafés downtown, thanked him for keeping an eye on his house when he'd been on vacation the week before.

It appeared everyone in the entire town was in love with him. Finally the last person left. Sara poked Colton in the back.

"Nice night for a date," Sara said. She knew full well she sounded catty but couldn't seem to help herself.

"It is," he replied, though he didn't turn around.

"Leave it to you to date the prettiest girl in town." Again with the catty. She needed to just keep her mouth shut.

"Not only is she pretty, she knows how to have fun too."

Ouch. "My pie must've not been very tasty, because it only took you twenty-four hours to get over it." *Why couldn't she stop?*

Finally he turned to look at her, and his gaze was steely. "A pie is just a pie, sweetheart."

And with that he turned back to the concession counter and handed her a Coke and two cotton candies. She took them, mollified and confused. His expression was business as usual. "Thank you," she said. "You didn't have to—"

"I wanted to."

Why did he always have to do something nice? She wanted—no, needed—to stay pissed at him. She tasted the Coke. Diet. "How did you know I drink diet?"

He shrugged. "Good guess." His gaze seared through her, leaving a burning trail of heat in its path. It burned through her insides and bloomed on her face in a crimson blush. "I've got to get back to Everly," Colton said. "Enjoy the fireworks."

He turned to walk back to his date, leaving her alone. The brief walk back to the blanket didn't improve her mood. She gave the kids a couple pulls of the cotton candy, even ate a bite herself, but she couldn't relax. The excitement she'd felt about bringing the kids here had faded.

"What's wrong?" Gabby asked her while Kaitlyn entertained the kids.

"Nothing's wrong. I'm just waiting for the fireworks to start." She sneaked a glance over at Colton and Everly, who of course had chosen to sit about ten feet away. She could see them chatting and Everly playfully pushing his shoulder. A time or two she heard his laugh, deep and sonorous. Everly must be very clever to get him to laugh like that. Sara didn't think anyone had ever laughed that way with her. And she wondered if anyone ever would. "Just that Everly's acting like the Eveready sex bunny."

"Sara! That's not like you."

"Well, maybe I'm not feeling like myself tonight. Am I fun?"

"Right now you're not, but you can be. You've got feelings for Colton, don't you?"

"No! Of course not. Why would I have feelings for him?"

"Because he's a nice guy. And because he might have feelings for you too."

"Colton doesn't do relationships. I'd be humiliated all over again, and the whole town would start gossiping. I could never subject myself to that again, believe me."

"You're scared!" Gabby wagged her index finger at Sara. "That's why you're running from your feelings."

"I made him a pie and he kissed me. But then I shut him down. And that was just last night and look who he's with today. End of story."

"You probably hurt his feelings."

She snorted. "I doubt it. If I did, he certainly recovered quickly."

The fireworks had begun, lighting up the sky with bursts of white light and loud rat-a-tatting noises that Sara felt reverberate clear through her chest. It had always been a fantasy of hers to watch fireworks with someone who kissed her as the *boom-boom-boom* of the explosions filled the night sky. Tagg had hated fireworks, so they'd rarely gone, plus he hated showing affection in public. Oh well, guess she was going to have to wait for another Fourth for a man who could make her see stars. Because she'd totally blown it this year.

She tried to take joy in her niece and nephew, but Michael was a little frightened and kept holding his hands over his ears. Sara tried to hold his ears for him and make a joke, but he wasn't buying it.

"I haveta pee," he said. Evie had warned her that he meant what he said. But where was she going to take him? The public bathroom was quite a hike away.

"Auntie Sara," he said more urgently. "I haveta pee *now*."

"C'mon, I'll take you," she said, scooping him up and heading to the back of the crowd. A patch of woods surrounded the baseball field, and in high school kids used to go in there to make out and smoke weed. She just hoped no one was in there now doing that or other worse things she didn't want to see. She walked about a foot into the woods and said, "Pee on that big rock."

He lifted his little face. "*Outside?*"

"Yeah. Um, Spider-Man pees outside when he has to, and this is an emergency." He liked Spider-Man as well as Barbies, didn't he?

"A 'mergency," he said, grinning. Then pulled down his pants and got the deed done.

"That was awesome!" she said as she carried him back to the field. "Don't tell your mom, though, OK?"

"I'm telling," he said, grinning and wrapping his little hand around her neck. His mother's son all the way.

On the way back to the blanket, Sara couldn't help but notice Colton and Everly again, but this time she did a double take because Everly was leaning over on the blanket, cleavage in plain view, feeding him cotton candy.

"Aunt Sara, why did you stop?" Michael asked.

Sara shook her head. "Oh, sorry, Mikey," she murmured. The intensity of her unkind, murderous feelings for Everly shocked her so much she'd stopped walking. And those same feelings bubbled up for Colton. How could he let Everly feed him cotton candy when yesterday he'd eaten Sara's *pie*?

She became aware Michael was tugging on her shorts. "What is it, sweetie?" she asked.

"You stopped again."

She scooped Michael up and kissed him and carried

him through the crowd back to their blanket, forcing herself to stay in the moment. But in the back of her brain, something niggled. The overt jealousy she felt at seeing Colton with another woman appeared to be above and beyond what she'd feel for someone she was merely attracted to. She couldn't possibly have real feelings for Colton.

Or could she?

Chapter 13

♥

Well, Sara had certainly acted jealous about Colton's date. And he had to admit that made him really...happy. He'd enjoyed sticking it to her too, and had taken a perverse pleasure in seeing her all riled up. Could it be possible she *was* interested in him, even after that just-friends speech?

"Colt, why are you chuckling to yourself?" Everly asked, scooting up close to him on their blanket. Instinctively, he leaned away from her overpowering perfume. He'd gone along with her feeding him cotton candy because he'd seen Sara walking toward them with Michael, and dammit, he wanted to make her jealous, but now that the fireworks were almost over he just wanted to go home.

He shook his head, as if it were easy to shake thoughts of Sara out of it. "I'm just thinking what a nice evening it is." He was spending way too much time thinking about Sara. Maybe he was losing it, because since when did he prefer someone who'd rejected him

over a beautiful woman who was right next to him?
Everly was close and getting closer. He could tell from
the looks she was telegraphing him, from the way she
kept showing him her cleavage, from her subtle little
touches, that she'd be more than delighted to join him
in bed tonight. Trouble was, he just couldn't work up
the excitement for it—for her.

Geez. Ruined by a smart, pretty type A woman
who'd turned him on by baking him a birthday pie.
Maybe he really *was* losing it.

Everly linked her arm through his. Fireworks lit up
the sky, booming and bursting.

But Colton barely noticed—the fireworks or Everly.
He was thinking of how cute Sara looked in shorts and
a T-shirt, her hair up in a ponytail. Out of the corner of
his eye, he could see her holding her nephew and pointing up at the sky. The little boy was leaning back against
her and watching the display with a look of awe, and
Sara was laughing.

His eyes wandered in her direction, only to find she
was looking right back at him. So she *was* staring at
him. Interesting. Maybe she was running scared. She'd
spent a lot of years with Tagg and had been through a
lot this past year. Maybe she was a little nervous about
jumping into something.

"It is a beautiful night," Everly said after the fireworks ended. "And it doesn't have to end." She gave
him a pointed look meant to telegraph her meaning.

"Gee, thanks, Everly, it's been a lot of fun, but I've
got to get home. Early day tomorrow, you know?"

Colton drove Everly home, then parked his cruiser

at the station and walked the short distance downtown. The shops were lit up. One or two people walked their dog, and there were a few stragglers from the fireworks, but the place was pretty dead. He kept walking to the bridge.

The angel statue greeted him as it had every day since he'd moved here.

"Don't look at me like that," he said to the angels. "She told me to get lost. Well, not in those words, but she friend-zoned me." He leaned over the bridge to look at the falls cascading over the rocks. The green was mostly deserted now.

"I'm the one that friend-zones people," he mumbled. "I'm the one who likes to date around. This is a good thing." Except even though Everly was beautiful and willing, he had no desire to go out with her. There was no challenge there. What was wrong with him?

Sara was able to raise his blood pressure like no other woman, that was for sure. And admittedly, he did sometimes take a perverse pleasure in baiting her, in watching her outrage rise in a pretty blush up her face. "I don't know why I do it," he told the angels. "In fact, I don't know why I'm attracted to someone I can't help sparring with half the time."

He had to let this go. But as he stood there on the bridge, the memory of that early spring evening came to him, with the blossoms blowing across the bridge, their sweet scent intoxicating and heady. He'd shared one hell of a kiss with Sara that evening. A kiss so full of promise that he could barely sleep the entire week.

That attraction was still there, regardless of her years

with Tagg, regardless of the fact that their date had
never happened. It buzzed between them like bugs
around a flame, and there was no denying it. Until he
saw it through, he would always have questions that
nagged at him. That kiss hadn't been the end of something. It had been a beginning.

* * *

In a small town like Angel Falls, the fireworks display
didn't last that long. Thank God, because Sara had a
splitting headache. Julia was tired and whiny, her small
hand literally stuck to Sara's like syrup on a pancake,
and Michael had fallen asleep, his head wobbling a
little on Gabby's shoulder. Kaitlyn had taken off with
Steve to have a big relationship talk, so Sara and Gabby
headed with the kids toward home.

"Remind me of why we decided to walk again?"
Gabby asked, adjusting Michael's dead-to-the-world
weight in her arms.

Sara peeled her hand carefully away from Julia's. It
made a sound like a zipper unzipping. "Oh my gosh,
Julia, here, sweetie, stick to Aunt Gabby for a bit while
I take Michael." She chuckled, but Julia just responded
with an "I'm tired" and rubbed her eyes, getting more
sticky stuff on her face, which was already coated with
a sparkly layer of cotton candy sugar.

Sara traded glances with Gabby. She saw the glint of
desperation plain as day. Gabby pointed to the picnic
bench on the far edge of the park, which stood on the
grass a few feet ahead. It would be their last pit stop be-

fore hauling the kids another half a mile home. Which wasn't that much, but it now seemed as impossible as a trip on foot across the Sahara with no water.

"Why is it children weigh twice as much when asleep than awake?" Gabby said as they sat. A soft snore emanated from Julia, whose mouth had dropped open in a soft little *O*.

Sara laughed. "I don't know, but I'm sorry I've been such a pill tonight."

Gabby patted her on the knee. "I forgive you. If it's any consolation, Colton kept looking over at you."

Sara shook her head. "I doubt Colton was looking at me when he had Everly to ogle."

"Oh my God, Sara. That man wants to do you, and you drove him into the arms of that horrible woman."

Sara rolled her eyes. "I didn't drive him into anybody's arms. I mean, it took him less than twenty-four hours to find someone else! Who does that?"

"An angry alpha male? Who maybe wanted to make you a little jealous? Or who wanted to try and forget you, but of course he can't because he's fallen deeply in love with you. Or maybe he's always been."

"My God, Gabby, you should write romance novels. Really."

"I'm just saying, I personally wouldn't write him off just because you're scared."

"I'm not scared!"

"Come on, Sara. I mean, if that were me, I'd be a little nervous too of someone whose nickname is the Revolver."

"I've only been with Tagg."

"Having only been with one person isn't the problem here. The trouble is, he wasn't the *right* person. And you've hinted to me before that maybe the sex with Tagg wasn't that great. A man like Colton has got to know what he's doing in bed. Maybe it would be...you know, a little fun to find out?"

"Gabby!" She looked down to check that the little ones were still asleep.

Her sister raised her brows in a *Well, I'm just sayin'* expression.

Sex with Tagg had been pleasantly predictable at its best...and, to be honest, generally lacking. She'd always covered up those feelings, thinking that that was the way it went when you were with someone for a long time, or blamed it on her own lack of experience. Thought that maybe if she tried new things, read *Cosmo* more, whatever, the sex would be better. After all, that's who she was at her core. Try Harder Sara. Out to please. Out to win everyone's approval.

"Thank you for being my sister," Sara said. "And I'm sorry everything's been about me lately. I was shocked when you announced your engagement. I felt bad. Like I'd been so wrapped up in my own troubles, I never even saw that coming."

"You didn't see it coming because I didn't see it coming. It had nothing to do with the fact that you just moved, started a new job, and are understandably stressed."

Sara picked her words carefully. "Are you happy with him?"

Gabby sighed and adjusted Julia's head on her shoulder. "What's happiness? If happiness is having a family one day, then yes, I'm happy, because I want that more than anything."

Oh God, that was not the right answer. "Gabby, you're young. You're talking like this is your last shot at marriage and a family."

"Let's get real, Sara. I'm twenty-nine, I have a job I dislike, and time is ticking away. I know Malcolm's not perfect, but he's smart, adventurous, and he's got a great job. Not to mention he's cute. Sometimes we don't get exactly what we want. We have to make do, or we miss out entirely."

"It's not like you to compromise for something so important. You're the romantic of the family."

"Maybe for once I'm a realist."

She tapped her sister's shin with her foot. "Don't settle, Gabs. I almost did. If Tagg hadn't been stupid, who knows how long I would've kept telling myself I loved him, trying to make it work, despite knowing in my gut there had to be more? I thought Tagg leaving me was awful, but now I see it in an entirely different light. It's a second chance for me."

A second chance with Colton. Which she'd blown.

Suddenly Sara began to laugh.

"What?" Gabby asked. "What is it?"

"We are never going to be able to carry these kids home. I mean…look at them." Michael was asleep with his cheek on Sara's shoulder, drooling, bless his heart. Julia was snoring, her head leaning back wantonly on Gabby's arm.

"I suppose we could call Joe and Evie to come get

us," Gabby said. She nodded in the direction of the road over Sara's shoulder. "Or...we could just get into Colton's cop car."

"Colton's..." Sara turned to see a car drive slowly down the road and stop directly in front of the park bench. Colton rolled down the passenger window and leaned over the seat. "Care for a ride home?" he asked. No one else appeared to be with him, including pretty buxom females who were cute and bubbly. Thank God.

"Yes!" Gabby said without compunction. She didn't even acknowledge Sara's glare. Fine. They were desperate. She'd take the ride.

Colton lifted Julia and carried her to the car, handing her to Gabby once she climbed into the back seat. Then he came back for Michael. "I've got him, thanks," Sara said, struggling to get up from the bench with a sleeping three-year-old who suddenly appeared to weigh as much as a sleeping elephant. Colton reached over and took Michael anyway, flashing Sara a don't-be-stupid glare.

"We don't have car seats," Sara announced from the back seat once they were all settled in.

She found her gaze level with Colton's in the rearview mirror. "Oh, you're right, Doc. Maybe you two should walk then."

"Now, Sara," Gabby said quickly, "it's only a few blocks, and Colton will drive really carefully, right, Colton? And we're so grateful for the ride, aren't we?" Sara felt a smack on her thigh. "Aren't we, Sara?"

"Yes, fine, Gabby, we're grateful. Very grateful."

"That's what I like to hear, ladies," he said, pulling

away from the curb. Sara didn't miss his grin in the mirror. "I promise I'll drive carefully."

They drove the short distance to Evie's with Gabby chatting exuberantly with Colton about cotton candy, the kids' antics, and the people she'd seen at the park. Which was fine with Sara, who couldn't wait to get out of the car. Evie and Joe met them in the driveway and carried their sticky sleeping angels to their beds.

When Colton offered to drive Gabby and Sara to Nonna's, Gabby wouldn't let Sara protest. As soon as they got out of the police cruiser, Gabby yawned loudly and stretched. "Those kids really wore me out, man oh man. Think I'll go in and check on Nonna. And Sara, you can just, you know, take as long as you want. Even all night, if you know what I mean. I've got things covered."

Gabby gave her a wink, jogged up the porch steps, and disappeared through the screen door before Sara could murder her.

She was ready to bolt up the stairs herself when Colton's hand on her arm held her back.

"It's a nice night," he said, his gaze steady and calm, his touch soft but insistent. "How about we take a walk?"

She scanned his eyes. He was looking at her in a way that seared clear through her like a lightning bolt, burning her to ash.

Why was she angry with him, again? Oh, Everly. But deep inside, she knew Everly posed no threat. The threat she worried about was much closer than Everly and her new boobs. It was inside Sara's own heart.

Colton seemed to have an uncanny ability to see her inside and out, X-ray vision kind of seeing. He constantly called her out on all her noise: her drive for perfection, going a million miles an hour, and trying so hard to achieve. Somehow she sensed that with him it might be OK to just *be*.

He took her hand as they walked down the tree-lined street. The moon was a bright crescent, and the sky looked like some magical fairies had tossed a bucket of glitter all over a backdrop of black velvet. It was one of those warm, wonderful midsummer nights when you didn't even need a sweater. Golden lights from inside the century-old houses made everything look picture-book perfect, and Colton strolled along as calmly as if they were old friends out for a walk.

Maybe she wasn't ready for this, for him, for any man. The past year had been so full of pain. The rejection she'd felt last summer at being passed over for someone who'd appeared on a whim still hurt. It made her question everything about herself, who she thought she was, what she thought she wanted, where she even belonged in the world. Being back home had just added to the unsettled feeling, since working with her dad seemed like a temporary stop along the way.

But Colton, he belonged somewhere, all right. As perfect a fit as a puzzle piece. He had that magic kind of personality that attracted people—he always had. Everyone loved him. He was woven into the fabric of their town, while she would always be the outsider looking in.

"I always like to imagine when I'm doing my rounds

and I see lights on in a house, a family is tucked in for the night," Colton said. "It makes me feel…"

She laughed, thankful to be dragged from her maudlin musings. "Like a voyeur?"

"Ha ha," he said. "I was going to say peaceful."

"When I was younger and I was walking home at night, I always looked into lit-up houses and imagined a family sitting around a table, the kids doing homework, the mom and dad supervising. Sort of like the fantasy family I was missing after my mom died."

He gave her hand a sympathetic squeeze. "I know the feeling."

Sara stopped on the sidewalk and faced Colton. He was so handsome, standing there in the glow of a nearby streetlight, the shadows highlighting his defined cheekbones, his strong jaw.

Was it possible that the two of them could be much more alike than different? Each of them had grown up missing a parent and longing to belong to a "normal" family, if there was really any such thing. They'd both ended up back here in Angel Falls for reasons not of their own choosing.

Sara took a deep breath. "Colton. I told you I wanted to be *friends* because you scare me to death."

"Yeah, I tend to have that effect on people," he said, chuckling a little, but she could tell it was a nervous laugh.

"I've been with one guy my whole life. I'm not ready for a relationship. I—"

He cut her off. "I don't care about any of that. I don't care about the past anymore, not our past or your past with Tagg. It's time to take a new course. For both of us."

Colton tugged her hand up very slowly to his mouth. His warm, masculine grip encased it as he slowly kissed her knuckles, one by one. A simple and easy gesture, but her pulse was doing the Indy 500 thing and it was making her dizzy.

"I'm sorry I brought Everly tonight," Colt said. "I was angry at you. Look, Sara, I don't want anyone but you. I can't eat or sleep, and all I do is think about how you'd feel in my arms. God knows why, because you're a real pain in the—"

She put a finger over his full lips. "Stop while you're ahead, big guy." Couldn't eat? Couldn't sleep? How she'd feel *in his arms*? Oh, wow. He'd had her at *Let's take a walk*.

His mouth curled up in the slightest smile. Then he kissed her finger.

The silly yet touching gesture melted her. He lowered her hand slowly from his mouth. The heat and fire of his gaze raised goose bumps up and down her arms despite the warm evening. "I want you, Sara. Every second of every—"

Sara cut him off, wrapping her arms around his neck and cutting off his words with her lips. He circled his big arms around her and kissed her back, deeply and urgently, pressing his body against hers. *He wanted her.* She could feel it down to her marrow, in the way he held her, tightly and possessively, the thorough way his lips moved over hers.

"How about we go back to my place and sit on my balcony?" he asked.

She crinkled up her nose. "That might sound a little like a line."

He stroked her cheek, and her knees almost caved. "It is a line," he said, his lips twitching. "But come anyway."

She sucked in a breath. Was he asking her to... Well, yes. Yes, he was. It wasn't like she'd never been propositioned before, but it had always been by semidrunk guys in bars. Usually with Tagg nearby to fend them off.

She glanced up at him, past the spinning, heady feeling, past her heart throbbing in her throat and every nerve standing on end. Once she saw the way he looked back at her, tenderly and calmly, her panic halted. He had a way of quieting her soul at the same time he filled her with anticipation and excitement, which seemed impossible but was the only way she could describe his effect on her.

"OK," she whispered, smiling. She gave him her hand and let him lead the way.

Chapter 14

♥

Colton led the way up the stairs and into his apartment, where he managed, a little shakily, to turn on a lamp. Around him stood his token bachelor living room, comprised of a leather couch, a La-Z-Boy, and a bunch of electronics along one wall.

"Nice TV," Sara said stiffly, looking around. She'd turned quiet during the last block, and dead silent on the way up the stairs.

"Thanks." God, he hadn't been this nervous since he had to read aloud in front of the class in third grade. He must *really* be losing his touch if he was thinking about that when he had a beautiful woman in his apartment.

Not just any beautiful woman. One who challenged him, and who brought out the best and the worst in him. A woman he could not stop wanting.

"I mean, there are no wires," she continued. "Some people have all those tangled wires." She made jumbled-up motions with her hands. "Not you though, nope. Tidy as can be."

"Do you want a drink?" he asked. His voice sounded a little higher than usual, their normal conversation having been replaced by Sara's waxing poetic about the quality of his TV setup. Her hands were shaking a little. He wanted to tell her his were too, but feared that would make her even more nervous.

She cleared her throat. "Water would be nice. I'll get it myself. I need to wash my hands." She held up her palms, which had a few blue streaks of cotton candy on them. He'd been thinking more in terms of a good, stiff shot of Jack Daniel's.

She walked into his kitchen and turned on the water while he poured a glass of ice water from the fridge and handed it to her.

"Thanks," she said politely, taking a few sips. "Are you nervous?" she asked over the top of the glass.

They were finally alone in a place where they could do something about it, and he could not blow this. Nervous? More like completely off the bell curve. "No," he said.

Sara, usually ready with some kind of retort designed to make his blood pressure skyrocket, was oddly silent. That was one thing about getting into it with her: they always had something to say. Getting *along* was a lot harder. He placed his hand lightly over hers, which was oddly cold. That little sign of cold, clammy vulnerability, plus the fact that she alternated between jittery small talk and complete silence, made him feel strangely tender.

"Red, I—" He wanted to tell her not to worry, but he faltered. Up close, he was drawn to all the multicolored flecks in her pretty green eyes—some dark, some honey colored—a beautiful unique mixture that took his breath—and his words—away.

"I—saw you giving money to those boys tonight," she said, filling in his awkward silence. "That was...sweet."

He looked down, not wanting to discuss how "sweet" he was. "Look," he said, rubbing the back of his neck, "don't make me out to be a hero. If I can do little things to help, I try to do them. Mainly because growing up, I understood what it was like—not to have stuff. Not to have fun."

She placed a hand over his chest. "You're very kind-hearted."

"I'm a small-town cop just doing my job." Why were they talking about his job when he wanted to be kissing her?

"I heard all those people who came up to you in line. Pulling down Christmas trees for elderly ladies and talking to kids and keeping an eye on people's houses when they're gone."

"Like I said, it's my job."

She shook her head. "It's more than that. Everyone in this town loves you. You look out for people—just like you look out for your family."

He sighed. Gently he took her glass and set it down. Then he lifted her up and set her on the counter next to the stove, stepping carefully between her legs.

She swallowed. He leaned his hands on the counter-top beside her, caging her in. "How do I get you to stop talking?" he asked, biting back a smile.

Gingerly she reached out and patted one of his biceps, as if she were examining it. Another avoidance technique, not a good sign. He massaged her shoulders. Yep, tense as a live wire. That made him back up a little and gesture toward the living room. "Come on. Let's watch TV. You can check out my sound system."

She laughed at that. But when he turned to go, she tugged on his sleeve, keeping him in place. "It's the over-ten-year thing," she blurted. "With Tagg. And no one else. Particularly the *no one else* part. Whereas you, on the other hand—"

With one swift move, he took her in his arms and pulled her close. She was soft and warm and he didn't know a damn thing about flowers but her scent reminded him of summer—warm sunshine and sweetness. "Sara," he said, smoothing wisps of hair back from her face. God, she was pretty. "I don't care about any of that. Unless, of course, you still want Tagg."

Her gaze met his. "I want you."

His heart was thundering crazily in his chest. He ached to touch her, but he needed to make certain she was all in on this. Wanted everything to be just right.

He took her smile as a good sign. So he bent closer to capture her mouth.

She held out a hand and pressed it against his chest. "I-I just want to make it clear, I'm in no position for a relationship. I—this is just for fun, right? I want us to be on the same page."

That surprised him, mostly because that was usually *his* line. He tried to figure out why it disappointed him a little too. Colton understood a woman like Sara wasn't likely to hang out for long with a guy like him anyway, no matter how people praised him ad nauseam for his good deeds.

All he knew was that he wanted her. And he'd take whatever she would give him. "Gotcha. Loud and clear."

Then he kissed her. Which, he was relieved to find, finally stopped all the talking. A funny thing happened when his lips met hers. Everything—the apartment, the hum of the fridge, the fireworks kids were setting off in the streets, the background humming of his nerves, ceased to be. There were just the two of them and his mouth on hers, their arms circling tight around each other.

Sara kissed him back, their tongues tangling, their lips searching, their bodies flush. She tasted like cotton candy and a sweetness he'd been missing for years. She fit perfectly in his arms, all curvy softness. With that kiss all the years of animosity disintegrated, and he thought he must've been an idiot to ever bother arguing with her about *anything*.

"You're beautiful," he murmured, running his hand under her shirt, over the warm, smooth skin of her back.

She blushed and shook her head, smiling.

"If you're forcing me to take compliments, I'm going to make you do it too," he said.

"Just kiss me," she said, curling her hand around the nape of his neck and kissing him deeply. A whimper escaped from her throat. When he pulled back to look at her, her eyes were dreamy, and, he thought, full of the same hunger he felt coursing through him. No nerves. A tidal wave of relief bowled through him.

"Sara, I—" Words lingered on his lips, the need to tell her something honest. But her words stayed with him: *just for fun.* So he traced his finger along her cheek instead. His hand was shaking a little, and he moved it before she could see.

When there was no sarcasm left between them, what was there? He wasn't sure, but it didn't feel like anything he'd ever experienced before. He tucked a strand behind her ear. "I always wanted to do that. Touch your hair."

"Take me to your bed now, Colt," she said, her mouth curving upward. "I don't want us to do it next to the coffee maker."

The magic words. "Whatever you say," he said, lifting her up, loving the way she wrapped herself sweetly around him. He carried her to his bedroom, kissing her all the way.

* * *

Good thing Colton carried her, because Sara's legs felt like marshmallows, weak and offering no support. She was trembling all over. Warm lava was pumping through her veins, and she thought she might be having a stroke, based on the hot and cold, the weakness, the leaden pounding of her heart. Whatever disease this was, she didn't want to get over it.

And oh my God, the man could kiss. She could spend *hours* kissing those beautiful, skilled lips.

He laid her unceremoniously on the bed and shucked

off his shirt and shorts in typical guy fashion, then stood there in all his male perfection, confidence flowing in spades. He was all sculpted hills and valleys, all tight muscle and golden skin. Then he was over her, their legs tangling, his erection pressing against the throbbing, aching pulse between her legs.

"Colton," she said. He was kissing her neck, behind her ear, tangling his hands in her hair, kissing her like she'd never been kissed, carefully, slowly, then suddenly demanding, consuming her, burning her up in flames. Somehow her blouse got undone and tossed off, her shorts pitched to the floor. He whispered sweet things, how beautiful she was, how happy he was that she was here with him, how he loved making love with her. She'd pegged him for a quiet man, not demonstrative at all, but again he'd surprised her. She'd never heard such words before, words that made her feel...treasured.

He unhitched her bra effortlessly, and then his mouth was on her breast and he was using his tongue in wicked ways. Heat built in her core and flashed all through her as he kissed and suckled, her body tensing and tightening and readying for him as her fevered need for him rose. When a moan escaped her, she felt him smile against her skin.

She drew her arms around him, up the sinewy cords of his back, fascinated by the hard muscle and contrasting softness of his skin. She slid her hand under his briefs, smoothing it over the taut muscle of his butt. "How's your tetanus shot these days?" she murmured as she stroked him.

"That's my girl," he said. "I was waiting for you to

mention that. I'm sorry, but I'm going to have to dole out some payback for that."

"No payback," she managed to say.

"Oh, don't worry. I think you might like it." He peeled off her scrap of panty and slipped a finger into her slick wetness, stroking her swollen flesh, kissing her long and slow and deep.

"Colton," she said, her voice urgent, grasping his arms, tugging him over her.

He put on a condom and she guided him into her body, clutching at his back while he entered her carefully, steadily, filling her, moving her. For a moment their gazes locked. Honesty, earnestness, connection—it all shook her. She met his gaze full on, tamping down an underlying sense of terror that somehow this man was different from any other, and she would never come out of this the same.

Waves of pleasure rolled mercilessly through her, every muscle tightening. She could tell from the way his muscles were tensing that he was very close to release too.

He kissed her mouth and began moving inside her, starting a rhythm that sent the little waves cascading into bigger, hotter ones, rolling through her one by one like a warm, languid summer tide. She opened to him, wrapped herself around him, embraced him with all her strength.

"Sara," he cried out, and then he let go, taking her with him. And she clung to him as they both plunged over the edge.

* * *

Colton was not a cuddler or a spooner, but he reached for Sara and pulled her to him, smoothing out her amazing hair as it fell against his neck. He inhaled its sweet scent, felt its silken weight run through his fingers. Around now was the time when he'd typically mention he had to get started early tomorrow, and the woman in question would take the hint and leave. A part of him had been hoping that once they'd made love, he would see Sara was like any other woman, that it was just sex, yada yada. Instead he'd found himself experiencing another feeling he had no real understanding of—contentment.

She surprised him by talking first. "Tomorrow's Sunday. I've got to get up early to help Nonna get ready for family dinner." She paused. "You should come sometime. To family dinner. I mean, you're good friends with Rafe, and Nonna loves you, so it's not like anyone would wonder why you're there."

He hesitated more than the usual time, finally deciding to be honest. "Thanks, but family dinners...just not my thing." It wasn't his thing. He didn't consider that maybe she'd be the exception to his rule, because she'd said she was in this for fun. There was no point in pretending otherwise.

"Oh, OK." Disappointment resonated in her voice.

"It's nothing personal. Just that...you know, it's...family." Great, that was making a lot of sense. "What I mean is..."

She kissed him quickly. "Sounds like we're both on

the same page. We'll keep this light. I'm not offended."
She still looked a little disappointed, maybe. He did
know her family's Sunday dinner was a big deal. Something he'd never show up to casually. And he knew her
family would never interpret his being there as a casual
thing.

She moved to get up. Impulsively he put a hand on
her arm to hold her back. "I said I didn't do family
dinners. Not that I wanted you to go." If she were anyone else, he'd encourage her to leave and get a good
night's rest. But he didn't want her to go. So he tightened his hold and draped a hand around her waist. She
gave in and lay back against him, resting a hand lightly
on his forearm. It looked pale and creamy—delicate—
compared to his much darker coloring.

"What are you thinking about?" he asked. Also new
for him. When had he ever asked *that*?

She smiled. "What we just did. How I still can't even
believe it. When I think about you and me in high
school—"

"I don't even want to talk about how I was in high
school."

"Why not? You were handsome and popular. You
had everything I wanted. Popularity, friends. I was just
an ugly little duckling."

"I was a jerk." He paused. "And I never thought you
were ugly."

"Oh, come on. It's all right. I had pimples and thick
glasses and braces until I was a sophomore."

He shrugged. "Everyone has an awkward phase."

"Except you."

He nuzzled her neck a little. God, she smelled good. "I almost asked you to homecoming senior year."

"What?" She propped herself up on one elbow, giving him a view of her pretty shoulders—and her cleavage, which she'd covered loosely with the sheet. "You did not."

"Remember when I'd hurt my knee and was hobbling around on crutches, and you'd sprained your ankle and were in an AirCast?"

"Oh yeah. I sprained it working at Outerspace Burgers while I was on those awful roller skates they made us wear."

"Yeah, well, we were sitting together at an assembly in the handicapped seats. Remember that?"

"I remember being nervous sitting next to you. Because you were so handsome. And I felt bad for you—it was right after you'd blown out your knee. The whole school was talking about it."

"Everyone was telling me I'd be fine, I was a great player, I'd come back. Basically blowing smoke up my butt when the doctors told me from the beginning it was bad news. You didn't say any of that. You just said, *I'm sorry.* That meant something to me. I think I understood deep inside my football career was over. I never thought I'd even make it to college without my scholarship."

She rubbed his shoulder. "That must've been a hard time for you."

"Honestly, I was more worried about the college part than the football part. I had to provide for Hannah. I couldn't do that without a decent job."

"You had a lot of responsibility for such a young man." Suddenly she grinned.

"What is it?"

"So what's the part about me? And homecoming. I can't wait to hear this." Her eyes were lit up in anticipation of what he was about to say. He couldn't help thinking he'd never seen this side of her, expectant as a little kid, her guard totally down.

"So you sat with me and we talked and I got to thinking you were pretty nice. That I'd been wrong about you."

"But I went with Tagg to homecoming that year."

"He uninvited you, remember? After you screwed up your ankle." Tagg had been an asshat—thinking she'd ruin his fun being on crutches. He'd eventually felt bad about it, but it had taken him long enough. "I was about to suggest we go together, as fellow invalids."

"Why didn't you?"

"Just then, Tagg came by and sat down with us. I was angry he did that to you. But he was my best friend, I couldn't move in on him."

"We never would've lasted back then anyway," she said with an exaggerated sigh.

"Why not?" He heard the hurt in his voice and silently cursed himself.

She smiled. "Because I always had my heart set on dating a professional athlete, and you clearly disappointed."

"Yeah, but I just might be professional at something else." He lifted his brows to let her know what it was.

She rolled her eyes and laughed. A snorty kind of

laugh he'd never heard from her before, and he loved it. This was the real Sara, and he liked her. A lot.

In response he rolled her over and kissed her until her laughter faded and was replaced by an entirely different kind of fun.

* * *

Judging by the gray light behind the shades, Sara guessed it was around five a.m. She knew because the summer light was always early, and the dark turned to gray long before the sun came up. It was one of the things she loved about summer.

Next to her, Colton was sleeping on his side, facing her. His long lashes made him look boyish, but the muscle of his arm traveling under his pillow, and the plains and valleys of his chest clearly visible above the sheet, were all man.

Consciousness fully dawned, and with it a surge of pure adrenaline hit her, jolting her fully awake, and suddenly she was completely freaked out. What had she been thinking, to fall asleep with him? To stay *all night*? That smacked of...relationship. Something she knew full well the Revolver wasn't interested in.

And while he might be very well acquainted with the "just fun" kind of thing they were embarking on, this was all new territory to her. She didn't know the first thing about navigating a fling, but she did know that last night with Colton had been too perfect, their lovemaking easy and natural, how they'd fallen asleep wrapped up in each other's arms. And she was pretty certain that thinking this way could only lead to heartache.

Panic hit her in bursts, each one bigger than the last. Suddenly she couldn't breathe, couldn't take in enough oxygen. She had to get out of here. She was not ready to face him in the light of day. Somehow, she had to find some sense of control.

Very cautiously she slid from the bed and found her bra, T-shirt, and shorts. God only knew where her panties had gone.

She slipped on her clothes in the living room and had just picked up her sandals near the door and placed her hand carefully on the knob when she met resistance.

In the form of a six-foot-two cop wearing nothing but navy boxer briefs, leaning over her with his hand on the door.

"Good morning," he said, his voice a little gravelly, the shadow of beard growth on his face sexy as sin. He moved to prop his hip up against the door and cross his arms.

"I—um—have an emergency." The emergency was that she was panicking and having a heart attack and she needed to get out of here. Fast.

"That right?" he said, one brow raised. "Funny, but I didn't see you with your beeper. And I seem to recall your saying you were off all weekend."

"Why could you not be a heavier sleeper?"

"Cop reflexes." He paused and let that sink in. "Don't leave. Stay."

"You should be glad I'm leaving. Isn't that what guys want? A woman who's not clingy and knows when to leave?"

"Stay," he said again, putting his arms on either side of her against the door, caging her in, which was sexy as hell. "Please."

Still she stayed strong. "We just *did it*! Like, three times. Aren't you exhausted?" *Three* times. And each time had been so, so good. Like walking-on-air kind of unbelievably good. Tagg clearly needed some lessons, because this man...

He bent to kiss her neck, and she shuddered. "Stay because I like you being here," he said. "And I'll make you breakfast." He was nuzzling her neck, and it was getting hard to think, with whatever he was doing with his lips between her neck and collarbone.

"Sounds like breakfast might come with a price," she said.

He smiled against her skin. She struggled to keep up the fight, trying not to smile herself, trying not to succumb to the warmth that was even now flooding through her.

Her thoughts were getting muddled, and the common sense that had led her to seek out the door was rapidly fading under the onslaught of his kisses. Sara reminded herself this was just for fun. Sex for fun did not involve hanging out for hours in bed talking and then staying for breakfast. It involved cutting loose and getting out before feelings got tangled up.

Yet his playful pleading got to her in ways she couldn't even describe. He liked her being here. He wanted to make her breakfast. He wanted her to *stay*.

He did a weird thing then. He lifted his head and hugged her. Put his arms around her and rubbed his hands up and down her back and just . . . held her. It was the sexiest full-body hug she'd ever had, and for a second she thought she was going to cry.

She couldn't talk. It felt like she had a Kleenex stuck in her throat. She didn't dare say it out loud but she felt it, clear through her bones. *Wanted.* She felt wanted.

He drew back and looked at her. Lord, she must be a mess. Crazed hair, wrinkled clothes, no makeup, plus she'd slept in her contacts and her eyes felt like a thousand needles were prickling them.

"I never had a woman get so emotional over the thought of breakfast." He reached over then and tilted her chin up so she had to make eye contact. The honesty in his gaze terrified her. It was as if he could see past all her bullshit. Before she could look away from that piercing blue gaze, he curled his hand around her neck very softly and gently and kissed her on the mouth.

Then, knowing full well he'd kissed all the fight out of her, he took her hand and tugged her back to his bedroom. He was irresistible. She had no choice but to push her fear aside and follow him.

Chapter 15

♥

Leonore, where's my dad?" Sara asked at work on Monday, setting a chart on the counter.

"He's still in with Mrs. O'Connor," Leonore said. "He told me to tell everyone he's running a little behind today."

A little? Sara glanced at her watch. It was ten o'clock, and the nine-thirty patient hadn't been seen yet. "I tell you what, I can see the nine thirty. But when Dad comes out, will you tell him I need to talk to him?"

"Sure thing."

Sara was already halfway down the hall when Leonore called out, "Hey, Sara...You forgot your pen, sweetie!"

"Oh! Thank you," she said, grabbing it from Leonore and making sure to stick it in the knit thingamabob around her neck, pleased to see Leonore smile.

"I told you that little thing would come in handy."

She held out another pen. "Here, stick this in there so you always have an extra." Sara had this terrible habit of forgetting pens everywhere. "Will do," she said, and ran down the hall.

She caught up with her dad after she'd seen the patient, who had a straightforward sinus infection. He was walking out into the reception area with Eva O'Connor. Her eyes looked a little puffy. She grasped Sara's hand unexpectedly.

"Hi, Mrs. O'Connor," Sara said, squeezing her hand back.

"Sara. I'm so happy you're back with us in town. We need a nice woman doctor like you. But I have to tell you, your father is a saint. Honestly, we're going through some tough times, but he made me feel so much better." She blew her nose, and Leonore pulled a few more out of a box on the counter and handed them to her. "I think I've held him up with my troubles."

Leonore patted her hand. "Oh, now, you know how Doctor is. He always has time to listen."

"Well, I am truly grateful for that, Leonore. You ladies have a good day."

Sara found her father back in his office, dictating the visit. "Patient's son is in the middle of a contentious divorce and got stopped for a DUI, her daughter's just moved back home with two little kids, and her husband just found out he's got to have back surgery." He looked up from dictating into his computer. "I'm sorry, sweetheart, for throwing off the schedule."

"Oh no, Dad. I'm really glad you made time to talk with her."

He smiled. "Me too. It's the part of my job I like the best. Sometimes people just need someone to listen."

Easy to forget that, in the hectic pace of the day. "Hey, Dad, I need to consult with you on one of your patients I just saw."

"Oh, sure," he said, walking around the desk and standing near Sara, crossing his arms. "Who is it?"

"Stacy Simmons. I know she's got irritable bowel syndrome, but she's having bad pain and her abdomen feels tight. It's concerning to me, like she might need a CT scan to make sure it's nothing worse. I thought I'd get you to take a look and see what you think."

Her dad rose from the chair. "I've been treating Stacy for years. I'm glad you asked me what I think." As he went off to see the patient, Sara couldn't help scanning his desk. Tidy piles of papers, pens with drug company logos, and a few goofy things his patients had given him, like a coffee mug that read, "I found that humerus." In the corner of the desk was a stack of charts. On the top was the name of a patient she'd seen the day before. She flipped through the stack. Yep, her entire afternoon lineup from yesterday. He was still checking them over as if she were an intern.

Just then her dad came striding back in the room. "I agree with you, her abdomen's tight. But she's really stressed, and her irritable bowel always acts up when she's overwhelmed. I told her you'd adjust her medication and to give us a call this evening if she's not better. Sound all right to you?"

Sara tucked her disappointment about the charts aside. She'd bring that matter up another time. "Yes, but it makes me nervous too. How can you be sure nothing's really wrong with her?"

He shrugged. "I can't be. I'm just willing to take the risk because I know her so well."

"But Dad—malpractice, lawsuits. Bad stuff happening to people." Sara shuddered just thinking about that.

Her dad laughed. "Yeah, yeah. That's why they call it the art of medicine. Or we'd spend all day ordering every test in the book on everybody." He pulled his beeper off his hip and squinted at it. "Say, can you help me turn on that newfangled EKG machine? It's like it has its own mind. This one asks you twenty questions before it decides to turn on. My old one just used to have a switch."

"Sure, of course I'll help you turn it on. Dad—"

"Yes, sweetheart?" He was already bolting down the hall. She caught up with him there.

"Thanks for that. It's—it's fun seeing you in action. I—hope I can be like you one day."

He rested a hand on her shoulder. "Give yourself a little time. I think you're going to be even *better* than me one day."

Wow, what? Did she just hear that out of her dad's mouth? A compliment? She took a minute to bask in the fact that her dad saw her potential. That she was doing OK, falling into a groove. Besides that, something more was happening. She was enjoying getting to know her patients, who were also her neighbors, friends, past teachers, and kids she'd babysat for. It made her feel a part of something...It made her feel like she belonged.

"Hannah Walker's in room three," Glinda said when Sara returned to the counter.

"Thanks, Glinda," Sara said, taking Hannah's chart and knocking on the door. She was a little nervous about seeing Hannah as a patient. Of course she would keep Hannah's concerns private, as she was obliged to do, but she wasn't quite sure if Colton would like that or not. Hopefully he'd be relieved that Hannah had gotten all the info she needed and be grateful to be spared the details.

Hannah's chart said she was here for a physical. A meningitis shot before college. And Sara couldn't forget about the sex talk. Part of her job. An important part, she reminded herself, whether it was a little uncomfortable or not.

"How's your summer?" Sara asked as she took a seat on the stool and put Hannah's chart off to the side.

"Fabulous. But it'll be coming to an end. I'm a little sad about that."

Hannah's tone was chatty, as always, the only evidence of nerves the fact that as she sat she twirled her long braid in one hand. "Are you nervous about college?"

"No, not really. Excited." She dropped her hands into her lap but fidgeted them a little. "Except I met someone. A boy."

Sara raised a brow. "A nice boy?"

"He's awesome, Sara. Kind and sweet and really handsome."

God, she loved this kid. Mentioning *kind* and *sweet* before *handsome*. Mature beyond her age. Colton would be so proud.

"My brother found out I was seeing him." Hannah looked Sara directly in the eye, which also impressed her. "You won't tell him any of this, will you?"

She wanted to make certain Hannah understood she had her trust. "Anything we discuss in this office is private."

"Aiden happens to be my brother's latest project."

"Project?"

"Yeah, you know. The cops helped Colton when he was a wild teenager or something and now he feels like it's his mission on earth to do the same for other kids. And he picked Aiden. He's painting Cookie's house, of all things."

"Have you had a talk with your brother about this?"

"Well, he confronted me because he found out I was hanging out with Aiden. And he basically went ballistic."

Colton going ballistic? Hard to imagine. On second thought, maybe not so hard, knowing how much he loved his sister. "Why's that?"

"Because Aiden doesn't come from a nice family—he's not going to college, and he wants to be an electrician. And he got in trouble last spring, but that was an accident. But he works three jobs and he's amazing."

"Three jobs. That *is* amazing." Sara made small talk but knew she had to somehow professionally broach the topic of sex while making the transition as natural as possible. She was just trying to figure out how to do that when Hannah spoke.

"I already know about the birds and the bees, if that's

what you're wondering. And no, I'm not having sex with him. Not yet. But I have a few questions."

"Well, I'd love to help you with whatever questions you have. Not just here in the office but anytime, right?"

"This isn't a fling. I love Aiden. But Colt will be so upset."

"Well, I know one thing—your brother adores you. He wants nothing but the best for you."

"My brother is stubborn. He can't see beyond Aiden's past. Geez, he practically broke out in hives when he found out I was seeing him." She grinned and waved her hands near her face. "I mean it, Sara, his face got all blotchy and he looked like he was going to pass out or something."

Sara couldn't help but chuckle. "My advice is to talk with your brother. And go slowly. Sometimes we think we're in love, but it's just infatuation."

"And sometimes it's love," she insisted.

"I'm just saying waiting to have sex might be a good thing. Slow things down a little. Really get to know one another. Proceed with caution." She certainly hadn't done that with Colton. But she was old enough to realize the starry-eyed feeling she felt around him was not love. She would not allow herself to get burned by that again.

Hannah was sitting there, her long dancer's legs dangling off the exam table, pretending to listen. Sara knew the look. Hannah was being respectful, but it looked as if she'd already made up her mind.

As Sara went on talking, educating, and informing, she thought about how dearly Colton loved his little sister and how she had to do right by him but also do right by Hannah. However that balancing act tipped, one side was bound not to be as happy as the other. But she had to do her job first.

* * *

"Hey," Colton said as he walked into Sara's office at twelve fifteen and found her writing up a chart at the counter. "Have time for lunch?"

"Yep. I'm done and I'm starving," Sara said, closing the chart and beaming a bright smile that told him she was happy to see him. He couldn't help grinning back like a smitten teenager, and bit down on his cheeks to control it. What was it about her that made him feel like he wasn't in control at all?

"I'm starving too," he said, giving her a look that let her know exactly what he was starving for.

She blushed at his comment, a fact that did not go unnoticed by Leonore and Glinda, who gave each other a knowing look.

He leaned through the open reception window. "Ladies," he said. "How goes it?"

"Great, Chief," Leonore said with a wave.

Sara hung her lab coat on the hook and walked into the waiting room. As they headed for the outside door, Glinda said, "Lord, I am having a hot flash. Did you see the way that man looks at her?"

"Like he's a sailor home after a six-month voyage," Glinda said. Colton held the door for Sara and gave her the most indecent look he could muster, which wasn't hard at all. As soon as they got outside, Colton swung her up against the side of the building and kissed her. "Ahoy there, matey," he murmured against her neck.

She giggled. "They said a *sailor*, not a *pirate*."

"I like the pirate better. Shiver me timbers, lass."

She groaned at his bad impression, but kissed him back just as eagerly, wrapping her hands around his waist and gazing at him with those stunning green eyes. In the cool shade by the door, under the old lilacs, he wished he could keep kissing her forever. "I hope you didn't mind I came in?" He grinned—again. He really had to stop with all the grinning. "I missed you."

She laughed. "But you just saw me yesterday morning."

He shrugged. "I know, but I missed you last night." Dammit, he shouldn't have said that. He knew she had commitments to her grandmother. Plus he was supposed to be treating this as casual and instead he was acting stalker-ish. What had gotten into him?

But then she grabbed him by the shirt and went in for another kiss. She tasted wonderful, felt so good in his arms. He skimmed her jaw with kisses, then trailed them down her neck.

She arched her neck to give him better access. "Maybe we should go to your place for lunch?"

"Can't," he said. "I have to be in court in Richardson by one. But I do have lunch for us in my car. And I thought I'd take you somewhere special to eat it."

She raised an elegant brow. "Somewhere special?"

"Yeah," he said. "You'll see." His gaze skimmed lightly over her. She was wearing a flowered dress and red sandals, and her hair, up in its usual ponytail, was catching golden highlights in the sun. *Gorgeous woman. Mine*, something primal cried out inside him. He started walking around the back of the building to his car before he could say something stupid. Sara was stirring feelings in him he had no business feeling. Ones he'd made it a point not to feel with women, and especially not her. Yet he couldn't seem to rein them in.

Just then they saw an older woman walking toward them with a cane. It was Mary Mulligan, the angel photographer. She must've seen them kissing outside the door in broad daylight. He uttered a curse under his breath. What had he been thinking? Did he really want the whole town knowing about them?

"Oh, hello, Chief, Dr. Sara," Mrs. Mulligan said. "Seems I always catch you two kissing."

Colton felt his face flush, a rare occurrence. He was suddenly at a loss for words. Fortunately Sara chimed in.

"Hi, Mary," Sara said, shooting a glance at Colton. "Headed to see my dad?"

"Yes, my stupid arthritis is acting up." She stopped and rummaged in her purse, then pulled out her iPhone. "Say cheese," she said, suddenly snapping their picture. "You two are such a cute couple. Are you headed out to lunch? It's such a lovely summer day."

A sense of apprehension spread through Colton. Terms like *couple* and *catch you two kissing* were the kinds of words that were apt to give him hives.

Mary replaced her phone, and Colton offered her his arm as she walked over to the office door.

"Have a nice day, Mary," Colton said.

"You too." She turned around at the top stair, grabbing on to the door frame for support. "It's nice to finally see you both together. But those angels are certainly taking their time with you two."

Colton waved to Mary and steered Sara to his car, reminding himself that this was only a summer fling. No big deal. It was only lunch. He couldn't allow himself to think further than that.

* * *

"Are you OK?" Sara asked as Colton drove them downtown and turned up a side street right after the falls. "You're not letting that angel stuff get to you, are you?"

"No, of course not," he said. But frankly it had, a little, and he wasn't quite sure why. Sara had said she wanted to keep things casual, which was exactly what he wanted too. What she'd said just now seemed to confirm that. Then what was his problem?

He'd decided on impulse this morning to show Sara his plot of land. But now he was having second thoughts. Maybe it was too personal. Half of him wanted to show her everything, tell her everything on his mind because his heart was bursting like a damn teenager's, but the other half told him he was a fool. A relationship wasn't what she wanted. Or what he wanted, right?

One more turn, and they were suddenly traveling up a gravel driveway surrounded on both sides by trees. He felt a little nervous about what she would think, but didn't want to even think about why that was important to him.

"Someone lives back here?" Sara asked.

He laughed. "Well, they used to." The car crunched along the road, which wound through a patch of woods and over a tiny stone bridge where a creek gurgled below.

"It's like a park back here," Sara said.

"It's next to the park. Pretty hidden, isn't it?" He felt the same peace come over him that he always felt making this climb. As if he'd left his world of problems back on the main road.

They continued through a clearing, and that's where Colton killed the motor. He got out of the car and grabbed a bag of food from the back seat and a blanket from the trunk.

"We're eating lunch in the field?" Sara asked.

He quirked a smile and signaled her to keep walking.

Suddenly, past the weedy field, a view opened up of a house that at one time used to be a showstopper but was now crippled with age. It was a big rectangular colonial, the bottom half covered in brown stone. The top half was made of wood and had been painted white, but the paint was now gray, chipped, and peeling. The front steps were crumbling, and a big tree alongside the house was growing through the roof.

"So who owns this decrepit old house?" Sara asked as Colton led her over to the tree and laid out the blanket. She seemed fascinated by the tree limb climbing through the window and popping out the roof. "I've never seen a tree do that before."

"I own the land, up to the house."

"You own this?" She squinted at him in the sunshine. "How could I not even know about this place?"

He shrugged. "Believe me, kids know about it, and sometimes they come out here and cause trouble. An elderly couple lived here, but it's been abandoned for years. Their grandchildren are finally selling it. They intend to knock down the house and sell this piece of land off too." Colton reached into the bag and pulled out two wrapped sandwiches. "Want to eat?" But she was already taking off toward the house, so he set down the food and followed her.

She climbed onto the porch, stepping around the crumbling stone steps, and peeked in one of the windows.

"Hey, be careful, Red. It's not safe. Plus it looks like *Hoarders* in there."

That of course made her peek in all the windows. "Oh, wow. I see all kinds of furniture. Newspapers, magazines. Lots and lots of stuff." When she turned, it surprised him to see excitement on her face. "So what made you buy the land?"

"Sometimes being police chief makes me feel like I'm in a fishbowl. I wasn't really ready for it with Hannah's college expenses, but sometimes you just know when something's right." He winced. That seemed to reflect some other feelings he might be having too. Ones he did not want to assess that deeply right now.

"So what are you going to do about the house? You have to buy it, or you'll have neighbors."

"The family asked me if I want it, but I said no. Too big for me. Not to mention it's a train wreck."

"It might not be too big if you have a family one day. Do you like old houses?"

A sudden picture popped into his head. Kids running around this field playing, dogs running right alongside. Some of the kids had red hair. *Oh geez.* He shook his head and made himself focus on the front door, which was coming off its hinges. "I'm not sure this one's worth saving."

She sighed. "There's something to be said about a house that's quirky and one of a kind. Have you been inside?"

He laughed. And remembered Tagg complaining when he and Sara had house hunted that she'd been drawn to houses precisely like this one. "There's not an inch of space in there not covered with junk. Plus it smells like mouse pee and other bad things. I know a lot of guys in the trades who can help me build a nice house from the bottom up. I've been clearing the field on my days off."

"Oh, c'mon, Colt," Sara said with a wink. "You're not afraid of a little challenge, are you?"

"No, but I'm also not crazy. Thanks for the pep talk, though." Then he kissed her, nice and long and slow, and it was the perfect kiss, on the most perfect day imaginable, being out here in the warm sunshine, the birds singing, the smell of summer grasses and growing things thick in the air.

"Can you stay over tonight?" he asked. He missed her in his arms, in his bed. If they'd had more time he would've made use of that blanket he'd brought, just sitting under that shady tree.

"I've got to stay with Nonna tonight."

"I understand. Disappointed, but I understand."

Impulsively she kissed him again, standing on tiptoe, tugging on his shirt to bring him closer.

"Woman, you are bewitching me," he murmured against her lips. Definitely not a safe thing to say, but nothing with her seemed to be following the rules.

"I tend to have that effect on men," she said, smiling against his lips. "Thanks for showing me this place. It was fun." Her phone went off with a text, and she looked at it. "Oh, how about that," she said incredulously.

"What is it?"

"It's from a friend of mine at Columbia. Looks like there's going to be a sudden opening in the type of fellowship I almost started last year. They're taking applications, and they want to fill the vacancy by Christmas."

Dread tore through him. "So you're going to apply?" he asked, hoping he kept a positive expression on his face.

"My dad assumes I'll just pick up where I left off last year and go back to doing research and working at a big hospital. I'm not sure he believes I'm cut out to be a family doctor."

"What is it you want?"

For a heartbeat, her gaze searched his. "I don't know."

He had no idea what to say. He wanted to cry out, *Don't go*, but who was he to hold her back? Or imply there would be commitments of any kind? He'd always known she wasn't long for Angel Falls, and this just confirmed it.

They ate lunch, but Colton had lost his appetite.

This reinforced what he felt in his gut: he did not want rumors to spread about them dating. He shouldn't have been so reckless as to kiss her outside her father's office. And it was of questionable judgment to be sharing his land with her too. The more he thought about it, the more he realized it was a bad idea to go too public with this—whatever it was. It was fantastic and amazing, but as far as he was concerned, it was too good to be real. Even if she didn't take that fellowship, she'd soon tire of him, a small-town cop still stuck in the same old place they'd grown up in. He'd just be happy for each day and stick to his rules—that he didn't get serious. Or do family dinners. Whatever it took to avoid a broken heart.

Because he could read the writing on the wall. Sara would be off soon, on to a big city, a big hospital, something much bigger than the life he had here. Keeping it casual would make it easier to say goodbye.

He dropped her off at her office. "Bye," she said, kissing him and lightly running her hand down his cheek. "Your land is awesome. Thanks for sharing that with me." She gave a little smile before she closed the door and walked away.

Leaving him more confused than ever.

Chapter 16

♥

Colton was working out at home that evening when Sara's text came through. OK to come over? He'd just set down his free weights and decided to hit the shower when his doorbell rang. He opened the door to find her standing there, holding her phone, wearing a gray T-shirt, leggings, and a long gray sweater with flip-flops. A flowery little overnight bag was slung over her shoulder. If she'd been in a gorgeous gown and heels, he wouldn't have wanted her any more.

"Surprise," she said.

His heart rolled over and surrendered right there. It struck him that it was an ordinary evening—he was sweaty from his workout, he still had earbuds in his ears from the audiobook he'd been listening to—and there she was, looking like everything he'd ever wanted.

He reached out and took her hand and guided her across the threshold, a little afraid he'd better do it quick before she vanished into the night. Champ bolted over, wagging his tail a mile a minute and nudging his nose into her hand. She laughed and cooed to him and stroked his back. Lucky dog.

"What happened with Nonna?" he asked, closing the door and tugging her away from his dog.

"Gabby understood how badly I wanted to come and shooed me out. Is it...all right? I hope you don't mind, but I brought my stuff for work tomorrow. I mean, just in case. Not that I have to stay that long, I just thought—"

"I want you to stay."

"Tagg told me once you don't care to have women leaving their toothbrushes and things around everywhere—"

He winced. "Tagg hasn't really known me for quite a while." He didn't want to talk about other women. Or about Tagg. "For what it's worth, you're the only woman I've ever had over here."

"Oh. That sounds like a compliment."

"It is." He slid the bag off her shoulder and leaned in to kiss her, then suddenly pulled back. "I forgot. I just finished working out and I need to hit the shower."

"Oh, go right ahead. Champ and I can hang out." He was about to suggest she join him, but no sooner did she sit down on the couch than Champ hopped up and settled right next to her, his head on her knee, giving him the eyeball. Fine, the dog won that round. But Colton could shower quick.

He was in the shower when he felt a gust of cool air. He turned to see her step in beside him.

His breath hitched. God, she was beautiful. He wasted no time pulling her into his arms. "What made you change your mind?" he asked, kissing the hollow between her neck and shoulder. "Champ didn't have gas again, did he?"

"No, but your country-western singing is terrible. This was the only way I could think of to shut you up." She waved something in front of him—a condom packet—and placed it on the high tile ledge.

He kissed her as they stood under the warm spray, steam fogging up the doors. Lathered up his hands with soap, then slid them all over her body, loving the feel of her, the satiny, slippery wetness.

He whispered sweet dirty things in her ear that made her blush and laugh, until she finally shut him up with kisses. After tracing a trail of kisses down her neck, he laved a sweet nipple with his tongue, then paid homage to the other, loving the way she writhed under his touch, the little sounds of pleasure that escaped her throat, and the way her hands roamed greedily all along his back, his hips, his ass.

For the moment all his worries had fled, and he decided right then and there that he would enjoy every moment he had with her. His mouth found hers again, tongues tangling and sliding, and his arms tightened around her waist as they stood pressed together.

He dropped a hand between her legs, slipped two fingers inside her, stroked her at her core until she arched under his touch. She slid her soapy hands up and down his length until he nearly lost his sense and his balance. She was driving him wild, and the heat was tearing through him like flames.

He put on the condom and managed to sit down on

the tiled shower seat. She hovered over him and slowly took in his length, took him inside her inch by inch. Her gaze was calm, direct, never deviating, her green eyes bright and intense in the misty shower. He never stopped looking at her either.

A shudder passed through him. He couldn't tell where his trembling stopped and hers began. Some kind of connection, intense, final, absolute, passed between them despite no words being spoken at all. They started a rhythm, at first slow, then more intense, as he moved inside her until she got dreamy eyed and a tiny frown creased her forehead. He was right with her, coming at the same time, driving into her, feeling her muscles clench around him. They came like that, in the hot, steamy shower, mist swirling around them, their lips melded, their arms wrapped around each other tight, her body tightening around him as they moved together to climax, his lips finally releasing a guttural cry.

For a while they didn't move, until the lukewarm water started to feel chilly. Colton was a little shaky as he stepped out and handed her a clean towel, wrapping it around her, then grabbing one for himself and tying it around his waist.

He tried to collect his sanity as he tumbled into bed. Good Lord, what was happening to him? He wasn't one to wax sentimental, but the words of every sappy love poem he'd ever heard were on the tip of his tongue.

Sara came out of the bathroom in a gray nightshirt that came down to her knees and had a cat on it or something. It looked old and well-worn and comfortable. And she had her glasses on. Her hand flew up to adjust them, and he knew she was self conscious about them. He pretended he didn't even notice, and got up to let Champ out for the last time, then turned out all the lights before climbing into bed beside her.

On impulse he reached over and took off her glasses, then set them down gently on the nightstand and kissed her good and hard. Then he pulled her into him and wrapped himself around her before Champ had an opportunity to sneak in himself. Mindlessly he fingered a curl of her wet hair, felt its silky texture, how it sprang back softly from his touch.

"Not too bad for a work night," she said, her hand draped over his. "We're even in bed on time. This isn't disruptive at all."

He kissed the top of her head. "Yeah. Not too bad for a work night." Except that being next to her was getting him aroused. He tried to focus on other things, like that he had to stop at the bank tomorrow and get an oil change for his car, and what would happen if he got awakened by a call in the middle of the night, but nothing was working. He hoped she wouldn't notice.

She'd definitely noticed and was reaching back and touching the evidence, stroking him gently with her hand. Oh God, there he went again. All it took from her was a couple of touches and he was hard as granite.

"Don't fan the fire unless you want to use the flame," he said, kissing her neck.

"In your case, it's not taking much fanning," she said, laughing. She turned around in his arms and kissed him, pulling herself flush against him, and before they knew it, playful, short kisses gave way to deep, long, wet ones, and hands started roaming. They just fell into it, plain and simple, and he could no more hold himself back than he could stop himself from breathing.

They lay there for a long time afterward, her head nestled between his chest and his shoulder, he softly stroking her arm. Finally she slid her nightshirt on over her head and snuggled back in next to him until this time they both fell asleep.

* * *

Sara slept like the dead until three a.m., when Colton's phone went off. "OK," she heard him say in a sleep-heavy voice. "He's drunk again? Be right there." He hung up and jumped from the bed, then tossed on his briefs and walked over to a chair where his uniform shirt, pants, and shoes were carefully laid out. She was fine until she saw him strap on the bulletproof vest. And the gun holster. He must've noticed her awake and staring at him because he said, "I'm backup on a 911 call. Got to fly."

Sitting upright, she watched him tug on his pants and tie his shoes. He opened his top dresser drawer and took out his gun, shoved it in his holster, and flew out the bedroom door.

She ran to the front door and opened it for him. "Be careful," was all she was able to get out as he gave her a quick peck on the cheek and was gone.

Sara closed the door and leaned against it, a new understanding of Colton's job fully sinking in.

Of course it had been a fantasy to think that his

job was all traffic patrol and lecturing kids about drugs and stopping to have breakfast with the locals at the downtown diner. Their town was quaint and lovely and friendly, but that didn't mean it didn't have a dark side, a side that Colton had to deal with on a regular basis. He could be going to a car accident, or a drunken brawl, or to confront a crazed lunatic with a gun.

In her world there were emergencies, but they were what she and her colleagues often joked were the "tucked-in kind": the EMTs had usually taken vitals, administered IVs, and begun the assessment process, so by the time the patients got to the ER, things were already under some degree of control.

Not like the situations Colton walked into. The complete unknown. He was a first responder. Anything could happen.

Sara didn't even try to go back to sleep. As she paced the apartment, Champ followed right behind her. She made coffee. Tried to watch TV. Prayed. Paced some more.

At five a.m. her cell went off. Her heart sank to her feet when she saw it was her father.

"Dad. What's wrong?" she asked.

"Hi, Sara," he said, his voice calm and soothing as always. "Everything's fine, but I'm working the ER tonight and Colton was just brought in by the squad. He's a little banged up, but he'll be OK."

Terror curled its limbs around her and squeezed, stole away her breath and her voice. "Dad," she managed in a raspy whisper. "What do you mean...banged up?"

"We've got George Carver stitching up his forehead, and he's got a black eye and a broken nose and a little concussion, but I think that's the extent of it. Disarmed a drunk with a knife but got punched out."

The words all ran together, *knife, black eye, broken nose*. Oh my God, a *little* concussion, what the hell was that? Tears flooded her eyes, the grateful and the frightened kind both.

George was the local plastic surgeon, who was often called in to suture up important places on bodies that most people didn't want to risk scarring, like faces. "I'm coming down." She paused. "Did you call Cookie?"

"Rafe suggested I start with you." Leave it to her dad to keep talking in the same calm voice. No evidence of surprise or even shock that his daughter was involved with the man she'd practically hated just a short time ago.

Explaining about her love life would have to wait. "Does Colton know you're calling me?"

"No. He went right to CT and I decided to call you myself."

"I'll be there in ten minutes."

"OK, sweetheart. Don't speed."

"Thanks—for calling me." She had no idea what her dad knew. Probably everything after talking to Rafe.

She wasn't sure how Colton would handle having her at his side. She didn't want to barge in and embarrass him, especially since they weren't officially a couple—in fact, she wasn't sure quite what they were. All she knew was she had to be with him. She couldn't bear not being there.

Sara put on her work outfit for morning, a simple print dress, brought her big gray sweater because the ER was always freezing, and brushed her hair back into a ponytail. She tried to calm down. Her dad had said Colton would be all right, but her doctor's brain kept imagining the worst.

Hearing upsetting news was an almost-daily part of her job. She understood how important it was to remain calm and objective when bad things were going on. But one look in the mirror showed that she was pale and shaking. What if he wasn't OK? A concussion was serious. Plus someone had blackened his eye and broken his nose. Just thinking that he'd been the recipient of that type of violence made her tear up.

Sara took a deep breath. Blew her nose and tried to hold it together. Where Colton was concerned, she was anything but calm and objective. And, she was coming to realize, he was anything but a fling.

* * *

"Since you're not next of kin," Sara's dad said when she arrived at the ER, "I can only give you the CT results if Colton allows it. You know that."

Sara rolled her eyes. "I slept with him, Dad. Please just tell me if something's wrong."

Besides the arch of a single brow, her father kept his same calm demeanor. Sighing deeply, he said, "OK, fine. As one physician to another, I can tell you it's just a concussion. He's got to take a week off. The rest you already know."

It was her turn to sigh. "He's going to hate that."

"I know he prides himself on never missing work." Her dad paused. "Maybe he won't give me such a hard time if you go in first."

She would've taken off if he hadn't grabbed hold of her arm. "He doesn't know I called you. Just warning you. And Sara—"

She was already walking toward the ER bay where Colton was resting when she heard her name and halted.

"Yes, Dad?"

He steered her away from the desk to an area where they could talk quietly. "Being a cop is a dangerous job, no matter how many Fourth of July parades you police or school talks on drugs you give or drivers' ed classes you help teach. The hours are terrible and you never know what you're going to walk into. Which means anyone who falls for a cop worries a lot. It's part of the package."

"I don't understand. Are you warning me away from him?"

"At this point I'm just trying to tell you to not go in there upset."

Oh, she was upset, all right. As much by the fact that he was hurt as by the fact that she'd been kidding herself. The moment her dad had called and told her Colton was hurt, she'd known that her feelings ran way deeper than she'd ever admitted to herself, and now there was no turning back.

She understood the subtle message her father was trying to convey. That if she walked past that bright-yellow

ER curtain into the room where Colton was lying, she had an obligation to respect his job. Not to fall to pieces. She tried to slow her heart down to the normal range and stuff down the panic. For Colton's sake.

* * *

"Someone's here to see you, Chief," said Sandy Feldon, the head nurse, rolling back the curtain, which opened with a satisfying *whoosh*. Colton looked up from the gurney with his one good eye, saw Sara standing there, and bit back the curse that threatened to roll off his lips.

Dammit, no. Not Sara. Not here. He didn't want her to see him like this. Wounded, weakened, looking like shit.

Her face said it all. Judging from that, he must look pretty damn bad.

Yeah, probably something like Rocky after a fight, bloodied and swollen. He'd sustained a lot of bruises and bumps in his time. Par for the course. Part of his job. But he'd never felt as helpless and uncomfortable as he felt now.

She was assessing the damage critically. The Frankenstein stitches on his forehead. His probably-still-bloody nose that they'd had to pack with gauze, and the gash on his arm from wrestling the knife from the guy. His nose and head hurt the worst.

"What are you doing here?" he asked. Not meanly, he just wanted to know who'd ratted him out. "What I mean is, they shouldn't have bothered you." His attempt to soften things didn't sound much better.

Her cheeks flared with color. And something worse happened—her eyes welled up with tears. *Shit.* He didn't want her shedding tears over him. That felt too—real. His mom had done plenty of that with his dad.

"Sara, no, don't—"

She sat down next to him on the bed and clutched his hand, hard. She was shaking. Her reaction took him by surprise—for someone used to seeing sick and bloody and injured people, she was taking it hard. For a woman who'd vowed to keep things casual, she seemed awfully upset.

His impulse was to hold her and tell her it was going to be OK. But another part of him wanted to tell her to just go and leave him be.

He reminded himself that this was his job. The job that had taken his father and made his mother go to pieces. It was a big reason why he kept things light with women. Why he needed to keep things light with her.

"You look terrible," she said.

"The other guy looks worse." He tried to smirk, but his lip was swollen and it hurt too.

"I bet he does."

"Who called you?"

"My dad. Rafe heard the call come in."

Just then her father walked in, looking distinguished as always with his gray hair and white coat. Colton dropped Sara's hand and sat up a little straighter.

Dr. Langdon scanned the room. To his credit, he didn't even raise a brow on seeing his daughter sitting on the bed. "Hey, sweetheart," he said. "Colton." He pushed his glasses down his nose and examined

Colton's forehead. "George said it took twelve stitches. I would've done it myself, but I like to leave stitching faces to the experts. I didn't think you'd want a reminder of your fight with a mean drunk the rest of your life."

"Thanks," Colton said.

Her dad rolled a wheeled stool over to Colton's other side and sat down. "Your face will be fine in no time. Your nose will require resetting in a few days when the swelling goes down. I could do it, but again, I think we'll send you to the folks who do this sort of thing every day. In the meantime you're going to need to take at least a week off because you have a concussion."

A week? Holy shit. Absolutely not. Colton shook his head. He tried to take a breath to calm down, but he couldn't breathe through his nose. "I can't miss work. There's not enough backup, sir."

"Well, here's where you get a little overridden, son. You just saved a woman from her drunken husband and protected all of us from his wrath, should he have gotten loose to wander our town. Or stepped into a car, God forbid. But you hit the concrete hard and you were out for a while. That earns you a week out minimum. No sports, video games, TV, no"—he cleared his throat—"no sex—until the neurologist tells you otherwise. And definitely no work."

Colton didn't miss Sara's head-to-toe blush. He was pretty sure her father didn't either. He looked at Dr. Langdon. "I've been in worse brawls than this back in college, sir, if you'll excuse my saying."

"Your head hurt?" Dr. Langdon asked.

"Yes, of course, but—"

"You were pretty stunned when you woke up, a little confused in front of the EMTs, and your balance was off."

If his head was hurting before, it was literally pounding like a bongo drum now. "I'm the only show in town." He looked up at Dr. Langdon and pleaded, "Please don't do this."

The doctor rested his hand on Colton's shoulder in that way he had, friendly but persistent. "Think of it this way. If you go back to work like this, some thug could take advantage of you in your weakened condition. So you wouldn't be able to protect your citizens like you usually can. None of us is indispensable. Surely you can get the sheriff's office to send a few days' coverage?"

"I'll work on it," Colton said, straining to be polite.

"Also, I didn't call your grandmother. I thought I'd leave that up to you. Didn't see the point of waking her up and scaring her half to death. It's best to stay with her a few days, son, where you can be watched and rest up." He patted Colton's leg, meaning their conversation was about through. "We'll get you those discharge papers and you can go home."

"My cruiser—"

"Is parked at the station. I might have forgotten to say no driving either."

Great. Sounded like all he was going to be able to do was stare at the walls for a week.

Just then Sandy the nurse walked back in. "Are we all ready for discharge here?"

Sara's dad gave Colton one final pat on the shoulder.

"I'm glad you're all right, son. You'll be back to work in no time."

"Thanks, Doc, for everything," he said, shaking his hand.

"See you later, Dad," Sara said, giving him a quick kiss as he left. She stayed at Colton's side. He couldn't help but notice Sandy glancing up from her paperwork, her gaze shifting between Colton and Sara.

"Just sign here," she said. "You're going to need a ride home, right?"

He really wanted to drive himself. Enough with the fussing already.

"I can drive you home," Sara said cheerily. "I'll go pull up my car."

"Sounds great," Sandy said. "I just have to run and get a wheelchair, and you'll be all set."

He knew the rules. But he hated them. Everyone would see him getting wheeled out. It wasn't good for his job, to have people know the chief was in a weak state.

Sandy handed Colton a copy of his discharge instructions. He sensed what she was about to say. "So you two. I had no idea you were a couple. I mean—"

"Sara and I are friends, Sandy," Colton said, cutting her off. "Thanks for the instructions."

Out of the corner of his eye, he saw Sara flinch. What was up with that? She couldn't think . . . Nah. She'd told him from the beginning she wanted to keep things light, and so did he. She was going to leave Angel Falls and find someone else who had an MD or some kind of Ivy League pedigree. He'd be left with only his pride, and he had to do anything possible to spare that. And to spare himself the humiliation of his whole community knowing that he was a fool to get things started up with her.

"Oh, OK then. Sorry. I'll go get that chair. Nice to see you, Sara."

Sara smiled. "See you around, Sandy." She turned to Colton, the same calm expression on her face. "I'll go get my car. Unless, of course, you'd like to call another *friend*?" Before he could answer, she gathered up her purse and walked out.

What the hell? Could it be possible she'd changed her mind? Did he *want* her to change her mind? Granted, he felt things with her he'd never felt with anyone else. Everything with her was different. But now that he'd had this scare, all he could think of was that look on her face when she'd first seen him. The same horrified face his mother had worn for his dad. The nights of worry, the stress of wondering every single day if it was going to be just another day shooting the bull in the coffee shop or something like this, only with even worse consequences.

It didn't matter anyway. Sara wasn't going to be around long, and he was going to stay the course. It was the only thing that made sense.

* * *

Colton's head might have been spinning, but Sara would bet not as much as hers, which was reeling over that *just friends* remark. Yeah, she knew that's what she'd told him at the beginning, but how could he say

that after how amazing everything had been between
them? Maybe he was protecting her from town gossip
by saying that in front of Sandy, quelling rumors, that
kind of thing. She'd been so afraid of that, but now that
someone close to her—her dad—knew about her and
Colton, it wasn't so bad.

She wasn't so afraid anymore of what her dad
thought of her choices. Hell, she wasn't so afraid of her
choices herself. Maybe she really did want more with
Colton. Was she even staying in town? Could this be her
actual home again?

The two minutes it took to wheel Colton out felt
like two hours. All the ER staff stopped to look at
his messed-up face and wish him well. He smiled and
waved at everyone, including the cop at the ER doors
who opened the car door for him, but he drew the line
at being helped into the car. He winced when he bent
his head to get in.

One look at him and she knew for certain she
couldn't pretend anymore that what she felt for him was
casual. She'd never felt so comfortable with someone.
So *herself*. And he'd seemed genuinely thrilled to see
her, and have her stay with him, and he'd even said she
was the only woman he'd invited into his home. Was
that all in the name of *friends*?

But he'd certainly hated seeing her emotional over
his wounds. And seemed to hate the fact that she'd
shown up at the hospital. She wondered if she was really
the only one feeling that this was something more. Perhaps she was off base, as she'd been with Tagg, thinking
he'd loved her. She'd pushed away all her uncomfortable

feelings, frightened to bring them out into the open. She'd vowed not to be like that anymore.

This time, she wasn't going to sit by unquestioning. This time, she knew what she wanted, and she was going to let Colton know, regardless of the consequences to her heart.

Colton breathed a heavy sigh as Sara finally pulled away from the curb, and Sara knew he must be exhausted and in pain. Not the best time for a relationship talk. They drove in silence the ten minutes to Cookie's house. The sun was coming up over the green hills and the forests just outside of town, the first light of another glorious summer morning.

Sara pulled into Cookie's little gravel driveway. "I let Champ out before I left, but I didn't feed him. How about I go do that now and bring him over?"

He turned to her, as much as he could with the stiffness. It looked as if his neck was hurting too, and who knew what other body parts. He assessed her through his one good eye.

"Sara, turn off the car for a sec, please?"

She cut the engine. "Colton, I'm sorry I showed up. I'm sorry I embarrassed you," she said before he could continue. "We can talk about this when you feel better. Just go in and rest, OK?" She managed a tight smile.

He took hold of her right hand, which was resting on the steering wheel.

"It's not good for citizens to see their police chief injured. I don't like people seeing me like that."

His words struck her as odd. "Like what—being a human?"

"Weak. Helpless."

"Human beings get hurt, Colton." What was he trying to tell her?

He swallowed and spoke again. "I hated seeing you cry over me."

He looked very vulnerable, upset even. "I didn't think I was going to cry," she said. "I thought I could handle it. But I took one look at you and I—"

Oh, hell, she felt like she was going to start crying again. "Part of the reason I don't like to get serious with anybody is I don't want anyone doing that," he said.

Oh dear, this was taking a turn. "Doing what?" she asked, her tone carrying a definite edge now. "Caring?"

Even in the dark, she could see something flash in his eyes.

"Look, sometimes my job is scary, and I don't know how I feel about letting anyone in on that." He shifted uncomfortably in his seat. "I mean, we did say we were going to keep it casual, you know?"

Oh God, she was tearing up. She didn't want to do that, and she didn't want to stress him any further. But she was afraid she'd lose her nerve if she didn't tell him now. "What we have...it doesn't feel casual to me." There, she'd said it. "I told you I didn't want a relationship because I've only dated Tagg. After his rejection, I was afraid to put myself out there again. But what's between us, I mean—" She swallowed and forced herself to continue. "What I'm trying to say is, to me, what we have is special. I care about you. Whatever's going on with you, I want you to know that."

The silence was getting deadly when he finally spoke.

"Thanks for driving me home," he said evenly, like she hadn't just spilled her guts. "And for coming to see me." He paused. "I just—I just don't want anyone worrying about me."

Well, that went well. Still a little stunned, Sara watched as Colton got slowly out of the car and righted himself. Somehow she managed to start it and put it in reverse. Before she pulled away, she turned and looked at him, still standing stiffly by the passenger door, his gaze impassive, his jaw stiff as granite. Her eyes were watery and her voice cracked a little with emotion. "You big fool," she said. "Don't you know it's too late for that?"

Chapter 17

♥

"You're super cranky," Hannah said as she passed through Cookie's living room with her car keys in her hand. She lingered near the couch, where Colton was sprawled out for the fourth day—and going stir-crazy. "Is that because you hit your head?"

He gave her a nasty look and went back to watching TV. Champ, who was sprawled on the floor, was handling his enforced rest well, more than happy to have Colton lying by his side all day.

Hannah went to grab the remote, which was lying on Colton's chest, but he was too quick, grabbing it instead. He could see out of his eye now, and nothing was wrong with his reflexes. And he was still a little dizzy and headachy but getting better each day. The only problem was that he was dying of boredom. And stupidity, considering how he'd treated Sara.

"Cookie," Hannah called. "Colton's watching TV again."

"Hannah, I swear—" He couldn't get away with anything around here.

"You know what the doctor said," Hannah said. "No TV, no texting, no computer, no paperwork..." At Hannah's scolding tone, Champ drooped his ears, ready to take the blame for Colton's indiscretions.

"Don't you have to go to work or something?" he asked his sister.

Cookie walked in, took the remote from his hands, and turned the TV off. "You know what the doctor said. No TV, nothing that strains your brain."

"I'll just lie here and stare at the ceiling all day." That was not a way to shut off his brain, just a way to make him insane. It also made it way easier to think of Sara. All. Day. Long. And how she'd said she cared about him. How she believed what they had was special. And how he'd pushed her away.

God, he'd screwed up. And the pain of missing her was worse than the pain in his head and his boredom combined.

He winced.

"Head still hurting?" Cookie asked. "Do you want some more Advil?"

"No, I'm fine," he said, trying not to sound irritated. He wanted to kick himself.

"Sara's grandmother brought us some chocolate chip cookies," Hannah said.

"That would make most people pretty happy," said Cookie.

"Don't you two have places to go? Geez." The hovering. The concern. He could do without both. Being left to wallow in his frustration and boredom sucked, but it was better than this.

"OK, fine then. I'm going to work," Hannah said. "I'd kiss you on the cheek, but I'm afraid you might bite me." She bent down and kissed him anyway, and gave Champ a pat, which turned into a belly rub.

"Thanks, squirt," he said.

"I'll be home at eight after dance class," Hannah told Cookie. "Oh, I forgot my keys in the kitchen."

Hannah ran into the kitchen, and Cookie sat down at the end of the couch. Colt moved his feet to make room for her.

"Your business isn't that private, you know. I ran into Sandy Feldon at the grocery store. She told me she'd seen Sara sit with you in the ER in the middle of the night and asked me if you and Sara were dating. She told me you said that the two of you were just friends. But she didn't believe it, by the way."

"Colton, you did not," came a voice from the kitchen. Hannah popped her head through the doorway. "Why would you do that?"

"Quit eavesdropping," he said. "Get to work already."

"I could be a few minutes late."

Colton sent her a glare.

"OK, OK, I'm going. But don't screw this up. I like Sara too much."

Hannah's phone buzzed, as it did a thousand times a day, and then she was tapping vigorously on it, sending a selfie, and running out the door. "Gotta go, good luck, love you."

When the dust settled, it was a little too quiet in the room.

"Thanks for worrying about me, Cookie, but I'm fine. You can get on with your day."

Instead of getting up, she crossed her arms and settled back into the couch. "I'm not going anywhere. Maybe Sara doesn't want to come around and upset you because of your head problem, but frankly I don't have a problem doing it. What's wrong?"

He felt like he was thirteen again, being stubborn and sullen and Cookie was telling him to snap out of it. "Nothing's wrong. Sara and I *are* friends. I'm just having a hard time doing nothing all week. It's all fine."

"Well, when I saw her yesterday she looked about as unhappy as you do. I'm old, and my clock is ticking. That means I have a low threshold for bullshit. What's going on?"

He was close to Cookie, and they'd sat here on this couch many a time throughout his growing-up years. Except now his troubles were a lot different. He didn't normally discuss his love life with her, and he felt at a loss.

"I know you feel you have to be the man of the house and take care of us all the time, but I can see you're hurting now."

Colton sighed. "I *have* been seeing Sara, but don't get your hopes up. She came right down to the ER the other night. Rafe called her dad and her dad called her and then...there she was, at my bedside. She took one look at me and..." He squeezed his eyes shut. It hurt to remember the look on her face when she'd seen him. He pinched the bridge of his nose. He didn't want to remember it.

"She was upset," Cookie offered.

He nodded. "I don't want to hurt her. Nothing good comes from a relationship with a cop. Families end up getting hurt. We all know that."

Cookie fell silent. She patted his calf before she spoke again. "Colton, you remind me so much of your father. You look like him. You have his big heart. You're handsome like him. But mostly you're stubborn as a mule. Just like him too."

"I'm not being stubborn, I'm being smart. She told me she's not ready for anything serious. So I don't know why she got so upset seeing me in the ER, or why she's upset I introduced her as my friend." Oh, he knew why. His gut was telling him why, with all its churning and pitching like a small vessel at sea. It was because their casual arrangement had gone to shit. For both of them.

"What happened with your father was a terrible tragedy," Cookie said. "And it led to other bad things. You were forced to act like an adult when you were only a child. You lost your father and your mother way too young. That's a lot of loss for a young boy."

"It is what it is, Cookie. We got through it."

"You're not understanding what I'm trying to say. This isn't about your getting beat up on the job and being afraid to upset Sara. It's about you being afraid of getting hurt yourself. You're not worried about Sara. You're worried about *yourself*."

Colton jolted upright. Champ startled awake, his dog tags jingling. "That's ridiculous," he said, but even he was beginning to see through himself. "I just wouldn't want to put anyone through a cop's life is all."

"Nonsense. You were all by yourself, as it were, taking care of Hannah when your mother couldn't be counted on. Your parents were both gone by the time you were a teenager. And so you protect yourself against more loss by not getting close to anyone. It's no wonder you're afraid to pull the trigger."

He shot her an incredulous look. "Afraid to pull the trigger?"

"Well, they call you the Revolver, don't they?"

"Geez, Cookie. Where'd you hear that?"

"The ladies at the beauty shop talk, Colton." She sighed. "Out of love for you, sometimes you need to hear things. I hope you understand that. Plus there is my need for great-grandchildren."

"Sara's not going to stay around here. She's meant for bigger things."

She shrugged, turning her palms up to the ceiling. "Well then, I guess there's no use in trying. Or asking her what *she* wants." She got up from the couch but didn't turn away. "I know you were sweet on her in high school, but you deferred to Tagg. But Tagg's out of the picture now. The only thing stopping you is yourself."

Was Cookie right? Had he been protecting himself? "I'll think about what you said."

She smiled and patted his calf again. "Well, you have plenty of time to do just that, don't you?"

* * *

Just Sara's luck. Of course she would get the job of chopping onions for the salad the night of the big family dinner, which happened to be at Dad and Rachel's house this week. And pungent onions they were, making her eyes leak and her nose run as she sat at the big kitchen island.

Rachel passed by on her way to the stove and squeezed her shoulder. "You OK?" she asked.

"Killer onions," Sara responded with a watery smile. Yep, her tears were all the fault of the onions. Not at all due to a certain cop who had friend-zoned her. Revolved her. Because that's what he did.

"Where's Malcolm, by the way?" Evie asked Gabby, who was tossing the salad. Through the big paned window, they could see their dad grilling his specialty salmon while Rafe and Joe played ball with the kids.

"He's lying down upstairs," Gabby said. "He had a sinus headache and needed a little quiet time."

Sara hoped he'd find it now, because once they were all around the table, quiet was going to go right out the window.

"Who's Malcolm?" Nonna asked. She sat at the island slicing strawberries for the top of the Jell-O salad.

"That's Gabby's sweetie, Nonna," Evie said, sneaking a strawberry. She turned to Sara. "Speaking of sweeties, how's Colton?"

"He's not my sweetie," Sara said, chopping more vigorously.

"You do know you're chopping the onions into microscopic pieces, don't you?" Evie asked.

"Oh! Sorry!" Sara set down the knife.

Gabby brought Sara a beer. "Everything all right?"

She smiled and took the beer. "I'm fine. Thanks,

Gabs." Or at least she would be, once she stopped thinking about *him*. It had been a week since she'd poured out her heart and he'd handed it back to her.

A loud siren bleat suddenly sounded from outside the house. Then another and another. It sounded like all the rescue vehicles the town owned had come to a stop in their driveway.

"Colton's here," Rachel announced as they rushed into the dining room to see what the commotion was all about. "And every other emergency services person in town."

Colton's here. The words hardly registered. Sara pulled back the dining room curtain only to find an EMS unit, a police car, and a fire engine, lights flashing. Dear God. She looked around, sniffed the air. Just the smells of a delicious dinner cooking. Was the house on fire and they didn't even know it?

"I saw Nonna pick up the phone a few minutes ago," Gabby said. "You don't think she could've..."

Oh Lord. Dialed 911. Nonna?

Nonna was at Rachel's side, innocently peering out the window. "Here comes Colton," she said. "My, that man is good-looking, even without his uniform on. And look, he's carrying flowers!"

"Flowers? To an emergency?" Rafe said, coming in from the backyard with the other men and the kids. Everyone gathered around the windows as if Sara were sixteen and getting picked up for a date. Except for the sirens wailing.

"Oh, I wanted him to come," Nonna said. "I called 911."

Evie rushed to Nonna's side. "You're kidding, aren't you, Nonna?"

Maybe Nonna didn't hear over all the commotion because all she said was, "I haven't seen a fire engine this close up in a long time."

It didn't appear that the house was burning down, Colton was here, and he had flowers. Anticipation fizzed up and bubbled over inside Sara like too much soft drink in a glass. She tried to tamp it down, and then finally just bypassed everyone and opened the damn door.

And there he was, looking amazing in a dark polo and khaki pants. And a suit coat, even though it was eighty-five degrees. "Everybody OK in here?" Colton asked, surveying the foyer. Sara couldn't help wondering what they all must look like, standing there gawking at him.

Nonna ran up to Colton, took the beautiful bouquet of flowers, and put them to her nose. "Oh, they're lovely! Just like the ones you brought Sara for homecoming."

Colton let that crazy comment pass and flashed a smile at Nonna. "Glad you approve, Mrs. F." His gaze scanned the foyer. "So we've got a report of a 911 call coming from this location."

"Nonna may have accidentally done it," Sara said quietly, so Nonna wouldn't hear. She rubbed her temple, where a massive headache was forming, despite the fact that dinner hadn't even begun. Sirens, trucks, flowers, Colton. Her entire family now staring at her.

A big burly firefighter appeared behind Colton, whom Sara recognized as Randall Ames, one of Rafe's friends. "OK if I go in and check around, Chief?" he asked.

"Have at it, Randy." Colt turned to Sara and smiled a big, wide smile, looking at her with an intensity that almost made her forget why they'd fought. "I think I better go out there and talk with the guys."

"Oh yes. Of course." She moved aside to let him do his job, staving the wave of disappointment that rolled over her. What was she expecting? An apology during a 911 run?

"I'll come with you," Rafe said, moving to the door.

"Just a sec," Colton said, pulling Sara aside. He dropped his voice. "I've been an ass. Forgive me." He raised her hand briefly to his lips and kissed it. "Talk later?"

Words caught in her throat. A shiver ran through her despite the warm day. Around her, her family became oddly quiet. "Um, sure," she managed.

"Oh, I almost forgot," he said, reaching into his suit coat and pulling out a long thin box. She recognized it immediately as being from the upscale candy shop downtown. "For you. Hope they're not melted."

Chocolate coconut nests. Her favorite. Stupidly, her eyes teared up, as if the chocolates were as precious as a diamond ring. "Thank you," she said, her voice sounding a little raspy and choked up.

He gave her a wink, then ran out the door to disperse the EMS people. As soon as the door shut behind him, her sisters swarmed.

"Oh, wow. He knows your favorite candy," Gabby said. "This is serious."

"He knows because he asked me," Evie said, reaching over her shoulder to steal a piece.

"So he really was coming for dinner," Rachel said. "Not just for the—um—emergency."

"I guess so," Sara said incredulously.

"Can I have one?" Nonna asked, nearing the chocolates.

"Hmm...I wonder what it means that he decided to surprise you and come to family dinner after all?" Evie said, with a little groan of pleasure over the chocolate.

"It means Sara has a boyfriend," Nonna said.

Evie reached over and tugged the apron tie at the back of Sara's neck. "Not that you don't look beautiful, but maybe you should take this off." She pulled off the apron and rolled it up in a ball.

"What's going on?" Malcolm asked, running into the foyer from upstairs.

"We had a misdialed 911 call," Gabby said quietly, nodding in Nonna's direction and putting a finger to her lips.

"Grandma did it?"

"Rachel, may I put these in a vase?" Nonna asked, holding up the bouquet.

Rachel smiled. "That would be lovely, Nonna."

"I'll help you," Gabby said, taking Nonna's hand and leading her into the kitchen. "C'mon, Malcolm, you can keep us company."

A few minutes later, Colton and Rafe walked into the kitchen, where the women were finishing up the meal preparations. Malcolm was perched on a stool at the island sipping wine, watching them work.

"Is everything OK?" Rachel asked.

"The crews were having a slow day anyway," Rafe said. "They enjoyed the excitement."

"Everything's under control," Colton said. "And the kids are loving the vehicles." He shook Rachel's hand and said, "Mrs. Langdon, hope you don't mind I showed up for dinner." He glanced at Sara. "Sara invited me off the cuff."

Sara raised a brow. Oh well, she supposed that was sort of true. But how had he even known dinner was here this week instead of at Nonna's?

"I don't know," Rafe said with mock seriousness, patting Colton's stomach. "He eats a lot, Rach. I may have to go to the store for more salmon."

"Oh, Rafe," Rachel said, chuckling. She turned to Colton. "Ignore him."

"Yeah, really. We usually do," Evie said, passing by and ruffling Rafe's hair. He scowled and smoothed it back down.

"Please, call me Rachel." Rachel took Colton by the elbow and steered him to a seat at the island. "And thanks for the flowers. We're thrilled you could join us. Your head is better?"

"Back to work tomorrow for a full day," Colton said. "Can't wait."

"Some cities charge big fines for false 911 calls," Malcolm said. "What does Angel Falls do? I mean, Grandma must've told them the house was burning down to get an engine out here."

Colton shrugged. "We have a pretty good sense of humor for accidents," he said. "A real nuisance call would be treated differently."

"Isn't anyone going to talk to her about that?" Malcolm asked. "I mean, old ladies can't just go around summoning every EMS vehicle in the county on a whim."

"Malcolm, it was an accident," Gabby said. "Chill, OK?" She turned to Colton. "It was my fault. I should have kept a better eye out. I saw Nonna hang up the phone. I didn't even think—"

"No one's to blame," Colton said. "On a positive note, the kids got to meet some firefighters and paramedics."

"I want to be a fireman," Michael said. "I wanna ride in the truck."

"I'll take you for a ride in the back of my police car after dinner, OK, Mikey?" Colton said, rubbing his head. "With your car seat, of course," he said with a wink at Evie.

"Hey," Rafe said. "Why would you want to ride in a tiny little police car when you can ride on the big engine?"

Michael jumped up and down. "I wanna go on both."

"Atta boy," Colton said.

"Maybe Michael would like to fly in my company jet," Malcolm said. "If you go to Wharton business school you could fly on a private jet one day too."

Sara didn't miss the subtle look Rafe and Colton exchanged before Michael spoke up. "No!," he said. "I want to go in the police car *and* the fire truck!"

Good boy, Mikey, Sara said to herself. She handed Colton a beer. "Are you on duty?"

"I'm on backup starting at midnight," he said.

"Then take it." She lowered her voice. "You might need it to get through this dinner." She tugged on his jacket. "Let me—um—take your coat."

"You sure I shouldn't keep it on?"

"Well, you can. But if you do, Rafe will never let you hear the end of it."

He took the beer and leaned over to whisper in her ear. "Did I tell you—you look pretty tonight."

She laughed. "You don't look so bad yourself. What made you come?"

"I missed you." He let that sink in. And oh, it did. The absolute intensity in his eyes told her he meant it. She felt it down to the marrow. Those simple words made her heart skitter and her usual redhead total body flush go into full-blown mode.

"I missed you too," she replied.

Then Rachel was calling everyone for dinner. Sara held Colton back. "Wait—how did you know dinner was here this week?"

"I didn't," he said, his lips curved up in a smile. "I was headed to Nonna's when the 911 call came in. I got lucky."

She shook her head in disbelief.

"You're important to me, Sara. I know how important this dinner is to you, and I wanted to show up."

"I'm glad you did," she said.

They all took their seats at a long outdoor table set with pretty blue dishes and matching napkins, Rachel's elegant doing. It was definitely a step above a normal backyard barbecue. OK, maybe a couple of steps. The patio was surrounded by antique statues and water features, gorgeous flowers blooming in spades. And of course her father's precious tomato plants, which he took every opportunity to explain in great detail.

"Rafe, you're the only one here without a date," Nonna said as everyone began eating. "You do like girls, don't you?" She took a sip of her wine. "I mean, it's OK if you don't. But who's going to carry on the family name if you don't, because there are no other boys in the family?"

"Grandma, rest assured," Sara said, patting Rafe on the back. "He likes girls."

"I don't need a date, Nonna," he said, wrapping an arm around Nonna. "Because I get to sit next to you." This made his siblings groan.

"Dinner's very good," Colton said, saving Rafe's ass. And gave him a look that told him so.

"Yes, dinner's fantastic," Malcolm said. "I took Gabby to a private chef tasting in New York City last month. It was around two hundred fifty bucks a head, wasn't it, babe? Every course was served in a little box, like a present you had to open. And when you'd open the box, smoke from the dry ice would waft out. Very elegant."

"Little boxes?" Nonna said. "It doesn't sound like there was much food."

"I was so hungry after that dinner, I ordered a pizza at midnight, Gran," Gabby said from Nonna's other side.

"Well, it was all about the presentation, the taste experience." Malcolm poured himself more wine—from Sara's count, his third glass. Not that she should be counting, but the more wine he consumed, the looser his tongue got.

After dinner Rafe left the table and came back with a football. "Would you boys like to play some catch?" he asked.

"Sure," Colton said. Sara tried not to give him a worried stare, but she must have, because he reached over and squeezed her hand. "It's only catch," he said and grinned.

"That's what I'm worried about. The men in this family are very competitive."

Her dad slid his chair back. "We'll keep it noncontact, sweetheart."

"Dad, not you too!" she said.

"Hey," Rafe said, smacking Colton in the stomach, "we can't have our police chief getting soft from all this sitting around."

Rafe, Colton, Malcolm, and her dad went out into the backyard and began tossing the ball while Rachel made coffee.

"So," Rachel said, giving Sara a conspiratorial look, "Gabby, sweetheart, tell us how things are going with Malcolm."

"Well," she said, "I know Malcolm can be a little direct and tell things like they are, but underneath that he's got a heart of gold. He's actually a lot of fun, and very spontaneous. He'll wake up on a Saturday and say, 'Let's drive to the beach,' and off we'll go on a wild adventure. He believes in not wasting a single second of time. He's always bringing me flowers or little gifts, and he's very affectionate in public."

That was an impressive laundry list, Sara had to admit. Seemed to her that Gabby, in her quest to get the life she wanted, was trying hard to focus on the positives and completely ignore the negatives. But Sara knew her sister deserved more than just to settle.

"Owww!" They heard a yelp of pain from the yard. Sara's first thought was that Colton had hit his head again. She was out of her seat and in the yard in an instant, but no one was on the ground. But Malcolm was standing beside the patio cursing a blue streak and holding a very bloody nose. Rachel arrived with a box of Kleenex she'd grabbed from the kitchen. "I sent Gabby for paper towels," she said to Sara. "What else do we need?"

"Maybe an ice pack," Sara said as she moved to inspect the damage.

"I threw him a pass, and it hit him in the face," Colton said sheepishly.

"Yeah, thanks a lot, Colton," Malcolm said loudly. "I think my nose is broken."

Chapter 18

♥

Colton understood that bloodying Gabby's fiancé's nose had probably not been the best way to make an impression. Between the 911 call and Malcolm's inappropriate comments, it had been a not to-be-missed dinner.

All he'd wanted to do was make up to Sara for pushing her away. Cookie had made him face up to some uncomfortable truths he hadn't wanted to face, but Colton was no coward. And Sara was more important to him than his fears. So he'd decided to show up at her family dinner, and with a little help from Nonna's 911 call, he'd made it. But the evening was degenerating fast.

"It wasn't your fault," Rafe said after Gabby and Sara led Malcolm away to ice his nose. "The jerk started to talk about what a great football player he was in the middle of the pass. He looked away."

"Did you hear how he talks about Gabby?" Joe said. "'I've been trying to get her to lift weights to tone up and lose those ten extra pounds.' I mean, who talks about their fiancée like that? You should've taken him out completely, Colton. Would've been better for everyone concerned."

"We cannot let Gabby marry this guy," Rafe said.

"Now, boys," Dr. Langdon said, catching up with them as they walked toward the perfectly manicured hill leading up to the house. "Let's not forget to be charitable." He paused. "Wait a minute. He said that about Gabby's weight? I may have to take him out myself."

"So Colton, how's your head?" Dr. Langdon asked after Rafe and Joe went to grab another beer. Colton refrained. He wanted to be clearheaded in case he got called out later.

"Much better, sir. I'm looking forward to getting back to doing everything I enjoy." Oh, hell, that came out wrong. "Like sports and stuff," he added hurriedly.

"You've got a tough job, son. You're on call more than we docs are. The worst thing I have to fear most days is a kid puking on me. I never give a thought to physical harm."

Colton shrugged. "This is my town and I'm responsible for protecting and serving every citizen in it. It's a privilege to do it, so I don't mind the hours. As for never knowing what you're going to walk into—well, I'm sure it's like that for you too. Medical emergencies are unpredictable too. I guess I don't spend too much energy thinking about that, just try to be as prepared as I can. In those situations, instinct tends to take over."

"You're a brave man. But you've chosen a tough life in which to raise a family. Hard on the wife and kids."

This conversation was taking a turn. Sounded like Dr.

Langdon was subtly warning him away from his daughter. Colton didn't know what to say. Because he'd lived that life firsthand ever since he was born. Everything Dr. Langdon was saying was the truth; he couldn't deny it.

Dr. Langdon's comments reminded him that he'd come here to make things right with Sara. That meant being honest with her—about his job, and about how he felt about her.

He was grateful when Sara interrupted their conversation. "Dad, Nonna's tired. I'm going to take her home."

Colton stood. "I'll come with you."

He liked and respected Sara's father, and understood he wanted the best for his daughter. Tagg had always spoken fondly of him. He used to tell Colton about how they'd golf together, talk about patients, and attend medical conferences. Dr. Langdon certainly hadn't found anything to disapprove of about Tagg's job.

Colton got up and shook Dr. Langdon's hand and thanked Rachel for dinner. Family dinner hadn't been so bad. Yet he couldn't quite help wondering if Dr. Langdon would prefer for his daughter a guy who wrote prescriptions and not tickets.

* * *

Colton waited on the porch swing with Rocket while Sara helped her grandmother to bed. She was a little breathless when she finally came back outside and sat down next to him.

"You made us coffee?" she asked, noting the cups set out on the little table.

"It's decaf." He handed her a cup. "Cream only, right?" She looked pleased about the coffee. Good, because he wanted to please her and let her know he was trying to be the man she needed. But he also needed her to understand a few things.

"Perfect, thanks." She took a sip. "Thank you for coming to dinner tonight," she said.

"No problem. It was…exciting. At least the 911 part was." He fell into silence, intent on balancing his coffee cup on his knee, but really working up the courage to tell her what was on his mind.

"I need to tell you something," they both said at the same time.

He set down his cup. "Can I go first?"

"Sure. Go ahead."

He took up her hands, half facing her on the swing. Gently, he rubbed his thumbs over the soft flesh of her palm. "My father was a city cop. You know that, right?"

"Yes, I remember Nonna told me you'd lost him a long time ago."

He kept holding on to her hand. "My mom used to worry about him a lot. She would stay up all hours of the night smoking cigarettes at the kitchen table, waiting for him to come home. Once he got hurt and she had to drag me out of bed in the middle of the night to go with her to the hospital. When I finally got to see my dad, he had an arm cast and his face was banged up. I was a little kid, and I guess I started crying, because he hugged me. I'll never forget what he said to me."

"Tell me," Sara said, sitting close to him, resting their joined hands on the swing.

"He said, 'Sometimes police officers get hurt so other people won't.' I think that's when I knew I wanted to be one too." He paused. "I was eight when he was killed on the job."

"Colton, I'm so sorry."

"It was during a bank robbery. He saved eight hostages."

"He was a hero." Sara's eyes were teary.

Colton smiled a little. His dad *was* a hero. Colton just wished the hero part hadn't kept him from actually having a dad. "The point is, small-town life isn't the big city. Most of my job is just being around, getting to know everyone, patrolling, keeping an eye on things. But not everyone is nice, Sara. You never know when a call's going to come that's going to take you way out of your comfort zone. It's a risk I have to live with as part of my job."

That made her tear up more. She reached out and touched the area around his stitches. "It was awful, seeing you hurt like that."

"The other night in the hospital, I thought I could push you away. I didn't want you to see me like that. I didn't want to put anybody through the kind of pain I saw my mom go through. It brought back too many bad memories."

"Colton, I couldn't not come." Her voice was low and hoarse. "When my dad called, I had to be with you. Seeing you was all I could think of."

Yeah, he got that—how upset she was, how much she cared. She'd worn it all over her face that night, and he could see the tenderness now in her eyes. He owed her more, the whole truth, so he forced himself to go on.

"Truth is, I told Sandy we were just friends because I was afraid."

"Afraid of what?" Her eyes were big and round.

He held her by the shoulders. Tucked a strand of hair behind her ear. "Of how I feel about you. I want to be more than friends, Sara. I want to give this a real shot. And I want to ask you if you'd be my girlfriend."

There, he'd said it, and oh God, she was really tearing up now. He held her face in his hands, wiped away her tears with his thumbs.

He moved his hands along her jawline, angled her face, and kissed her, slowly and tenderly. Her lips were soft—hell, she was soft and sweet in his arms and he got lost in the simple act of kissing her, of exploring every inch of her mouth, of holding her in his arms. Nothing had ever felt so absolutely right.

"What happens if I say yes to the girlfriend thing?" she murmured.

"You get more kisses," he said with a grin. Their lips met again, more thoroughly, more insistently. God, he'd missed her. It had been a week since he'd kissed her, but it had felt like a year. He moved his hands through the silky thickness of her hair and tugged her closer while she slid her arms around his waist.

He was just contemplating the pros and cons of doing her under the porch swing when he became suddenly aware of headlights spotlighting them. Rafe's truck pulled up the drive, the wheels spitting out gravel. He got out and walked up to the porch.

"Rafe, what's wrong?" Sara asked.

"I came to spend the night with Nonna."

Oh my God, Colton loved this guy. "You sure you don't have a date or something?" Colton asked.

"Nope. So I can sleep here, right? That's all I have to do? And when I get up in the morning, if I'm lucky she'll make me breakfast?"

"Something like that," Sara said.

Colton stood up and pulled him in with a bro handshake. "Thanks."

Rafe lowered his voice. "You know I love you, but if you hurt my sister you're a dead man."

"Got it," Colton said.

"See you tomorrow, Sis."

Sara hugged her brother. "Thanks, Rafe."

* * *

Sara followed Colton into his apartment. Champ was happy to see her but even more happy to go outside with Colton to relieve himself. Sara had just enough time to dash into Colton's bathroom and use his mouthwash. OK, so she'd managed to relax quite a bit, but she still couldn't help having some type A moments.

Colton found her on the couch, leafing through a *Time* magazine she was pretending to read. Champ came bounding over, grabbing a tennis ball from somewhere and depositing the wet slimy thing in her lap. She petted his glossy black coat. "Well, hello there, handsome. You're in the mood to play, aren't you?"

Colton sat down next to her and threw the ball for his dog, who tore off across the living room chasing it. He looked at her with an unholy gaze that sent a shiver racing down her spine. This time, when Champ dropped the ball into her lap, Colton tossed it as far away as he could. "Champ can wait," he said, his mouth curving into a smile.

Then he was kissing her, toppling her to the couch, his delicious weight over her. He kissed her thoroughly, his hands roving everywhere, murmuring wonderful things like how much he'd missed her and how lucky he felt to be with her. This was her crack, this love talk, which, she was discovering, he used quite frequently. He could mumble his grocery list like that and she'd surely melt just as easily into his arms.

Speaking of arms, somehow his shirt was off, and she found herself encased by a pair of rock-solid biceps. She wrapped her arms around his lean waist, slid them up his back, feeling the hills and valleys of muscle, the soft skin over the flexing, sculpted firmness.

Of course the dog trotted back, tennis ball in his teeth, nudging both of them with it. Colton turned to Champ and patted him on the head. "Sorry, buddy. Go in your bed."

The dog crossed the room, tail between his legs, and slunk into his bed. No surprise he listened. Who wasn't under this man's spell?

Colton smiled from above her on the couch. He had such full lips for a man, and skillful too, running them along her stomach, using one hand to open her bra with one quick flick. Then his mouth was on her breast, and she was arching and reaching for him, and somehow in the shedding of the clothes they ended up on the floor. Sensation spilled over her in waves, and all she knew was how he was touching her, kissing her, using his clever mouth to bring her to a place where words couldn't form, where there were only the two of them and nothing and no one else. She marveled at how perfectly they fit together, how they moved, how everything felt so...effortlessly right.

"Sara, I...Now. OK?" She smiled at his lost words, the struggle for control. In the fever pitch of the moment, all she could do was nod. He reached for a condom and before he entered her, he looked at her. No, not just looked—he *saw* her in a way no one had ever seen her before. That one resounding moment shattered her and she knew—just knew—this was it. *He* was it. She wrapped herself around him and clung to him, telling him with her body what she could not say. How could she say it? His coming to family dinner was a big deal. It had been difficult for him just to ask her to be in a relationship. Mentioning the L word would surely send him running for the hills.

Then he was inside her, moving, starting a rhythm that swept all thought away. And there was just him, his body, his lips, the clean scent of him that was so familiar and comforting, the confident way he moved and touched her—it was all him, only him.

They came together, shattering quickly and absolutely, and when it was done they lay there on the floor, tangled up in each other. Colton drew her into him so that her head was resting on his shoulder, his big arms wrapped around her perfectly. They were both a little sweaty. He smoothed her hair back from her face. She curled an arm around his waist, and they lay there together, their breathing slowing.

He kissed the top of her head.

"Was this our first makeup sex?" she asked, running

her hand along his chest, over the soft, light coating of hair that lined his muscles.

"Um, I think so. Why?"

"Because if it is, I mean—wow. Maybe we should disagree more often."

"Or maybe I should come to family dinner more often." He chuckled. And then he kissed her again.

* * *

Colton found her on his couch at four in the morning, writing on a legal pad and glancing at her laptop, and took a seat beside her. He kissed her cheek, then asked, "What are you doing awake?" They should both be sleeping like the dead, in his opinion.

"I'm a little excited. We've got a decorator coming to the office tomorrow who wants our input about paint, and we're ordering new waiting room furniture and some paintings to hang on the walls. And I had an idea about how we could actually schedule my dad more half-hour visits so he could spend time with his more complicated patients and still keep the office moving. My goal is to actually have us all leave the office by five p.m. I've already got us starting a little earlier, and I even blocked a half hour out for lunch."

She seemed happier and more relaxed than he'd ever seen her. Well, except during their lovemaking. She definitely seemed happy and relaxed then. "Sounds like things at the office are going better."

"I'm learning tips from my dad, like how to focus down on the immediate problem. He's got so much experience. Plus he knows any rash this side of the Mississippi. And he's been asking me about new treatment options he's not as familiar with. It's...I don't know. I feel like it's starting to work."

"That's great. Sounds like a real partnership."

She looked at him and smiled. Her hair was mussed. She was wearing one of his T-shirts and a pair of his boxers, and she looked like the sweetest thing he'd ever seen. "Yeah. I hope so."

"I'm really happy for you," he said, gently nudging the laptop from her hands and shutting it. Then he nuzzled her neck.

"Well, it's getting there. And I'm really getting to know people again. Guess who I saw yesterday? Mr. Campanella."

He continued to kiss her neck. This time she extended it, giving him better access. "Our trig teacher?"

"Yep. He retired, did you know that? I'm starting to feel like I'm becoming part of the community. Or at least I hope so. I keep working towards that."

"Sara, all you have to do is be yourself and I'm certain you will." She liked her job, she liked Angel Falls. Music to his ears. "Besides, I'd certainly love it if you stayed. And I've been thinking."

She blushed, which he took as a good sign. "About what?"

"I have a few new ideas I'd like to discuss with you too."

"Oh, is that right?"

He took the pen out of her hand. Placed the legal pad on the coffee table. And proceeded to show her exactly what he meant.

Chapter 19

♥

Sara went into the office early Monday morning to catch up on paperwork, entering through the staff entrance in the back. At 8:10, she remembered the meeting with the decorator about the waiting room redo. As she walked into the hallway from her office, she heard voices from beyond the reception window. She was on her way to join everyone when she saw that the green flag had been lifted in front of one of the exam room doors, which meant the room was occupied. Sure enough, a chart was in the door.

She walked around the counter and peeked into the waiting room to ask her dad if it was one of his patients, but everyone was excitedly weighing in on fabric swatches.

"Burnt sienna is really popular right now," the decorator, Claire Hutton, was saying. "We could do that in a vinyl on the waiting room chairs and alternate with aqua chairs. And I've got this fun pattern here that we could mix and match in between the other two. What do you think?"

Her dad pulled his bifocals down on his nose, deep in contemplation.

"I think after thirty years anything's an improvement," Leonore said, catching Sara's eye through the window and winking.

Sara decided not to bother them and go see the patient for herself. She'd just pulled the chart from the slot and turned the doorknob when Leonore came bursting into the back office. "Sara, wait!" she said excitedly, waving her arms. "He insisted on seeing your father as a sick visit. Don't go in there!"

Too late. She'd already opened the door. There, sitting with his long legs dangling off the exam table, was Tagg

Tagg. After an entire year. She didn't trust herself to close the door behind her. She might murder him, and with the door open, maybe someone could stop her before it was too late. On the other hand, she didn't want anyone hearing whatever he had to say. Closing the door won, after she'd signaled to poor Leonore that everything was OK. Maybe.

"Tagg," she said on an exhalation, trying to suck in deep, calming breaths as she approached him. "How did you get in here?" She'd known that sooner or later their paths would cross, although he seemed to be making every effort to ensure that that didn't happen. Except for the paperwork she'd had to fill out to give him her half of their house, she hadn't heard a peep from him. So why was he here, masquerading as a patient?

His big brown eyes swiveled over to her. She used to love those dark, mysterious eyes—used to think they were honest eyes. His shiny ink-black hair and full lips were so familiar to her, yet knowing him seemed like a lifetime ago.

She thought of all the times she'd looked at that face. Loved that face. They'd shared a lot together, over ten-plus years of life, there was no denying. For just a moment, it was as if none of the ugliness had happened and it was just another day, when he'd somehow come to joke around and say hey before his own workday began.

But Tagg's face wasn't the same innocent face she'd once loved. He wasn't the person she'd once thought he was.

"What are you doing here?" she asked.

"I had to see you, Sara. I'm dying." He placed his hands over his chest.

He was sitting there calm as could be. Definitely not in any distress. "Quit clowning around."

"I'm not clowning around. Look at my chart." He pointed with a fine, long-fingered hand to the manila folder resting near the sink.

She did. It read, simply, "Chest pain."

Chest pain? A nagging feeling in her gut told her something was up. Even if he was serious, she wasn't about to collect his medical history. And she certainly wasn't going to examine him.

"I can't see you as a patient." She walked to the door and put a hand on the doorknob. "Let me get my dad."

"Wait," he called out. "Why can't you just see me? I'll cooperate, I promise."

Who cared if he cooperated? She was too annoyed

to see him, and the fact that she was truly irritated with him filled her with relief. That pining feeling, that yearning she'd felt in spite of herself for much of the last year was... gone. In the past year she'd often imagined meeting him again, and the thought had filled her with dread. She'd pictured running into him and his girl-friend on the street, maybe even seeing them strolling an adorable, drooly baby, Valerie wearing a diamond the size of a golf ball and proclaiming their love. And the same feelings would overtake her, that she simply hadn't been enough. She'd been the woman someone could bail on two days before their wedding and never think of again.

But strangely, she didn't feel like that lonely, dis placed person, the object of pity. She felt no sadness, no dread, no longing. Her heart wasn't racing. Nor were her thoughts. She just wanted to move on with her day.

Colton had already sent her a pic of Champ looking adoringly into his phone, captioned We both miss you already. And just then, as if she'd conjured him, her phone vibrated. Is Tagg in there? read the text. I see his car out front.

Of course Tagg had probably parked his Popsicle-red Porsche on the street, with its license plate TAGG IM IT. Conspicuous consumption at its finest, that was Tagg.

She ignored the text for now. She doubted Tagg was having a heart attack, but if he was, she didn't want it to be on her conscience that she'd botched the diagnosis. Although it was tempting to do just that.

"Just a minute," she said, and walked out into the hall. She avoided the reception area, instead going to the only other exam room with a closed door and knocking.

Her dad poked his head out.

"Dad, how long will you be in there?" she asked.

"I'm seeing Clara Ridgeway."

Oh God. A lonely senior who was also a hypochondriac. That meant a half hour at least.

"Anything I can help you with, honey?"

"It can wait until after you're through."

Her phone vibrated again. Are you OK? She shoved it into her Leonore-pouch and reentered the exam room.

"Are you having chest pain now?" she asked.

"Yes, yes I am." He splayed his fingers over his chest and grimaced.

She glanced at her watch. Chest pain could be a complicated diagnosis, but the workup was fairly straightforward. Tagg was also a smart guy—and a doctor. If something were seriously wrong, he would have taken himself to the ER. This whole situation smelled like bad cheese.

"Maybe you should head over to the ER," Sara said.

"No," he said, quite adamantly. "I came to see you. I-I want to discuss my problem with you."

"Where does it hurt?"

He moved the palm of his hand over his chest. "All over."

"How often and how long does it last? And does it happen during activity or at rest? Any fever or shortness of breath?"

"It's come and gone for about a year now, but it's been nearly constant for the past month."

"How severe is it, and any radiation down your arm?"

"No radiation. But it nearly doubles me over sometimes."

"Palpitations, skipped beats, strange rhythms?" She ran through all the usual questions, although the hair on the back of her neck was prickling. Nothing was adding up, but at the same time she didn't want to ignore a weird or unusual problem that needed to be dealt with ASAP.

She unwound her stethoscope from her neck and approached him. "Let me have a listen and then we'll do an office EKG, OK?" She took his wrist and timed his pulse. "It's steady, and you're not tachycardic."

Suddenly he grabbed her hand. The abrupt movement startled her.

"Sara," he said, looking her in the eye, "I screwed up. Bad. I'm so sorry. My life's been hell without you."

Sara pulled her hand away. "Tagg, what are you thinking? I'm at work. There are people who are *sick* here, for God's sake."

"I didn't think you'd talk to me any other way."

"You were right." Her boldness shocked her a little, and her heart thumped hard in her chest. But she wasn't backing down. This time she was going to say what she should've said long ago. "It's been a year, Tagg. One whole year. Surely you've had other opportunities to contact me."

He at least had the decency to look sheepish. "I was embarrassed. With every day that passed, I felt more and more ashamed about what I'd done." She shook her head and backed up, but he grabbed her elbow. She used to love that he'd always been a little touchy-feely, but not anymore.

"Look," he continued. "We dated for such a long time. As it got closer and closer to our wedding, I kept thinking I never got to sow my wild oats. It was like I had this monster inside of me, always wondering what it would be like to date someone else because I never did."

She crossed her arms. "You'd think you'd have come to that conclusion sooner than two days before our wedding."

"I panicked. Maybe there's even something admirable about that, wanting to get that out of my system, not committing because I wasn't ready. I mean, what if we'd gone through with it? Imagine starting a marriage feeling like that."

The look in his eyes told her he believed what he was saying. Although she had an entirely different word for him, and it wasn't *admirable*.

"I know I embarrassed you and you're right to be angry with me, but I understand myself so much better now. And I've come to understand there's no one like you, Sara. No one. You're beautiful and good and kind, and you were the best thing that ever happened to me. I was a huge fool. I hate myself every day for what I did to you. I hope you can forgive me."

"Where's Valerie?" Sara asked. "Is she in the waiting room?"

"We...broke up." He looked embarrassed. "OK, she left me. But that was because I kept comparing her to you."

He was the picture of earnestness. Sara knew him well enough to know he was in pain. But she also understood what had happened to them so much better now. Tagg hadn't admitted to himself that he hadn't loved her the way he needed to until he'd done something really stupid. And she hadn't had the courage to leave their relationship because it had been too damn comfortable.

As with so many other things in her life, she'd gone with the flow to live up to other people's expectations. Getting A's, going to the best schools, achieving, achieving, achieving. Staying with Tagg because he was the "right" kind of guy, one who lived up to her dad's expectations. Not that the achieving part had been a bad thing, but why had she been so afraid to rebel a little? Choose what *she* wanted?

"Tagg, you're forgiven," she said, placing her hand over his. She meant it too. She now saw the whole embarrassing event as a relief, an opportunity to start over that she would've missed. She would have missed *Colton*, and never known what the possibility of true happiness looked like.

Speaking of Colton, her phone vibrated again in her pocket.

Tagg stood and took both her hands. Maybe it was the blue gown that made him seem extra vulnerable, but she did feel sorry for him. "I hope you can see it in your heart to give me another chance. If you do, I promise I'll be faithful to you until the day I die."

"Tagg, you were my first boyfriend. My first everything. We supported each other through those really tough med school years. We believed in each other's dreams. But the rest of it…it wasn't right. *We* weren't right. I'm sorry." She dropped her hands and walked over to the door.

He followed her. "I want to prove to you I've changed. Give me another chance, Sara. Please."

She felt really…bad for him. But his feelings weren't her concern anymore. It was Colton she needed to check in with, which meant responding to his texts ASAP. "I'm sorry, Tagg." Then she opened the door and left.

In the hall it was so quiet you could've heard someone slice cake. She walked through the office to the reception desk. Leonore and Glinda were staring at her, wide-eyed. Her father was leaning on the counter, writing up a chart, and to his credit, he didn't even look up. Behind the open reception window was Colton, standing there quietly.

Thank God. She didn't want him worrying, and now she could put his mind at ease in person.

The exam room door opened, and Tagg stepped out into the hall, tucking in his shirt.

"Dr. Langdon! A pleasure to see you, sir." Tagg extended a hand. For a long second, her father stared down his nose over the top of his bifocals in that way he had of quietly assessing everyone he met.

"Hey, Colt! How's it going?" Tagg asked, giving Colton a wave. Colton nodded back, his jaw spring-loaded like a mouse trap, ready to crush and kill.

"Taggart," her dad said cautiously. "What brings you back to town?"

"I came to beg Sara for forgiveness," he said, his eyes darting around at everyone. Judging by the looks on their faces, Leonore and Glinda were definitely thinking this was better than Netflix. As were the handful of people in the waiting room. Leonore sat at the reception desk, arms folded staunchly across her ample chest. Glinda held a syringe in her hand, ready to inject at a moment's notice.

"And you've got it," Sara said, her face turning its usual fifty shades of red. Now would he just leave already?

"But I want more than that. I want you. And I want everyone to know. Complete honesty from here on out."

"Isn't it a little too late for that?" Colton asked. He was frowning, and his steely gaze was boring a hole through Tagg.

"Oh my," her dad said. His gaze swung back and forth between Tagg and Colton, but he didn't say anything, just cleared his throat. Maybe he'd decided not to touch that one with a ten-foot pole.

In the old days her dad would have made small talk, or hugged Tagg, or at least given him a friendly slap on the back. Not so today—thank you, Daddy. He did, however, turn to Colton. "Have a nice day, son," he said, giving him a wave before he left to see his next patient.

Colton, in true cop form, scanned all the players, nodded at her father, and addressed Sara. "How are you?"

"Oh, good. Thanks for asking." She couldn't help

the near-hysterical giggle that bubbled up her throat. God, she just needed Tagg to leave already.

Colt eyed her carefully. Then his gaze flitted to Tagg, his eyes narrowing a little. It struck Sara that this was how he might look during target practice.

"Colton," Tagg said, walking past Sara and out into the waiting room to embrace his friend. "Long time no see. What are you doing here?"

Colton's gaze landed on Sara, who held her breath while waiting for what he was about to say.

"I saw your car out front," he said casually. "Came in to say hello."

"I was just leaving. Walk out with me?"

"I have a minute, sure."

Tagg actually walked back into the reception area and kissed Sara on the cheek. "We'll talk more later, OK?"

Ugh, that was just like him. What had she not made clear? After a year, did he actually think simply waltzing in and apologizing would bring everything back to the way it had been?

Oh man, Colton's jaw was so tight you could bounce a quarter off it, and a muscle at his temple was twitching. Maybe she should have shut Tagg down immediately by telling him about Colton. But she didn't want drama in front of the entire office. Colton would understand and no doubt tell Tagg himself.

"Take care, folks," Colton said a little stiffly. "Have a good morning, Sara," he said, as he and Tagg walked out the door.

Her morning schedule was on the counter. First up

was Troy Cummings, a two-year-old whose mother Holly worried endlessly about every sniffle. Holly's own mother had passed away shortly before Troy was born, and she needed lots of reassurance. Sara would also be seeing an elderly patient from the nursing home with diabetes, a bad heart, and lung problems, and a recent widower, Mr. Stevens, whose bunions were bothering him for the second time in a week but who probably just needed a little TLC.

Despite all the turmoil this morning, Sara was really looking forward to her day. Seeing her patients. Plus she felt that a huge weight she'd been dragging behind her for a year had been cut free.

"You OK, sweetheart?" her dad asked in a quiet voice. "If I would have known it was that pea brain, I would have taken care of him myself. You should've told me."

God love her dad. He never said an unkind word about anyone, but calling Tagg a pea brain was about the most wonderful thing anyone could say to her right now. She even teared up a little.

"Dad, I always thought you liked Tagg."

Her dad took off his glasses and eyeballed her. "No, honey, *you* always liked Tagg. I just supported your choice, like I've supported whatever you wanted in life."

Sara blanched. Could she really have gotten it so wrong all these years? "But I always thought you thought he was the perfect guy for me."

"I appreciated his ambition, but I always felt he had his eye on anything and everything beyond his reach. The most prestigious job, better cars, better fiancées, that kind of thing. He was never one to be happy with what he had. But then, he didn't really show his true colors until last year, did he?"

"How could I not know you felt this way?"

"I try to think the best of people. Sometimes I'm wrong, of course. But you're an adult now. You can figure out what you want for yourself."

What else had she been wrong about? Her dad's constant push to have her succeed—his hints about her continuing the fellowship she would've started last year—how did he really feel about that? And hadn't he just told her now it mattered more what she wanted for herself than what he wanted?

Well, she finally knew what she wanted. Colton.

* * *

Colton turned over in his brain what he'd just seen and heard. Tagg was going to talk to Sara later? He'd kissed her on the cheek and she'd said . . . nothing?

Jesus, Colton's stomach was churning as he walked outside with Tagg.

It was a bright morning, but clouds were building, making the sun look a little watery.

"It's great to see you, man," Tagg said, slapping him on the back. "And Sara. God, I've missed her."

The acid feeling in Colton's stomach crept up to his esophagus. He was definitely going to have to break out the Tums.

"I've been such an idiot." Tagg paused and leveled his gaze at Colton.

"Things not working out with Val?" Colton asked. Shocker if they weren't.

"I knew Val and I weren't going to last forever. It just ran its course. But being with her helped me understand how much I'm really in love with Sara. Thank God she's still single." Tagg smiled and Colton clenched his fists.

"A year's a long time. Anything could happen."

Tagg didn't seem to hear. "The one good thing that came of this was that I finally cut myself free and got to explore who I really was. After ten years of dating one woman I felt entitled to that."

Yes, entitled. Something Colton had come to realize was part of Tagg's character. He'd never really noticed it before. Or he'd ignored it. Now Colton felt entitled to pick him up by his skinny neck and shake him, but somehow refrained.

"I screwed up, Colton. I'll do anything to get Sara back. I heard you two are on good terms now. I may need you to go to bat for me, to tell her this was just a crazy phase."

A crazy phase, canceling your wedding to the woman you were supposed to love on a whim and moving in with someone you barely knew?

Colton was reminded of the times he'd deferred to Tagg, because Tagg and his family had done so much for him. They'd given him a real family as an example, and Tagg's dad had helped Colton stay on the straight and narrow, and for that he'd always be grateful. For years he'd had Tagg's enduring loyalty—Tagg had always thought Colton was cool, and Colton had liked that. It had made him feel important.

He didn't need to feel important anymore. Tagg had lied and had potentially cost Colton years with Sara. Water under the bridge, but still. Once upon a time, his dedication to Tagg had known no bounds, but maybe it was time to consider that debt repaid in full.

More important, he wanted to tell Tagg to stay the hell away from Sara. *Mine* was the word that kept drumming through his head. But something stopped him. His own fear, maybe, that Sara might possibly want Tagg back? She'd certainly tolerated that kiss on the cheek. And the fact that she was going to talk to him later? He didn't know. She'd looked a little shocked, a little confused. All he knew was he needed to talk to her.

"I want to ask Dr. Langdon to set up a meeting for me with the new neurology group in town. And hopefully he'll drop a bug in their ear that I'm a hometown son and a perfect future candidate for their practice. Dr. Langdon golfs with them, and I'm pretty sure he'll put in a good word for me."

Colton wasn't so sure that Sara's father would put in a good word for the guy who'd broken his daughter's heart. "So you're planning on moving back to town?" Colton asked. Tagg lived about an hour away, nearer to his job.

"I want to be closer to Sara. She forgave me, even though I can tell she's still angry. I know I hurt her. Part of me was rebelling against my parents pushing so hard for our marriage, but now I understand why they love Sara so much. She's the best. I'll never find anyone better. I don't know how you've done it, going from woman to woman all these years. It's exhausting. All I want is my old life back."

Save it for your shrink, buddy, a voice in Colton's head said.

Colton wanted to hit something. A punching bag, Tagg's pristine face. Both decent-size targets. He clenched his fists repeatedly to try to knead out some of the tension. Wasn't working.

He'd heard this same speech from Tagg in one form or another for years, the gist being that he'd always wondered what else was out there. He'd always defaulted to Sara, though, until the bachelor party. As far as Colt knew, Tagg had never cheated on Sara before then. Colton had never said anything to Sara—hadn't felt it was his place— but maybe he should have.

The difference this time, despite the subtle dig about Colton's love life, was that maybe Tagg really *had* learned his lesson. This time he seemed dead serious, and when Tagg set his mind to something, he usually got it. What if Sara wanted him back too?

As Colton's mind wandered, he noticed a white blur moving in the shrubbery next to the office. Sure enough, there was a little white dog peeing in the boxwood. On closer inspection he saw it wasn't just any dog, but a poodle, a super-groomed one, with painted toenails and bright pink bows in its hair.

"Dolly?" he called. The dog stopped peeing and froze.

Tagg's beeper went off. "I've got to get this. I've got a head trauma patient in the unit who's really sick. Hello," he said into his phone while Colton walked toward the dog. "His intracranial pressure's increasing? Let's give him more Solu-Medrol and call neurosurgery to schedule him for craniotomy, OK? I'll be there as soon as I can."

Colton bent down and pulled out the emergency dog biscuit he always kept in his shirt pocket. "Come here, Dolly. We'll find your mama, OK? Come get a cookie." He looked up and down the street. No one running down the street frantically panicking...yet.

At the sound of *cookie*, the dog practically leaped onto the biscuit, making it easy for Colton to scoop her right into his arms.

"What the hell?" Tagg said, laughing, as he looked at the dog, who was now sniffing Colton's pocket for another biscuit.

"Mrs. Nelson's dog," Colton said.

Just then Maggie Nelson, who ran Angelfood, the gourmet chocolate place, and Cindy Madison, the dog groomer, came running down the street, exclaiming over Dolly's misbehavior.

"Gotta go, buddy," Tagg said, climbing behind the wheel of his car. "Let's have dinner one night soon."

Colton stood there holding the poodle, who was now licking his face. Tagg was off saving critically ill people while he was here nipping an overgroomed poodle's dream of freedom in the bud. The question was, which guy would Sara prefer?

Chapter 20

♥

Later that afternoon, Colton was standing on a stepladder working on his grandmother's porch roof trying not to think about upsetting things, like Tagg wanting Sara back. Aiden had told him he'd seen a loose downspout, and Colton thought he'd give it a quick fix before he met Sara for dinner at Fallside, the popular multideck restaurant downtown that sat practically on top of the falls.

Logic told him Sara cared for him, a lot. But Tagg could be persuasive and charming, and he and Sara had a long history together. Plus they had similar backgrounds and their parents belonged to the same social circles. The list of how they were alike and he and Sara were different seemed a mile long.

Tonight was his first real date with Sara. But he wasn't really in the mood for it. He'd kept thinking of Tagg all day, wondering about Sara's reaction. There'd been no time to talk with her this afternoon, and it was eating him alive.

That was probably why he cut himself on the jagged rim of the disconnected spout. Nothing serious, but his thumb started bleeding.

He stopped in the kitchen to run water over his cut and wrapped it in a paper towel while he hunted for a Band-Aid. No luck in the kitchen or the downstairs bathroom, so he ran up to the bathroom at the top of the stairs, the one Hannah had appropriated. The narrow sink was lined with bottles of stuff he didn't recognize and a curling iron that looked ready to fall into the sink. He'd have to warn her about that hazard. He opened the medicine cabinet above the sink.

He found the Band-Aids, all right. Right behind a little pink wheel of birth control pills.

He forgot all about his bleeding finger and stared at the thing. Picked it up, even though he knew it wasn't his business. Some of the pills were popped out of the foil backing. He flipped it over. There was a pharmacy label. "Sara Langdon, MD, Langdon Family Practice."

With fumbling fingers, he replaced the wheel and shut the cabinet. Leaned over the sink. He felt a little sick. One, because his sister was taking the pill. Having sex. With the guy he'd brought to the house, a kid he'd tried to help get into electrician school. Two, and worse, because Sara had prescribed them.

He forced himself to calm down enough to wrap a damn Band-Aid around his finger, but it took him two tries.

Colton leaned over the sink and heaved a big sigh, avoiding his reflection, which looked panicky. He was the father figure in Hannah's life, and sometimes the boundary between that and being her big brother got blurred. But he was responsible for her. It was his job to protect her future, to make sure she had a great life. That meant sending her to college and making sure she was free to make choices he'd never been free to make. That didn't include something like this. A guy who was wrong for her, who could alter her future plans. A guy she was having sex with at eighteen!

Dammit, why hadn't he talked to her himself? He'd trusted Sara to do the right thing.

This was not the right thing. This was disaster.

* * *

Sara hadn't minded at all when Colton suggested they cancel their dinner reservations and pick up Chinese instead. In fact, she told him he was welcome to bring the food to Nonna's, since Nonna was with Rachel at the big senior center Italian meatball cook-off.

She couldn't wait to see him. Tell him all about the stupid things Tagg had done in the office. Mostly she just wanted to feel his arms around her. Be reassured that what they had was real and good and so different from what she'd had with Tagg.

As soon as Colton's cruiser pulled into Nonna's driveway, Sara ran to the driver's side and bent down to kiss him on the cheek. "Hi!" she said. An enthusiastic greeting, because she was starving—for food and for him. A couple of brown bags of takeout sat on the passenger side. The smell of ginger, sesame oil, and soy sauce wafted up, and her stomach grumbled.

As soon as Colton looked up, Sara sensed something was off. He was too quiet. Not smiling, his mouth drawn in a tight line. His brow was furrowed, and a muscle twitched in his jaw. Plus he had a white-knuckle grip on the wheel.

"What's wrong?" She was learning that cops often kept a lot of things to themselves, things that would be upsetting to those that they loved. Maybe he'd had a terrible day at work.

He met her gaze briefly but didn't smile like he usually did, or try to kiss her back. "I thought we might eat first, but I'm a little too upset." He was staring straight ahead out the car window, and that unnerved her. It wasn't like him not to look at her. My God, what was wrong?

"Do you want to come sit on the porch?"

"OK." He walked up the porch steps and set the takeout bags on the table.

She took a seat on the edge of the swing while he stood against the porch railing, glancing out over the backyard.

He sighed heavily. Turned to face her. "I found Hannah's birth control pills. The ones you prescribed for her."

"You're angry?" she asked.

He snorted. Well, that answered that.

"I sent her to you for information and you gave her license to fool around." The anger in his eyes wasn't what slayed her, but rather the hurt. He felt betrayed. By her. She could see it, all over his handsome face, and it devastated her.

She chose her words carefully. "Regardless of how I counseled her, she's old enough to make her own decisions."

"Why couldn't you have told me?"

"She's my patient. I couldn't discuss what she told me in private."

"Did you not think I had a right to know?"

"God, Colton, it has nothing to do with that. Look, I gave her all the facts, including my opinion on waiting. It was never my intention to encourage her to run off and have sex—just to protect her."

Another heavy sigh.

He didn't believe her, and that broke her heart.

The sound of a car idling down the road made her turn. A red Porsche was pulling up in front of the house. She saw that idiotic license plate, TAGG IM IT.

"Looks like your fiancé couldn't stay away."

"Ex-fiancé," she said. This was getting worse by the minute. "Oh, come on, Colton." She folded her arms. He could *not* be serious.

"You didn't tell him about us this morning."

"I was in the middle of my office. He was...emotional." She paused. "You're his oldest friend. Did *you* tell him?"

"Maybe there's nothing to tell."

Really? He was actually doing this? "Are you really going there? Before we do, let's make it clear—is this about Hannah or Tagg?" Tagg got out of his sports car, shut the door, and took off his sunglasses. He was going to be up on the porch in a minute.

"It's about everything. It's about us and how different we are. Our families, our education, our back-grounds—*different*."

She'd looked on their differences as complementary. Apparently he thought they were insurmountable.

"Colton, I'm sorry you're angry. If you just talk with your sister—"

"This isn't working," Colton said, still staring out over the backyards where next door, a couple of kids chased each other around, laughing and playing.

"What's not working?" Sara sucked in a breath. He was angry. Furious, even, about her interference with his sister. But was he so angry he wanted to *break up*?

"*We're* not working."

"We—us? Wait—are you breaking up with me?" Oh God. He couldn't be serious. This was their first fight about something other than their relationship. How could it be their *last*?

Her heart was drumming inside her chest as if she were having a heart attack. She felt sick. And angry. He was being obstinate. And she had no defense. She'd done what she felt she'd needed to do for Hannah.

Tagg was striding up the lawn. "Hey, babe," he said, approaching her and giving her a side hug, which she quickly stepped out of.

She did not need this now, not ever.

"Babe, huh?" Colton said, clearing his throat. He rolled his eyes, his fists balled into a death grip at his sides.

Jealous. Could he be jealous of Tagg? His comment about their differences, about calling Tagg her fiancé...it was all making sense now.

"I stopped by so we could continue that discussion we started in the office," Tagg said. "Guess what? Turns out my dad's friends with the head of the neurology department at Falls Hospital and he's arranged to have lunch with me. I'm really excited."

Sara glanced at Colton, who seemed...shut down. Distant. She wanted to shake him.

"Tagg, this is a bad time," Sara said.

"Hey, I'm glad you're here, Colt," Tagg said. "Maybe you can tell Sara how much I missed her. How sorry I am. How much I—"

"I meant what I said this morning," Sara said to Tagg. "I'm not getting back together with you. I—I'm seeing someone else." She looked pointedly at Colton, who seemed very busy checking his radio.

Tagg stared at her. At least that had temporarily shut him up. Unfortunately Colton didn't say a thing.

"I love somebody else." She looked at Colton, but he still wouldn't make eye contact. God, the man was impossible. She frowned at him, but inside she was starting to panic. "So that's it?" she finally said. "You're not going to say anything?"

This time he turned cool blue eyes on her. Emotionless. "I need some time to think."

"You're really breaking up with me?" Her voice was shaky now.

Tagg had gone silent but suddenly began to sputter. "Wait a minute...You two...?"

"I love you," Sara said softly to Colton. Oh God. Look what she'd done. The words had slipped out at the worst time. They came out sounding like a desperate attempt to keep him, a statement of outrage instead of a tender profession. As if she were really saying, *I love you, how could you possibly break up with me?*

He looked at her then, his gaze detached and level. "I'm not sure that's enough, Sara."

"Of course it's enough," she said, starting to cry. How could it not be enough?

"I—I've got to go." He barely glanced at her as he walked down the porch stairs and to his car, leaving her standing on the porch with Tagg.

Sara wanted to escape into the house and get away from Tagg, but her muscles were paralyzed. She stood frozen, arms wrapped around herself. She was afraid if she moved she might fall to pieces.

"You've been dating Colton while I was gone?" Tagg asked, irritation tingeing his voice.

"Tagg, go home, OK?" Tears rolled uncontrollably down her face. She needed to move. If only her legs would obey. She didn't care about Tagg or his unjustified outrage. She just wanted to get inside before the whole damn neighborhood caught her outside bawling.

"I can't believe it. I mean, you two hated each other."

OK, that was it. All the anger she'd kept bottled up inside for the past year finally burst out. "Maybe Colton and I wouldn't have hated each other if you hadn't lied."

"What are you talking about?"

"That time you and I broke up in college, I made a date with him. You made sure it didn't happen."

For a second his eyes widened. "Oh, come on, Sara, that was years ago. I've always loved you. You can't blame me for trying to hold on to you."

"Tagg, you've always *thought* you loved me. What did we know of love? We were kids."

His voice got quiet. "I know what love is now, Sara. You have to believe me. I've learned my lesson."

Sara frowned. "Does this have something to do with the fact that you and Val broke up?" Of course it did.

His brows knit down. "Of course not."

"I don't know, why else are you suddenly here after an entire year?" He looked a little uncomfortable, but what did she know? And you know what, she didn't really care. Tagg was not her problem anymore. "Maybe you need to stop searching for the right woman and try living with yourself for a while."

"I've found the right woman. And she's standing right here."

"It was never right between us, Tagg, but I didn't see it. Thank God things happened the way they did. Because you'll always be looking over your shoulder, looking for something—some*one*—other than me."

His mouth dropped open. He looked hurt and maybe even a little shocked. The Sara she'd been a year ago would never have made that speech. It was her only consolation now when she was aching, body and soul.

Sara turned and walked into the house. She couldn't help but be reminded of the day before the wedding last year, when Tagg had shown up at her parents' and told her he'd slept with Valerie. How devastated she'd been.

She'd hated being rejected, hated the cheap way it had happened, with Tagg sleeping with Cake Girl instead of having the guts to tell her to her face that he didn't love her enough to marry her.

But now she felt only relief. Thank God she hadn't married him! Who knew how long she would've kept telling herself she loved him, kept trying to make it work, despite the nagging in her soul that surely there must be more.

With Colton she felt love the way it was meant to be. He knew her so well, her vulnerabilities and her strengths, and he wasn't afraid to call her out on either. But now he was rejecting her too.

* * *

Colton found the door to Hannah's room closed. On it was a little magnet board covered with pictures of her and her friends and some goofy signs her friends had made for her eighteenth birthday. Typical teenager stuff.

The photo that caught his eye was of Hannah hugging a scraggly teddy bear whose left eye hung a little lower than his right. Elmer. Colton had sewed that eye back on when he was sixteen, after they'd all hunted for it for over an hour on Cookie's front lawn.

He remembered how Hannah had cried about that lost eye, big, heaving sobs that had made him vow he'd search high and low all night if he had to, until the thing was found.

Where had the years gone? And why couldn't today's problems be as simple to fix as yesterday's? Sewing on a teddy bear eye was nothing compared to worrying about the consequences of bad choices.

He hated that Hannah was growing up. He *really*

hated the thought of her getting serious with someone. Someone who was a tattooed troublemaker, who would probably dump her for some other girl in a heartbeat. Someone who could get her pregnant and narrow her choices and alter the course of her life forever.

He rubbed the heel of his hand over his forehead. It was no secret that he had a difficult time talking about feelings. Add the birds and the bees into the discussion and he felt beyond helpless. But now he had no choice. Hannah's life was too important to him. He wanted her to have the best life ever—full of love and happiness and fulfillment. Every choice that had been taken away from him—through his parents' deaths, his heaped-on responsibilities, his blown-out knee—he wanted to be hers for the asking. He'd been a coward to depend on someone else to do what he should've done himself.

He knocked on the door.

No answer, but he was pretty sure she was in there, so he knocked louder.

"Come in," Hannah said. "Is it Cookie?"

"Colton."

He opened the door to find her sitting on her bed in a jumble of blankets, talking into her laptop. Elmer stared at him with his uneven, oddly suspicious gaze from her side.

"I'm FaceTiming Sydney," she said, laughing at something. "What's up?"

"I wanted to talk with you. Can you call her back?"

"Hey, Syd, I gotta go. I'll text you later, K?" She closed the computer.

There were clothes tossed all over the floor, makeup

strewn across her dresser top, some smudged into the carpet. Photos lined her vanity mirror on both sides, mostly of her and her friends hamming it up for the camera. A lacy purple bra dangled off the edge of the mirror. He was really, really glad he never came in here.

He headed for the desk chair. "Can I sit here?" She jumped off the bed and moved the clothes that hung over the back of the chair. "I wanted to talk to you about something I probably should have brought up a long time ago."

Hannah bit back a smile. "I've already had my period, Colton. It's all good."

"Ha ha. Look, I'm just going to come out and say it, OK? I found some pills in the cabinet when I was searching for a Band-Aid. I-I wondered if you'd talk to me about that."

"About why I'm on the pill?"

He nodded. His hands were clenched so tightly on his knees he was pretty sure he'd leave bruises, and his jaw was stiff from clenching. But he had to stay the course on this, or he'd never forgive himself.

"Wait—no," he said. "It's not really about that. I feel like I've let you down as a brother."

"What are you talking about? Most boys are terrified to ask me out because you're so scary." She was smiling.

That was the idea, but clearly Aiden hadn't gotten the *scary* memo. And Colton didn't feel very intimidating now.

Who the hell was he to give a sex talk anyway? He hadn't had a serious relationship in his life. He'd cultivated that lifestyle on purpose. Carefree, easygoing

Colt, who had enough responsibilities at home. Who didn't want to be tied down to anyone.

Until now. Until Sara. And now he'd wrecked that.

"I screwed up because I was afraid to talk to you about what's important because it made me uncomfortable. Because I told myself it was easier to send you to someone else who could help you."

"That was great advice. I love Sara. By the way, she said she'd take me to the Young Adult Bookfest in Coventry next weekend. My favorite author's going to be there and there's food and a street party. Wanna come?"

"Maybe. The point is, I passed something off on Sara that I should have done myself. Should have *said* myself." He took a deep breath. "Don't have sex just to have sex. Or because a boy is pressuring you. Do it because you love someone."

"I haven't had sex, Colton."

His exhalation was audible. "You haven't?"

"No. And I'm not going to have sex with randos or just to hook up."

"If you aren't having sex...then why are you taking those pills?"

"Because I've been seeing Aiden since March. I love him. And I'm *thinking* of having sex with him."

March? Jesus, it was July. He'd had no idea.

"I'm sorry I hid it from you," she said. "I was afraid you'd go ballistic."

"Look, Hannah, Aiden has a lot of things to overcome. He's already gotten into trouble and my whole reason for bringing him here was to..."

"I know, Colton. Get him on the straight and narrow. He appreciates it. He knows he screwed up with the
pot, but he's a good guy. And very driven. His dream is
to own his own company one day."

"Hannah, there are lots of guys out there. Ones with
intact families who don't have all that turmoil at home
and lots of stuff to overcome."

"*We* come from a family with a lot of turmoil and
lots of stuff to overcome, and look how we turned out.
Well, you can speak for yourself, but I'm personally
planning on being terrific."

Colton cracked a smile. God, he loved this kid.
"Hannah, you *are* terrific. And you've got your whole
life ahead of you. Decisions like sex can lead to permanent consequences—babies." There, he'd said it. "I
want you to have every choice, every opportunity you
dream of. I don't want something like an unplanned
pregnancy or a boyfriend that ties you down to this
town to make you alter your dreams. So I still wish
you'd wait."

"Sara told me the same thing. She told me to talk to
you because she said you'd probably be afraid to bring
it up. She said you weren't going to like that I was starting the pill, but it was my decision. And she told me
how to be safe. I really like her, Colton. Honestly, you'd
be an idiot if you didn't marry her."

Sara told her the same thing. Yet he'd been so angry,
accusing her of dispensing birth control with little
thought. And of course she'd told Hannah to talk to
him because she herself could not.

God, he was an ass.

He stood up and went over to the bed. Hannah's phone with the pink sparkly case was next to her, pinging every few minutes. He remembered when she wore pink sparkly tutus and pink sparkly ballet slippers and pink sparkly everything. Not everything had changed, apparently.

He put his arm around her and hugged her. "I'm really proud of you. You have a lot of good sense. I love you."

She wrapped her arms around him. "Oh, Colty, I love you too." After a few seconds, he heard sniffing.

"What is it?" he asked, drawing back to look at her.

"It's just—sometimes you're a kick-ass brother. I want you to know that. You've taken good care of me and Cookie."

Sometimes. He'd take that as a compliment. He smiled against her hair. "I still don't want you to have sex. Ever."

She hugged him back. "I'll take it under advisement. Now what about you? Don't screw things up with Sara, OK?"

Don't screw things up. Yeah, he was pretty sure he'd already done that.

Chapter 21

♥

There were times when not having your own place was a very bad thing. Like now, for instance, when Sara sat numbly on her grandmother's old sofa, Rocket lodged next to her hip. Gabby, Rachel, her dad, and Nonna were due back any minute from the senior center meatball competition. She didn't want to see anybody. She just wanted to watch *The Notebook* and ugly cry.

She checked her phone every ten seconds, but there were no texts from Colton saying he was sorry for being an ass and couldn't live without her. Dammit.

She was rummaging through the cupboards looking for Nonna's Christmas Eve bottle of Crown Royal when Gabby walked in. "Nonna won the sauce contest and Rachel and Dad took her for ice cream to celebrate. And I stopped at the liquor store because Dad told me Tagg's back and causing trouble—" Gabby took a good, hard look at Sara. "Geez, you look terrible."

"Colton broke up with me," she said, her voice cracking. She gave up on the liquor search and poked around in the freezer. Through the blur of tears, she saw a bunch of things wrapped up in tinfoil and labeled with masking tape with dates on it. A quick perusal showed random packages marked "2013" and "2014." No ice cream. She shut the door.

"Did you say liquor store?"

Gabby held up a brown bag. Sara didn't care what was in it. She'd take it.

"Oh, Sara. Maybe he just needs time—"

"He hasn't called me to make up." Gabby pried her phone out of her hand and set it on the kitchen table. "He's not going to, Gabs. He broke up with me. Done. *Finito*. Kaput."

"What happened?"

She took the bag from Gabby and pulled out a bottle of wine. "I could tell you, but then I'd have to kill you."

"What are you talking about?"

"I saw his sister in the office at his request and . . . and I can't really talk about it but he's upset with me."

"You gave her the sex talk?"

She nodded. "And other things."

"He should be thanking you."

"Well, he's pissed." She rolled the cold bottom of the wine bottle against her forehead. "Really pissed. And then Tagg was here, being an idiot, and it just snowballed. And then Colton said he wanted to call it quits. Said we're too different. Just like that."

"Have you had dinner?"

Sara's eyes suddenly filled with tears. "I don't want dinner, Gabby. I want Colton."

Gabby guided her over to Nonna's table and pulled

out a chair. As Sara glanced out the big bay window, she saw the old oak tree, steadfast and solid, but somehow it didn't provide her with any of its usual comfort.

"Sit here," Gabby said. "I'm going to make you something to eat, OK?"

They'd gotten used to taking care of each other after their mother died, depended on each other for comfort and confidences. Gabby's mothering was familiar and welcome.

Gabby opened the wine and poured them each a glass in one of the many plastic cups in every color of the rainbow that filled Nonna's cupboards.

Her sister handed her a cup, and Sara took it gratefully. Gabby had just started to crack eggs into a bowl when they heard voices coming up the walkway.

"Oh, they're home," Gabby said.

"Don't say anything." Sara wiped her eyes and blew her nose.

The door opened, and Nonna, her dad, and Rachel walked in. Nonna was clutching an old iron pot with a blue-and-white-speckled lid to her chest.

"I won first prize in the meatball contest," she said.

"The best meatballs this side of the Mississippi," her dad said, giving Nonna a hug.

"And there were ten other contestants," Rachel said, looking elegant as usual in jeans and a sleeveless black blouse.

"Oh, Nonna, that's wonderful," Sara said, a note of false cheer in her voice. Rachel, always intuitive, looked at her a little strangely, but kept a smile on her face.

"I got a gift certificate to Giuseppe's. So it can be my

treat next time we all go." Nonna looked at Gabby, who was beating the eggs. "Who are those for?"

"Sara. She's feeling a little low and hasn't had any dinner yet."

Nonna shooed her away and took over the cooking in that way she always had. "Go, go, sit down. Sara, want some mushrooms in your omelet?"

"Anything you want, Nonna," Sara said. She wanted nothing but Colton. That big stubborn jackass.

"Why are you feeling low?" Rachel asked, narrowing her eyes.

"Colton and I broke up." There, she'd said it. They might as well know.

"Damn that Taggart," her dad said. "Thinking he can come home with his tail between his legs like that and stir trouble. You're not taking him back, are you?"

"No, of course not."

"Oh, honey," Rachel said. "I'm so sorry."

"Colton's jealous," her father said. "That's got to be it. He certainly didn't appreciate Tagg showing up in the office today."

"I have no idea why he'd feel threatened. I don't love Tagg anymore. I don't *want* Tagg anymore. I love Colton."

"Did you tell him that?" Rachel asked.

"I tried to, but he was too busy being angry with me about seeing his sister in the office to listen."

"I know about that visit," her dad said, frowning a little. "The pharmacy called me about the prescription."

She nodded. She thought her father would understand the difficulties of seeing Hannah in the office, even if they couldn't really talk about it now in front of everyone.

He patted her knee as if she were twelve again. Kissed her forehead. "Hang in there, sweetheart."

She attempted a smile. "Thanks, Dad."

Rachel hugged her. "I'm sorry, sweetie."

She squeezed Rachel's hand. "Thanks, Rach."

After her dad and Rachel left, Nonna served her up a perfect mushroom-and-onion omelet, and made one for Gabby too, but Sara was barely able to stomach a bite. Then they all sat on the couch, Nonna in the middle covered up with her favorite crocheted afghan, and turned on an episode of *Friends*, which Nonna loved.

Nonna wrapped her arm around Sara's shoulders and Sara leaned her head against Nonna's shoulder. She smelled like baby powder and spaghetti sauce, not a bad combination, actually.

"Nonna, where are our mom's journals?" Gabby asked during a commercial. She tended to ask every once in a while. *You never know when Nonna's memory could be triggered*, she'd say. "We've combed through every box in the attic."

"In my bedroom closet," Nonna said. "Want a meatball?"

Gabby got up and came back into the room a few minutes later with a box.

Sara saw the elated expression on Gabby's face and threw back the afghan. "Oh my God."

"What is that?" Nonna asked.

"It's a box of Mom's things. I found it exactly where you said it would be."

Gabby set the box down and knelt on the floor to rummage through it. It was filled with bundles of computer-printed paper rubber-banded together.

"These aren't journals," Gabby said excitedly. "They're stories. Typed out."

"Oh, your mother was always writing stories, from the time she was in third grade," Nonna said.

Gabby pulled out a fat bundle. "What kind of stories did she write, Nonna?"

"Oh, adventures with animals mostly. Kid stuff. She always did have an amazing imagination. She stopped writing once she got married, but after Rafe was born, she got back to it. She even had a writers' group. I think she may have been writing a romance novel. You know, like that one about the girl falling in love with the priest."

"Good God, Mom was writing a *Thorn Birds* story?" Sara said. "Maybe you don't want to read that. There might be *love scenes*." She made a silly gagging gesture for Gabby's benefit.

Gabby was completely enthralled, leafing through the bundles and the notebooks. "Nonna, is it OK for me to have this? Sara, it's all right with you, isn't it?"

"Oh, have at it," Sara said. It felt good to see Gabby happy. Excited about something other than Malcolm.

"Well, this was a lovely surprise," Nonna said.

"I know!" Gabby said, grinning.

Despite her pain, Sara couldn't help but be happy for her sister. She put a hand on her shoulder. "You always loved to write. Maybe it will give you some inspiration." Now if only it gave Gabby some inspiration to dump that idiot Malcolm. But Sara didn't want to ruin things by saying that.

"Just knowing Mom did this inspires me. I don't even need to read what she wrote, although I will. Every word."

Gabby emptied all the papers out until they were piled all around her. Then she tipped the box toward herself and reached into the bottom. "Oh my God, Sara."

"What is it?"

She pulled out a small rectangular box wrapped in pretty pink-and-green paper, with a silver bow.

Under the bow was a tag.

Gabby exchanged glances with Sara. Sara knew Gabby was thinking the same thing she was.

Her long-lost birthday present from so long ago. Somewhere deep inside, she knew it. Even more fitting, because tomorrow was her birthday. Her eyes filled with tears yet again.

Aw, hell. As if there hadn't been enough crying today.

Gabby handed it over. She was getting teary too.

"Open it, sweetheart," Nonna said.

Sara flipped over the tag. Her name was written in her mother's beautiful script, with the usual flourishes and swirls she'd used for special occasions.

"Better late than never," Nonna, always the practical one, said.

Sara studied the perfectly wrapped package meant for her thirteen-year-old self. She was never one to carefully unwrap a present, but this one made her hesitate.

"Hurry up, I can't stand it!" Gabby said.

Sara smiled a little. If Evie were here, she'd make Sara wait until the whole family was present, but there was no way she was doing that. She put her finger under a seam to start tearing the paper but stopped herself. Like a piece in a museum, this package seemed almost as if it shouldn't be touched. And certainly shouldn't be ruined.

She carefully pulled up the tape without tearing the paper. Almost immediately she could tell it was a book.

Her vision blurred. Then, without thinking, she ripped into the rest of the paper. Her mother wouldn't have wanted her to treat it like a museum piece.

It was a copy of *Pride and Prejudice*. A collector's copy, the kind with gilt edges. A special edition that had the original text on one side of every page and footnotes explaining all kinds of things on the other.

Her mom had known how much that book meant to her. She'd bought her a copy that would allow her to fully learn every last detail. The perfect gift.

"Open it," Gabby said.

Sara stilled with her hand on the cover. She knew what she'd find when she opened it. Every book their mother had given them had been inscribed by her at the front.

"My sweet girl," the inscription read. "Welcome to your teenage years! A wonderful, scary time. Just a warning, there will probably be a Wickham or two to deal with before Darcy comes along. My wish for you is to know the difference. Love always, Mom."

Oh, Mom. A landslide of tears hit her, not just for

the beautiful gift but also because her mother's message seemed so spot-on in an eerie way. She wanted to cry out to her mother that she did know the difference! It had taken her over ten years, but by God, she knew. Too bad that when she'd finally figured it out, her Darcy had flown the coop.

"Colton's your Darcy," Gabby said.

"You're *such* a romantic," Sara said, rolling her eyes.

"He's liked you for a long time, Sara," Nonna said.

"You're thinking of Tagg, Nonna," Gabby said gently. "We're talking about Colton."

"I love Colton," Nonna said with a sigh. "Such a nice man."

Sara felt tears coming on again. He *was* a nice man. He took care of Nonna and his own grandmother and everyone in town. He'd stood up for her to her dad and shown up at her family dinner and handled all the craziness really well. She thought of how he'd taken off her glasses so carefully, setting them on the nightstand, and kissing her. Yeah, he'd loved her for who she was, all right. Or at least she'd thought it was love.

And she loved him in a way she'd never loved Tagg. Tagg had given her validation that being smart was OK. He'd been a shield of sorts for her to hide behind during those years when she wasn't confident enough in herself. But he wasn't the one. Not the *right* one.

No, the right one was a man who at the beginning couldn't have been more wrong. She'd gone from hating him to loving him. What a fine line that was, between love and hate.

"Are you all right?" Gabby asked, because sure enough, Sara's eyes were leaking again.

"Gabby," Sara said, wiping her eyes and leaning forward so Gabby would know what she was about to say was important. Her words came out shaky. "Don't marry a man who doesn't treat you like you're the best damn thing that's ever happened to him. Because if I learned one thing from all of this, it was that Tagg could always take me or leave me. But with Colton, I thought... Well. I clearly don't have it all figured out, but..."

"I get it," Gabby said, putting her hands up. "I get what you're saying."

"Don't ever marry a man who doesn't look at you like you're chocolate ice cream," Nonna said out of nowhere.

"Chocolate ice cream," Sara said, smiling through her tears.

"Perfect," Gabby said, laughing.

"I wish I had some of that," Nonna said.

Gabby rose from the floor and stepped around all the piles of paper. "I'm going to run and get us some."

"Get the half-gallon size," Sara called after her.

"Hurry back so we can watch more of the *Friends*," Nonna said.

Sara leaned back against the couch and linked her arm with Nonna's. Maybe Nonna didn't always get the facts right, but she was still very, very wise.

* * *

"Hey, babycakes." Carmen's voice blasting through the police radio on Colton's desk startled him awake. "I'm coming in there."

Colton bolted upright. His neck had a crick, his back ached, and his left leg was asleep. Champ's tags jingled as he shook himself awake too. The smell of police station coffee, strong and a little burnt, reached him through the door. He rubbed his neck and tried to pretend he hadn't spent the entire night at his desk.

Carmen walked in, holding a cup of coffee in one hand and a box of chocolates in the other. She was wearing a bright-orange sleeveless blouse, print pants with yellow pineapples on them, and hot pink pumps. It was hard not to be wide awake after looking at her.

"Carmen, what are you doing here? I thought you were supposed to be dispatching from the sheriff's office today."

"First, Maggie Nelson brought these in to say thank you for rescuing Dolly the other day." She waved them under his nose. "They're delicious, by the way. Second, I went out of my way to tell you to your sweet baby face personally that you're making a big mistake with Sara and to get your head out of your ass."

"How do you know anything about my personal life?"

"Tagg's mother told everyone what happened at the Angel Statue Preservation Society meeting this morning. Apparently she's rooting for her son to get back together with Sara."

He sighed. "Thank you, Carmen. You can go to work now."

"Did you sleep in those clothes? You look terrible."

He sent her a glare. The best he could do right now. Maybe if he didn't talk much she'd go the hell away.

Wishful thinking, because she parked her butt in one of the chairs in front of his desk. "I watched you grow from a cocky kid who was angry at everybody to a kind, gentle guy who watches out for every single citizen in this town. You hold your head high, Chief." Her voice cracked a little. She shook her finger at him emphatically, her bright-fuchsia polish sparkling. "Don't you let someone move in on your life who doesn't have half the integrity you do. Even if he does have double the degrees."

"And a better car," Evan said from the other room.

Colton scrubbed a hand over his head. "When did everybody get to be Dear Abby around here?" Still, he felt a warm little tightening in his chest.

Evan appeared in the doorway. "Hey, someone's here to see you, Chief." He lowered his voice. "It's that kid you gave the painting job to."

Carmen leaned over, grabbed Colton's chin, and shook it. "Think about what I said. Sara's too good to let her get away."

"Thanks, Mom," he said as she headed out the door. He was only half kidding. "Hey, Carmen," he called after her.

"Yes?" she asked, turning around.

"Seriously, thanks. I...appreciate your concern."

She grinned. "No problem, boss." She blew him a kiss as she left and patted Aiden on the shoulder as she passed him in the doorway.

Colton managed to grab a slug of his coffee before he told the kid to take a seat.

"So, Aiden," he said, leaning back in his seat and tenting his fingers. Where to begin? *The paint job looks terrific. Now get the hell away from my sister.*

Aiden had taken a ball cap off his head and was holding it to his chest. He looked contrite and humble—and nervous. But Colton didn't fall for that kind of thing easily.

As soon as the kid plopped into a chair, Colton said, "Look, Aiden, I'm glad you're here. Let's get a few things straight." He was going to get the upper hand on this. Attack the problem head-on. Make it clear where he stood in terms of Hannah. Which was, he didn't really want him near her but it was clear he wasn't going to be able to stop them. But he could scare the shit out of Aiden. That might help. It would at least make him feel better.

Colton felt a sudden burning in his chest. Heartburn. He choked it down with a slug of coffee, probably not the best remedy.

"Before you start, I want to tell you I'm grateful for what you've done for me, Chief," the kid said. "And I came to show you this."

Colton wondered if the kid was being a kiss-ass. Aiden was smart enough to know when he was in trouble and clever enough to wheedle his way out of it. Colton might have tried the same back in the day. One look in Aiden's eyes as he handed over a long envelope showed Colton otherwise. The kid looked eager. Proud. He was also shifting nervously in the chair. What in the world?

Colton pulled out an official-looking piece of paper. He took a minute to skim it. It was a letter of acceptance to the electrician program at the local technical college.

Well, I'll be. The kid had followed through. Applied and gotten in. And looked darn proud of it.

"I start in the fall," Aiden said. Despite his tough appearance, he was practically beaming.

Colton sat forward. The kid was grinning broadly. Colton couldn't help breaking into a grin too.

"Congratulations," Colton said. "Wow. I mean, this is great."

"I owe it all to you, Chief."

"You got the grades, Aiden. You got yourself in."

"When I interviewed, the guy told me you'd personally put in a good word for me. I'll never forget how you helped me."

Aw, geez. This was killing him. The kid really meant it.

He stood up. "Look, Hannah told me you were upset about us. I didn't tell you about me and Hannah because I knew you wouldn't approve. I want you to know I'd never hurt her or mistreat her. I-I love her, sir. Hannah's... amazing."

There went his heartburn again. But somehow, the pain wasn't so bad. He couldn't not like this kid, who reminded him so much of himself. Who had so much potential. Who'd been dealt a shitty hand but was trying to overcome that. All he needed was a little bit of help.

"I'll always be grateful for what you did for me. I'm going to do good, you'll see."

Colton put down the letter. He pinched the bridge of his nose, trying to find the right words.

"I expect you to keep working until your community service hours are done," Colton said. "That will take the rest of the summer."

"Will do."

"And I expect you to turn in all your grades to me from school—as part of your court supervision, of course. No slacking, right?"

"Absolutely." The kid was grinning widely now.

"And if you ever hurt my sister I will personally kick your ass, understood?"

"Yes, sir."

He knit his brows down low. "And if you ever encourage her to get a tattoo I will come find you, is that clear?"

"Yes, sir."

He escorted the kid out, wrapping his arm around him and squeezing his shoulder. "I'm proud of you, son," he said. It suddenly occurred to him that this was the first time he'd ever called anyone *son*. It reminded him oddly of Chief McGregor, who had seemed ancient when Colton was a teenager but who probably hadn't been much older than he was at the time.

The kid flushed and shook his head, a little embarrassed. Colton slapped his back and sent him on his way.

As he walked back to his desk, his eye caught the framed picture of Chief McGregor with his three buddies that hung on the wall. The buddy in the middle was his dad, whose smiling face looked up at him through time.

Colton wasn't his dad. He had to live his own life his own way. But he liked to think his dad would be proud that he'd become an officer and was serving their hometown.

Colton hadn't exactly chosen this job, but it suited him. Every once in a while, he was able to do some good. Besides, he loved it. Especially on days like this when something actually went right.

So maybe he wasn't saving lives, not the way Sara and Tagg did, anyway, but he'd built himself a place here, a life. Made a few people smile. Listened to their complaints. Tried to alleviate their worries and make their town safe. Saved their dogs when they were roaming loose. Not such a bad job after all.

He'd messed up with Sara. And he hadn't spoken honestly with her. He'd let things get in the way, like Tagg and the feeling he'd harbored that he was somehow not as good as Tagg. He'd been afraid of her slipping out of his fingers, thinking she wouldn't want to stay here in this town, but had he actually asked her what *she* wanted?

Maybe it was time to let her know how he felt. And maybe he really was right where he belonged.

Chapter 22

♥

The next day in the office, Sara noticed her charts from the day before were missing, so she walked into her dad's office, where he was sitting behind his desk reading a medical journal on his iPad.

"How's it going, Dad?" she asked. His desk was gorgeous glass-covered cherry, his office complete with all his diplomas hanging in neat rows on the wall beside his desk. She'd always loved coming in here as a child, if only to sit in the big leather swivel chair or experiment on tapping Gabby's knees with her dad's reflex hammer.

The old Sara would never have made waves, just quietly suffered in silence. Not that things had been bad in the office. She felt there was real potential for her there. But first she had to get her father to look on her as a partner. And if she kept saying nothing, nothing was going to change.

She took a seat in one of the upholstered chairs across from his desk, where over the years he'd given a myriad of patients news about their health, both good and bad. "Dad," she began, "what do you think of me coming to work here with you? I want the truth."

He looked up from his iPad. "I think you're going to be a successful physician no matter what you do."

"That's a canned answer. What do you really think of me being here? I mean personally?"

What had gotten into her? Well, a breakup would do that to someone, but she couldn't really blame her boldness on that. She'd told off Tagg, and that had felt really good. And she'd told Colton that she cared about him, and even if that didn't work out, she wasn't going to crack. So she was on a self-assertiveness roll. She waited with her arms crossed.

"You want the truth?" her dad said, folding his arms and setting his jaw in a stubborn way that reminded her of... herself. "I hate to tell you my personal feelings because I don't want it to cloud your judgment."

"What do you mean?"

"Well, I don't want you to stay because we love having you here. I want you to stay because it's the best *opportunity* for you."

"I really like seeing families. Talking to them about their concerns, educating them about health issues. I'm not going to apply for the fellowship again, Dad." She suddenly spotted a familiar pile of manila folders on the corner of his desk. "And Dad, for God's sakes, quit checking my charts every day!"

"First of all, I thought you *wanted* to go back to your fellowship. And secondly, I'm studying your charts. Not for errors. Well, maybe a little bit. Maybe. With the more complicated patients, but I must say, you have excellent clinical judgment. But I'm learning the new medicines you prescribe. I'm keeping up to date."

"You don't need to read my charts to learn that. I can teach you. More importantly, I thought you hated me doing family medicine. I thought you wanted me far away, on the East Coast somewhere."

"I would never hold you back from what you want. If opportunity takes you far away from home, I want you to feel free to take it."

"But sometimes it's hard to figure out what exactly you're thinking, you know? You just don't... say much. And you're all about academia. Reaching for the stars. Going as high as you can go. I've always wanted to please you, Dad, but I can't help thinking that I always fall a little short."

At that he took off his glasses and set them down on a pile of magazines. "Well, I'll say one thing. Your assessment of me is just wrong."

"Maybe it's because you rarely say anything. Not that I'm begging for praise, but a nice word or two goes a long way, you know?"

"Sweetheart, I couldn't be more proud of you. I've always encouraged all of you kids to reach for the stars—what kind of parent would I be if I didn't?"

"Yeah, but Dad, sometimes you're just pushy."

He raised a brow. "Well, it appears that you've learned to push back, now haven't you?"

She smiled at that. "All right then, while I'm on a roll, I'd like you to treat me like a partner. That means letting me see some of your more complicated patients—you know I'd talk over their treatment plans with you. I just don't want to be treated like a med student."

That was good, but she had one more thing to say. She took a deep breath and plunged in. "But mostly, Dad, I want you to treat me like your daughter. I want you to tell me you love me and are proud of me, because you are, aren't you? Sometimes I just feel like you can't express it or something. Or else you're deeply disappointed."

He looked at Sara and smiled in a sweet, nostalgic way that caught her off guard. "I delivered you, you know. Your eyes were green. Most newborns have blue, of course. You were wide awake with these big, round eyes, putting your tiny fist in your mouth, and I just... Well, I just fell. As purely and simply as I fell for your mother standing by the punch bowl at the senior prom. Anyway, I examined you and made sure you had all your parts, and there you were, my beautiful daughter."

Oh, that did it. Sara started to cry. Her dad got up from his chair and met her on the other side of the desk, wrapping his arms around her.

"Oh, Dad," she said, hugging him tightly and inhaling the spicy old-fashioned aftershave he'd worn for years.

"Your mother's death wrecked me, sweetheart," he said quietly. "There was a time when I didn't think I could go on. Just because I don't talk about her doesn't mean I don't still love her very much. Or you."

She mopped at her eyes. "Maybe sometime we could have lunch and you could...talk about her a little. If you wanted to. Gabby and I want to know more about her—I mean, now that we're adults."

"I can do that." He paused, and Sara noticed something she'd never noticed before. His eyes were watery. "I love you, sweetheart," he said. "I'm sorry I don't say that often enough."

"Got it, Dad," she said. "I love you too." *Open the floodgates, the whole dam just broke.* "That's all I wanted to hear."

Her dad reached over to a mahogany-covered tissue holder and handed her a Kleenex. Then he surprised her again. "You love the cop?"

"Really a lot." Oh God, there she went again. "And I think...I think you might have given him the impression he wasn't good enough for me."

"No one's good enough for my daughter."

"I think he assumed you were comparing him to Tagg."

"Tagg's an ass." Her mouth dropped open. Her dad never cursed, yet now he was up to twice in one day. "And I wouldn't be so sure the cop's done with you yet. He looks at you like you're chocolate ice cream."

He'd clearly been hanging around Nonna too long.

A loud rap sounded on the door. "Doctors, let's get the lead out," Leonore boomed. "We've got people waiting out here, you two." The firefighters probably heard her at the station two blocks down.

Her dad began walking toward the door but suddenly turned around. "I might want to go golfing on Wednesday afternoons and leave you in charge. What do you think of that?"

"You should take Wednesday afternoons off." She grinned. "But then I would get Thursday afternoons off, how's that?"

"Fair enough."

In the hallway, her father passed a longtime patient. "Hey, Bill," he said, stopping to shake his hand.

"Hey, Doc, how's it going?"

"Great. Hey, this is my daughter, Sara, and she's going to be seeing you today. She trained at Columbia, one of the finest hospitals in the country. You're gonna love her," he said, giving Sara a squeeze and beaming. "I know I do."

After Bill passed by, her father said, "By the way, I never told you this, but I got the Hopplebauer Award in my residency class too."

Sara's mouth dropped open a little. "How did I not know that?"

He shrugged. "It was your moment."

"Like father, like daughter then."

"I'm really proud of you, sweetheart," her dad said, giving her a fatherly squeeze. "And I'm so glad you came back home to work with me. We're going to make a great team."

"Got it, Dad," she said, grinning. "I love you too."

* * *

"Hi, honey," Rachel said as Sara walked into family dinner, which was at Rachel and Dad's house that evening. "Oh, I'm so glad you came!" Rachel said from where she stood working at the kitchen island. She pecked Sara's dad on the cheek. "How did you get her here?"

A corner of Dr. Langdon's mouth turned up, and he gave Sara's shoulder a squeeze. "I told her we didn't want her to be alone on her birthday."

Rachel gave her an enormous hug that made her tear up. "We're your family. We know you're hurting. But I'm so glad you're here."

Sara saw the pains Rachel had taken to make a nice birthday dinner. On the island two pies sat, half-covered with fresh whipped cream. Coconut cream, Sara would venture to guess. But she didn't have the heart to swipe a sample. She checked her phone, as she had a million times that day. Colton still hadn't called. Apparently he'd meant what he said about breaking up. OK, well, let him be like that. She'd be fine.

She wasn't fine.

Rachel moved to finish putting the topping on the pies.

"They're beautiful. Thank you." Sara was touched by the gesture, but she was starting to feel really bad about this whole pie thing. Now that she'd spoken to Tagg, her aversion to cake was dimming, and she was ready to move on from it.

"Well, you've got to eat something. Right?"

Actually, she had about as much enthusiasm for dessert as a patient post gallbladder surgery, but she didn't tell Rachel that.

"Rafe's bringing Nonna over," Rachel said. "We'll all be together." Well, that did it. She certainly wasn't going anywhere now. Who knew how many birthday celebrations she had left with her grandmother?

Her dad had gone out in the yard to pick a few tomatoes for the salad. Rachel finished topping the pie and placed the spatula in the bowl.

Sara sat down across from her at the big island. "Rachel," she said.

"What is it, honey?" Rachel asked as she slipped the bowl into the sink.

"Sit down a second." Sara patted Rachel's hand. "Look, this thing with Colton got me to thinking a lot—not just about my relationship with him but with the whole family. Sometimes I go a mile a minute and lose track of what really counts, you know? I just want to tell you you've been a sweet, wonderful stepmother to me, despite my holding you at arm's length. The only thing you did wrong was you weren't my mother. And I want to say... I'm sorry. I never allowed us to grow closer. I never gave you a chance."

"Oh, sweetheart. You were a teenager, too old to accept a mother substitute. And you were awfully independent. All you girls were. You all stuck together so tightly and mothered Rafe. If anything, I consider that strong bond a tribute to your mother."

"Those years after Mom died—we didn't know what else to do. We had to pull together. What that must've been like, to enter a house full of teenagers..."

"You had fierce loyalty to your mother. That's as it should be." She squeezed Sara's hand. "There's nothing to forgive."

"Well, you've always been kind and openhearted. I'm trying to take an example from you. And... I hope we can finally get to know each other better."

"Oh, Sara. Honey." Rachel's eyes got a little watery. Sara suddenly realized she could do a lot better. She got up from the island stool and hugged Rachel. "I love you. I just want you to know that."

"I love you too, sweetheart." Rachel squeezed her back for a long moment. Then she walked over to a built-in hutch and took out two wineglasses, grabbed a bottle from the cupboard, and poured them each a glass of red wine. "Happy birthday, Sara," she said. "May this be your year."

Sara clinked glasses and forced a smile, for Rachel's sake. She didn't think her year was exactly starting off on the right foot, but she didn't want to be any more of a killjoy on her birthday. "Any ideas about Gabby?" she asked.

"Have faith, my dear. Sometimes bad things self-destruct on their own."

"Sometimes good things do too," came out of Sara's mouth before she could censor herself.

"Oh, honey," Rachel said, giving her another hug, which Sara took gratefully. Sara brushed away a tear. "I don't know about that. Part of love is learning to iron out your differences. Don't give up yet."

Just then, Evie and Joe showed up with Julia and Michael. Rafe and Kaitlyn had ridden together and picked up Nonna and Rocket, and Gabby had actually convinced Malcolm to forego his usual late-afternoon workout and join the family, although Sara wouldn't have minded if he hadn't. Her dad had grilled chicken and vegetables tonight and thrown on some nice unhealthy brats just for Sara.

Julia shoved a little flat rectangle into her hands, wrapped in bright-pink tissue paper with lots of tape. "It's a pwesent." She grinned, showing a huge gap where one of her top teeth had recently fallen out.

"For me?" Sara asked, shaking the package. "Hmm. What could it be?"

"Open mine, open mine!" Michael said, running up and shoving another package at her.

Sara caught Evie's eye as she hugged her niece and nephew. "You better open them now, Sara. They've been driving me crazy all day."

"Hurry up, hurry up!" Michael said.

Sara unwrapped a package of sparkly hair barrettes from Julia and a pair of Spider-Man socks from Michael. "My favorite things!" Sara exclaimed as she brought both kids in for a hug. Julia was already trying to get the barrettes into her hair. "I love you both so much," Sara said, winking at Evie. "I'm so lucky to be your aunt." She wasn't kidding. The day might pretty much suck, but these kids were a huge bright spot.

"Can we have pie now?" Michael asked as his mother led him and Julia to the table. The dog followed close in tow, confident he would get food dropped, accidentally or intentionally, by the little ones.

Rafe came in at the last minute and slid into a seat beside Malcolm. "So how's business going, Mal?" he asked.

"Fantastic," Malcolm said with a wolfish grin. "Stocks are up and life is good. I'm making a killing."

"I heard on MSNBC today that Wall Street is robbing Main Street," Nonna said. "Hedge fund guys are all crooks."

Malcolm stiffened and shot Nonna a disgusted look. "Hey, watch it, Grandma. That's my job you're talking about."

"Take it easy," Gabby whispered, giving Malcolm an elbow. "She has dementia, remember?"

"This one political reporter said it," Nonna said. "I forget his name."

"You don't know what you're talking about," Malcolm said. Sara looked up. Rafe stopped serving himself potatoes. Evie frowned.

Gabby stood up. "No, Malcolm, *you* don't know what you're talking about, and I've had enough. No one talks to my Nonna like that."

Malcolm raised his hands in surrender. "Hey, I'm just defending my job."

Gabby crossed her arms. "Is it really necessary to do that? Geez!"

"Settle down, sweetheart," he said, sipping his wine. "Your grandmother just insulted my livelihood. The one that's going to make both of us very comfortable."

"Make that one of us, Malcolm." Gabby pulled the giant stone off her finger and placed it on Malcolm's plate, where it landed with a *chink*. "I think you should leave."

Malcolm made the mistake of glancing over at their father for support. Her calm, mellow father, who had welcomed anyone and everyone to their table over the years, was holding his fork with a death grip. His face was red. Maybe he was contemplating using it as a weapon. He quietly set the fork down and tossed his napkin on the table. "You heard her, Malcolm. I believe she's asking you to go."

Just then there was a knock on the door. Rafe, who had stood up and assumed the crossed-arm stance of a bouncer, complete with massive biceps, reluctantly glanced in the direction of the front door, torn between answering it and booting Malcolm out on his well-dressed rear.

Fortunately he was spared the decision. Tagg walked in, bearing a small wrapped package. Rafe took the opportunity to escort Malcolm out.

Sara moved to get up. She didn't need Rafe as her bouncer. She'd get rid of Tagg herself.

"Hi, everybody," Tagg said sheepishly. "I hope you don't mind, but I just stopped by to wish Sara a happy birthday."

Her father met Sara's gaze across the table and gave her a do-you-want-me-to-take-care-of-this look. Rafe remained on standby, ready to do the same.

Sara got up to deal with Tagg in private. And to get him out of the house, because he was definitely not staying for dinner. She tugged him by the elbow back to the front door, opened it, and went out onto the front stoop.

"I'm not here to try to make up to you," he said. She shot him a puzzled look. Was this a joke too, like the chest pain? If it was, she was definitely getting Rafe to bounce him. "I mean, I am, but not romantically. Here," he said, handing her the package. "Open it."

"Tagg, you didn't need to—" The last thing she wanted right now was a present from Tagg. Yet he stood there looking contrite. Not exactly humble, but his demeanor was different in a way that threw her.

"Please," he said. "I wanted you to have this."

She ripped open the elegantly wrapped gift. It was a Montblanc pen, black and silver and sleek. It must've cost a fortune.

"Oh, thank you," she said, fighting tears. Not because it was a sinfully expensive gift, or because she wanted such an expensive pen, but because she knew exactly why he'd chosen it for her.

He flashed her a smile. "I figured if I got you an expensive one, you'd be a little more careful about where you put it."

"For this price, I may have to wear it on a string around my neck." Which she literally had, thanks to Leonore's thingamabob.

"You like it?"

She ran her finger along its smooth wooden surface and nodded. It was too fancy for her, but he meant well.

"I thought about what you said," he said. "I've decided to try something new. I'm leaving next week to do a year of research at Stanford. Check out a whole new place. See what it's like to be alone for a while."

"That's wonderful, Tagg."

He turned his beautiful brown eyes on her. "I want you to know I'll always love you, Sara."

"I'll always love you too." She kissed him on the cheek and stepped back, amazed that Tagg was taking this so well.

"But if, in the future, you're ever up for a fresh start..."

She should've known he'd qualify that. "Tagg—"

"The only one she's starting fresh with is me."

Sara jumped. There, standing in Nonna's front yard, was Colton. Also carrying a box. But his was bakery big, a square white box. His intense blue gaze locked on to hers, and in that instant Sara saw something that stole her breath away. Their future. Babies with beautiful blue eyes. A house with a fireplace. Two toothbrushes side by side on the sink.

Maybe this birthday wasn't going to be so bad after all.

Sara's eyes flooded because, God, he was here.

Colton acknowledged Tagg with a nod, then walked right over to Sara. Behind her, in the house, the family had gotten up from the table and gathered in the foyer. She could see Gabby and Nonna straining to stick their heads out the front door.

Turning to Sara, Colton took her hands in his big, calloused ones. His hands felt warm and steady and wonderful, and she gripped them with all her strength.

"I told you he came for homecoming," Nonna said in a horrible version of a stage whisper.

He turned to Nonna. "Yes, I did, Nonna." He said to Sara, "Nonna's right. I decided that night that if Tagg wasn't going to take you to the dance, I was going to. That we'd go together, hopping along. But I was on the way up to your door when Tagg called me, feeling guilty that he hadn't taken you. And I backed down for him." He looked over at Tagg, who was standing off the porch. "I'm done doing that, by the way."

"I told you," Nonna said. "He brought such pretty flowers too. I found them in the shrubs."

"You said you almost asked me to homecoming, not

that you almost picked me up at my door," Sara said. "Geez, Colton!"

"Yeah," he said. "Funny, isn't it? Don't blame Nonna. At the time I begged her not to tell you." He turned to Tagg. "You've been a good friend to me over the years, Tagg, but I love Sara. I can't step aside anymore for you."

Tagg walked up to Colton and extended his hand. "You've been a good friend to me too. Be happy, you two." Tagg pulled Colton into a hug, and then gave Sara a longer one before heading down the driveway.

Colton pulled Sara away from the family threatening to spill out the door and led her toward a big shady maple at the side of the house.

"I overreacted about Hannah. I didn't want to accept that she's growing up. But I finally had that talk with her, one I should've had years ago. Anyway, I'm sorry for blaming you."

"I'm sorry I couldn't talk to you about it. I didn't mean for you to be blindsided."

He shrugged. "It wasn't really about Hannah. I've been in a kind of mental competition with Tagg for half my life, and in most cases he won. But I learned that life's not really a competition, is it? I didn't exactly choose my path, but it all worked out all right. I think I'm where I'm supposed to be."

"Colton, I just hope that one day I could serve the people of our town half as well as you do."

"You think you'll end up staying?"

She grinned. "I love it here."

"Oh, good. Well then, I guess you can have your

birthday gift now." He nodded toward the box in his hands.

"I'm always up for dessert."

By the time they walked into the house, the family had somehow managed to pretend they'd been sitting at the table all along, making small talk. Colton said hi to everyone and nudged the box over to Sara.

Colton's eyes twinkled mischievously. Sara couldn't help grinning wildly. She couldn't care less what was in the box, because she already had the best birthday present ever. And he was standing right in front of her.

Kaitlyn gave a little sob. Rafe handed her a birthday napkin, which she used to blow her nose.

"Don't cry, Kaitlyn," Nonna said, patting her shoulder. "It's not like it's a ring box."

"Happy birthday," Colton said.

Someone handed her a knife to slit the tape. She lifted the lid to the fragrance of chocolate and sweet icing. Inside the box sat the most beautiful chocolate cake she'd ever seen, decorated with intricate multicolored flowers, tiny gilded leaves, chocolate shavings, and "I love you, Sara" written in gorgeous pink swirls.

"Colton—it's beautiful."

"Thank Kaitlyn for that," he said, giving her a nod.

Sara looked over at her best friend. "You made this?"

"I got up early to do it this morning. Just for you, babe." She was blubbering pretty hard now. Rafe had grabbed a roll of paper towels from the kitchen and ripped one off for her.

Colton walked over to Sara and took her hands. "I

love you and I want to celebrate a lot more birthdays with you." He gave her a big, wonderful smile. "And I want to give you a reason to like cake again."

Her heart was in danger of melting right there, into a huge puddle on the braided rug. That was about the sweetest thing she'd ever heard.

"No surprises popping out of this one?" Nonna asked.

"Well, actually, I can't promise that there's no surprise in the cake," Colton said, winking at Kaitlyn.

Sara imagined one of Kaitlyn's exquisite fillings—chocolate ganache, fresh strawberries and whipped cream (her favorite), or maybe raspberry custard or amaretto.

Rachel was suddenly lighting candles. Everyone sang "Happy Birthday" and cheered.

"May I cut it?" Kaitlyn appeared at her side, taking the knife. "I know how you hate to cut cake."

"You're the professional," Sara said. "Can I take a picture of it first?"

Rafe did the honors, capturing the beautiful cake for posterity, then Kaitlyn cut it into slices and passed them all around.

"Take the first bite," Rafe said. It was a tradition they'd had since they were little kids. The birthday person always got the first bite. Except Rafe really pissed her off one year by biting into her cake before she did, and she never let him forget it.

She bit into the cake, everyone watching. "Eat, everyone, eat," she said, waving them on. "Oh my God, it's delici—"

Her teeth chomped down on something hard. She covered her mouth with her hand and ran her tongue over the hard object that had nearly broken her teeth.

And suddenly stopped chewing. Heat blazed into her face. Colton was staring at her, a very broad grin spreading across his face.

"Make sure you don't swallow that, OK?" he said, a little too seriously.

She turned her head away and spit out the bite into a napkin.

Holy shit.

A chocolate-covered...Oh, wow. She tossed it into her water glass and shook it and fished it out.

A gorgeous, shimmering diamond, none the worse for wear, surrounded by a circle of tiny diamonds, and it was the most beautiful thing she'd ever seen.

Except for the stunning, wonderful man next to her, who had dropped down on one knee. Sara's eyes misted over and everything blurred—the cake, the ring, the smiling faces of her family, and Colton, kneeling on the floor with Rocket trying to jump on him.

"Down, boy," he said. Rafe pulled the dog away as Colton looked up at her. "I love you, Sara. Will you marry me? Be my wife?"

She couldn't see very well through her tears but she could see Colton right there in front of her, and that was all she needed. "Yes, yes. Of course." Her lips found his and she kissed him with everything she had. He kissed her back, his lips sliding softly against hers, his hands reaching up to caress her cheeks, all just this side of PG-13.

"They're kissing," Julia announced. "They *love* each other."

"Yucky," Michael said, putting his hands over his mouth and giggling.

By this time all the women were crying too. The men looked awkwardly at their drinks, and Rachel was running around pouring—was that champagne? And the whole family was getting ready to toast them.

"This is the best birthday ever!" Nonna said. "Can I have more cake?"

"I have to agree with you on that, Nonna," Colton said. "The first of a lifetime of birthdays together," he said, sneaking a kiss. Then he set down his plate and kissed her again, good and hard, in front of everybody.

Nonna smiled. "Life is just too short to hate cake."

Epilogue

♥

The bachelor party took place in mid-December in the back room at Giuseppe's, which had craft beer on tap and the best sauerkraut balls in town. Rafe was there, and all of Colton's cop and firefighter buddies, and Joe and Sara's dad. Colton tried not to get drunk, but there were definitely more than a few rounds bought. But at the end of the night his friends stuffed him into an Uber and he asked to be taken to Nonna's house.

Sara met him at the front door wearing flannel pj's, thick red slipper socks with reindeer heads on them, and an old terry robe. *Perfect.*

"What are you doing here?" she asked, a little alarmed, pushing up her glasses. "It's two in the morning."

"Sorry. I just—wanted to be with you."

Her eyes softened, and she gave him a kiss. He probably smelled like booze and cigarette smoke, but she didn't say anything.

"You look pretty in flannel," he said.

She snorted. "Oh, you are a little drunk." But he'd meant it. And he couldn't wait to show her something. Then she'd never think badly of a bachelor party again.

She pulled him into the little foyer. "Did you have fun?" She was whispering, so as not to wake up her grandmother.

"Yeah. I have great friends." He paused. "Hey, can you drive us somewhere?"

"Do you mean can I take you home? Of course. Let me get my keys."

"Not exactly home." She scanned his face for clues, but he just smiled. He was a little buzzed, but it was wearing off.

"OK. Give me a sec."

She ran upstairs and came back a minute later with her phone. Then she pulled on boots and a winter coat and followed him out the door.

A few minutes later they pulled up to his plot of land. There was enough snow to cover the grass, but not so much that the car had much difficulty climbing the long gravel drive. The snow crunched under the wheels as she passed over the tiny bridge and parked at the edge of the woods as Colton instructed.

He reached in his pocket and pulled out a wool scarf. "Give me your glasses and cover your eyes with this," he said.

She eyeballed the scarf a little reluctantly. "You sure you're sober enough to make sure I don't fall in a ditch and break my leg?"

"Just put it on, Red."

"All right. Here goes." She handed him her glasses and wound the scarf around her head. He helped her out of the car and held her hand while they trudged through the snow. After a few minutes, he tugged on her arm to get her to stop walking and lifted the scarf from her head.

"Surprise," he whispered, placing her glasses into her hand.

* * *

In front of her the old, dilapidated house slowly came into focus. But it had been transformed by hundreds of tiny white Christmas lights on every window, the door, and on the awful overgrown bushes They were wrapped tightly around the trunks and branches of the trees too.

With the blanket of snow, bluish now in the moonlight, and the softly glowing lights, the house had been transformed into a fairy tale.

She had no words. Colton was watching her, smiling.

"It's so beautiful," she said. Before her, delicate lights sparkled and twinkled.

"I think it could be, one day," he said.

"How did you..."

"Generator. Rafe helped me."

"It's spectacular." The old house, its flaws subdued by the night and the glow of the lights, looked elegant and proud.

"Come on." He pulled her by the arm, but she resisted.

He walked up to her. His breath was turning into

white puffs of steam, and his eyes were watery from the cold, but they held something irresistible in them...more than amusement. A...gravity. Whatever it was he wanted to show her, it was important. "Stop thinking of *Hoarders*, OK? You're going to have to trust me on this one."

She nodded and let him lead her up to the front of the house. Digging into his jacket pocket, he pulled out a flashlight. "Here, you'll need this."

She flicked it on. There was a wooden ramp where the crumbling steps used to be. "You do know I hate spiderwebs? Like, they completely freak me out. And I saw this old abandoned house on HGTV that looked just the same—filled to the brim with newspapers, broken furniture, raccoon poop, mouse pee..."

He cut her off by pushing the door open, scooping her up, and carrying her though the doorway. She gave a little squeak at being swept off her feet.

"Welcome to the foyer," he said, turning in a slow circle. Surprisingly the foyer was empty. And it smelled like sawdust, not mouse pee. "Here, flash that light over there." He pointed above the door. A semicircle of leaded glass panes sat above the door. Similarly paned glass sidelights with the lead in a vine pattern ran the length of the door on either side.

"Ohhh, it's beautiful," she said, curling her hand around his warm neck. She was thrilled to be in his arms, thrilled to see him so excited. And thrilled to be swept up and carried over a threshold, which made her heart race crazily. What had he done?

"I knew you'd like that." He set her down and took

the flashlight, his fingers grazing hers. When her eyes adjusted to the dim light, she noticed the house was empty. No boxes, no papers, no broken furniture, no hoarder stuff. What in the world?

He took her hand and walked to one side of the big staircase. "This is the hallway—where our dogs will come falling over each other with excitement to greet us every day."

"Have you been drinking? Oh yes, you have. Did you just say *dogs*—as in more than one?"

He shrugged. "I always wanted two. Champ could use a buddy. How many do you want?"

She laughed. "I guess two's fine. But what about some kids running to greet us?"

"Oh well, they might do that too. Until they get older and leave it to the dogs."

He pulled her through a doorway to the right. They stood in a big rectangular room with two white china cabinets built into the corners. The ceiling was rimmed by a wide and intricate crown molding. A wire dangling in the middle indicated the presence of a chandelier at one time. "This is the dining room, where we'll have big family dinners on Sundays with your family. But Cookie and Hannah will probably be there too. And Rocket, who will hang out with Champ and our new puppy. And I know Cookie will love to hold our babies. She'll tell us it's to help us have time to grab a bite to eat, but in reality she won't be able to get enough of holding them. And our kids will have a million birthdays and other celebrations here, and we'll listen to them tell us how their day was every night over dinner."

That's what started the tears. That he'd cared enough
to do all this, and say all the touching things he was saying. Colt stood there, stroking her hand, his low voice
echoing a little in the empty rooms.

A smoky scent suddenly drifted through the chilly
air. "Is everything all right?"

"That just means Rafe has done his job," Colton
said. Before she could ask what that meant, he pulled
her along again. "C'mon."

The next stop was an enormous formal living room
with a big fireplace, where a hearty fire was blazing and
crackling. Candles burned on the mantel and on the
floor surrounding an air mattress heaped with blankets.
Everything looked a little blurry because she was crying down the insides of her glasses. She rubbed them
against her robe. "You had Rafe do all this?"

"I set it up earlier today, but his job was to come
light the fire."

"Wow," she said.

"Don't worry, he's already planning payback. I think
it involves taking his truck somewhere to pick up furniture or something."

That sounded more like the Rafe she knew and
loved. "Colton, I-I don't even know what to say. Everything is...amazing."

"There's no family room—yet," he said, pointing toward the back of the house. "That will have to be a
future addition, but when we build it, it will be spectacular, with a view of the backyard. It overlooks the creek.
Of course we'll need a fence, to keep the dogs and kids
out of there. Are you OK with fences?"

"Sure, I—"

He paced a little around the room. "This is the formal living room, except I don't expect we'll be all that formal." He swept his arm around the room. "But for tonight, it's the bedroom."

Her legs just melted right there. The chill in the room was nothing against the warmth that suddenly spread through her entire body. Was this man real, or was she still asleep under the eaves at Nonna's, dreaming of a man like this, a life like this?

Colton's eyes were dancing, and she knew deep inside that she'd remember how he looked at this moment for the rest of her life—the firelight playing on his face, accentuating the dark, dangerous brows, the chiseled jawline, the full lips that quirked up in a tiny smile.

He led her closer to the fire and tugged her into his arms. Lowering his voice, he said, "Once we make love here, the house is ours, you know that, don't you?"

Sara's heart was pounding so furiously she thought surely Colton could hear it. She felt weak and dizzy and suddenly hot, but overall so, so right. Her voice came out sounding strange and muted. "No refunds, huh?"

He laughed. "Actually, the Wrights told me I could have another day to try and convince you."

"Colton, you had me at *Hoarders*."

"So you like it? Enough to live in it?"

She was really crying now. He reached over and wiped her tears with his glove. "Hush now." He cradled her face in his hands. "This was meant to be happy. And if you hate it, we'll bulldoze it. Simple as that."

She grabbed him by the arms, shaking him a little. "I am happy. Happier than I ever thought possible. And from what I can see, the house has beautiful bones. I can imagine us living here. But honestly, I'd live in a one-room shack with you if that's where you wanted to live. I love you, Colton. So, so much."

He drew her close and kissed her forehead. "I can't wait to spend my life with you. Have babies with you. Share our days over dinner and go to bed holding you and wake up with you every morning." He bent to kiss her but stopped. "Oh, I almost forgot." He grabbed a package off the built-in bookshelf next to the fireplace and handed it to her.

"Open it," he said.

"Is it a wedding gift? Because I have yours back at Nonna's." She'd made him an album of photos of them taken over the past months. Even found an old one Tagg's mother had taken of the two of them standing unhappily together during some awards ceremony for Tagg. It was a fitting reminder of how far they'd come.

"It's just something little," Colton said. "Go on."

She tore into the package. It was a framed photo. One she'd never seen before. She and Colton were standing in front of the angels on the bridge. They both looked flushed and...happy. It was the one Mrs. Mulligan had taken when they were nineteen, on the day of Hannah's dance recital. Right after he'd kissed her.

"How did you get this?"

"Mrs. Mulligan sent it to me. She swears the angels are never wrong."

She was quiet. And swiping at her eyes again.

"We could've been together all these years."

"The way I see it, you're getting a much better version of me than the one from ten years ago. Maybe things happen as they do for a reason."

She wrapped her arms around his waist and looked tenderly into his eyes. "I'm so glad they happened, Colton."

He wrapped his big arms around her, and she curled into his warmth. They stood like that for a minute.

"It's warmer by the fire," she said. "Plus there are blankets. I'd hate to waste that nice little bed you set up. I mean, since it would probably be a good idea to inaugurate our new home, don't you think?"

"I thought you'd never ask." Then he kissed her. "I love you, Sara."

"I love you, Colton. And I always will."

Acknowledgments

Many thanks to Jill Marsal, my agent, who is always in my corner. Thanks also to Amy Pierpont, my editor, who worked tirelessly to help me to realize the vision of this story

Many of us are walking the Alzheimer's journey with a loved one. The way can be fraught with stress as families must navigate a complex medical care system and care options. This experience during the past decade with my mother-in-law has taught my own family kindness, patience, and love, and has brought us closer together, as I am certain she would have wished. A friend told me, when you have a loved one with Alzheimer's, you lose them twice. I believe this to be absolutely true.

My husband is my rock, and he also has a wicked sense of humor. If Colton has any whopping good one-liners, you can thank him. Thanks also, sweetie, for sharing with me the ups and downs of Sara and Colton's path to love. At one point I think he said, "I think I know their problems as well as you do," and that is probably true.

Thanks to my older sister, who has given me many wonderful books through the years, the same ones on Sara's mother's shelf, in fact. She has also inscribed the front of each one with a beautiful message. I'll keep all those books forever, Mar.

Writer sisters, you know who you are. We live far apart yet we are only an email or phone call away. Your friendship means everything to me.

Pride and Prejudice is one of my favorite books. The edition Sara is given as a gift with text on one side and notes on the other is actually not a fancy gilt edition. It's called *The Annotated Pride and Prejudice*, edited by David M. Shapard, and is a must for any true Austen fan.

Lastly, thank you, dear readers, for sending me messages about things in the books that made you laugh or cry. These thrill me to the core. I've said before that writing can be a lonely job and getting to the end of a book is a struggle, but you make it all worthwhile. Thank you from the bottom of my heart.

xo
Miranda

About the Author

Miranda Liasson loves to write stories about everyday people who find love despite themselves, because there's nothing like a great love story. And if there are a few laughs along the way, even better! She's a Romance Writers of America Golden Heart winner and an Amazon bestselling author whose heartwarming and humorous small-town romances have won accolades such as the Gayle Wilson Award of Excellence and have been *Harlequin Junkie* and Night Owl Reviews Top Picks.

She lives in the Midwest with her husband and three kids in a charming old neighborhood that is the inspiration for many of the homes in her books.

Miranda loves to hear from readers! Find her at mirandaliasson.com, Facebook.com/MirandaLiasson Author, or on Twitter @mirandaliasson. For information about new releases and other news, feel free to sign up for her newsletter at http://www.mirandaliasson.com /#mailing-list.

Fall in love with these charming contemporary romances!

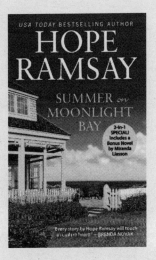

SUMMER ON MOONLIGHT BAY
by Hope Ramsay

Veterinarian Noah Cuthbert had no intention of ever moving back to the small town of Magnolia Harbor. But when his sister calls with the opportunity to run the local animal clinic as well as give her a break from caring for their ailing mom, he packs his bags and heads home. But once he meets the clinic's beautiful new manager, he questions whether his summer plans might become more permanent. Includes a bonus novel by Miranda Liasson!

WISH YOU WERE MINE
by Tara Sivec

When Everett Southerland left town five years ago, Cameron James thought it was the worst day of her life. She was wrong: It was the day he came back and told her the truth about his feelings that devastated her. Now she's having a hard time believing him, until he proves to her how much he cares. But with so many secrets between them, will they ever find the future that was always destined to be theirs?

Find more great reads on Instagram with @ReadForeverPub.

ALL I WANT FOR CHRISTMAS IS YOU
by Miranda Liasson

Just when Kaitlyn Barnes vows to get over her longtime crush on Rafe Langdon, they share a sizzling evening that delivers an epic holiday surprise: Kaitlyn is pregnant. While their off-the-charts chemistry can still melt snow, Rafe must decide if he'll keep running from love forever—or if he'll make this Christmas the one where he becomes the man Kaitlyn wants...and the one she deserves. Includes a bonus novel by Annie Rains!

SNOWFALL ON CEDAR TRAIL
by Annie Rains

Determined to give her son a good holiday season, single mom Halona Locklear signs him up for Sweetwater Springs' Mentor Match program. Little does she know that her son's mentor would be the handsome chief of police, who might know secrets about her past that she is determined to keep buried. Includes a bonus novel by Miranda Liasson!

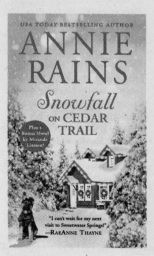

Follow @ReadForeverPub on Twitter and join the conversation using #ReadForver.

IT STARTED WITH CHRISTMAS
by Jenny Hale

Holly McAdams loves spending the holidays at her family's cozy cabin, but she soon discovers that the gorgeous and wealthy Joseph Barnes has been renting the cabin, and it looks like he'll be staying for the holidays. Throw in Holly's charming ex, and she's got the recipe for one complicated Christmas. With unexpected guests and secrets aplenty, will Holly be able to find herself and the love she's always dreamed of this Christmas?

CHRISTMAS IN HARMONY HARBOR
by Debbie Mason

Evangeline Christmas will do anything to save her year-round Christmas store, Holiday House, including facing off against high-powered real-estate developer Caine Elliot, who's using his money and influence to push through his competing property next door. When her last desperate attempt to stop him fails, she gambles everything on a proposition she prays the handsome, blue-eyed player can't refuse. Includes a bonus novella!

Connect with us at
Facebook.com/ReadForeverPub.

THE AMISH WEDDING PROMISE
by Laura V. Hilton

After a storm crashes through town, Grace Lantz is forced to postpone her wedding. All hands are needed for cleanup, but Grace doesn't know where to start—should she console her special needs sister or find her missing groom? Sparks fly when the handsome Zeke Bontrager comes to aid the community and offers to help the overwhelmed Grace in any way he can. But when her groom is found, Grace must decide if the wedding will go on…or if she'll take a chance on Zeke.

MERMAID INN
by Jenny Holiday

When Eve Abbott inherits her aunt's inn, she remembers the heartbreaking last summer she spent there, and she has no interest in returning. Unfortunately, Eve must run the inn for two years before she can sell. Town sheriff Sawyer Collins can't deny all the old feelings that come rushing back when he sees Eve. Getting her out of Matchmaker Bay when they were younger was something he did for her own good. But losing her again? He doesn't think he can survive that twice. Includes a bonus novella by Alison Bliss!

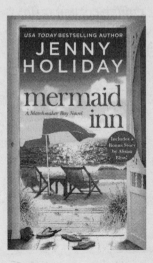